The *Water's Lovely*

RUTH RENDELL

The *Water's Lovely*

A NOVEL

RANDOM HOUSE
LARGE PRINT

Copyright © 2006 by Kingsmarkham Enterprises, Ltd.

All rights reserved.
Published in the United States of America by
Random House Large Print in association with
Crown Publishers, New York.
Distributed by Random House, Inc., New York.

Library of Congress Cataloging-in-Publication Data
Rendell, Ruth, 1930–
The water's lovely / by Ruth Rendell. — 1st large print ed.
p. cm.
ISBN 978-0-7393-2724-1
1. Sisters—Fiction. 2. Drowning victims—Fiction.
3. Large type books. I. Title.
PR6068.E63W38 2007b
823'.914—dc22
2007022200

www.randomhouse.com/largeprint

FIRST LARGE PRINT EDITION

10 9 8 7 6 5 4 3 2 1

This Large Print edition published in accord with
the standards of the N.A.V.H.

The *Water's Lovely*

Chapter One

Weeks went by when Ismay never thought of it at all. Then something would bring it back or it would return in a dream. The dream began in the same way. She and her mother would be climbing the stairs, following Heather's lead through the bedroom to what was on the other side, not a bathroom in the dream but a chamber floored and walled in marble. In the middle of it was a glassy lake. The white thing in the water floated toward her, its face submerged, and her mother said, absurdly, "Don't look!" Because the dead thing was a man and was naked and she was a girl of fifteen. But she had looked and in the dreams she looked again, but at Guy's drowned face. She had looked at the dead face and though she would forget from time to time what she had seen, it always came back, the fear still there in the dead eyes, the nostrils dilated to inhale water, not air.

Heather showed no fear, no emotion of any kind. She stood with her arms hanging by her sides. Her dress was wet, clinging to her breasts. No one spoke then, neither in the reality nor in the dreams, neither of them said a word until their mother fell on her knees and began crying and laughing and babbling nonsense.

When she came home the house was a different place. She had known, of course, that it would be two self-contained flats, the upper one for her mother and Pamela, the lower one for her and Heather, two pairs of sisters, two generations represented. In her last term at university, four hundred miles away in Scotland, what she hadn't understood was that part of the house would disappear.

It was Pamela's idea, though Pamela didn't know why. She knew no more of what had happened than the rest of the world knew. In innocence and well-meaning, she had planned and carried out these drastic changes. She showed Ismay the ground-floor flat and then she took her upstairs.

"I'm not sure how much Beatrix under-stands," she said, opening the door to what had been the principal bedroom, the room they had walked through to find the drowned man. "I can't tell how much she remembers. God knows if she even realizes it's the same room."

I can hardly realize, thought Ismay. The shock of it silenced her. She looked around her almost fearfully. It was one room now. The door to the bathroom had been—where? The French windows to the balcony were gone, re-placed by a single glass door. The whole place looked larger, nearer to the dream room, yet less spacious.

"It's better this way, isn't it, Issy?"

"Oh, yes, yes. It's just that it was a shock." Perhaps it would have been better to sell the house and move. But how else would she and Heather afford a flat to share? "Has Heather seen it?"

"She loves all the changes. I don't know when I've seen her so enthusiastic about any-thing." Pamela showed her the two bedrooms that had once been hers and Heather's, the new kitchen, the new bathroom. At the top of the stairs she paused, holding on to the newel post and turning her eyes on Ismay almost plead-ingly. "It's ten years ago, Issy, or is it eleven?"

"Ten. Coming up to eleven."

"I thought changing things like this would help you finally to put it behind you. We couldn't go on keeping that room shut up. How long is it since anyone went in there? All those ten years, I suppose."

"I don't think about it much anymore," she lied.

"Sometimes I think Heather's forgotten it."

"Perhaps I can forget it now," said Ismay and she went downstairs to find her mother, who was in the garden with Heather.

Forgetting isn't an act of will. She hadn't forgotten, but that conversation with Pamela, that tour of her old home made new, was a watershed for her. Though she dreamed of drowned Guy that night, gradually her mindset changed and she felt the load she carried ease. She stopped asking herself what had happened on that hot August afternoon. Where had Heather been? What exactly had Heather done—if anything? Was it possible anyone else had been in the house? Probing, wondering, speculating had been with her for ten years and at last she asked herself why. Suppose she found out, what could she do with the truth she had discovered? She wasn't going to share with Heather, live with Heather, to protect her from anything, still less "save" her. It was just convenient. They were sisters and close. She loved Heather and Heather certainly loved her.

She and Heather downstairs, her mother and Pamela on the top floor. The first time Ismay saw her mother in the new living room, in the corner she had made for herself with her radio, her footstool, the handbag she carried everywhere, she watched her to see if her vague dazed glance wandered to the end of the room that was most radically changed. It never did. It really was as if Beatrix failed to understand this was the same room. Heather went up there with her when Pamela invited the two of them for drinks, and it was as Pamela said. She behaved as if she had forgotten, even going up to the new glass door and opening it to check if it was raining. She closed it and came back, pausing to look at a picture Pamela had newly hung on the wall where the towel rail used to be and Beatrix's bowl of colored soaps had stood. Ironically, the only thing to remind you it had once been a bathroom was that picture, a Bonnard print of a nude drying herself after a bath.

If they could forget or dismiss it or accept it, whichever it was, she must too. She had. She was almost proud of herself for doing what people said you had to do: move on. The next time she was up there with her mother, sitting with her while Pamela was out, she got up and walked across the polished floor, stepped over the two rugs, stood in front of the table where the shower cabinet used to be, and picked up a glass paperweight patterned with roses. Holding it up to the light, she felt her heart beating faster. The beat steadied, became rhythmic and slow, and, with deliberation, she turned to look at the place where Guy had died.

Beatrix had turned on her radio, had contorted her body as she always did, leaning to the left, so that she was almost resting her head on the shelf where the radio was, her ear pressed against it. If she noticed where Ismay was she gave no sign of it, managing a distracted smile when her daughter smiled at her.

Not long after that she found her job in public relations and Heather hers in catering. They got on well, they always had. Besides, long ago and almost unconsciously, Ismay had appointed herself, not Heather's guardian, never that, but her companion. Not exactly to watch over her, not in the commonplace phrase to "keep an eye on her," but just to be there and to see. Each time she came home, each time they met during those four years apart, she had watched and inquired and listened to what Heather had to say. She never thought much about the future, the inevitable separation which must come one day—must come or be avoided at a terrible cost to both of them.

Living together, they never discussed the changes to the house, still less what had happened on that August day when she was fifteen and Heather was two years younger. If they had, Ismay would have had to ask the question she had never asked. Each of them paid her share of the rent to Beatrix. It was what she lived on.

A year went by and half another. Ismay fell in love. To Pam, who listened, and to her mother, who never seemed to care or even hear, she described it as falling fathoms deep in love. There had never been a passion like her passion for Andrew Campbell-Sedge. Heather also listened but had nothing to tell her in return. Heather's love affairs, if she had any, must have been brief, superficial, and lukewarm. In Andrew's presence she hardly spoke and Ismay knew why. She was silent with the people she disliked, but there was more to it than that.

Andrew looked like Guy. He belonged to

the same type. He might have been Guy's younger brother. Was that why she loved him and Heather didn't love him? The night she understood that, Ismay had the dream again but it was Andrew's face she saw under the clear, pale-green water.

Chapter Two

Marion was there when Edmund came home from work. That was the second time this week. His mother said, "Marion kindly did my shopping for me, so I asked her to stay and eat with us. I knew you'd be pleased."

Did she? Why did she? As far as he could remember he had never expressed an opinion of Marion, apart from saying some months past that it was a mystery to him why women dyed their hair that unnatural shade of dark crimson. She smiled at him and sat at the table, starting to chat in her lively way about all the old people she visited and loved to help—"We'll all be old one day, won't we?"—the National Health Service and her late mother's deferred hip operation, sedatives and analgesics and alternative medicine. She thought it was his "field," she aimed to please him. Later on he would have to walk her to the station. It was only at the bottom of the hill, but he couldn't let her go alone through the dark streets. She would chat all the way about how marvelous his mother was in spite of her health problems.

His mother had produced avocado with shrimp, followed by spaghetti carbonara. "Absolutely delicious, Irene," said Marion, no mean cook herself in her own estimation. She had brought a Bakewell tart with her as a gift. "If I shut my eyes I might be in Bologna."

I wish you were, thought Edmund. So it was "Irene" now. Last time she was here they had still been on "Mrs. Litton" terms. Marion's hair was redder and darker than it had been at the beginning of the week and her little marmoset face more brightly painted. He had never known a woman to be such a fidget. She couldn't sit still for five minutes but was up and down, bouncing about on her little stick legs and her kitten heels.

"You mustn't think you have to come with me," she said to him when she had served and cleared away the coffee. Another first time.

"It's no trouble," said his mother as if she

were doing it herself. "Suppose something happened. He'd never forgive himself."

She smiled. She made a conspiratorial face at Marion, a sort of can't-you-see-he's-longing-to-go-with-you face. And then he knew. Marion was intended for him. His mother's chosen present for him. Not from the first probably, not from when they first knew each other a year or two years back, but for perhaps six months. Like a fool he hadn't seen it coming. He saw it now. She was older than he but maybe by no more than five or six years. She was to be his girlfriend, then his fiancée, in a year or two his wife, a wife who would happily share a house with his mother.

Desperate situations call for desperate measures. He walked Marion down the hill, listening with only half an ear to her prattle about his mother's arthritis and her courage (as if Irene were ninety instead of sixty-two), then the latest doings of old Mr. Hussein and old Mrs. Reinhardt. All the while he was thinking what steps to take. Outside the station, as she thanked him for his escort, she lifted her face quite close to his. Did she expect a kiss? He stepped back, said good night, and left her.

"Such a sweet woman," said his mother. "Girl, I should say." She paused to let this sink in. "We've got a new neighbor. I saw him move in today. A Mr. Fenix. Marion says he paid over a million for that house and she should know."

Next day, at the hospice, he reviewed his fellow nurses. The women were all married or living with a boyfriend. At his mid-morning break he went downstairs to the catering department, for a slice of gingerbread or a piece of strudel to go with his coffee. The Jean Langholm Hospice was known for the high standard of its food. As Michelle, one of the cooks, said, "Let's face it, folks come here to die. The least you can do is make their last meals cordon bleu."

She was helping Diane prepare vegetables, cleaning broccoli and scrubbing carrots. Heather, the chef, was making wafer-thin pancakes for lunch. Edmund went up to Heather, as he sometimes did, to ask her how she was and tell her about Mr. Warriner, a cancer patient on his ward in whom she had shown an interest. She simply smiled at the first inquiry and nodded at the news of Mr. Warriner. She was a quiet girl and plain-faced, calm and reposeful, sturdy and full-bodied without being fat. She always looked as if she had just had a bath and washed her hair. Her eyes were the blue of willow-pattern china, and her beautiful thick fair hair was cut in a short bob with bangs. She asked him if he had come for his cake and could she offer him an almond slice or a piece of Battenberg. Edmund chose the Battenberg cake, then he said, "Would you like to come out for a drink one evening?"

She was surprised to be asked. He could see that. "All right," she said.

"Well, this evening?"

She didn't have to think. She stared at him. "If you like."

"What time do you finish here?"

"Six."

"I'll come down for you at six."

It would mean hanging about upstairs for an hour, but never mind. He could have a chat with Mr. Warriner about his son and his dog and his once-splendid stamp collection. However awful the evening might be, however many long silences and glum stares, it wouldn't be Marion and her blather. It wouldn't be a step into the trap his mother and Marion were setting for him.

"What do you think," said Ismay. "Heather has a boyfriend."

Andrew, pouring wine, was so astonished that he let the glass overflow. Ismay ran and fetched a towel from the bathroom. He laughed and kissed her. "Who is this hero?"

"Oh, Andrew, that's not kind. She **is** my sister. I love her if you don't."

"I'm sorry, sweetheart. I suppose I judge the way she's likely to treat other guys by the way she treats me. She's a mistress of the persistent silence. It would matter less if she didn't live with you." Andrew handed her a glass, sat down beside her, and lit a cigarette. Ismay disapproved of everyone's smoking except Andrew. He smoked, she thought, with the elegance of an actor in a Hollywood film of the thirties. "D'you know," he said, "I think I deserve some credit for actually sticking around once I'd learned that little gorgon I found ensconced on this sofa was **your** sister and **your** flatmate. All right, don't be hurt, you know I love you. Who is he? Tell me about him."

"He's a nurse."

"You're joking. You mean a male nurse?"

"Of course he's a male nurse if he's a man, Andrew. He's a nurse in the Jean Langholm Hospice where Heather works."

"That figures. Have you met him?"

"Not yet. He's called Edmund Litton and apparently he's got about as many nursing qualifications as you can get. He lives in West Hampstead and he's thirty-three."

"Just how do you manage to get all this info out of a brick wall? I can barely get a word out of her. Quite a contrast to how you prattle on. Frankly, I sometimes wonder if she really is your sister. Maybe she's a changeling. You're so lovely and she's no oil painting, is she?"

"No **what**?"

"Something my grandmama says. I rather like it. It's so graphic. There's just one more thing I want to know: Will he marry her? Will this courageous paramedic marry her and take her away from here so that you and I can move in together as I've been trying to do this past year?"

"Oh, Andrew, I shouldn't think so," said Ismay. "He lives with his mother."

It was quite a big house, of mid-thirties vintage. Irene Litton would never have expected her son to live with her in a flat or a small place. Or so she told herself. But surely, when you had a four-bedroom house at your disposal, it was simply imprudent not to occupy it—well, prudently. Edmund might have all those certificates and diplomas but he didn't earn very much. Now if he had been a doctor, as his father and she had wanted . . . As things were, it would have been simply foolish for him to take out a mortgage on a flat on his salary. Of course, ignoring how much she loved the house in Chudleigh Hill, how it had been her home for thirty-six years, her home she had come to as a bride, she could have sold it and divided the proceeds with Edmund. He would never have allowed that. He had too much respect for her feelings and her memories.

Besides, she wouldn't live long. She wouldn't make old bones. She had always known that from the time Edmund was born and she had had such a dreadful time, thirty-eight hours in labor. They had gone to her husband and asked him whom they should save, his wife or his unborn child. Of course he had said his wife. As it turned out, after a nightmare of agony, when she thought she was dying, the child was born and she was still alive. But from that moment she had known her constitution wasn't strong. It couldn't be when she had so many things the matter with her: migraines that laid her low for days on end, a bad back Edmund said was neither arthritis nor scoliosis—but he wasn't a doctor—M.E. that made her perpetually tired, acid indigestion, a numbness in her hands and feet she knew was the start of Parkinson's, and lately, panic attacks that frightened her nearly to death.

She hadn't expected to live to fifty. By a miracle she had and past that, but it couldn't go on much longer. When she died, in two or three years' time, the house and everything in it would be Edmund's. Marion's too, she had hoped, but that was not to be. Well, young people had to make their own choices. And their own mistakes. She hoped, for his sake, Edmund hadn't made a mistake in picking this Heather. He had brought her home to Chudleigh Hill. She couldn't exactly say he had brought her home to meet his mother. No doubt he was shy of doing that, the girl was gauche, to say the least, and with a disconcerting stare out of over-bright blue eyes. You could say she had **rude** eyes, thought Irene, pleased with the phrase. Irene had met the pair of them coming downstairs. It was the middle of a Saturday afternoon, so there was no question of their having been upstairs doing anything they shouldn't have been. Edmund wouldn't do that. Not before he was married. Or not perhaps, Irene thought bravely, moving with the times, before he was engaged.

"This is Heather, Mother," Edmund said.

"How do you do?"

The girl said "Hello, Mrs. Litton" in the sort of tone too casual for Irene's liking.

Nice hair, thought Irene, but otherwise nothing much to look at. "Can I get you some tea?"

"We're going to the cinema," the girl said.

"How nice. What are you going to see?"

"The Manchurian Candidate."

"Oh, I'd love to see that," said Irene. "Nicole Kidman's in it, isn't she?"

"I don't think so." Heather turned from Edmund to face her with a smile. "Will you excuse us, Mrs. Litton? We have to go. Come on, Ed, or we'll be late."

Ed! No one had ever called him that. She couldn't help thinking how different Marion would have been. For one thing, Marion would certainly have asked her to join them when she had said she would like to see the film. It was only polite. Come to that, Edmund might have asked. A twinge gripped her in the region of her waist and she tasted hot bile in her throat. She wondered if she could possibly have gallstones. When Edmund came home she would ask him and he would know, even though he wasn't a doctor.

Waking in the night after Andrew had gone and unable to go back to sleep, Ismay lay alone in the dark thinking about her sister. Was there a chance this man might marry Heather? She hadn't even considered the possibility until Andrew suggested it. Edmund and Heather had been going out together for less than a month.

But Heather seemed to like him, to be always out somewhere with him. Ismay had never known her to be absent from the flat so much since they had come to live here. And though Heather had had a boyfriend or two while at catering college, nothing, as far as Ismay knew, had been remotely serious.

She got up to go to the bathroom. Dawn had come and with it the gray light that is the precursor of sunrise. Heather had left her door open and Ismay stopped to look into the room at her sister lying fast asleep. Her beautiful hair lay on the pillow like a gold silk cushion, her strong and capable right hand spread out beside it. It was early days to think about Edmund marrying her, but on the other hand, there had never before been a situation like this. Ismay admitted to herself that she had somehow taken it for granted that Heather would never have a serious relationship, let alone marry. When she asked herself why, she came up with an unsatisfactory answer. Because she was Heather, because she's not like other girls, because she's not attractive to men. Yet she must be attractive to Edmund.

Of course, she had never committed herself to staying with Heather, the two of them sharing forever. There would have been no point in that. Heather was an independent person, quite capable of looking after herself, living alone or, she supposed, being a wife. She shouldn't even be thinking about her the way Andrew did, as someone vaguely incapacitated. She could separate herself from Heather and they could be like any other normal sisters who loved each other, of course, but weren't bound together. . . .

It was the night, that was what it was, five o'clock in the morning, a mad sad time. She went back to bed and lay there, her eyes open in the pale-gray light and seeing at last that this was nothing to do with the time of day or wanting to live with Andrew or Heather's temperament. It was to do with what Heather had done twelve years ago. Must have done, surely beyond a doubt had done.

No one knew but the three of them—herself, her mother, and Heather. The knowledge had driven her mother over the edge into the shadow world of schizophrenia. They had discussed Heather's involvement, Heather's guilt, she and her mother, but between themselves, never with Heather. Guy might still be alive, be on the other side of the world, lost or vanished, for all Heather ever spoke of him or his death or even, it seemed, remembered him. But he was dead, and that was due to Heather. Sometimes Ismay felt she knew it as if she had witnessed the act and sometimes that she knew it because there was no other possibility.

If Heather married Edmund Litton, should he be told? That was the great question. Could she let this apparently nice, good, intelligent man—or, come to that, any man at all—take on Heather without knowing what she had done? But if he knew, would he take her on? I love my sister, she whispered to herself in the dark. Whatever Andrew says, she is lovable. I can't bear to hurt her, deprive her of happiness, cut her off from life, like they used to shut girls up in convents, just because . . . But, wait a minute, because she **drowned** someone?

She heard Heather get up and move very softly into the kitchen. Should she hand over her stewardship of Heather, halfhearted though it had been, to Edmund? It's early days, she told herself; but she couldn't get back to sleep.

Chapter Three

Unless you are very young, it is difficult to have sex if you haven't a home of your own or the money to provide a temporary refuge. Edmund had had no sex for five years now. The last time had been with an agency nurse at the hospice Christmas party in a room full of washbasins known as the "sluice." And that had been a one-off. Since going out with Heather he had looked back on his largely sex-free twenties with shame and incredulity. Those were the best years of a man's life as far as desire and potency were concerned, and he had let them pass by because he balked at telling his mother he was bringing back a girl for the night. Regret was pointless. It wasn't too late and he intended, this evening, to tell his mother he would be going away for the weekend—and why.

For some time now he had been standing up to her. Long before he met Heather he went home for a meal with his friend, the hospice palliative care doctor, Ian Dell, and saw Ian with his own mother. He had never imagined that his strong-minded decisive friend could be so enfeebled and conciliatory, and under the rule of a parent, as Ian was. Mrs. Dell was a little old crone (as Edmund put it unkindly to himself) quite unlike Irene Litton, but their dictatorial manner was similar. It seemed to him that Ian yielded in almost everything to Mrs. Dell, even apologizing to Edmund afterward for having refused—very gently—to take a day off from the hospice the next day to drive her to see her sister in Rickmansworth.

"I expect you think I should have taken her," he said. "I do have time off owing to me and we aren't that busy at the moment, are we? But I suppose I felt, rather selfishly, that it might be the thin end of the wedge. I'll make it up to her. I'll take her for a day out somewhere at the weekend."

In Ian, Edmund had seen himself mirrored. He must change. If he failed to take a stand now when he was only a little over thirty, it would be too late. Although he and Heather had never discussed his mother, somehow it was Heather's presence in his life that helped him. Gave him confidence and cheered his heart. So when Irene told him—told, not asked him—to come with her to his aunt and uncle in Ealing on the first free Saturday he'd had for a month, he took a deep breath and said no, he'd be busy. The ensuing argument became acrimonious and culminated in his mother having a panic attack. But it is the first step that counts, as Edmund kept telling himself, and after that things gradually got easier. He would be able to tell her about the planned weekend and its purpose and, he thought, screwing up his nerve, she would just have to get on with it.

When he first asked Heather out for a drink with him he had hardly thought of their relationship as coming to much. A few weeks, he gave it, and no sex because there never was. Besides, Heather hadn't really had much attraction for him. She was a better prospect than white-faced, skinny, crimson-haired Marion, but almost anyone would have been. Now, though, they had been out for drinks, three meals, two cinemas, and one theater, and to a food-through-the-ages exhibition she had been keen on, and he looked at her with new eyes.

One evening she said to him, "I'm a silent

person. I talk to my sister but not much to others. I can talk to you."

He was enormously touched. "I'm glad."

"It's easy with you because you don't say stupid things. It's nice."

He saw her home to Clapham. When he didn't leave her at Embankment but came the whole way, she said, "You're so kind to me. I don't much like walking home from the station on my own."

"Of course I'm coming with you," he said and when they began to walk along the edge of the Common, he took her hand.

It was a warm hand with a strong clasp. He looked into her face under the lamplight and saw her eyes fixed on him, large blue eyes, opaque and cloudy as the glaze on pottery. Then there were the other markers, more obvious to any man, her full breasts and rounded hips, her plump lips and that hair, that glossy, dense, radiant hair whose color varied from flaxen through cornfield to eighteen-carat gold. She never wasted words but when she did speak her voice was soft and low, and her rare smiles lit her face and made her pretty.

The house where she lived was much bigger than he had expected, a detached house in a row of others like it but the only one with a glazed-in walkway from the gates to the steps and with stone pineapples on the gateposts. Lights were on upstairs and down.

"My sister, Ismay, and I have the ground floor, and my mother and her sister the top." She stopped at the foot of the steps, keeping hold of his hand. "Ismay and her boyfriend," she said softly, "will be away next weekend."

"Can I take you out on Friday?"

She lifted her face and in the gleaming half dark he thought he had never seen anyone look so trusting. He brought his mouth to hers and kissed her the way he'd been kissing her these past few weeks, but something new in her response made him ardent, passionate, breathless when their faces parted. She held him tightly.

"Heather," he said. "Darling Heather."

"Come for the weekend."

He nodded. "I'll look forward to it so much."

Edmund said to his mother, "I shall be away for the weekend, back on Sunday."

They had just sat down to eat. Irene lifted her first forkful, set it down again. "You never go away for the weekend."

"No, it's time I started."

"Where are you going?"

"To Clapham."

"You don't have to go away to go to Clapham. Clapham's in London. Whatever you're doing in Clapham you can do it in the daytime and come back here to sleep."

Strength came to him from somewhere. From Heather? "I am going to spend the weekend in Heather's flat."

Edmund continued to eat. His mother had stopped. She shook her head infinitesimally from side to side, said, "Oh, Edmund, Edmund, I didn't think you were that sort of man."

He was still wary of her, but he contrasted how he now was and how he had been. There was a world of difference. His efforts had paid off and there was no doubt that now he sometimes got amusement out of their confrontations. "What sort of man, Mother?"

"Don't pretend you don't know what I mean."

"I am going away for the weekend with my girlfriend, Mother. I don't suppose you want me to go into details." It was the first time he had referred to Heather as his girlfriend. Doing so now seemed to bring him closer to her. "And now I'd like to finish my dinner."

"I'm afraid I can't eat any more," Irene said, leaning back in her chair and taking deep breaths. "I feel rather unwell. It is probably the start of a migraine."

Edmund wanted to say something on the lines of, "You always do feel ill when I say anything to cross you," or even, "It couldn't be psychosomatic, could it?" But he stayed silent, unwilling to argue further with her or defend himself (God forbid). Of course she would revert to the matter again—and again.

She did so at the moment he laid his knife and fork diagonally across his empty plate. "I shall be all alone in this house."

"Unless you can get Marion to stay."

"It's hard when you're my age and not strong."

"Mother," he said, "you have a good neighbor in Mr. Fenix next door and good neighbors opposite. You have a land line and a mobile phone. You are only sixty-two and there is nothing wrong with you." Even six months ago he couldn't have summoned the strength to say that.

"Nothing wrong with me!" The words were repeated on a note of ironic laughter. "It is extraordinary how one's good little children can grow up so callous. When you were first put into my arms, a tiny child, after all I went through to give you life, I never dreamed you would repay my suffering with this kind of treatment, never."

"I'll get Marion on the phone for you, shall I, and you can ask her?"

"Oh, no, no. I can't become dependent on strangers. I shall have to bear it alone. Please God I won't be ill."

In the event, Edmund left for Clapham on Friday but only after more battles. Irene "went down" with a cold the evening before. It was a real cold. Unlike acid indigestion, which needs only one's word for it, sneezes and a running nose cannot be faked. Irene pointed out that it was only three weeks since she had had her last cold. It was a well-known fact that "cold upon cold" was the precursor of pneumonia. She had had it as a child as the result of a series of colds, **double** pneumonia.

"You aren't going to get pneumonia, Mother," said Edmund, the nurse.

Discouraging whiskey toddies, he made her a honey-and-lemon drink and advised aspirin every four hours. "You're not a doctor," she said, as she so often did. "I ought to be having antibiotics."

"A cold is a virus and antibiotics don't work against viruses."

"It will be a virus all right when I get viral pneumonia."

Irene Litton was a tall, well-built woman,

having much the same sort of figure as Heather Sealand. Edmund had noticed this and refused to draw the psychologist's conclusion, that he was attracted by women who looked like his mother. In any case, the resemblance ended there, for Irene's hair was dark, barely yet touched with gray, and though English through and through, she had much the same features as Maria Callas: large, aquiline, striking. She was aware of this herself and had been heard to say that she might have had the same operatic success if she had only been able to have her voice trained. She dressed in draped or trailing clothes in strong jewel colors—garnet-red, sapphire, deep green, or amethyst—mostly with fringes, hung with strings of beads she made herself, and she moved slowly, straight-backed, head held high. Her usual good health suited her type and she was at her worst when red-nosed and sniffing.

Marion noticed at once and poured out sympathy. She had arrived just before Edmund left for the weekend—timed her arrival, he thought, for he was sure that his mother had invited her, in spite of her avowals that she had not. That she knew where he was going and with whom he was also pretty sure, for while they were alone together in the hall, before she danced in to see Irene, she gave him a look of deep reproach, half smiling, yet sad. "I brought some of my homemade fairy cakes," she said. "Fairy cakes have come right back into fashion, you know. They're such comforting food and she'll need comfort."

When he had walked down the path and let himself out of the garden gate, he looked back to see them both watching him from the bay window. Those women were sure to make him—thoughtless, immoral, unfilial, callous, and not a doctor—the principal subject of their conversation. His ears ought to be burning all the evening. He was determined not to let thinking of it blight his weekend, and it didn't.

Letting fall the beige damask curtain and returning to the fireside—a realistic-looking gas fire of smoldering yet everlasting coals and logs with flickering flames—Marion bustled about, feeling Irene's forehead, refilling her water carafe, fetching echinacea drops and cough lozenges, and finally thrusting a thermometer into her mouth.

"You'd have thought Edmund would have done all this," said Marion.

"Hmm-mm-hmm-hmm."

"After all, he is a nurse."

"Mm-hmm-hmm," more vehemently.

The thermometer reading was normal.

"It can't be!"

"Maybe there's something wrong with it. I'll try again later, shall I? Or shall I run out and see if I can get another one from the all-night pharmacist? Or I could run home and fetch mine."

"Would you, Marion? You're so good to me. I'm beginning to think of you as my daughter, you know. Or—dare I say it?—my might-have-been daughter-in-law."

Marion ran to the station, changed her mind, and ran home through the winding streets to the Finchley Road. She ran everywhere, just as she talked all the time. Though she had made an attempt at courting him, Edmund's defection hadn't troubled her as much as Irene believed. What she wanted was not a young man's desire but the devotion and admiration of elderly people with money. As well as Irene, she had old Mr. Hussein and old Mrs. Reinhardt, her sights on a couple of others, and she had had old Mrs. Pringle, only old Mrs. Pringle had died the previous year. True, she hadn't bequeathed her enormous house in Fitzjohn's Avenue to Marion, but she had left her a large sum of money and some very nice jewelry. This had enabled Marion to buy the ground floor and basement flat of the house in Lithos Road she now entered to find a thermometer. Since she was obsessively neat—a place for everything and everything in its place—she found it at once in the bathroom cabinet on the shelf next to the brown bottle of morphine sulfate, and she skipped back to get the tube this time, one stop to West Hampstead and Irene.

Heather would be shy and perhaps nervous, Edmund had believed. She might even be a virgin. As he made his way by Jubilee Line and Northern Line to Clapham, the joyful anticipation he had felt earlier in the week began to fade and he wondered if she was so inexperienced that he would have to—no, surely not, teach her. The idea was enough to chill him in highly undesirable ways. For one thing, he was sure he was incapable of educating a woman in the art of love and for another, suppose she was unresponsive and frightened. He told himself, as the train came in to Clapham South, that he wasn't in love with her—maybe it would be easier if he were—and that if this split them up rather than consolidating their relationship, it wouldn't be the end of the world. There were other women to be found. Marion wasn't the only alternative.

But as he climbed the steps under the glass

canopy he remembered the kiss she had given him and that look of utter trust when she had taken his hand. Here at the top the lower door-bell said, I. AND H. SEALAND, the upper one, SEALAND AND VINER. He pressed the bell and as he waited found quite suddenly that he was longing to see her, that when she answered the door he would take her in his arms.

Things were very different from what he had expected while in the train. Once he was over his amazement, he found himself with a passionate partner, enthusiastic and uninhib-ited. Not silent and calm as she was when they were out together or she was busy in the kitchens of the hospice, but yielding yet active, sweetly tireless and delightfully greedy, promis-ing an inventiveness to come. If education were needful, she was the teacher, not he.

"The first time is never good," she said at some satiated moment. "Or that's what they say. But ours was, very good."

From thinking of her as the "blocking tackle" that defended him from Marion, a girl with a good figure and not much to say for her-self, he had come to be enchanted by her. Leav-ing her on Sunday afternoon with passionate embraces—he had no wish to meet the sister and her boyfriend—he found himself making a date for the Monday evening and the Tuesday.

Both made faces in mock despair over having nowhere to go, then laughed at their own absurdity.

"Issy has Andrew here for the night," Heather said. "You could come here."

"Could I?" he said. "I'd love to."

He couldn't tell her of the scene with his mother he must face. A thirty-three-year-old man under his mother's thumb is a comic figure, emphatically not the dashing lover. But he wasn't really under his mother's thumb anymore, was he? He still had a way to go, he could see that, and he must persevere. Remembering his two nights with Heather brought him such luxurious delight that he seemed to gain strength, and when he let himself into the house in Chudleigh Hill he was determined to speak out at once.

Unfortunately, Marion was there. The minute he walked into the living room she ran out of it to return very rapidly with a tray on which was a hot drink for his mother, a fairy cake on a plate, two aspirins on a saucer, a bottle of inhalant with dropper, a tin of Fisherman's Friend lozenges, and tissues in a box as glittery and brightly colored as a Christmas decoration.

"Aren't you rather gilding the lily?"

He could see that his mother was far better

than she had been on Friday. She said nothing but looked at him with raised eyebrows.

Marion managed an uncertain smile at his waspishness and began administering her remedies, chattering away. "Have you had a lovely time, Edmund? What did you do?"

What a question! Made love, he thought. Fell in love. Had two days and two nights of bliss. . . .

"It's been so frightfully cold, hasn't it? I met Mr. Hussein while I was out this morning and I said to him, this cold must be worse for you than for the rest of us, I said, coming from such a hot place. And do you know what he said? He said, I come from the north, from Ladakh—I think it was Ladakh, though it might have been Lahore, some name like that—and it's far colder there than it ever gets here, he said. I was amazed. You think of India being hot all the time, don't you? Well, I know I do. It's going to get milder tomorrow, no frost at any rate."

When she paused to draw breath, he rushed in with his announcement, afraid that if he left it till Marion was gone he would never make it. "I shall be away overnight on Tuesday too." On Monday, he had decided, he would go to the flat in Clapham but leave before midnight. His courage increasing with every word, "I am taking Heather out to dinner and I shall be spending the night with her."

"I see."

His mother's words dropped like pebbles into still water. Even Marion was silenced.

Irene had flushed a deep red. "Do you think it's very nice," she said, "to speak about a young woman in those terms? Personally, I doubt if ever in the history of the world it has been acceptable for a man to talk about a respectable girl like that. Spending the night with her, indeed. Now I've heard everything."

Marion giggled. She stood, screwing back the cap on the inhaler bottle. "Yes, I must say it rather took my breath away," she said in a conversational tone. "I couldn't help thinking to myself, how would I feel if my—well, my sweetheart, I suppose—talked about me like that. I wouldn't like it. I'd feel so embarrassed. I think these things call for a certain amount of discretion, don't you?"

"Since you ask," said Edmund, made strong and brave by the delights of a full sex life, "I don't give a stuff what you think. You should mind your own business."

A little shriek from Marion and a loud "Heavens above!" from his mother drove Edmund from the room. He went upstairs, furiously angry but doing his best to stay calm. From downstairs he could hear Marion's feet tap-tapping swiftly about. God knew what she could be doing. He unpacked his bag, thinking about Heather, her eyes sleepy with satisfied love, her rounded white arms resting softly around his neck. The front door was lightly closed, the kitten heels clack-clacked down the path to the gate, then up Chudleigh Hill. All sorts of frightfulness awaited him downstairs but he went down; first to the dining room, where the drink was kept. Instead of pouring himself a vodka and tonic (at five in the afternoon) he resisted that bracing elixir and strolled into the living room. His mother was lying on the sofa with her eyes shut. Without opening them, she said, "After being so grossly abused, I doubt if Marion will ever come near me again."

"Oh, yes, she will," he said. "A pack of pit-bulls couldn't keep her away."

Chapter Four

If only it were possible to tell how serious it was. With any of Ismay's girlfriends it would have been quite a different matter. They would have talked about the affair in every possible aspect, how good he was in bed, but how attentive he was too, how generous, how well-mannered, how funny, how laid-back, how faithful he was likely to be. With Heather this was impossible. To inquiries she would respond with a "yes" or a "no" or more likely a "don't know," and if Ismay became persistent, with "I don't want to talk about it, Issy. You don't mind, do you?"

Had she always been like this? Before she did what she did, or probably did what she did, was what Ismay meant. Before she came down these stairs in her wet shoes and her wet dress. She had never been very talkative as a child, but withdrawal came later, along with coolness and control. It was impossible to say—Ismay thought that even a psychiatrist couldn't say—whether Guy had caused this or if it had come about because of what Heather herself had done.

She was upstairs now with Pamela and her mother. "Bea's very quiet," Pamela said. "She's taken against the telly and she's listening to the radio all the time. Shall we have coffee or a drink or something? I was prepared to force her to take her tablet this morning, but I didn't have to. She was as quiet as a lamb."

She let Ismay into the hall, which had been a first-floor landing in the old house. "Why is it that people who've got what poor Mum's got always go to such lengths not to take their medication?"

"Apparently, they're afraid it will change their consciousness."

"But that's the point, isn't it? You'd think they'd want to change their consciousness, seeing how miserable it makes them."

Pamela shrugged. They went into the kitchen, which had been Heather's bedroom before the conversion. Her head was so full of

Heather and Edmund that for a moment Ismay almost forgot that Pamela knew nothing about Guy's death except that he had drowned in the bath when weak from illness. She nearly said she was worried about leaving Edmund in ignorance, but she stopped herself in time.

While Pamela put on the coffee, Ismay put her head around the door and said hello to her mother. Sitting in her usual chair, listening to the radio turned very low, the useless, unused handbag in her lap, Beatrix ignored her. Ismay sighed. She thought how good it would be if she could talk to someone about all this Heather business. Andrew was out of the question. He disliked Heather and had, as he said, "no time for her." Her mother was what Pamela called "away with the fairies." As for Pamela herself, now was too late to start telling her even if it wouldn't be an unbelievably rash thing to do. This was something she had to keep to herself, argue out with herself, come to a decision alone.

All that should matter to her now was to assess how far Heather's relationship with Edmund had gone and how far it was likely to go. She couldn't let the man marry Heather, perhaps not even let him become engaged to Heather, without telling him. But her heart quailed at the thought of coming out with it, all of it in its bare awfulness, not to mention the part she and her mother had played.

She and Pamela took their coffee into the living room where Beatrix sat. She leaned a little toward the radio, which stood on the top shelf of a low bookcase, and inclined her head toward it, her ear pressed up against its gray laminated surface. Ismay knew it would be quite useless to suggest turning the radio on a little louder or moving her chair closer. She went up to her mother and kissed the uplifted cheek. Beatrix took no notice of her. She seldom did, though she sometimes shouted out the more violent passages from the Book of Revelation at any of them indiscriminately. None of them was religious and Ismay had never seen her mother read the Bible, but now, mysteriously, she was able to quote long passages from it.

When their father died, Heather had suffered intensely. They had both missed him, but Ismay not half as much as Heather. Both were too young for the possibility of their mother remarrying to cross their minds. They would just be alone, the three of them, with Pamela coming around to see them quite often or them all going to Pamela's. The only change that Ismay could remember was when Pamela met a man called Michael Fenster and Beatrix was always saying how nice he was and they were bound to be married.

But it wasn't Pamela who got married. It was Beatrix. Unsuitably, incomprehensibly, to the last man in the world anyone would have considered possible.

Ismay's mobile rang while she was there. Of course it was Andrew. He had already phoned her twice that day, but that wasn't unusual. Pamela smiled, but fondly, when she realized who it was and heard Ismay say, "In an hour then. Love you."

Beatrix, as usual, behaved as if there were no one in the room with her and no phone conversation had taken place. She moved her head away from the murmuring radio. "Before the throne," she said in a mild tone, "there was a sea of glass like unto crystal; and in the midst of the throne, and around about the throne, were four beasts full of eyes before and behind."

"Yes, Mum, I know." Ismay, who had heard that one before several times, used to wonder about those beasts, apparently with eyes in the back of their heads, but she accepted them now. "You don't need me here, do you?" she said to Pamela.

"Absolutely not. You know she's no trouble while she's like this. I could go out and be gone for hours and she'd still be sitting there like that. Are you going to meet Andrew somewhere?"

"At a pub."

Pamela talked about her latest date, this time with a man she had met through an Internet chat room "for the more mature." For the first time in years, Ismay thought, she mentioned Michael, only saying she wished she could meet someone like him. Ismay remembered how Michael had treated her, living with her and getting engaged to her and then walking out a week before they were to be married. She kissed her mother's unresponsive cheek and, while Pamela talked, glanced toward the single glass door. She always did this, she couldn't help herself.

Where there was now polished floor with scattered rugs, a small table and wing chair, the bath had once stood up against the wall. Where there was a circular table with painted surface had been the shower cabinet. Under the picture of Madame Bonnard drying herself, the basin had stood and the bronze curlicued towel rail. At the end of the bath a cane chair had stood ready for a bathrobe to be draped across its back. It wasn't always there but it had been that afternoon. . . .

Did the others think like this? Did they remember when they looked at this extension of the room that the conversion had been done to hide what had once been there? To make it utterly different, just as houses where murderers had lived and bodies been concealed were razed to the ground and gardens planted where they had been?

She hadn't heard a word Pamela had said, though she had made replies, a "yes" and a "no" and a "why not?," had drunk her coffee, given Madame Bonnard another glance, and gone off to meet Andrew. It was a coincidence, she thought, that Pamela had mentioned Michael, whom she had been thinking about just half an hour before. He had been Guy's friend, she thought as she walked along the edge of the Common, or at any rate, he had worked with Guy, and it had been he and Pamela who had introduced Guy to Beatrix. Ismay couldn't remember what Michael had looked like. Dark, she thought, not very tall. Not as good-looking as Guy. He never appeared in that recurring dream, the one where Guy was dead under the water, or in other dreams peopled by her mother and Pamela and Heather, and once by the older of the two policemen.

Six months after Pamela and Michael arranged that meeting, Beatrix married Guy. He was a few years younger than she, and people thought weird, dowdy Beatrix lucky to get him. She was, and always had been, one of those women who look like witches, young fey witches with pointed features and wispy hair when they are young, and gray witches in trailing garments hung on their skinny frames when they are older. Heather disliked Guy from the first and he seemed to make no efforts to endear himself to her. With Ismay it was a different story. He said he regarded himself as her father, wanted her to call him Daddy but didn't try to force it when she was reluctant to do so. Ismay had often wondered since if he realized why calling him Daddy wasn't acceptable to her. Perhaps he thought this usage would be painful to her since her real father had been dead so short a time. This was not, of course, the reason.

He showed her a lot of affection. For instance, he often took her to sit on his knee. This, which would have been inappropriate for Heather, who was nearly as tall as he and with a womanly shape, seemed simply charming toward slight, dainty Ismay, though she was the elder. He kissed her good-bye when he went to work in the morning and kissed her in greeting when he came home. He called her his sweetheart and his angel.

"You can't **like** it when he does that," Heather said, referring to the kisses.

"I don't mind," said Ismay.

One day he told her something he said was a secret. She must never tell anyone. He had seen her long before he had met her mother. Both girls had been staying with Pamela, and he and Michael and several others were her guests for dinner. Ismay and Heather hadn't been able to sleep and had come down to say there was a wasp in their room. Did she remember? No, he knew she wouldn't. But he had seen her and never forgotten the little blond child who had come downstairs crying.

Even when she was nearly fifteen she could look very innocent and younger than she was. Guy was thirty-four but could be taken for ten years younger. He was attractive to women, a source of jealous misery to Beatrix, his wife. Ismay sat on his knee and when they all went out together she held his hand. Sometimes he kissed her when no one else was present and then the kisses were different from those given and received under Beatrix's and Heather's eyes. Until one day Heather saw. She saw Guy kiss Ismay on the mouth, her face held in his hands in the dark hall, and Ismay pull away, turn, and run. She was close to fifteen when that happened and Heather was thirteen, five feet seven inches tall with a straight back, full breasts, muscular arms, and considerable physical strength. Ismay had run away because Heather had seen, not because she disliked the kiss. She thought now, not for the first time, that Andrew was like Guy to look at. If you saw them together you might have taken them for brothers. But of course no one could ever see them together.

Ismay went into the pub, and Andrew was sitting on a bar stool waiting for her. Other people were with him but he left them, came up to her, and took her in his arms. He smelled of smoke and some rather sophisticated herb. She had never told him anything about Guy. As he led her up to the others and bought her a glass of wine, she thought that of all the appalling things that could happen, the worst was that Andrew should ever know, ever find out, about Heather.

Influenced by Andrew's estimate of a male nurse as "a bit of a nerd if not a closet queer," Ismay was pleasantly surprised to meet a good-looking fair-haired man, well built and as tall as Andrew, a man with plenty to say for himself and a considerable grasp of current events.

He had brought with him a bottle of champagne in a cooler. "This is to celebrate my meeting Heather," he said. "The best thing that's happened to me in years."

Heather wasn't the sort of girl to blush or demur at such an accolade. While Edmund opened the bottle of Lanson, she sat calmly, a Mona Lisa smile on her lips.

He raised his glass, said, "Heather!" Ismay and Andrew followed suit, Andrew with an undertone of amusement. They talked about a political scandal, which was the lead story in the **Evening Standard,** then about the uncontrollability of what Andrew called "the print media," and after that he and Ismay went off to the going-away party for a man in his chambers.

"Not what I'd expected, I must admit," he said in the taxi.

"Not a nerd?"

"It would appear not. To be frank, I don't in the least care what he's like so long as he likes her and she likes him. The burning question of the hour is, will they get together to the extent of moving in together or, better still, get married?"

"It's early days, Andrew."

"Ah, but they are exactly the sort of people who would fall madly in love, marry in haste, and repent at leisure."

"Don't say that, please."

"I'm sorry, my darling, but I do want your sister out of there. I don't frankly know why she has to be there in the first place and nothing you tell me seems to me an adequate explanation. You earn twice what she does. You don't need her share of the rent. . . ."

"Oh, but, Andrew, I do. My mother does."

"Yes, but if I were there she'd have my share. Or suppose you were to leave and move in with me? She need not be alone. Finding someone to share with her would be easy as pie."

"It might be easy but it won't do."

"But it would do if it were this Edmund?"

Would it? He was very nice, Ismay thought, and he seemed sensible, mature. In some ways he reminded her of their father. Of course, he was a bit older than the rest of them. But was he mature enough, **responsible** enough, to take something like this on board, accept it, be sure his love was strong enough to encompass even this? Ismay felt very doubtful about Heather's ability to love—to be in love, that is. Of course Heather loved her, there was no doubt about that. Indeed, there was a grim certainty about it. But would she love Edmund and love him enough to overcome the inevitable cooling off or settling down which must come after a year or two of marriage? Or must come, according to what Ismay had read. For her part, she knew she could never cool off Andrew or settle with him into a humdrum existence. Her passion and her devotion would endure until death. "Till death us do part" would have real meaning for her when she came to say those words at the altar or before the registrar . . . if only the saying of them might not be too long deferred.

The taxi drew up outside the Charlotte Street Hotel, where the party was, and Ismay and Andrew walked in hand in hand.

Christmas was a grim affair in Chudleigh Hill. It made little difference if Edmund managed to fix things so that he worked on Christmas Day. In that case the celebrations would be postponed until Boxing Day. In the unlikely event of his succeeding in working Christmas Day, Boxing Day, and the following day, the Great Feast was put back to Christmas Eve. There was no escape. And should he manage to bring forward or defer the huge culinary excesses, the present giving, and the ecstatic watching of the Queen's Speech (recorded on video), his mother's bad-tempered reproaches, prolonged for hours, made his efforts to rearrange his days off hardly worthwhile. It was in vain that he told her he cared very little whether he celebrated Christmas or not. She simply said, "You don't mean that. I can see how you love it—like a small boy again."

This year he was taking December 25 off. He had given in. Over the preceding months he had stuck out so much for nights away with Heather, weekends with Heather, once a weekend in Paris with Heather, that giving in now seemed less wimpish than it otherwise would have. Besides, he was making plans. "Plotting," his mother would have called it. Having had little to spend his earnings on over the barren years, having inherited money when his father died, he had enough in the bank to put down a good deposit on a flat in a "nice part" of London, almost to buy a flat outright in a less nice part. Heather never talked about the future, never said things like "We could do that in a couple of years' time" or "One day we might go there."

But when he told her how much he liked being with her, what a lot she was beginning to mean to him and even how he couldn't imagine life without her, she smiled at him, gave him a kiss, and said, "Me too, Edmund." So he was becoming sure that when he suggested the flat as a home for him and her together she would agree to that too. The difficulty was his mother.

He had lived with her too long. He had

stayed here, with her, too long. To have made a break ten years before when he was twenty-three and she was fifty-two, that would have been the time. When a son remains under his mother's roof for half the span of a lifetime, she thinks—she is almost entitled to think—he means to stay forever. Irene was fit and strong, and physically young for her age. She made herself old and feeble artificially. He knew that, but saying so outright wasn't easy. Wasn't kind; wasn't filial. And meanwhile, here was Christmas looming, in the shape of endless visits to supermarkets, notably Marks and Spencer and Waitrose, but Safeway and Asda too. In the absence of a car, huge bags had to be carried (of course, all of them by him) into bus queues and onto buses or, occasionally, into taxis. When they got home he had to unload (because she was exhausted) quantities of food he mainly disliked, ingredients to be made into other things he disliked and as far as he could see, she didn't much like. But this was Christmas fare and the guests would like it. Woe betide them if they didn't, he thought.

He could see—had done for years, and his mother surely could see—that the people she invited didn't want to come, would go to considerable lengths to avoid coming but couldn't always achieve this. The ones who couldn't find an excuse came under duress. They were her sister, his aunt Joyce; Joyce's husband, Duncan Crosbie; an old relative called Avice Conroy; and Marion. Of those four, only Marion really wanted to come. Probably had nowhere else to go, Edmund thought unkindly. After all, her other rich lame ducks wouldn't be celebrating the festive season. Old Mrs. Reinhardt would be having a spot of Hanukkah with her son in Edgware and Mr. Hussein was a Moslem. I wish I were, thought Edmund, not for the first time.

Cooking started on the twenty-second. With the exception, that is, of the Christmas pudding and the mince pies. The former had to be made a year before—a January treat for him, that would be—and the latter three weeks before. So much brandy went into them that they would probably keep for a thousand years without benefit of cryogeny and be a future archaeologist's dream find.

It seemed to him that everyone was obliged to spend Christmas in the company of people they would rather not be with, not just Aunt Joyce, Uncle Duncan, and Avice Conroy. Heather and Ismay would be with their mother and the sister she lived with, Andrew Campbell-Sedge with his parents in Shropshire, and Edmund's friend Ian Dell with his aged mother and an even more aged uncle in Leeds. All these people, he supposed, would rather be with someone else, Heather with him as he would have liked to be with her, Ismay surely with Andrew. Even Avice would have been happier at home with her rabbits. He knew from experience that she would fret about them all the time she was in the house in Chudleigh Hill.

Several years had passed since he stopped calling Joyce and Duncan "uncle" and "auntie," but his mother continued to tell him it wasn't respectful to use unadorned Christian names to people so much older than himself. They must be offended even if they never said so. As for her, she winced each time she heard this solecism committed. He saw her recoil when they arrived on Christmas morning with Avice Conroy and he greeted them with a simulated heartiness.

"Hello, Joyce. Hello, Duncan. How are you?"

They appeared unoffended and were still talking about the cost of the taxi they had been obliged to take in the absence of any public transport, all the way from Ealing, making a detour on the way to pick up Avice who lived in Pinner, when Marion arrived ten minutes later. Marion was oozing Christmas cheer, her arms full of Christmas presents, brilliantly wrapped and tied with silver and gold thread.

One of them was a knuckle of bacon she had cooked herself to augment the dinner. Another, she announced, was not for giving away but a gift to herself from Mr. Hussein, on whom she had just called.

"He lives in a tiny little house in Hampstead. In Perrin's Grove, as I'm sure you know." Her listeners smiled uneasily. Living far away as they did, they had never heard of Mr. Hussein and had no idea what kind of house he lived in. "He's all alone, very isolated really. He needs someone to look after him. I sometimes wonder how he manages."

"My next-door neighbors will make a terrific noise this afternoon," said Avice. "The crashing and banging and the music are actually quite frightening. Susanna and Figaro huddle together in fear."

"Mr. Hussein is always so well-dressed and smart but I wonder if he's just putting a brave face on things."

"I ask myself if I'm right to leave them. Going out hardly seems worthwhile when I worry about them so much."

"Your pets are your jailers, Avice," said Joyce. "That's what I'd call not worthwhile, keeping those animals. Anyway, rabbits should be outdoors, in a hutch. Think of the droppings!"

"My rabbits are thoroughly house-trained, I'd have you know."

"My friend Mrs. Reinhardt has a cat," said Marion. "She puts it in a cattery at holiday time. That way she's free as a bird with nothing to worry about. You won't mind if I open Mr. Hussein's present, will you?"

Edmund poured drinks and handed around plates of sausages on sticks, mini-pizzas, mini-quiches, smoked salmon on bread squares, and salmon roe on biscuits. Marion talked, mostly about Mr. Hussein, but also about Mrs. Reinhardt and that elderly lady's irritable bowel syndrome, varicose veins, and impending knee replacement. She opened her present, but very slowly because the silver string had to be untied, not torn off, and wound around two of Marion's fingers, "to come in useful at a later date." The scarlet, holly-leaf-strewn paper had to be meticulously folded edge to edge, and finally a British Home Stores gift box of soap, bath essence, and cologne was disclosed.

Affronted by the lack of sympathy she had received, Avice said, "That didn't cost him much."

Plainly disappointed, Marion said that Mr. Hussein hadn't much money to spend. It was all tied up in his house, which she knew for a fact was worth two million, small though it was. She worked for an estate agent so could calculate exactly what everyone's house was worth. It was the thought that counted, anyway. The poor old man must have been all the way to Oxford Street to buy that. She thought it very kind and she elaborated on the themes of kindness, generosity, and present giving for several minutes. The scent of roasting turkey wafted through open doorways from the kitchen. While Marion proceeded to talk, now on the curious coincidence of so many religions celebrating a feast around the end of December, Edmund poured more drinks. He had made up his mind in advance that when someone said it was the thought that counted, he would leave them and phone Heather.

In the kitchen Irene's temper was worsening. "I don't know why she brought that ham. If ever there was a case of corn in Egypt!"

"Or coals to Newcastle," he said. "I'm going to phone Heather. Better not leave them alone."

"For heaven's sake, haven't I got my hands full?"

"You invited them, Mother," said Edmund.

He went upstairs, phoned Heather at her mother's house, and wished her a happy Christmas.

• • •

Sometimes Ismay thought that Guy had only married Beatrix in order to have access to her elder daughter. Hadn't he said himself that he had seen her at Pamela's house long before he ever saw Beatrix? Beatrix might have been attractive when their father had married her, but by the time he was dead and more years had passed she was already growing strange, a disheveled creature with wild eyes, long uncombed hair, and an apparent inability ever to make herself neat or smart or elegant. But handsome Guy had married her, against all likelihood. To live in the same house with Ismay, see Ismay every day, assume with Ismay the rights and privileges of a father?

After he was dead and they made their plans, she and their mother, plans to save Heather and protect her, Beatrix had grown even more strange. It was as if the decision they took and the consequent acting out of parts, of ignorance, grief, helplessness, was too much for her. Something fragile in her mind cracked. Something gave way and she began to justify what they had done (because of what Heather had done) by casting Heather as an avenging angel and herself as a kind of holy mother, one destined to bear this special child. Schizophre-

nia was diagnosed and as a result no one believed her when she said her younger daughter
was a good spirit, appointed to stand with
flaming sword between her sister and harm.
When she failed to take her medication and
could escape from Pamela's guardianship, she
wandered the streets of Clapham, declaiming,
"And the fifth angel poured out his vial upon
the seat of the beast; and his kingdom was full
of darkness; and they gnawed their tongues for
pain."

Heather was sometimes the fifth angel and
sometimes the second, the one "who poured out
his vial upon the sea; and it became as the blood
of a dead man." There was no doubt Beatrix was
mad, but Ismay thought the author of Revelation was mad too, and probably in a worse state
than her mother. Fortunately, Pamela usually
managed to get Beatrix's pills down her and,
apart from the occasional foray into Saint John
the Divine, she was quiet and dull and staring.
The dosage had been carefully administered on
Christmas morning well before Ismay and
Heather came upstairs with bags full of presents
and food, for Beatrix hadn't cooked anything
for years and Pamela called herself an expert in
microwaving ready meals.

They had only been there five minutes
when Edmund phoned. Ismay, unloading

everything in the kitchen, a large glass of Sauvignon already beside her, heard Heather whispering, then laughing, then saying, "Me too." This obvious response to a declaration of love was quite unlike her sister, or unlike how she used to be. Ismay knew she ought to be pleased for Heather and she was in one way. As far as she knew, her sister had never before had a happy love affair, one which wasn't a case of one loving and the other permitting the loving, but mutual pleasure and happiness. It was developing in just the way these things did when they were going to lead to engagement and marriage. And then . . . ?

In the living room Beatrix sat under the influence of a calming drug, a drowsy skeleton with shoulder-length gray hair and staring pale eyes, dressed in the kind of robes worn by Dürer's **Melancholia.** She never drank alcohol, never seemed to want to, which was a blessing as it might have reacted with the drug. She was a prey to obsessions, the present one being gum chewing.

Pamela fought a losing battle with the dropped and squashed gum circles on the floor, scraping away from time to time with a blunt knife. She looked the way Beatrix might have looked if Heather hadn't gone into the bathroom that day or perhaps if she had never married Guy in the first place. Pamela was an upright, well-built woman with a young face and white hair discreetly tinted blond, and alone since Michael's departure, she made no secret of the fact that she wanted a lover. "I don't mean a partner," she said to her nieces. "That wouldn't be possible, not with Beatrix the way she is." And, seeing Ismay's stricken look, "I'm perfectly happy living here with Beatrix. It's fine. I don't think I want to live with a man on a permanent basis but I—well, I would like someone."

An industrious accountant, she had enough clients for her needs, and modern technology had made it possible for her to work from home. An aunt to her nieces when they were children, she had become a friend almost as if she were their contemporary. She got down on her knees and began scraping blackened gum off the floor. "It's as bad as the pavement in Bedford Hill down here," she said and laughed. Beatrix's only sign that she had heard was a shifting of the handbag on her lap.

Heather came back into the room, looking pleased and happy. "I told him to ring off," she said. "I thought Andrew might be trying to get you."

Pamela, who knew nothing about what had happened twelve years before, asked Heather whom she had been talking to. Always calm and self-possessed, Heather said, "A friend."

"A boyfriend?"

"Well, yes. There's a difference, isn't there?"

"A big difference," said Pamela. "I envy you."

The meal eaten on December 25, whether at one p.m. or two or four, is always called dinner and never lunch. The turkey was precooked by Heather, the potatoes ready peeled by Heather, and the Brussels sprouts cleaned and washed. The bread sauce she had made at home the night before. Pamela, after going through the **Spectator**'s dating columns, drank a bottle of wine entirely to herself. Beatrix picked at her food, remarked that an angel had told her not to eat sprouts because, though they were like unto an emerald, they came from the lake which burneth with fire and brimstone.

The Queen's broadcast was listened to at Beatrix's insistence, not watched, the washing up done by Ismay and Heather. Pamela fell asleep and Beatrix chewed gum. Ismay watched Heather to see if her eyes strayed to the French windows and the Bonnard, but they seemed not to. She even went into what had been the bathroom to place an open box of chocolates on the table there. When it got to five and Andrew hadn't phoned, Ismay began to think whether she should phone him, but she didn't much like the idea of one of his parents answering the phone. They had tea with Waitrose mince pies because Heather hadn't had time to make any, and at seven she and Ismay went downstairs.

Ismay fretted rather. It wasn't the first Christmas Andrew had failed to phone. Last year she had been seriously worried because he hadn't been in touch for a week around that time, though he had a perfectly reasonable explanation for why not. That wasn't going to be repeated, was it? She lay awake a long time, thinking he still might call at midnight. When the phone rang at nine next morning she rushed to it, certain it was him. The voice was Edmund's for Heather. Andrew finally phoned just after eleven.

"What happened to you? I was worried."

"Really? Why ever? Such a crowd turned up, I didn't get the chance. There was this chap Charlie Simber my father was at school with and he brought his daughters, and my uncle turned up with all his brood. Grandmama was her usual queenly self. Daddy wasn't very well, and Ma said I should play the host. My God, it was exhausting. Have you done what you said and thought about moving in with me?"

"Did I say that?"

"Indeed you did. You said you'd give some serious thought to leaving the flat to Heather and someone to share with her. Don't you remember, Ismay?"

"I must have done if you say so," said Ismay. "When am I going to see you?"

"Probably never if you go on dodging the issue like you do. Sorry, darling, I don't mean that, but do give it some serious thought and I'll see you tomorrow."

"Love you."

"Love you too," said Andrew.

Chapter Five

Disliking the ornate and elaborate furnishings of his childhood and the Harrods stately home interiors that had been his late wife's taste, Tariq Hussein had sparsely furnished his cottage with Swedish blond wood and stainless steel. His marble floor was bare but for the occasional kilim. Slatted blinds hung at his windows. For flowers he might have a single lily or a single fern frond in a tall black jar. A Giacometti nude sculpture stood alone in one corner.

"If this place was mine," Marion was saying, "I'd carpet these floors and have some velvet curtains." The little rugs seemed threadbare to her, and as for that rusty iron thing in the corner, it looked as if it came off a scrap heap. "Don't you feel this house needs some warmth?"

"It is warm enough for me."

"Backing up your heating with one of those big gas fires is not to be sneezed at."

"Atishoo, atishoo," said Mr. Hussein with heavy humor. "I sneeze at it. I don't want it, my dear young lady. I won't do it. My house stays as it is."

Marion rather liked being called his dear young lady, especially the "young" part. Tariq Hussein was old but not very old like Mrs. Reinhardt, no more than, say, seventy. He was small and thin with copious white hair and the profile of a handsome hawk. When she called to see him he produced a pot of very strong coffee and they drank it in the living room Marion called a lounge. She thanked him for his Christmas present and he smiled. Christmas meant little to him, but he kept the custom of the country.

"When in Rome," he said, incomprehensibly to Marion, "do as the Romans do."

He had made it a rule some years before never to spend more than five pounds on presents for those people who expected them—the cleaner, for instance, his driver, and the paper boy. But inflation had become so shocking that two years ago he had been obliged to raise that ceiling to ten pounds. He had no objection to spending money, but he had his priorities. Apart from the value of the house, he had almost five million, appreciating fast, he had made from the bridal garment shops he had owned in Kilburn and Willesden until recently when his eldest son had taken them over. His eye on Marion, talking now about her friends the Littons and various other people he had never heard of, he wondered what she wanted of him. Was it possible she thought he was poor? Or could the reverse be true and she thought he was rich? Perhaps she hoped he would marry her. He looked no more than sixty or possibly fifty-five and she was forty if she was a day. Although he got a lot of amusement out of her visits, secretly laughing at her, he intended soon to terminate them. He owed it to his sons not to remarry. His money, his house, and his home in Derbyshire were reserved for the three of them to share. But even if he had considered remarriage he wouldn't pick her. For one thing, she was as skinny as his Giacometti and far less valuable.

Absently pouring more coffee, Marion chatted away about someone called Joyce and a man called Edmund who had deceived her or betrayed her in some way. She had given these people and several others Christmas presents and all she had got in return was a scarf from Mrs. Litton. This reminded her that she had a gift for him. He was very thin, she was sure he didn't look after himself, so she had taken the liberty of bringing something to eat. She had cooked it herself. All he would have to do was slice it up and eat it with some Branston pickle. She had taken the same thing to the Littons and they were so grateful, it was quite touching.

In the middle of Marion's disquisition on a rabbit keeper who lived in Pinner, Mr. Hussein got up and said he must send her away now. "Mrs. Litton and Mrs. Reinhardt and Mrs. Pringle will be wondering where you are."

Marion wasn't clear what he meant by this. She had told him several times that Mrs. Pringle was dead. Perhaps he was losing it. Perhaps this was the start of Alzheimer's, though of course he was an Asian and it might be no more than that. When she had gone Tariq Hussein opened his present. Inside the red and gold wrapping, the clear plastic and the grease-proof paper, was a knuckle of ham. Recognizably pig, he thought. A good mosque-attending Moslem, he recoiled and pushed it a little way away across the ebony and silver table. He found a long kebab skewer and stabbed the ham, holding it at arm's length and carrying it into the kitchen, where he dropped it in the waste bin. He could see the funny side of it now and thought it would make a good story to tell his friends.

Then he called his driver and asked him to bring the Rolls around at one. Elegantly dressed in a light-gray suit with lilac tie, he set off for the Ivy to take his mistress, Fozia Iqbal, out to lunch.

It was done to protect her from Guy Rolland, to keep her safe. Afterward Ismay told her mother many things, but there was one thing she didn't tell her: that she **wouldn't have minded** if Guy had made love to her, that she would have **liked** it. He was her mother's husband and it would have been wrong. Those were the considerations that held her back from overtly encouraging Guy, not that she didn't want it, wasn't excited by him, didn't used to hope he would one night come to her bedroom. Heather knew nothing of this. All Heather saw was a man of thirty-four touching and kissing her beloved sister, a girl of fifteen, in an improper way. All Heather assumed was that her sister must dislike it because she herself would have disliked it.

Or that is what I believe happened, thought

Ismay. I think it was like that. She realized then that every time she dwelled on those events of twelve years ago, she always prefaced them with that sentence or something like it. That is what I believe. It had to be that way. How else could it have been? She had disclosed it to no one. Only she and her mother knew, and it was hard now to tell how much of anything Beatrix knew anymore. For all Ismay could tell, the whole thing had passed utterly from her mother's mind. It had marked her mind, wounded it, mutilated it, and then slid away as a disease may do, leaving ineradicable scars behind.

Early in their relationship she had considered telling Andrew. She loved him now, would love him forever, but then her passion had been starry-eyed, it had been worship. She had been able to find no fault in him and had seen him as a just judge, wise, forbearing, and kind. Knowing him better now, she told herself she must have been mad even to think of it, even to imagine she could reveal such a thing about Heather, who he already held in contempt. Anyway, it was basically nothing to do with Andrew and everything to do with Edmund.

But tell him that she was sure Heather had killed their stepfather? She couldn't see herself doing it. She couldn't see him and herself sitting opposite each other while she told him. Nor could she imagine what the result would be. Almost certainly to split him and Heather up. He seemed a good person, but was he good enough, magnanimous enough, **saintly** enough, to take Heather on in spite of what she told him? No man would. And once he knew, other possibilities would arise. Suppose he went to the police. He was a nurse, a part of the medical establishment; he might see it as his duty to tell the police what she had told him. A terrible urge took hold of her not to tell him. To say nothing and let things take their course.

What was she afraid of if she never told him and he married Heather? That Heather would do it again? Only perhaps if she, Ismay, were in danger as in Heather's eyes she had been then. If someone threatened her as Heather saw Guy as threatening her. But that wasn't going to happen. She was young and happy. She had Andrew, who loved her, as well as a good job and plenty of friends. Her mother was a perpetual worry, of course, but there was no crisis over her home or her care or her carer. The present arrangement worked well and would do so while Pamela was willing to live with Beatrix and her nieces lived on the floor below.

Ismay asked herself if there was anyone else Heather loved and would feel it her duty to protect or avenge but came up only with Edmund himself as the possibility. Was this what she had been afraid of from the start of Heather's love affair? That she would marry Edmund and love him, devote herself to him, and when someone harmed him—this was bound to happen—take revenge on that person? It could be in connection with his job, some figure in authority failing to promote him or sacking him unjustly. Suppose someone brought an action in court against him for negligence. In the compensation culture this was happening all the time. And there would be children. Would Heather wreak vengeance on a child who bullied her child or fought him in the playground or a teacher who spoke harshly to him?

You're letting this get out of hand, she told herself, you're going over the top. This is all conjecture. She's not a psychopath. There's no rule that someone who kills once is bound to kill again, is there?

But they say it happens. The first time is the enormity. The next time would be easier. . . . If only, she thought, before I told him, I could get Edmund to promise not to desert Heather. Even if he did undertake that (which no one would) he'd break his promise when he knew what she had done. She couldn't tell him. He must take his chance. And if Heather killed the man who had sacked him or the doctor who had failed to diagnose his illness or the driver of the car who hit his car or the little boy who teased their daughter—well, she would blame herself for the rest of her life.

"My son wants to buy a flat," said Irene. "I don't know why. I tell him that he already has a house. I regard this place as much his as mine."

This was said in the presence of both Edmund and Marion, Edmund and his mother having already thrashed the matter out to exhaustion point earlier in the day. Excited as another woman might be by sexual desire or some great treat in prospect, Marion was stimulated by family rows, any sort of row and anyone's family. Her face had taken on youthful color, her cheeks red and her eyes gleaming. Irene, by contrast, looked pale, even wan. Stately in a long black tunic over a long black skirt, her hair piled up on top of her head and kept in place precariously by silver pins, she sat like Patience on a monument, wondering at the vagaries of men. In her lap lay the coral beads she had been stringing onto a length of thread.

"You'd think he had everything he wanted here," she said. "He doesn't have to lift a finger.

Even though I say it who shouldn't, the food here is as good as anything cooked by that Jamie Oliver." She turned to Marion. "You know who I mean."

"Oh, yes," said Marion. "Frankly, I think your cooking is better."

"Cleaning the house from top to bottom, too. Bed making, the windows shining like—like diamonds—washing, ironing, all done for him."

For a moment Edmund thought his mother was going to compare herself with some television star who demonstrated the arts of the laundry on screen, but instead she said, "What do you think, Marion, about this idea of leaving, of setting up home elsewhere? Have you ever heard anything so absurd?"

"I'd rather not discuss this in front of Marion," said Edmund.

"Why on earth not?"

"Believe me, Edmund," said Marion, "I have nothing but your interests at heart. Who knows? After all, I am practically an estate agent and I may be able to help."

"Marion, you force me to say I don't need your help. I don't need anyone's help. I shall move out of here the moment the purchase of my flat is completed and that's all there is to it."

Having already said more in front of Marion than he intended, Edmund went upstairs where he phoned Heather and told her there had been a row but he intended to move just the same. He sat in his bedroom, thinking about how Heather had said of course she'd move in with him once he had possession of the flat in Crouch End, how easy it had been to find the flat and how smoothly things appeared to be going, and that he must assess the size of Heather's ring finger—and propose.

Downstairs, tactful Marion thought a change of subject would be the most acceptable course to take and had begun chatting about Avice Conroy. Three times since Christmas she had called on her in her house in Pinner and once she had done a stint of rabbit-sitting while Avice had gone away for the night to a friend's funeral in Harrogate. Avice herself was very frail, Marion thought, though of course marvelous for an eighty-year-old. As for those rabbits—well, it took all sorts to make a world, didn't it?

"She's eighty-four," said Irene in a doleful voice, and then, "I suspect he's going to get engaged to that girl. I don't see why they can't live here. Not that I would allow it until they were married."

"I wouldn't think much of a girl who lived with a man without being married under his mother's roof." Realizing that she had got into a mess with that sentence, Marion amended it to, "I mean, I wouldn't think much of an unmarried girl living with an unmarried man in his mother's house."

"Wouldn't you, Marion?" said Irene wistfully. She sighed. "I wish things could have been otherwise."

This was not a line Marion wanted the conversation to take, implying as it would that she had been left on the shelf. She reverted to her lame ducks and began talking about poor old Mr. Hussein, his few sticks of furniture, his single lily, and his childlessness. How he had loved the knuckle of ham! Irene interrupted her.

"I'm making this necklace for you, Marion, though I wonder if it's quite your color. Would malachite perhaps be better?"

Having no idea what color malachite was, Marion said, "Anything you made would be delightful, I'm sure. May I look?"

Irene held out the uncompleted necklace listlessly. "I'm sure I don't know when it will be finished. I can't work when I'm upset. You'd better run away now, Marion. I've got terrible heartburn or it may be the start of a hiatal hernia."

"Running away" was something Marion did all the time. It wasn't in her nature to walk or stroll. She went home at breakneck speed, galloping down Chudleigh Hill and along Acol Road to Lithos Road. Though shabby, her flat was neat and pleasantly scented with floral air freshener.

Irene's saying she had heartburn reminded her that it was time to check on the morphine. When her mother died a year earlier, a whole unopened bottle of morphine sulfate had remained among the medicaments, as well as an already opened bottle containing about half the quantity. Like a good citizen, Marion had handed the half-empty bottle and all the remaining vials and jars and packets to the nurse, but since no one asked for it, she kept the unopened bottle. At that time she had considered trying it on Mrs. Pringle, convincing herself that "putting her to sleep" would be a merciful release, a natural peaceful exit. The idea would be for Marion to pour a little on her homemade rhum baba, for instance, or a slice of tarte Tatin. She was always taking such delicacies to the house in Fitzjohn's Avenue. But Mrs. Pringle forestalled her and in the course of nature achieved an even more merciful release than Marion had had in mind, leaving behind her that thoughtful will.

On the principle of where do you hide a leaf

but in a tree, she first put the morphine in her bedside cabinet. But mistaking it for a dyspepsia remedy about six months later, she was on the point of unsealing it and unscrewing the cap before she remembered. Goodness, she might have killed herself! She took the morphine out and put it in the back of the bathroom cabinet along with items no one would consider consuming, a bottle of hand lotion and some vapor rub among other things. As soon as she got in she checked that it was still there. It was. Of course it was. Who would have moved it?

Well, Fowler might have. He'd drink anything if he thought it would intoxicate or stimulate him. Once, soon after Mrs. Pringle died and she'd first moved in here, he made his way in while she was out and drank a whole can of silver polish and half a bottle of Lancôme eau de toilette. It wouldn't be easy for him to get in now, not easy even for him since she had had the locks changed. Still, it would be wise to take precautions. She found an adhesive label, one of many neatly stacked in the stationery drawer, wrote POISON. NOT TO BE TAKEN on it, added INTERNALLY, and stuck the label on the morphine bottle.

. . .

"It may seem trivial to you," said Andrew, coming back into Ismay's bedroom after his shower, "but I don't actually much like sharing this place with those two. I don't like joining the queue for the bathroom. And most of all I don't like coming back here after being out with you somewhere and finding them sitting on the sofa, then having to get up after half an hour and say, 'Well, good night. Ismay and I are going to bed now.'"

"Oh, darling, you can't mean it embarrasses you."

"Not particularly. What I mean is I want to be allowed a bit of spontaneity. To make love to you on the sofa, for instance. On the floor—why not? In the bath. I don't want to be treated like half of an old married couple stopping the night with friends."

"It's not like that, Andrew."

"It is just like that. Are you going to tell me you don't keep quiet because they're there? You're not careful to stop the bed from creaking? If you have to go to the bathroom you're not conscious that one of them may be in it? Now that's embarrassing, if you like." Andrew was dressed by now, peering into the mirror to fix his tie. "And don't say it's as bad coming to me. You know Seb mostly stays in his room.

Besides, I can't live in my place without his rent."

"I wasn't going to say anything." Getting up, Ismay wondered if the bathroom was free but knew that if she asked Andrew another storm of protests would begin. "Edmund's found a flat, and he's expecting to sign the contract soon. He and Heather are engaged, and as soon as he can move he will and she'll go with him."

"And how long is that going to be? In my experience it's only when people pay for property with ready cash that these deals get done fast. Someone I know in chambers waited a year from signing a contract on a house until completion." He turned around and put out his arms, holding her naked body against him. "I love you. I love holding you like this whenever I want. I want to be alone with you and I don't want to wait a year."

"Of course it won't be a year, darling." Ismay took her dressing gown off the bed and wrapped it around her. "April is what Edmund's solicitor says."

"Look at you. You have to cover yourself up to go to the bathroom. In case your sister's boyfriend sees you. And in half an hour we're all supposed to sit around the kitchen table having breakfast together like two married couples sharing a **gîte** in the Dordogne. Oh, please. But I'm not doing that. Not this time. I'm going to leave now and call into Starbucks on my way."

But they were engaged, Edmund and Heather, she thought when he had gone. They would marry as soon as they had somewhere to live. Heather would go and Andrew could move in. It wouldn't be long, a few months at most. This will all work out, she told herself. It will come right. And as she made her way to the bathroom and passed Heather's door, which was a little ajar, she caught a glimpse of Edmund and Heather standing as she and Andrew had stood a few moments earlier. Quickly she looked away, but not before she had seen that Heather was naked, Edmund's arms enclosing her. The difference was that they were kissing.

Looking back, Ismay supposed she had been in love with Guy. He was her type, the prototype of her type really, the first one of a few that ended in Andrew: thin, tall, dark men with fine-drawn features and beautiful hands. When her mother first brought Guy Rolland home, she and Heather had been antagonistic, loyal to their father's memory, absolutely unable to understand that Beatrix, at not quite thirty-nine, might not yet be past the age for love. And that attitude had continued as far as Heather was concerned. She liked Guy as little as she was to like Andrew. In fact, when Ismay thought about it, she saw that her sister reacted to both men in the same way, had been similarly hostile—though rather less so—to those boyfriends who had come in between. Was it that they all looked a bit like Guy?

The first evening that Guy came into the house with Beatrix they had been to the theater and Guy brought her home. It was only their second date, the first being the dinner with Pamela and Michael. Guy was the marketing manager in the firm Pamela worked for at that time. There had been no matchmaking intended, she said afterward, and it was hard to see how she could have seen Guy as a suitable husband for her sister. For one thing, he was five years her junior and, since her husband's death, Beatrix had looked older than her age. Perhaps Pamela, only just over thirty at the time, had had her eye on him herself, Ismay had wondered, and considered he would be safe with Beatrix.

If that were so she couldn't have been more wrong. That first date led to another and another, and very soon Guy and Beatrix were a couple, an item. And Ismay developed a "crush" on him. She kept it dark; she was ashamed of it. He was her mother's, and Ismay, young as she was, understood that her mother needed Guy, even deserved Guy, after the years of nursing their father and her long-drawn-out suffering after his death. Besides, she was only thirteen, a child in appearance. That was how Guy must see her, as a child. Heather, on the other hand, eleven years old, was already beginning to look like a woman. But she was childlike, innocent, even naïve, Ismay thought. At school Heather worked hard. She worked earnestly, her eyes too close to the book she was reading, her handwriting slow, deliberate, and round. Far more than she and her mother did, Heather talked about their dead father. "Daddy" might not be still alive, but he was present with Heather, a rock to lean on, male perfection and the role model she would look for in the men in her own life.

"Why did Daddy have to die?" was a question she still occasionally asked. She didn't expect an answer. She knew there wasn't one.

For weeks she wouldn't speak to Guy. To do him justice—and Ismay was very willing to do him justice—he tried doing what he called "drawing her out." He wasn't stupid. He didn't bring her presents or call her darling, as he soon did call Beatrix and Ismay, he didn't ask her how she was getting on at school or ask her anything except her opinion, come to that. She was almost twelve but he talked to her as if she were ten years older, making it his business to find out what things she liked doing at school and after school, and trying to discuss these subjects with her. "Trying" was the word, Ismay thought. He never succeeded. Heather was learning Spanish and Ismay remembered— with pain now and a kind of fear—how Guy had talked to Heather about Spain and its history and language and the perils of the Spanish subjunctive, about tennis and Andre Agassi and Pete Sampras, and about cooking, which she was already good at. Heather didn't ignore him. She answered with a "yes" or a "no" or an "I don't know."

Ismay remembered the first time he had kissed her. He and her mother were engaged by then and due to be married a month later. When they got engaged Ismay expected Guy to move in. Every couple she knew or came across who were engaged, lived together. But Guy went on going out with Beatrix and bringing her home, and half an hour later kissing her good night. One evening he kissed Ismay too. She knew very well from films and television how men kissed women they were in love with and Guy's kiss wasn't like that. The way he kissed her mother wasn't like that either.

Ismay asked Heather why she thought he wanted to marry Beatrix. He didn't act as if he wanted to marry her. He just said he did and went along with all the arrangements.

"I expect he wants a house to live in," said twelve-year-old Heather.

"Oh, grow up," said Ismay. "You are such a baby. Men don't marry women for a house to live in. He's got a flat. Pam said he earns good money. I heard her say that to Mum when he first came here."

"Our house is nice and big. It's worth a lot. His flat is quite small with just one bedroom. I heard him say so. I expect he's got a big mortgage. You don't even know what a mortgage is, do you?"

"Of course I do." Ismay was bored by the kind of practical things that interested Heather. "I do know," she said, though she didn't really. "If he likes this house so much why doesn't he come and live here? They're engaged. It's normal to live together when you're engaged."

Their grandmother was alive then. "Gran says he respects Mum too much for that." Heather laughed. "I should think that if you respected someone you'd want to live with them. Won't he respect her after they're married?"

"He doesn't love her," Ismay said. She had never put that into words before. Now she did she knew it was true.

"Perhaps he won't marry her then. I hope he won't. We were better without him, just you and me and Mum."

Ismay and Heather went to the wedding, but they weren't bridesmaids. Beatrix liked the idea but Heather refused even to think of it. She hated dressing up. Once Guy was in the house, living there as much as they did, Heather changed. As she entered her teens she became the archetypical teenager, moody, intractable, and isolated. She wanted no one's company but Ismay's and she clung to Ismay, associating herself with her in every possible area of life. "I" almost disappeared from her vocabulary as "we" took over. It was "we don't want any breakfast" and "we didn't sleep well last night" and sometimes even "we've got a cold." One day, when Guy was talking to Ismay about what sort of job she thought she would have when her education was finished and where she would like to live, Heather said, "We shall live together. We always will."

The first time Ismay sat on Guy's knee was when he offered to help her with her homework. It was chemistry and she had to learn some of the periodic table. Guy, who had done chemistry to A level, called her over for them to study the book together. "Come here," he said. "Sit on my knee."

Beatrix was there and so was Heather, a look of horror distorting her face. Ismay sat on Guy's knee and immediately remembered that she had never sat on her father's. Close beside him, yes, his arm around her, in bed with him and her mother when she was little, on the arm of his chair, leaning against him, but never on his knee. If she had, would she have felt like she did sitting on Guy's? She thought not, she recoiled from the idea, because, with Guy's arm around her, his lean thighs under her slender delicate thighs, she felt—not something new, not quite that, but a sensation she had once or twice had when watching on television the kind of film put on after the nine o'clock watershed.

If she had told Heather about that feeling, about her sensation of some indefinable excitement, would Guy be alive today? It didn't bear thinking of. She had never told Heather and certainly never said a word to her mother. As far as Heather knew, she disliked Guy's putting his arm around her, kissing her, calling her his sweetheart and his angel. She didn't dislike it. Because she was so young, necessarily without experience, she thought she must be in love with Guy and only knew she hadn't been once he was dead. He attracted her and she desired him, that was all.

It was interesting, she often thought later, how everyone had a type who they were drawn to above all others. She had guessed the type that attracted Heather would be a man who resembled their father or at least had his qualities. That was why, when she first met Edmund, she almost committed the awful solecism of bursting out laughing with delight. He was the same height and build as Bill Sealand and, though with quite different features and hair color, had the same sort of voice and manner. Because of all that, she knew he would be right for Heather, just as she knew Andrew was right for her.

From the first, she pitied Beatrix. Poor old thing, but she hasn't a hope. Now she knew this was a typical adolescent girl's reaction to a mother's lover. What does he see in her? He can't be in love with her. She's old, she's a mess, she's let herself go. What wasn't typical, perhaps, was her thinking he must prefer me. Guy began kissing her when he left in the morning and when he came back in the evening. Just a kiss on the cheek or on both cheeks. But subtly she felt the kisses change. If her mother was there the kiss would be like the one he gave Pam or her mother's friend next door, an air kiss really, which barely brushed the skin. But when he and she were alone his lips stayed for a few seconds and moved closer to her mouth. He always got home at about six and she began making a point of happening to be out in the hall around that time. She had tennis lessons on Thursday evenings and more and more she began missing them so as to be in the hall when Guy came home.

If her mother came out just as Guy's key turned in the lock, Ismay would feel a sharp, almost panicky disappointment, and resentment, too. Heather was often there, but Guy took no notice of her. That is, he would say, "Hi, Heather," and smile at her, but he wouldn't let it stop him giving Ismay those kisses that had moved to her mouth by then. Heather was too young to bother about, Ismay knew he thought. Heather couldn't understand. She sometimes wondered when it was too late, why Heather hadn't said something to her, something on the lines of, "You shouldn't let Guy kiss you that way." At the time she had felt the way Guy felt: it doesn't matter about Heather being there, Heather doesn't count.

She never thought about what it would lead

to, what might happen, though she began to imagine a step farther on, a mile farther on. Guy might come to her bedroom one night. If only Beatrix would go away somewhere, go away on holiday, for instance, on her own with Pam. Or with Jill and Dennis, the people next door. A scenario developed in which Beatrix and Guy were planning a holiday, and she and Heather were to stay with Pamela. At the last minute Guy couldn't go. He was too busy at work. But Beatrix could still go and she went alone or maybe she took Heather with her and her old school friend Rosemary. Guy would be working all day but he'd come home in the evening and she'd be there and that first night Guy would. . . .

That was a fantasy and didn't happen. But when they were alone (except sometimes with Heather) Guy's kisses became real like in the kind of films she and Heather were still too young to see unaccompanied. His tongue exploring her mouth and his hands on her breasts. The first time that happened Heather saw. She stood in a corner of the hall where the phone was on a table as if she meant to make a call. Ismay seemed to remember her starting to dial just after Guy had said "hi" to her, starting to dial and then putting the phone down quietly when Guy took Ismay in his arms. Staring and noting what happened, no doubt, only Ismay was too rapt and excited to see.

It happened that way three times, with Heather there the first and second times but not the third. By then she was showing him she liked what he did, she responded to him, returning his kisses. After that Guy must have been busy at work because he started getting home later. Weeks went by without those kisses. And then he got the flu. Beatrix called it flu, though actually it was a virus, the kind that brings a high temperature, a headache, a sore throat, and congestion of the lungs. It was high summer, the time when no one is supposed to be ill. The first day Guy went to work but had to be brought home in a taxi. He almost collapsed in the hall. Ismay and Beatrix had to walk him upstairs between them, supporting him until they could get him onto the bed. Beatrix thought the doctor wouldn't come. It might be July, but the virus was raging and half the patients in the practice had it. The doctor would tell him to take acetaminophen or aspirins, drink plenty, and keep warm. This last wasn't difficult because a heat wave had begun and the temperature outside was approaching Guy's. But the doctor did come and said she would come again. Guy might have to go to hospital if he didn't improve.

Ismay helped Beatrix nurse him. Heather wouldn't. Ismay carried upstairs jugs of fresh water and glasses of orange juice. Because he soaked the sheets with sweat, Beatrix changed them every day while he sat shivering in a chair, wrapped in blankets. Ismay had another fantasy, that as he got better and his health and strength returned he would hold out his arms to her and as she sank into them, pull her into bed beside him. Her mother, of course, would be out shopping at the time.

Reflecting on this years later, she thought how little she must really have loved him, for she never worried about him. His illness lasted for a month and in all that time she slept as well as ever, she never thought about him except how he might make love to her. Thinking like that was when she realized she'd never had a real conversation with Guy. They never talked. Apart from Spain and Spanish, marketing (whatever that was), and watching sports on television, she had no idea what his tastes were. She never saw him read a book or listen to music. He had a degree in business studies, so he must know about them, but she didn't know what they were either. Something about keeping accounts, she supposed, or filing things. Making love with him was all she thought about, and even then she didn't know what lovemaking was like or, come to that—though the basic facts had been known to her since she was five—how you went about it. If she had loved him, wouldn't the possibility have occurred to her that he might die? Wouldn't she have been so anxious that she couldn't eat or sleep or do any of the normal things she did?

He did die, of course. Bathwater, not the virus, killed him. He drowned, his handsome face bleached by long immersion, his dark hair streaming and his long white hands floating just below the surface of the cooling water.

Chapter Six

Seeing Heather and Edmund's happiness, she
wondered how she could ever have considered
telling him. There was something else as well:
how she could never be absolutely irrefutably
cast-iron sure Heather was guilty of Guy's
death. No one could be positive Heather had
killed Guy. She couldn't and her mother
couldn't. They had the evidence, of course.
Heather coming downstairs with that look on
her face and her dress and skirt all wet down
the front, Heather never actually denying it,
Heather falling in with their plans to say she
hadn't been in the house but out with them. In
court, if it had ever come to it, a clever lawyer
could have demolished all that.

But if Heather hadn't done it, who had? Beatrix had put forward the theory of the mysterious intruder, in spite of the front door being locked and the back door locked and no sign of any break-in. The door to the balcony was open, Beatrix had said. Or she had said it until Ismay pointed out that in order to come into the bathroom through that door, the mysterious intruder would have had to break down the locked side gate into the garden or traverse neighboring gardens and climb over a six-foot-high wall. Then somehow climb up the sheer back of the house where there were no drainpipes or creeper vines and haul himself onto the balcony. All this with no one seeing him? On a fine summer's day when people were in their gardens?

But that was Beatrix's theory because she so much wanted it to be true. Besides, who but Heather would kill Guy and for what? Nothing had been stolen from the house. Nothing had been disturbed. Perhaps Guy had drowned himself. It is extremely difficult, Ismay had found out, to drown oneself in the bath, or anywhere else, come to that. Then her mother had said Heather wouldn't have had the physical strength to do it. She was not yet fourteen. But Heather was as tall and strong as a grown woman. Momentarily closing her eyes, Ismay saw her sister coming down the stairs once more, her eyes staring and her pink dress wet, drops of water on her shoes.

Weak as he was from his illness, he had struggled. He must have thrashed about in the water, for the bathroom was wet. Not wet as if water had come through the ceiling or a flood had come up through the floor, but wet enough. Heather's dress was wet down the front and the skirt was wet. She wasn't soaked. Could she have been in that bathroom and drowned a struggling man without getting soaked? If only she could remember twelve years later just how wet Heather's dress had been, how wet her shoes. But she couldn't. She couldn't remember if Heather had seemed frightened or shocked, but she retained an impression of Heather's calmness and of her steady voice.

The two choices before her seemed like two columns standing side by side in her mind. Written on one, like graffiti, were the words, TELL HIM, and on the other, NEVER TELL HIM. She asked herself, how can I ever make up my mind? Perhaps there might be a halfway house, a middle course. She knew she could never ask to see Edmund alone, then sit opposite him and tell him these things. There was no point in even considering this, ever thinking about it again. She couldn't do it. At the last minute, when they had met in some pub or hotel lounge or café, she would smile and kiss his cheek—they had begun these brotherly-sisterly kisses—she would come up with some completely different subject, where the wedding was to be, how to arrange some surprise for Heather. She would never tell him. So what could the middle course be? Write to him? Then she imagined seeing him later, after the letter had been read. It was as impossible as the meeting.

I could have this weighing on my mind for years, perhaps for the rest of my life, she thought. How to get rid of it without telling him face-to-face or taking the passive course and saying nothing? There must be something she could do. An idea came to her. She could record what she had to say, she thought, put it on tape, not give it to him but keep it. Get it off her mind, speak it aloud, then keep the tape until—what? There was always the chance—the curious, unlikely, but possible chance—that Heather herself would tell. Or they might split up. They hadn't known each other long. But far from agreeing with Andrew's rather callous forecast that they would marry in haste and repent at leisure, Ismay saw them as one of those rare monogamous couples who would never even consider straying from each other.

They were like those creatures she had read about imprinted with the image of their mates. If that mate died the other would be eternally inconsolable.

Making a tape seemed her only choice. Not ideal, perhaps cowardly, perhaps never to find its destined recipient, but just the same the sole possible solution. She could make it and wait. She admitted to herself that this was evading the issue, passing the buck. Of course, it was therapy for her. Perhaps that was all it would be. It would all be on tape and she wouldn't have to agonize about it anymore. Psychotherapists sometimes advised their clients to take hold of unpleasant thoughts or beliefs or fears and put them away into boxes in their minds. You could put the person you didn't get on with at work away in a box. You could put away a worry like that or an old but persistent unhappiness. The tape would be her box and she could put it away.

When Ismay was fourteen—for her fourteenth birthday, in fact—Guy had given her a tape recorder. She had got everyone to talk into it, Beatrix and Heather and Pamela as well as Guy himself. Michael Fenster fancied himself as the lead tenor in the local amateur operatic society

and he had sung an aria. Poetry was Beatrix's
choice and she had read a long poem of Ten-
nyson's. In time Ismay got tired of it. Almost
the last thing she recorded was a long apology
to her mother for having been rude to her.
Rude to her in what way she couldn't now remember, but she had said she was sorry at great
length and said it on tape because she felt better about giving Beatrix the tape than saying
the words to her. Tape recorders must be almost
obsolete now. Only journalists used them. She
hadn't used hers for years and she didn't know
where it was, but it must be somewhere in the
house and she could find it.

She walked about the flat, searching for the
tape recorder. It was just as likely to be upstairs,
more likely, seeing that Heather's and her bedrooms had been up there. It would be in a cupboard in one of those rooms. Pausing at her
own bedroom window, she looked down into
the street below and saw Pamela on her way out
somewhere. Beatrix would be sitting with her
ear to her radio, chewing gum or eating chocolate. She would take no notice if Ismay went up
there and hunted for the tape recorder. Maybe
she wouldn't even see her; certainly she would
show no curiosity as to what she might be doing. Ismay didn't much like using her key to get
in, but it was only for once. She could ring and

ring the bell and Beatrix would never answer the door. Beatrix wouldn't notice if someone broke the door down.

Ismay looked first in the rooms that had been Heather's and her bedrooms. They were Beatrix's and Pamela's now. They had been painted but not otherwise altered. Ismay looked inside the built-in cupboards, which were full of the older women's clothes just as they had once been full of hers and Heather's. No sign of the tape recorder. She tried the kitchen, though it was an unlikely place. As soon as she set foot inside the living room she knew where that recorder was going to be. When the conversion was made, cupboards and shelves had been built into the walls around the area where the bathroom had been. Open one of those doors and there it would be.

Although Beatrix invariably ignored her, Ismay never liked to be in her mother's presence without acknowledging her. It was as if she feared that if she did it once she would always do it and Beatrix would disappear, become worse than she was now, a nothing, a shadow, a ghost muttering madness. So she went up to her, kissed her cheek, and did something unusual with her. She took her mother's hand and held it for a few seconds. The hand in hers seemed the limpest thing she had ever han-

dled, cool but not cold, utterly relaxed and im-
mobile, until suddenly it tensed shockingly and
was snatched away.

The tape recorder was where she thought it
would be, in that changed place, in the box it
had originally come in. She said, "Good-bye,
Mum. See you later," and went downstairs, carrying the box.

In the bathroom was a shower cabinet in which
Guy and Beatrix took their daily showers, but
as he slowly recovered from his illness and no
longer needed to be sponged down from a
basin of water, Guy started taking an afternoon
bath. It was more restful and relaxing. Standing
up with hot water spraying him was still too
much for him. The bath (or "tub" as Americans
called it) wasn't free-standing but flush against
the wall on the right-hand side. The end nearest the doors was also against the wall but the
other stood free, and between it and the inte-
rior wall was sometimes the space for the
soiled-linen bin and sometimes, when Beatrix
changed things around, for a chair or a dark-
leaved ficus in a ceramic pot. The taps were in
the middle of the long side of the bath. At the
time of Guy's recovery from his illness the chair

stood in the space between bath end and door so that a bath towel could be hung over its back within easy reach of Guy when he got out of the water.

Neither Ismay nor Heather ever went into that bathroom. Having their own, which they shared and was between their bedrooms, they had no need. The last time Ismay had been in there was after Bill Sealand died and Beatrix was so wretched and desperate that Ismay crept into bed with her for a few nights so that she shouldn't be alone. Heather, as far as she knew, had never been in that bathroom. Of course she knew Guy was in the habit of taking a bath in the afternoons at about four. He had just begun coming downstairs afterward, wearing sandals and wrapped in a toweling dressing gown. It was on one of these descents of the stairs that he had kissed Ismay for the first time since the virus had struck.

She waited for him at the foot of the stairs. First of all she clock-watched. It was always between four-thirty and four-forty that he came down. At about twenty past four she was in her bedroom and she heard the water begin to drain away down the plug hole. She waited a bit longer and then she went downstairs, treading very softly, and slipped into the little room

Guy and her mother called their study. Beatrix was in the garden. She had been a keen gardener in those days.

Heather was nearby, though she hadn't known that at the time. She was also just inside a door, the living-room door, waiting. Because she had seen what was about to happen, or something like it, before? Perhaps. Ismay heard the bathroom door open and close, Guy cross the floor on bare feet to his bedroom, then come out again wearing sandals. She emerged nonchalantly from the study. A vase of flowers stood on a little console table against the wall between the living room and study doors. A pink chrysanthemum had fallen from the arrangement onto the polished surface of the table. Since that day, Ismay had always disliked chrysanthemums.

She was replacing the flower when Guy began to descend the stairs. She turned toward him, holding it up to her face.

"Do you know how very charming you look?" he said in a voice she had never heard before, a voice that was no longer intense but light and gentle and charged with something she couldn't define.

"Do I?" she said like the child she was.

He took the flower from her, lifted her face on one hand, and kissed her. But the kiss was different, light and somehow remote, just missing her mouth. Behind them, Heather made a sound, an intake of breath. Heather wasn't out in the hall but standing concealed by the living room door, which stood just ajar. Guy must have known she was there, and that accounted for the kiss that was so different and so disappointing. Ismay broke away from him once she knew Heather had seen and later she understood how Heather must have interpreted this move: as dislike on her part of what was happening, as resisting Guy, perhaps as fear of him.

Guy smiled, hugged her in a stepfatherly way, and gave back the flower. "You should wear it in your hair," he said, "or behind one of your ears."

But she hadn't. She wanted to explain to Heather but didn't know how to begin. Heather wouldn't understand. The fact was she didn't understand what was happening herself and now that twelve years had passed she knew that this was part of why child abuse was wrong. Because children didn't understand.

None of that excused Heather, though. If Heather had killed Guy—and she must have killed him—because she had seen him kiss her sister in a sexual way, she was wrong, wrong, wrong and perhaps Ismay and Beatrix had been wrong all along in shielding her.

Guy and she had gone into the living room after that. The pink chrysanthemum was back in the flower arrangement. Beatrix had come in from the garden with a pair of pruning shears in her hand and gone to make tea. As for Heather, she was sitting on the sofa reading a set book for holiday homework. It must be finished by the time school started on September 5, and she scarcely glanced up when they walked in.

Three days later Guy was dead.

Ismay recorded nothing of that. It wasn't necessary.

After the first awful dawning fear that Heather had done this thing, after seeing her wet clothes and that look in her eyes, she and her mother decided to test it themselves to see if it was possible. To see if a teenage girl could have done it. It was Beatrix's idea, and at first Ismay said no. She wouldn't, she couldn't, it was too horrible.

"We must," Beatrix said. "We must be certain."

Even then, aged fifteen, Ismay knew they would never be certain, whatever they did, because they could never precisely repeat the conditions of the drowning or reproduce the two people involved. All they could do they did.

While Heather was out at a school friend's house—that same Greta she had been going to visit on the fateful afternoon—Beatrix said they must carry out their plan. She was adamant about not getting naked into the bath. She had been prudish in just the same way when she and Ismay found Guy drowned. Even then, **in extremis.** "Don't look," she had hissed at Ismay. "He's naked, don't look at him."

She got into her red one-piece swimming suit and a ridiculous rubber bathing cap with waves and curls embossed on it and fastened the strap under her chin. Ismay positioned herself at the end of the bath behind the taps and waited. Beatrix finally got herself under the water, the hot steaming water that seemed to make her shiver and cringe.

"Why are you wearing that?" Ismay had asked. "It's grotesque."

"I'm not letting you see me naked."

"Oh, Mum, you're mad."

Afterward, she wished many times she had never uttered those words.

They didn't speak, or if they did Ismay had forgotten. Her mother's long thin white feet floated just under the taps. The toenails were painted red and the varnish had started to chip. Hating what she was doing, the play-acting part of it and its macabre side, Ismay took hold of

Beatrix's feet and in a strong fast movement lifted them up high above the surface of the water. Beatrix's head plummeted backward and plunged below the water, her arms and hands thrashing. She tried to pull her legs backward and as she did so bubbles rose in streams from her end of the bath. The beating arms and struggling feet sent cascades of water over Ismay's dress. Her mother was under there for no more than fifteen seconds before she let her go.

"I thought you were going to drown me, too," Beatrix said, coughing and spluttering.

Ismay was drenched, her blouse clinging to her chest. There was water everywhere. The towel draped over the chair at the head of the bath was soaked, and the bath mat was sodden. "I'm three inches shorter than Heather," Ismay had said, "and I weigh about fourteen pounds less, but I could do it. It was easy." She began to cry, shivering in her wet clothes. She had thought then, my mother was strong and well but Guy was weak; he'd been ill.

"What shall we do?"

Ismay, the tears running down her face, thought her mother shouldn't have asked her that. It was a question no woman of thirty-nine should ask a fifteen-year-old.

. . .

She need not tell Edmund that part. When he had heard the tape, he would ask her questions and she would tell him. If he didn't simply ignore it, pretend it didn't exist. Who knew? She sat down on the sofa, put the tape recorder on the coffee table, and switched it on. First she tested it, then she began.

"My stepfather was called Guy Rolland. He was thirty-three when he married my mother and she was thirty-eight." That was the bit she played back. Her voice sounded clear and steady, better than she had dared hope. "My father had been dead for three years. When Heather was thirteen and I was fifteen, Heather got it into her head that Guy was abusing me. Nothing had really happened apart from some kissing and a little—well, a very little—fondling, but Heather thought I was in danger from Guy. All I thought was that he was very fond of me, as I was of him." That wasn't completely true, but Edmund wouldn't want to know about her sexual feelings for Guy. Better to let him think she had none. It would look better for Heather. "What Heather did she did to protect me. Not from revenge, I don't think that, but to protect me from—rape, I suppose. This would never have happened, I'm sure of that, if Heather had told me what she was afraid of, but she never told me.

"When Guy and my mother had been married for about two years, Guy got a very bad virus. He was ill for three weeks and there was some idea of taking him into the hospital because he wasn't responding to treatment. Just as our GP was talking of getting him a bed in the hospital, Guy started to get better. My mother had barely left the house for a fortnight, she had been at home caring for him, but by that Thursday—it was the end of August—he seemed nearly well again, though without much strength. My mother wanted to take me out to buy a school uniform, some items of school uniform—a skirt and blazer, it was. It was the summer holidays. We went out at about two in the afternoon, leaving Heather at home because she was going around to a friend's house. Apparently, soon after we went out, the friend—Greta—phoned to say not to come because she had to go out with her parents, so Heather was alone in the house with Guy.

"They had never liked each other. Heather always had as little to do with him as possible and although he tried to be nice to her at first, he gave up on that. What happened in the house between the friend phoning and, say, four p.m. I don't know. I suppose Heather knows but no one else can. At about four Guy got up to have a bath. Since he'd been getting better he'd regularly had a bath at around that time, and then would put on his dressing gown and come downstairs to sit with us and have a meal before going back to bed. Sometimes he'd sit in the garden. It was hot weather. So on that Thursday he got up to have his bath in the en suite bathroom which opened off the bedroom he shared with my mother. There were French windows then from the bathroom onto a balcony, but of course it's all changed now.

"I don't know where Heather was, possibly in her own bedroom, adjacent to his. Probably she came out when she heard him get out of bed. She would have heard him walk rather slowly into the bathroom and run the bath. When she was sure he was in the bath she went into the bathroom. Perhaps he didn't see her— she would have gone in very quietly—but when he did I expect he shouted out, asked her what the hell she was doing, told her to get out. She took hold of his feet in her hands and pulled them upward. I don't know if you know what happens when someone does that. Your head goes under. Guy's head went under and no doubt he struggled and thrashed about but he was weak from the flu. You'd try to get hold of the sides of the bath with your hands and pull your head out, but that takes strength and Guy was very weak. . . ."

Was a lot of that conjecture? How could she be sure of exactly what Heather had done? Perhaps only because there could be no other way. She stopped the tape recorder and went out of the flat into the hall. It was very different now from what it had been when the house was in single occupation. A wall had been put up to divide the hall into two, half leading directly to the stairs and the upstairs flat. The other half was the lower flat's hallway. Their own front door was halfway along the wall, and both flats shared the common front door. She stood in this hall by the front door and looked up the stairs. They were unchanged. Here her mother and she had come in from shopping. A table stood there once, a console table, usually with a bowl of flowers on it. They had put their shopping bags down on the floor by this table and, hearing a footstep, had looked up the stairs and seen Heather.

Ismay went back inside and switched the tape recorder on again.

"Heather came downstairs. She was wearing a pink cotton dress and the front of it was wet, the bodice and the skirt. Her shoes were wet. I don't remember what she said. Maybe she didn't say anything. My mother said, 'Why are you so wet, Heather? Where have you been?'

"Then Heather said, 'I've been in the bathroom. You'd better come.' We went upstairs. My mother went first. She told me afterward she thought one of the pipes was leaking. We'd had trouble with it before. We went into the bathroom. I don't remember if there was water everywhere. I suppose there must have been. The bath was full of water and Guy was in it. He was lying under the water and he was dead."

That was the first time she had ever seen a man's naked body. Strange that the first one she had seen should be a dead man's. Dead, Guy looked very young, a boy. Beatrix screamed once, then fell on her knees and the crying and muttering began. She clapped both hands over her mouth. Ismay looked and then looked away, trembling, shaking all over. She stumbled back into her mother's bedroom and fell on the unmade bed. Beatrix came in and silent Heather with her. That was how it had been. Ismay returned to the tape recorder.

"My mother asked Heather what had happened and Heather said she didn't know. Then she asked her what made her go into the bathroom. Neither of us ever went into that bathroom. The last thing Heather would have done was go in there where Guy would have been naked. But she had. It didn't occur to me for a while that Heather might have had something to do with that death. Heather said nothing in answer to my mother's question. Then my mother asked her if she'd been in her own bedroom when Guy got up. 'I went into the bathroom,' Heather said. 'I was in there a bit and he was dead. He was like he is now.' My mother screamed aloud when Heather said that, and she clutched at me. She said to me, 'Phone a doctor. No, phone for an ambulance. Dial nine-nine-nine.'

"I couldn't. I'd lost my voice. After a bit my mother phoned Pam and Pam came. I think it was she who phoned for an ambulance. The police came eventually. I don't know who sent for them. It was evening by then. There was a detective inspector and a detective constable, I think. The inspector had a name like a bird, Sparrow or Peacock but not one of those. I can't remember anything about the constable except that he was young.

"An ambulance came with two paramedics and they took Guy's body away. Or it may not have been an ambulance. There may have been a doctor. I don't remember. Before the police came Mum said to Heather, 'These people who are coming will ask. The police will have to come and they will ask.' Heather didn't say anything. I think she was terrified. Mum thought for a moment and then she said, 'You were out with us. All three of us were shopping. You complained about Issy taking so long trying on clothes.' Heather gave her such a strange look. She looked like an old, old woman for a moment. 'Did I?' she said.

"It was like a game. I got into the spirit of it, me, aged fifteen. I said, 'You were fed up because they hadn't got a blazer in your size.' 'All right,' she said. Mum said, 'No, Heather, it wasn't like Issy says. You came with us but you didn't come into the shop. You waited outside while Issy tried things on.' Heather shrugged; she said, 'I was with you. It's simpler that way, isn't it?' And that was all. That was all she said and all she's ever said. The inspector with the bird name and the other one came and said there would be an inquest. They believed everything we said, the nice and sensible but distraught widow, her well-behaved teenage daughters. We said what we'd rehearsed saying.

"My mother and I knew we should tell the police the truth—what we both thought, that is—but we couldn't. This was Heather, her daughter, my sister. My mother had lost her husband, a man she'd loved, at any rate when they were first married she'd loved him, but

Heather was more important to her. Far more.
We both understood by then why she had done
it. My mother said she half knew, she guessed,
about Guy and me. She had seen things. 'You
should have told me,' she said and she sounded
very angry. I said nothing. What could I have
said to his wife? She had considered separating
herself from Guy, but she hadn't yet said a word
to him and now it was too late. If she'd left
him—or turned him out; it was her house after all—if she'd done that he'd be alive and
Heather not guilty of anything. We never told
anyone. We agonized over it, separately and together. We wept together. If it's possible for
grief and horror to turn someone's brain, and
all those old dramas and operas and whatever
said it was, this turned my mother's."

She stopped there. All this wasn't necessary.
He only had to know, if it ever came to this, the
basics of what Heather had done. No need to
tell him about the inquest and the verdict of ac-
cidental death, the bruises on Guy's ankles dismissed as due to some other cause. No one but
Guy, after all, had been in the house at the
time. Beatrix had been out shopping with her
two daughters. They had all returned home together.

And Heather? How had she and her mother
confronted Heather? The answer was that they

hadn't. Beatrix manifested signs of schizophrenia after a year had passed and slipped away into madness. Ismay never again mentioned the way Guy had died, already afraid that Heather might come out with it and tell her the truth. Much as she wanted to know, she was afraid of Heather telling her. She couldn't imagine a situation in which she asked Heather straight out and Heather said, yes, she had. Yes, she'd drowned Guy. To save Ismay from being raped by Guy. Not so much from dislike, hatred even, but to save her beloved sister from her stepfather.

And Heather seemed just the same afterward as she had been before—but perhaps not quite the same. Calmer, quieter, steadier, the kind of person you would tell your fears to and know they would be safe with her and stay hidden. Not a gorgon, as Andrew described her, but a quiet, reposeful woman who seemed older than her years, the woman Edmund loved so much.

Chapter Seven

The temporary hiding place Ismay found for the tape was in the bottom of a ceramic pot under the dry roots of a cactus. The cactus had vicious thorns instead of prickles and putting the tape in there made her fingers bleed. She scratched them again two days later when she decided the hiding place wasn't safe, moved it out, and put it inside a case that had originally contained a cartridge of Indian classical music. It wasn't long sinnce she'd been mad about the sitar and the tabla, but most of her collection was on CDs. This tape was Aashish Khan's **Rainy Season Ragas,** which no one in this flat was remotely likely to want to listen to. She put it on the shelf where all the other tapes were, station and the La Marquise café it had fallen through a hole in his pocket.

"Is there anything to eat?" he asked.

"Only sardines," said his sister, "and some Brussels sprouts, but they're a week old. I haven't had time to go shopping. Some of us work, you know."

Fowler stared glumly into space, scratching his head. "People like you don't seem to realize that begging is work. Very hard work. You're outdoors in all weathers, you can never relax, you never take a break. You've got to be polite all the time, you've got to be humble. If you speak your mind you're done for. And there's nothing of what you'd call job satisfaction. Even in Piccadilly or Bond Street you can stand about for three or four hours and those rich bitches'll walk past you on their way into jewelry shops. And then the Prime Minister has the nerve to tell people not to give to beggars. As if they needed telling. I think I'll make myself sardines on toast."

Marion followed him into the kitchen, not to help with the preparation of his meal but to stop him raiding her liquor supplies.

"Do you remember when we were kids you used to have to open sardine tins with a key stuck through that ring thing? And the key always broke and you had to put something stronger into the ring. I used the poker. I bashed myself in the mouth and knocked one of my front teeth out. You must remember."

"You were always accident prone."

"Can I have a drink?"

"No, you can't."

"Come on, Marion. Don't be like that. I tell you what. If I can have a drink and a couple of aspirins—well, four, say—I'll have my sardines and a bit of that Christmas pudding I saw in the fridge, if I can have that I won't stay. I'll go straight after. Come on, be a sport. A gin—well, a double—and a few aspirins and I'll make myself scarce."

"All right," said Marion, relieved she wouldn't have him sleeping on her sofa. Mystified as always by his choice of narcotics, she poured the gin herself, carefully calculating the amount in a measuring glass. She was more generous with the aspirins, dropping six strong ones into a saucer. She ate nothing herself, having made an arrangement to rabbit-sit for Avice Conroy. She'd pop in again on Mr. Hussein before she went to Pinner. Avice was so grateful. As well as paying her, she always left her a Marks and Spencer ready meal and half a bottle of wine. Marion looked forward to it. While she was in her bedroom, changing into her coral tracksuit, Fowler spotted her handbag on top of the fridge. Go easy, Fowler, he cautioned himself. If you don't take more than a tenner the chances are she won't notice. He took a ten-pound note and two pound coins, called out to her that he was leaving, and closed the front door gently behind him. Be careful not to lose those oncers, Fowler, like you did the fifty pence, he told himself. In his inner monologue he always addressed himself as Fowler. He was proud of his given name. It had been his mother's before she married and, when he was feeling low, he reflected that it was the only distinguished thing about him.

The evening was mild and he was in no hurry. He strolled down the Finchley Road, disappointed because the gin and aspirins had had little effect. The twelve pounds he had stolen from his sister he had originally intended to spend on a slap-up greasy spoon meal, the sardines being inadequate, but the rival claims of lager or skunk competed, and of the two he could get more drink for his money. Three pubs later, with not quite his bus fare left, he set off unsteadily on foot for the dossers' hostel, known to its denizens as Jimbo's, in Queens Park. It closed its doors at eleven sharp. If you don't make it in time, Fowler, he said to himself, you'll find yourself sleeping in a doorway. It wouldn't be the first time.

In spite of his dislike of the women who frequented it, Fowler was again in Bond Street three days later, loitering outside Lalique's doorway and wishing he had a dog or, better still, a baby. That was a brilliant idea. It was always women who begged with babies, but there seemed no reason why a man shouldn't do it. Could he borrow a baby? More feasibly, could Marion?

Rooting through the rubbish bins of Bond Street and Piccadilly was part of what he told Marion was his day's work. Not every day, of course, but three times a week. If, as occasionally happened, he saw someone else with his hand plunged up to the elbow in, for instance, the one in Piccadilly outside the Ritz, he took it as a personal affront. If there were a dossers' union and he were a shop steward, it was the kind of thing he'd bring the workforce out on strike over.

The sort of bins you found in the less salubrious suburbs contained too much perishable food waste, burger remains, curry containers, and chicken bones. Fowler wasn't fastidious but he disliked bad smells apart from his own, and the bins of Harlesden were a bit much. Mayfair was something else. There was a bin in Piccadilly, outside the Royal Academy, in which he had once found a pink satin toilet bag full of freebie cosmetic samples he'd given to Marion for Christmas and on another occasion a watch that only needed a new battery. The bin outside the Ritz had yielded a jar of Fortnum's marmalade—why?—and an umbrella with a Mickey Mouse face on it, while another in Bond Street gave him two stalls tickets for **Phantom of the Opera** for that evening. The watch and umbrella he had sold in Church Street market, the tickets outside the theater; and he'd eaten the marmalade.

Fowler regarded the bins of Piccadilly, Jermyn Street, and Regent Street with Bond Street and its offshoots as his manor, his golden square mile. He particularly disliked seeing anyone else investigating them and made himself unpleasant if there were confrontations. This evening he had caught a more than usually filthy dosser at the Bond Street one **in flagrante delicto,** so to speak. It was no wonder his own probings into that particular bin had been disappointing. The harvest he had gleaned was merely a single badly bruised cigarette in an otherwise empty packet and a condom. To be fair, it was an unused condom still in its pack but an article for which Fowler had no possible use. If he tried to sell it, potential buyers would think he'd stuck a pin through it first out of malice. He had smoked the cigarette in Lalique's doorway, thought a bit more about the baby plan, and sat down with half a cardboard carton, once containing porridge oats, beside him on the marble step, hoping for what he had once heard grandly called "eleemosynary alms."

It was there that Edmund passed him on his way to buy Heather a birthday present in the Burlington Arcade. Knowing Marion had a brother but never having seen him, he merely felt that slight pang of guilt we all feel when passing a beggar. But on his way back, carrying the newly gift-wrapped pale-blue cashmere sweater, he saw the man still sitting there with an empty carton beside him and felt in his pocket for change. He had spent so much already that another couple of quid would make no difference.

Fowler said, "Thank you very much, sir. You're a gent."

Ashamed of his warm feeling of righteousness, Edmund went on up the hill and turned into Brook Street, heading for Bond Street tube station. It was just after seven on a Thursday, late-night shopping evening, dark but brilliantly lit. Ahead of Edmund a taxi coming from the direction of Berkeley Square pulled up to the curb and stopped. Two people got out and one of them was Andrew. Edmund had ample time to make sure it was Andrew, watching him pay the taxi driver from the pavement. His companion, who he at first thought must be Ismay, was a different girl, fairer than she, just as slender, wearing shoes with golden heels of an impossible height and a fur wrap. And apparently not much else, thought Edmund. They didn't see him, being too engrossed in each other, Andrew's arm around the girl's shoulders as they disappeared down the exquisitely cobbled entrance to Lancashire Court.

Sitting in the train, he thought about what he had seen. There was no doubt about it. The girl couldn't have been Andrew's sister (if he had a sister) unless they were committing incest, which, when you came to think of it, also amounted to infidelity. What should he do, if anything? Nothing, of course. Telling Ismay wasn't to be considered. But tell Heather? He thought not. It would only upset her. He had long since perceived how close Heather and Ismay were, how deeply his fiancée loved her sister. She would no more tell Ismay than he would, but she might make some sort of row

with Andrew, have it out with him. It sometimes amused him to see how much she disliked Andrew. Better tell himself it wasn't his
business and try to forget it. He was already
learning that his future wife could be fierce and
direct as well as calm.

He got to Clapham just before eight. The
girls were having champagne to celebrate
Heather's birthday. He handed over the sweater
and it was rapturously received. It hardly
seemed fair that Heather should cook her own
birthday dinner, but she seemed to like doing it
and she was, naturally, a very good cook.

"When we're married," Heather said, smiling at him, "Edmund's going to do all the
cooking forevermore because I'll be doing it at
work."

He thought he saw a kind of shadow pass
across Ismay's face or perhaps it was more a
stiffening, a setting, of the muscles into a fixed
smile. He had experienced his own face doing
that when something painful or embarrassing
had been said (usually by his mother). It was
accompanied, in his case, by an inward sensation that was close to nausea but not quite that.
Was that how Ismay was feeling and why? Was
it possible she knew about Andrew's defection?

Within a few moments it appeared not, for
she was expecting him to phone her. She re-

marked on this omission with surprise. He wasn't coming around, she said. He had had to work late. But he had promised to phone. Just before Heather put their starter on the table, Ismay phoned him. Or tried to.

"His mobile's switched off," she said.

"He's probably in a meeting," said Edmund, wondering why he seemed to be furthering that philanderer's deception. But it was to protect Ismay, who would soon be his sister-in-law. After all, she might never need to know. It wasn't inevitable that she find out, and if she could be kept in ignorance for a while, Andrew might get over this attraction and return to her. Strangely, for he had not found this other woman particularly fetching—too pale and childlike—he thought of her high golden heels and glistening wrap before he turned his attention to his dinner.

Ismay, who normally had a healthy appetite, found she couldn't eat much of Heather's avocado mousse with pears and arugula or her roast quails with sweet-sour orange sauce. She had only once before known Andrew to turn off his mobile, and that had been on Christmas Day when he was with his parents. If he was working late he should be in chambers, but when she called the number there was no reply. Pamela had given Heather the latest six DVDs of **Sex and the City** for a birthday present, and she and Edmund put on the first one of them after they had finished eating. Ismay went into her bedroom and tried Andrew's mobile number again. It was still switched off.

She attempted to think of other things, but all that came to mind was Heather's remark that began, "When we're married." It had brought her a faint feeling of sickness. Every mention of the coming marriage did that. The only one of "the other things" that came to mind was the tape. A plan to find out about safe deposit boxes had come to nothing. It seemed too grand a project and there was a flavor of espionage about it. People like her didn't possess and conceal secret documents—for this was what the tape amounted to. Anyway, she was beginning to think the whole idea of the tape had been rather silly. She was a little ashamed of making it, of sitting there and talking into a recording device about her beloved sister. Especially when, though it was designed for that sister's future husband, she knew she never would give it to him.

She slept badly, waking every hour or two to ask herself why Andrew had turned off his mobile. The next morning, she tried it and got a message that he wasn't available. Strange how every time her glance took in the shelf where the tape was (and where the CDs and her iPod and Walkman radio also were), the first thing her eyes rested on was that tape. **Rainy Season Ragas.** It was quite safe where it was, she reminded herself. The eyes of others wouldn't see it or would not see it any more than they would see the Mozart or the dangling headset on her radio.

In the train she began once more worrying about Andrew. He'd behaved like this at Christmas, true, but Christmas was an exceptional time when the usual rules hardly applied. There had been another occasion, the summer before, when he had seemed to disappear for a few days and she had been frantic with worry. He soon explained that his mother had been ill. He had been in the hospital with her in some remote place in the Scottish Highlands where, for some reason, his mobile didn't work. She had worried then. She always thought of an accident in that fast sports car of his father's he liked to borrow. If he was injured who would let her know? She wasn't Andrew's partner or his fiancée but only his girlfriend. His parents might not even know of her existence. It brought her a shaft of pain to think that might be true. Did he talk about her to other people? She didn't know but she was sure Edmund talked to his friends about Heather.

. . .

Now that Edmund was regularly absent from Chudleigh Hill three nights a week, Irene had begun to understand he really did intend to get married. He really meant to move out and buy a flat five miles away. Her making it plain that she disapproved, disliked what she knew of Heather Sealand and believed that "anticipating marriage" doomed any subsequent union to failure, had had no effect on his conduct.

She devoted a large proportion of her thoughts to plans for showing him what a grave mistake he was making. Mostly these schemes came to no more than telling him to wait a little longer, that she was not well enough to be left on her own and that he couldn't afford to get married. She even asked him if he knew as much as a putative husband should about his future wife's background and antecedents, but this, as even she could see, had a fatal effect and resulted in his changing his mind about inviting Heather for Sunday lunch. Heather had only twice been to the house in Chudleigh Hill, the first time when she had more or less told Irene outright that Edmund's mother wouldn't be welcome to join them at the cinema and the second when she and Edmund had come home together after work.

Edmund had phoned but only half an hour ahead of their arrival. Naturally, she hadn't been very welcoming to Heather—how could she be after the way the girl had snubbed her about the cinema?—but when she had said she couldn't possibly produce a meal at a few minutes' notice, Edmund had chosen to take it badly. He and Heather would go out to eat, he had said, and come back to see her later.

"I don't think so," she had said quite reasonably. "It's nearly eight now and by the time you get back I shall be thinking about bed." His shrug annoyed her. "You're here so seldom I expect you've forgotten I go to bed quite early."

Surprisingly, the girl had suddenly said, "Why don't you come with us?"

Edmund had probably told her off for her behavior over going to see that film. That would be it. "Oh, no, my dear, that wouldn't do. I don't suppose Edmund's told you but I'm not a very well person. This has been one of my bad days."

They had gone and not come back. Irene told Joyce, first on the phone, then face-to-face. Joyce was unsympathetic, but that was only to be expected; they had never been close as sisters. "That's a game you can't win," she said. "The mother always loses. All you'll succeed in doing is alienating your son. He won't stay away three nights a week. He'll stay away every night. I wouldn't be surprised if you didn't get an invite to the wedding."

"What do you know?" Irene said rudely. "You've never had any children."

She painted a different picture for her new neighbor. "My son and his fiancée are always begging me to come with them when they go out, but I seldom feel up to it. I've never been strong, you know. Between ourselves, I shall be relieved when he's married and in a home of his own. I shall be left to my own devices at last."

Barry Fenix was a tall, soldierly-looking man with thick white hair and a small mustache. Every inch the colonel of the regiment was how Irene saw him, though he had told her in a burst of confidence that while doing his National Service he had never risen above the rank of lance-corporal. Another thing he told her was that he had a unique collection on DVD of films about the Indian Army and the Northwest Frontier. "You should think about going," he said, speaking to her over the garden wall. "You ought to get out more, a fine-looking woman like you. This could be your opportunity. Your son's wedding, I mean. Seize the day, Irene, seize the day."

"Do you mean, go out with them or go

out—well—with other people? You seem a bit confused." She smiled encouragingly, sure he was going to invite her out. For a drink, wasn't that what they said? Or maybe to watch his DVDs. "Now which is it?"

"I was only trying to be helpful." He went back into the house.

Andrew was back. His mobile was on all the time, and he was taking Ismay out in the evenings and spending the nights with her. Perhaps it was his imagination, Edmund thought, that he was less ardent, less **fixed** on Ismay than formerly. It must be imagination, it must be an illusion created in his mind by what he had seen that evening in Lancashire Court. And the girl in the fur with the golden heels? Someone from Andrew's past, a former girlfriend, a cousin, or even a one-off evening's companion, picked up somewhere in a moment of madness, of aberration. . . . Anyone could see he was in love with Ismay—or did he mean that anyone used to be able to see?

When he had first met Andrew, Edmund fancied that he had complained less. Now it seemed that he was always grumbling and mostly that the flat was overcrowded. Without quite coming out with it and saying Edmund wasn't welcome there overnight, he constantly harped on the nuisance of having only one bathroom between four people, of one couple being obliged to go out in the evening so as to leave the other alone, of what he called the "chaos" of breakfast eaten standing up or sharing the tiny kitchen table. Edmund discussed it with Heather, even suggesting most unwillingly that he should cut his overnight stays down to twice a week. Or, tired of waiting for the seemingly interminable chain to show its last links, rent a flat somewhere.

Prudent Heather didn't encourage this. She had paid her rent up to the end of April and couldn't ask Ismay to reimburse her. Her suggestion was that they share his room in his mother's house.

"It will only be for a few months."

"It will be hell," he said.

She said in a very serious tone, "We can get married first if you like."

"Of course I like. But I know her. I know how she can be. I don't want her breaking up my marriage when it's only just begun."

Ismay was beginning to see that marriage as inevitable. She was tempted to take the easy option, to relax and let it happen. But what she had foreseen—that once she had made the tape she would cease to think about its contents—hadn't happened. She dwelled on it nearly as much. And now she began asking herself if she could be quite sure, positive, certain beyond a doubt, that Heather had killed Guy. There was of course the evidence of the wet dress as she came downstairs when they arrived home. The very fact of her coming downstairs counted against her. So did her agreeing with Ismay and her mother when they said she had been out, buying her school uniform, with them. An innocent person would surely have denied that. Ismay had expected her to deny it and had felt sure of her guilt when she didn't.

But there was—just—an alternative. There was the inquest's version. Enfeebled Guy, taking a bath in water which was too hot, had lost consciousness. Fainted, she supposed you would call it. His head had sunk below the surface of the water and in his weak state he had been unable to struggle out. So the coroner had said. Or there was the fact that, however inaccessible it seemed to be, the door to the balcony had been open. It would have been hard to get into the garden but not impossible. As for climbing up a ladder to get to it, a neighbor seeing that would have assumed it was the window cleaner.

These solutions dwindled into thin theories against the evidence of the wet patch on Heather's dress or the lie Ismay and her mother had told and Heather confirmed, the lie that gave her an alibi. Would she have needed an alibi if she had been innocent? Of course, it might be that she had let Beatrix lie for her because it saved trouble. Seeing how it looked, the wet dress, the wet shoes, her dislike of Guy, she might only have been **relieved** that her mother intended to protect her from police questioning. It was a strange answer to the dilemma of Heather, but it was a possible one.

Everyone accepted the coroner's verdict. Pamela had never questioned it. Nor had their mother's brother nor any friend or neighbor. She wouldn't have questioned it—except that she had been there and seen Heather and heard what she said. Perhaps what she should try to do now was attempt to see that verdict as true and right, the way others saw it. The trouble was that, looking back, she saw that she and her mother had modeled their subsequent lives on the assumption that Heather had done it. They lived the way they lived, Beatrix in madness, Ismay watching over Heather, because they had been convinced Heather had murdered her stepfather. Could they undo the structure of that after all these years?

Chapter Eight

The man in Crouch End who was selling Edmund his flat insisted he wasn't backing out of the deal. He couldn't help it if his vendor wanted a further month's delay on signing the contract for the sale of his house. Edmund couldn't expect him to sign the contract on the sale of his own until he was sure of somewhere to go when he moved out. Edmund, of course, agreed. The alternative was to start again with another property. He and Heather loved the Crouch End flat, already thought of it as their future home, and hated the idea of trying to find somewhere else.

Meanwhile, a row had taken place with Andrew one Saturday morning. He found himself

alone with him while the girls were out shopping. Edmund had no idea what Andrew
wanted to say when he asked if he could have a
word, but he soon found out.

"Are you and Heather any closer to moving
into this place you're buying?"

"The vendor keeps delaying. It's not likely
to be much before May." Edmund hadn't particularly liked Andrew's adversarial tone. "Why
do you ask?"

"Well, frankly, because there isn't room for
four in this flat."

"I think that's down to Ismay and Heather,
don't you?"

"Not entirely, no, I don't. It's a matter of
priorities. I was here first. From what Ismay
tells me you have a home in West Hampstead
that is a considerable size. What stops you taking Heather there until this elusive purchase of
yours is available—if it ever is?"

"That house belongs to my mother. My
mother lives there." Edmund wasn't about to
go into reasons why Heather and his mother
wouldn't get on. Now, he decided, was the time
to clear the air, though air clearing was seldom
what a row achieved. "I don't see what this has
to do with you. Two sisters are the tenants of
this flat, and you and I are here as in my case
the fiancé of one of them and in yours as the

boyfriend of the other. On equal terms, in fact." Because he was growing angry and remembered the scene in Lancashire Court, he said, "I at least am going to marry Heather."

"What's that supposed to mean?"

"That you," said Edmund, again seeing the girl with the golden heels, "are not going to marry Ismay. You're seeing someone else, aren't you?"

Andrew, who had been walking up and down like a lawyer in an American courtroom, stopped and stood very still. "Who told you that?"

Almost an admission, Edmund thought. He hadn't intended things to go as far as this, but now he thought he had better come out with what he had seen. "I saw you getting out of a cab in Brook Street with a girl."

"You mean that in your philosophy sharing a taxi with someone who's not Ismay amounts to infidelity? If that's so, God help you."

"The way you and she were together amounts to it in anyone's view."

"Have you said anything to Ismay?"

"No, and I shan't. I haven't even said anything to Heather."

The sudden change in Andrew was shocking. He came over to Edmund and stood over him, pointing one long finger in his face. "You stupid, lower-class, puritanical bastard!" he shouted. "You, you paramedic, you **male nurse.** A so-called man who lives in his mother's house till he's thirty-five, a queer, a pansy, who takes up with the ugliest girl he's met because that's all he can get. You make me puke, you fucking mummy's boy!"

Edmund got to his feet, pushed the quivering finger away with his right hand, and thought of hitting him. It would make matters worse. He turned and walked away into Heather's room, closing the door behind him and sitting on the bed until he heard Andrew bang out of the flat. When Heather came back she came alone, Ismay having gone to her yoga class. Edmund told her what had happened, leaving out his accusation of infidelity and Andrew's unjust and untrue description of her.

"Why did he get so angry, Ed?"

"I suppose because I—well, I suggested that while I wanted to marry you he'd no intention of marrying Ismay."

Heather laughed, then looked grave. "Well, what shall we do now?"

"It's pretty clear I can't come here again. Not after the things he said. It wouldn't be possible to be in the same room with him."

"That means we may be apart for months."

"You'll have to let me rent somewhere, darling."

"Let me think about it. It's such a waste of money. I could come to you. I wouldn't mind about your mother. Or you could smuggle me in after dark. It might be fun."

Fun when you were sixteen, thought Edmund, on his way home to Chudleigh Hill. Not now. He wanted Heather, he wanted to go on making love to her, but he wanted to eat his meals with her too and sit and talk to her, and listen to music with her and hold hands on the sofa in front of the television. He wanted to be able to sit in the same room with her, both of them reading but without awkwardness, in close companionable silence. She would sometimes raise her eyes and smile at him and he would sometimes raise his eyes and smile at her. Or she would get up and come to him and nestle in his arms. Of all this he naturally said nothing when he got home and met Irene in the hallway.

"Hello, stranger," she said.

If she had heard anyone else say it she would have called them common. Edmund nodded and smiled, though he didn't feel like smiling.

"I don't suppose you'll be staying."

"Yes, I shall. For this weekend."

Irene put down the duster she was holding, approached him in much the same manner as Andrew had done before his outburst, and said in the voice of a TV detective who has made the discovery that solves the case, "You've quarreled with her."

Patience extends only so far, but Edmund still kept his. "No, Mother. Heather and I haven't quarreled. I shall see her this evening."

"Oh, Edmund, I know you so well. Your mother knows every look on your face and the look I see there now tells me you've had a serious row, perhaps even an engagement-breaking row. Isn't that so?"

Perhaps he was catching it off Andrew, but his control broke. "For God's sake, Mother," he said. "Be quiet and mind your own business."

"Those two are going to be living here till midsummer," Andrew said. "Or beyond."

A cold note in his voice Ismay found disquieting. "May at the latest was what Edmund said."

"What that man says and the actuality are two very different things. I'm not sure how long I can put up with it, my darling. I'm used to your sister, but her paramour is rather beyond the pale."

Ismay looked at him in dismay. "I'll talk to them," she said. "I'll—oh, I don't know what I'll do, Andrew, but if you've quarreled with him, I'll ask Heather if she can't go to Edmund's place and not bring him here."

"He has quarreled with me," said Andrew. "He has insulted me and drawn intolerable conclusions."

"What sort of conclusions?"

"Never mind."

Ismay found she couldn't do as she had promised. She couldn't speak to Heather and perhaps she wouldn't need to, for Edmund ceased to come to Clapham and her sister was out a great deal more than she had used to be. But her worry about Heather's part in their stepfather's death had receded. It is difficult to be worried about two things at once, and concern as to whether Andrew would be driven away had forced Heather's past into the deeper recesses of her mind. She had even ceased to be troubled about the tape—perhaps the putting of her worry into a box had worked—whether it was safe where it was or should she move it somewhere more secure, even destroy it? Worry about Andrew was more important. It always was and always would be.

After that conversation they had had when
he had complained about Edmund and
Heather and she had promised to try to alter
the situation, she sensed that he had changed
toward her. He was less—ardent. He came to
the flat, spent nights with her, took her out for
the occasional evening, but he often seemed
absent-minded, and when he talked to her it
was almost exclusively about the awkwardness
of Edmund's and Heather's presence, even
though Edmund hadn't been there for the past
week. He seemed to have become fixated on it,
as if he thought of nothing else, yet Ismay felt,
strangely, that his obsession wasn't quite real,
was assumed, to cover some genuine preoccu-
pation.

"Edmund doesn't come here anymore," she
protested when he accused her of doing nothing to change the situation.

"**She** does. I still have to put up with her
silent presence and those eyes on me."

"But you said you were used to her."

"Please don't pick me up on every little
thing, Ismay."

The more he seemed to grow away from her
the more she felt she must be placatory. She
wanted to say that he must know she wasn't
willing to separate herself from Heather. Even if
it was in her power to turn her out, she couldn't

do it. A rift would open between the two sisters that nothing would heal. They would be apart forever.

"I don't actually see why you couldn't move her upstairs. They've got a spare room, haven't they? He could be there with her if he can't control his lusts for five minutes. And it would only have to be endured until—when did you say? May?"

She said miserably that she would suggest it, but if she did, Pamela and perhaps even her mother would have to agree as well. She even came close to the point of asking Pamela, but thought she should mention it to Heather first. The prospect made her feel sick and she was relieved when Heather phoned to say she wouldn't be home that night. Andrew asked her, of course, and she said she intended to speak to Heather. She was just waiting for the right time. Andrew phoned the next day as usual, but she noticed he didn't end their short conversation with "Love you" as he invariably did. Then, instead of daily, his phone calls became more widely spaced. Monday, Tuesday, Wednesday went by without the sound of his voice, without a sight of him. She was distraught. Heather was always out—at Edmund's mother's? In a flat borrowed from a friend? Edmund had that friend who was a doctor and

Heather had Michelle at work and that Greta whose home she had intended to visit the day Guy died and whom she was still close to. Andrew says he's not here because of Heather, but he could be here now, she thought, with me and without Heather. When she tried to phone him his mobile was switched off. On the Thursday evening he arrived without warning. As might a husband who had been married for years, it seemed to her.

"It's wonderful to see you," she couldn't stop herself saying. She got up, went to him, put her hands on his arms and looked up into his face. "Andrew? They're not here. They haven't been here for days."

"You haven't spoken to them, have you?"

She shook her head.

"You haven't asked your mother to take her in upstairs and you haven't asked her to go upstairs?"

"No, but she hasn't been here. That's the point."

"The point seems to be that you prefer her company to mine. Is there anything to eat? No? I suppose I'd better go out to a restaurant then. D'you want to come?"

She thought it a strange question and wondered why he hadn't said, "Shall we go out to eat?"

"What's wrong, Andrew?" She now knew what that expression meant, "her heart was in her mouth." "What is it?"

"Nothing."

"There is something. You've changed."

"Yes, I expect I have. Haven't you understood yet that I'm fucking fed up of having those two about the place? I thought I'd made it plain. Can't you see it's getting me down?"

"But they're not here," she said. "Heather says Edmund won't come back. Not after what you said to him. And she's out every evening with him."

"Oh, yes, and we know what that amounts to. A week or two and they'll both be back." He sat down beside her, but he didn't touch her. "I have serious doubts about this flat he's supposed to be buying. Does it exist, one wonders?" He had been addressing the bookcase or perhaps the door to the hall, but now he turned and looked at her, stony-eyed. "You once told me I was the most important person in your life, yet you can't do this small thing for me. You haven't the spirit to tell your gorgon of a sister to remove herself upstairs."

Tears sprang to her eyes. "Andrew, tell me, I have to know, is it really Edmund and Heather that's the trouble or is it something else? Because I can't bear it, the way it is now between us."

"I need a drink," he said. "I need my dinner," and he left, slamming the door behind him and then the front door.

Alone that night, she dreamed the dream. This time, however, Guy was alive, contemplating Andrew's drowned body floating in a glassy lake.

Chapter Nine

In a hotel room in Shepherd's Bush, a very small room containing a double bed, wall hooks for clothes, an Ikea table with a mirror hanging above it, and a chair that was part of a 1930s dining suite, Heather and Edmund sat up in the bed, drinking tea out of a thermos flask. It was eight o'clock in the morning.

"You've a home in your mother's house," she was saying to him, "and it's a big house. I'll come to you there. We can do it, Edmund. It will just be hard at first. I'll be nice to your mother, I'll help her in the house if she'll let me."

"You know I've found this so-called studio flat."

"And from what you say I'll hate it. I'll especially hate it because it's three hundred pounds a week. We need every penny we've got for our own place when we get it."

"We can't go on staying in these ghastly hotels like adulterous couples in the fifties." He hesitated, then said grudgingly, "I suppose we could try Chudleigh Hill."

"I love you," she said, "and I know we ought to be together. A lot of people would say that the worst thing we could do would be to live with your mother, that it would separate us, but I think it would keep us together. I think it would make us a united front, while spending two thirds of what I earn on that studio and the other third on Ismay's flat would—would divide us. Don't forget I'd have to go on paying my share of Ismay's rent up until the end of April."

"I'm afraid my mother will set out to make trouble between us," Edmund said.

"Yes, maybe, but Andrew set out to make trouble between us and he hasn't. Don't you see she can't succeed if we know it beforehand? If we're determined? You say you're afraid, but I'm afraid too. Not of that, never of that. I don't think I'm superstitious, but what I'm afraid of is something I don't understand, something out there that will—well, strike us and part us forever and there'll be no going back."

"I've never heard you talk like this before."

"Maybe not. But I've had feelings like this before. When I was—well, younger."

He took her in his arms and held her close to him. "I think we ought to get married," he said. "I know we're going to get married, but I think we should do it now, as soon as we can. It takes three weeks, doesn't it?"

Alone at home, Ismay waited for Andrew to phone. He had said he would phone "around six" and now it was nearly seven. She had brought work home with her, but writing her ideas for a new client presentation was beyond her. She could settle to nothing and had slipped into the fraught and impotent mind-set of those who only stand and wait. Only she wasn't standing but trailing about from room to room, looking out of windows into the winter darkness. At the Victorian double-fronted houses opposite, the houses she had been looking at almost all her life, the shallow roofs and unused chimneys, the carved stonework around window frames, the lights between open curtains behind glass, the leafless trees with peeling trunks. Why did the bark peel off plane trees and not off other trees? Like skin off diseased people, but the trees weren't diseased.

Cars lined the pavement edges; wind-blown litter left behind by people who ate in the street was tossed about in the gutters. A vandal had stuck an empty Coke can on a garden wall and a graffitist had painted a swastika and a Maltese cross in red on a white gatepost. Scaffolding and builders' materials were stacked outside at least four houses and the part of the street that was being dug up was encircled by cones, some of them on their sides. It often seemed that the whole of London was gradually being dug up or rebuilt. She turned away and went to look out of a rear window at the garden, the darkness that lightened and grew gray if she stared at it long enough, lights in windows which were just lights, but which always made wistful watchers think that inside were happy people partying and enjoying each other's company. She carried the phone with her in case it rang and she couldn't reach it before it went on to message, though ten rings had to sound before that happened.

A glass of wine, which at first, at six, had seemed unwise, at seven was indispensable. She must have something to quiet her, to calm the beating of her heart, release her held breath, slacken her tense muscles, even take away that feeling that eating would never again be possible. While she was opening the bottle of wine with shaking hands, the phone rang. She picked it up, said a breathless "Hello?" only to hear her Pamela's voice. Immediately she thought, suppose he phones now and the line's busy? She heard herself making all sorts of promises to Pamela. Beatrix had been restless, had been wandering about, shouting the more extravagant effusions of Saint John the Divine. Pamela didn't care to go out and leave her. . . . Yes, she said breathlessly, yes, she'd sit in with her mother anytime Pamela wanted, tomorrow, Thursday, whatever, making wild excuses for ending the conversation.

When at last it was over, she poured herself a large glass of wine, drank half of it, and felt warmth flood through her. Not comforting warmth, though. She knew she would worry now half the night, perhaps all night, that he had phoned while she was talking to Pamela. Things would be marginally better if Heather were here. But that was what he wanted, wasn't it? That Heather shouldn't be here and Edmund shouldn't, but together in a place of their own? Or anywhere so long as it wasn't here. If he phoned she could tell him. She could tell him they had gone off to Edmund's mother's house, the very thing he wanted. It was "if" he phoned now, not "when." She thought, he is punishing me, that's the way he is. He will punish me for a few days and then he will phone. And I'll tell him they're gone. I've done what he wanted. Maybe I'll tell him a lie and say I did speak to Heather and asked her to go. It will please him to know I've obeyed him.

A momentary qualm visited her. Was this to be her life, abject obedience to a man in order to keep him? She would once have called herself a feminist. She was behaving like a masochist, relishing subservience. But how can I do otherwise, she asked herself, when I love him so much? When I long for him? She marveled that a week ago the thing which worried her was what Heather had done to Guy. Or might have done. Or very possibly had done twelve years ago. It wasn't her responsibility. Who said it was someone's job to be a guardian to her able-bodied, strong, healthy, capable sister? Now Ismay could hardly understand why her mother and she had undergone such stress, such pain and so many struggles over what Heather might have done. Stress and pain over such a thing seemed nothing compared to her present agony. Draining the glass of wine, she said aloud, "He doesn't care about me any-

more. I know he doesn't. And I can't live without him."

The worst thing was that she would have to
live. Alone here, carrying on, putting a brave
face on it. But wait a minute . . . there must
have been a thousand reasons why he hadn't
phoned. Well, two or three. As she poured another glass of wine, she tried to think of reasons
but couldn't find one. He always had his mobile
with him. Once, she thought, even if he was expecting a brief or a client, even if he was due in
court in a minute's time, he would have phoned
her. Just to hear the sound of her voice. Those
days were over. Could this be solely due to his
dislike of Heather and Edmund? There was
something else. She began to shiver in the
warm room. Something else was always only
one thing. . . .

Dropping in on Mr. Hussein, Marion found
him entertaining a lady in a red-and-gold
shalwar-kameez with glasses of mint tea and a
plateful of sticky sweetmeats.

"May I introduce Mrs. Iqbal," said Mr.
Hussein. "This is Miss Melville. She won't be
staying."

Had she ever heard anything so rude,

Marion later said to Irene Litton. As if she were a child or a servant.

"Well, I suppose you are a servant," said Irene.

"Maybe, but not his."

"Did he give you anything to eat?"

"It would have choked me. That woman he had there was a great big fat thing with black hair and bright red lipstick and loaded with jewels. Goodness knows how she got those diamonds. Mind you, I can guess."

Irene wasn't interested. Edmund had phoned a few minutes earlier, she now told Marion. "He's bringing that girl back here."

"You don't mean for the night."

"I do. Would you like a glass of Bristol Cream?"

They were drinking sherry when Edmund and Heather arrived. Edmund came into the living room alone. He frowned when he saw Marion.

"Well, where is she?" said Irene. "Not shy, I hope."

Edmund fetched Heather, who said, "Hello, Mrs. Litton. How are you?"

"Much the same as always. I'm never very well. This is my dear friend Marion Melville. You've heard me mention Edmund's friend Heather, Marion."

"Heather is my fiancée," said Edmund.

"When I was a girl," said Irene, "I was always told that was a very vulgar word. Only common people used it. One said"—when she reflected that what one said involved such expressions as "going to marry" and "engaged to," she cut herself short—"something more decorous."

"Right," said Edmund. "Heather is my betrothed, my promised spouse, my affianced bride. We're going to take her things upstairs and then we'll eat." He looked around him. "We'll go out to eat."

"Yes, you'll have to. I haven't felt well enough to cook anything."

"You do look rather peaky, as white as a sheet." Smiling Marion was in sycophantic mode. When Edmund and Heather had gone she said in a voice not much above a whisper, "I can't say I admire his choice. You'll have to put your foot down about her sharing his room."

Support from Marion was one thing, advice quite another. "I think I can manage my own son, thank you very much. And now, if you've finished your sherry, I'd really like to be on my own. I've got a splitting headache."

Dismissed twice in the same day, Marion went home, running through the backstreets to Lithos Road. Fowler had been in the flat in her absence. She could smell him. He had left a glass in the sink and she saw that the gin level had gone down alarmingly. Time to get the lock changed and new keys cut. . . . It was coming up to eight and she was due back in Pinner by eight-thirty. The idea of the long tube journey made her yawn in anticipation. She would have preferred to trot and run and dance all the way except that it would take hours.

The drugs Beatrix had been prescribed were highly effective, and under their influence she was docile and compliant. Silent, adhering to her radio as if it were an extra limb, she retreated into some secret space. No one knew what was in there, whether it was turbulent and demon-ridden or empty where thought was absent. But she had contrived cunning ways of not taking the drugs, hiding the capsule under her tongue or sticking it to the piece of gum she incessantly chewed. Then her wildness returned and if she could escape, she roved the streets declaiming the texts she had once mysteriously learned.

When she could be sure her sister had taken the drugs prescribed for her, Pamela could go out without fear. In the evenings, though, she worried and never stayed out long. Mostly, when she intended to be out late, one of her nieces would "keep an eye" on their mother, sometimes sitting with her. Beatrix was never left alone overnight.

Neither Ismay nor Heather ever referred to Pamela's habit of dating men to whom she had introduced herself by means of a newspaper or through the Internet, unless she did so first. This was tact on their part, and it occurred to neither of them that their silence on the subject made Pamela feel awkward.

Pamela never advertised her own attractions. An essentially modest woman, she wouldn't have known how to describe herself. She was fifty-six and a size sixteen, and though her face wasn't too bad, her neck was wrinkled and her hair thinning. Looking dolefully into the mirror, she saw these defects but never her advantages: her large blue eyes, clear smooth skin, and excellent teeth. One of the men she met on a date told her she had "American teeth," which she knew was a great compliment. In spite of that, he didn't want to see her again.

She was getting tired of going to a rendezvous with a man who had described himself, for instance, as tall, dark, sexy, and young-looking, and meeting a sexagenarian of five feet six with gray hair and appearing every year of his age. She was tired of men looking her up and down as if she were a cow in a cattle market. So tonight she was set for an adventure in speed dating. Not that Pamela approached the Kensington hotel where the function was held in an adventurous spirit. She was more nervous even than she had been the first time she met an unknown man. Getting off the bus, she told herself as she had often done before, that she only did this because without it her existence would be a pathetic apology for a life. Without it, tasteless as it often was, she would spend her days sorting out other people's money and as companion to a woman who was only bearable when stunned with drugs.

The speed-dating session was held in a rather cavernous place called the "small ballroom." It made Pamela wonder what the large ballroom was like.

She had paid quite a lot for her ticket so was glad to see a number of tables laden with canapés and, even better, bottles of wine. Before she arrived, she had imagined the setup might be like a dance hall of her youth, the girls all giggling at one end and the young men eyeing them at the other before one dared make a move and ask a girl to dance.

Here the room was more luxurious than any provincial dance hall, the floor being carpeted and the windows festooned. There were numerous gilt tables and chairs as well. As for the hopefuls who stood about, the men were on the whole congregated at the end where a dais stood, and the women were grouped nearest the food and drink. No one was young and, as far as Pamela could see, no one was beautiful. Music was soft and sweet, the numbers one heard in every hotel lounge the world over: "Never on Sunday," "Un Homme et une Femme," "La Vie en Rose." The idea was to approach someone of the opposite sex and enter into a conversation. Five minutes was allowed and then you had to move on. Pamela spotted a man in a dinner jacket who appeared to be some sort of master of ceremonies. She was so afraid that this person, who looked to her like a Latin star of thirties movies, might come up to her, take her by the hand, and lead her to the man of his choice, that she took the plunge herself.

The old formula that he couldn't kill her came to her aid and she boldly marched up to a man of about fifty who looked quiet and shy. In spite of his downcast eyes, she said, "Hello. I'm Pam." She had never called herself that before, though others did, and she cringed a little as she said it. "This is my first time here. What's your name?"

. . .

When the entry phone bell rang, of course she thought it was Andrew forgetting or losing his key. No, she didn't really think it was. She hoped, that was all. Breathless, she opened the door. Heather and Edmund stood there.

"Now I'm not living here I didn't like to use my key. We've come for more of my clothes. You look awful. What's wrong?"

"You must both come in," Ismay said. "I was supposed to be mother-sitting for Pamela but Mum's taken her tablet so she's okay. I couldn't face it." She hesitated. "Andrew won't be here. I haven't seen or heard from him for ten days."

"Where is he? What's happened?"

"Nothing's happened to him, if that's what you mean. It's not something that's happened to him that's stopping him. I've phoned his chambers. Lots of times. I was desperate. They just say he's in a meeting. That's what they always say."

"Oh, Issy. Oh, darling." Heather put her arms around Ismay and held her close. "I'm so sorry. What can we do? We'll do anything."

"Of course we will," Edmund said.

"There isn't anything." She had been dry-eyed, but now she sobbed and the tears poured down her face. "I love him so much. I've never been in love with anyone before."

"D'you want me to stay here with you? We could both stay here with you."

Edmund read it all in Ismay's anguished face. It was the two of them, in her estimation, or more likely him, who had driven Andrew away. Suppose he reappeared tonight and they were back again?

"Or just me," said Heather, intuiting the same thing.

"Better not." Ismay scrubbed at her eyes with tissues. "I'm better alone. I'll have to get used to being alone, won't I?"

"I'll phone you tomorrow."

"I suppose he's with his new woman now."

"You don't know that, Issy."

"It's either that or that he's dumped me because he didn't like having you two around. Is that likely? Would he do that if he loved me?"

Carrying the two suitcases into which Heather had packed her clothes, Edmund and she walked back toward the tube station.

"We don't seem to be anyone's favorite people," Edmund said. "Your sister doesn't want us and my mother doesn't. We are like orphans of the storm or babes in the wood."

"We want each other," said Heather, "and that's what matters."

"Do you know, I used to see couples kissing in the street and I thought, how wonderful to

do that, how I'd like to do that, and now I can."
He suited the action to the word. She clung to
him, kissing him with passion. "In two weeks
we'll be married. Tomorrow we'll go and buy a
wedding ring."

She stepped away from him and smiled. "I
shall like that. I like the things they say when
they know we're soon to be married, the jokes
and all that. I want to hear them call me Mrs.
Litton."

He laughed. "You're an old-fashioned girl."

"D'you think it's true Andrew's found another woman?"

That was when he made up his mind to tell
her. "I know he has."

The house in Chudleigh Hill was in deep darkness, though it was only just after nine. It had
been that way every evening since Heather
had come to stay there with Edmund. Irene had
taken to going to bed very early and when she
went to bed she turned off all the lights. Edmund asked her why and she said she couldn't
bear to see him go up to his room "with that
girl." And he should remember she'd be an in-
valid by now if she hadn't struggled against it.
After that, Heather stayed upstairs almost all
the time she was there. If they went out—and

they mostly did—they went straight upstairs when they returned.

Because he had always done this and long before he met Heather, Edmund put on the hall light, which he turned off from the top of the stairs. His mother was never asleep and always called out, "Is that you, Edmund?" as if a burglar would let himself in with a key, put a light on, and walk upstairs talking in whispers to his female companion. Edmund invariably called out, "Good night, Mother," as he switched off the light. Irene never called out, "Is that you, Heather?" So far she had never called Heather by her Christian name or spoken a word to her on the rare occasions she and Edmund were downstairs together.

They went into Edmund's room, which by now was taking on the look of a bedsitter. It was large and comfortable, with a big bed and built-in cupboards and its own bathroom. Edmund had added two armchairs and a table and a desk, a bookcase, and a standard lamp. Neat, methodical Heather would normally have emptied her suitcases and put the contents away. Instead she sat down in one of the armchairs and said, "But you don't actually **know** Andrew's seeing this girl?"

"Do you think anyone could see us together

and not know we're lovers? It's in the look. He was looking at her like that."

"Maybe she was a one-night stand."

"Then why hasn't he come back to Ismay, all contrite and telling her of his undying love?"

"I'm sure you're right," Heather said. "I just don't want you to be. When I shared the flat with Issy I used to see them together and think they were the perfect lovers, the way a couple ought to be, the way I thought I'd love to be—and never would."

"Why not?" Edmund sat on the arm of her chair and put his arm around her. "Why on earth not?"

"I don't know. Well, I do. I just thought a happy life with someone I loved wouldn't ever be possible for me. It sounds silly, I know. But never mind me. What can we do for Issy, Ed?"

"Nothing. No one can do anything. Two hundred years ago I could have called him out and had a duel with him on Primrose Hill, and a hundred years ago I could have horsewhipped him. If I did something like that now I'd spend five years in jail."

"Yes," said Heather thoughtfully. "Yes, you would." She smiled up at him. "We're the perfect lovers now, aren't we? The way a couple ought to be. Let's go to bed."

"Yes, please," said Edmund.

Chapter Ten

There was a place in the Strand he regularly went to for his lunch. Not always but at least twice a week. If I go there every day at lunchtime, Ismay thought, he'll come in one day. With a friend perhaps or with several people. It will be humiliating and horrible, embarrassing for him and worse for me, but he will have to speak to me, he will have to tell me. Terrible though it will be, can anything be worse than now? Won't anything be better than what I suffer now? And is there any other way I can find him?

She had phoned him at work until it was pointless to try anymore. Seb Miller, the man he shared a flat with, had told her at first, repeatedly, that Andrew wasn't there; then, when she persevered, that he "seemed to have moved out." Seb was kind and reassuring but she hadn't believed him. He had moved out only in the way a man sometimes does; because he is spending nights elsewhere and with a new woman. His flat was in Fulham, the area estate agents call "Chelsea borders," picturesque but unsafe after dark, the lawless precinct of muggers and car thieves and hunters whose prey was mobile phones. It was a long way from Clapham and her job in Regent Street. She had been there only two or three times and always with Andrew. She went there, searching for him, before she tried Brief Lives.

It hadn't occurred to her that she would be so frightened. She had thought her longing for him, her anguish at his absence, would overcome all other emotion, just as it had overcome her dilemma over Heather, Guy, and the tape. It was early evening when she got there, nearly six, the time he would reach home if he were coming home. She waited, walking up and down because keeping still adds to the stress of someone in her situation. The street was shabby, shaded by the same peeling planes, the trees of London, terraces of Victorian houses of grayish stucco with turnings off which looked much the same, the lights dim, without shops or bus stops or people at this hour. No stranger to London would have believed how high the rents were. She walked up and down, around the block or half around it so that by looking over her shoulder she could keep the house in view. No one was about except the occasional resident who came out and got quickly into a car. A solitary man on foot spoke to her.

"What are you playing at? I've been watching you. Can't keep still, can you?" She didn't answer but began to walk back the way she had come. "I'm talking to you," he said.

Then she was frightened. The only sanctuary was a phone box. She went inside it. The door wouldn't close. The phone itself was unusable, the broken receiver hanging by a shredded cable. She stayed there, breathing in short gasps, until she saw the man pass the box and head for the Fulham Road, talking to himself and laughing. After that she resumed her pacing. At nine, when Andrew hadn't come, she went up to the front door and rang his bell. It took immense nerve to do this. As soon as she had done it she was praying no one would answer. A sort of hiss came out of the entry phone and Seb Miller's voice said, "Yes?"

"It's Ismay."

"Oh," he said. "Oh, yes." There was a pause. "He's not here, Ismay."

She felt like a creature people trod under-foot. Something whose natural habitation is subterranean. "Yes," she said. "I see."

"Are you all right?"

"No," she said and walked away to get a bus home.

A point must be reached, she thought, when I shan't care about humiliation anymore. I shall be so low I can get no lower. That's when I'll wait here all night. Men will come and rob me of my bag and beat me and probably rape me. I'll think I deserve it because I'm so low. He's with that girl now and if I think about that I'll scream out loud.

Next day she tried Brief Lives.

The way to do it was just to go there. Turn up in the clothes she normally wore for work, a plain black or navy suit, her long black coat over it. She couldn't do it. He had once said he liked a clinging blue knitted dress she had, he liked her best in that. She wore it to go to this grimmest of rendezvous, over it a blond faux-fur jacket. Her haggard face, overly made up, contrasted badly with the soft pale colors.

Breaking her rule of not drinking at lunchtime, she asked for a glass of the house wine. She had eaten so little in the past days that it went to her head, increasing the beating of her heart. But still she had another. One o'clock went by, half past, ten to two. He wouldn't come now and she had to go back to work. Dressed the same, she returned to Brief Lives next day. And the next. He never came.

She thought, Seb has warned him. Whether he still shared the flat with him or really had moved out, Seb would have alerted him. And he would have deliberately avoided old haunts, especially those to which in the past he had taken her. If she went to Fulham, he would get Seb to watch for her, phone him when he spotted her outside, warn him off. How did he get people to lie for him? Charm, she supposed, the barrister's persuasive tongue. That heart-stopping smile, that authoritative voice. She wasn't the only one tied to him by invisible, unbreakable cords.

Avice Conroy had gone to a Scarlatti recital with Joyce Crosbie, leaving Marion to guard the rabbits. Guard them from what, Marion asked herself. Figaro and Susanna, brother and sister, were large but lean, Abyssinian cat colors, one of them chocolate, the other pale blond, their coats like thick soft plush. Avice got angry when people called them bunnies. Both had mild brown eyes and little in the way of personality. They hopped about, sometimes leaving

currant-like droppings in spite of what their
owner said, and sometimes lolloping through
the rabbit flap into a large hutch with a window
and an exit door, which like a conservatory ex-
tended six feet or so into the garden.

Apart from sucking up the currants with a
hand-held dustette, Marion had absolutely
nothing to do and this suited her fine. Money
for old chicken feed, it was, or rabbit food. In
case Avice got wise to the fact that no rabbit-
sitter was really needed, she thought she should
perhaps invent some hazard or alarming incident she could say had occurred during the rabbits' owner's absence. A firework going off
nearby would do—such explosions were no
longer confined to Guy Fawkes Day—or even
a German shepherd barking next door. Meanwhile she explored the house.

Marion brought all the enthusiasm and pre-
cision of a scholarly researcher to investigating
other people's desks, drawers, and other private
places of concealment, leaving no scrap of paper or even used envelope unturned. Looking
for Avice's will, she finally found a copy in, of
all unexpected places, a drawer in one of the
kitchen cabinets where she kept the brochures
of instructions for using the oven, fridge, microwave, hair dryer, and alarm clock radio. The
large brown envelope contained not one will

but four, each invalidating its predecessor. There were approximately two years between them and the most recent had been made some twenty months earlier. Of course Marion's name appeared in none of them. She would have been astonished if it had, considering the shortness of their acquaintance. But it was apparently time, or soon would be, for Avice to make a new one.

The contents of a will shed a good deal of light on the testatrix's circumstances. Who, for instance, would have supposed Avice to own not only this place but a terrace of houses in Manchester? Or so many Tesco shares? No wonder she could afford to part with twenty pounds for the unnecessary services of a rabbit-minder. The beneficiaries were the Small Mammals' Protection League—Marion, a realist, knew she couldn't shake that—a nephew with an address in Berwickshire and a woman, not apparently a relative, in the Isle of Man. Avice, who was given to making her testamentary dispositions in elaborate language, had left the Isle of Man woman fifty thousand pounds "in fond memory of our happy schooldays when we first learned of friendship's joys and consolations."

If she'd been at school with Avice, thought Marion, she was no chicken. Might drop off her perch at any minute. All this required a good deal of careful consideration. She put the will back exactly where she had found it and when Avice came back half an hour later told her she had caught—and killed—a flea which she had found on Figaro's back.

"Oh, dear, how dreadful," said Avice. "I'll have to take him and his sister to the vet. I didn't actually know rabbits had fleas. But it's half a mile away and taxi drivers won't take them, you know. Afraid they'll spend a penny, which they very seldom do."

"I could take them. Well, separately of course. If you'd like to make the appointments. I wouldn't at all mind carrying one of them in a basket half a mile. They're so sweet, it would be a pleasure."

"Would it?" Avice beamed. "I really do need more help with them than I have. Well, I don't have any. And they deserve the best attention, don't you think?"

"I absolutely do. And by the way, a fox came into the garden and came quite close up to the windows. I don't think Figaro or Susanna saw it but I couldn't help thinking what might have happened if one of them had been out-side. If I was here on a more or less regular ba-sis I could see to things like that."

"Dogs and cats have owners, Marion," said

Avice with a friendly laugh, "but rabbits need staff."

Arrangements were made to their mutual satisfaction. Marion was to have a regular job with Avice as rabbit manager but to include a little shopping, limited cooking, and occasionally staying overnight. Giving up her job at the South End Green estate agents came as a relief. Of course the sum Avice had named was pitifully small, well below the minimum wage, but no worse than what Mrs. Pringle had provided and look what the result of that had been. Marion was never worried by illegality and had reasoned that the perks would almost make up the shortfall. For instance, she would be doing the household shopping and could manage to make Avice's weekly budget include all her own eatables. There were, too, a great many nice things lying about the house, silver ornaments, porcelain and glass, not to mention jewelry. Avice, whose sight was fast deteriorating, would hardly miss them. In a burst of confidence she had told Marion she had diamond rings, which had been her mother's, she could no longer squeeze over her arthritic knuckles. A plan of gradual abstraction must be made.

"It's quite pathetic the way my poor old dad looks forward to my visits," Marion said in a suitably lugubrious voice. "I really do need to see him three times a week."

Avice had just heard from her managing agent that she would be permitted to raise the rent of her houses in Manchester, so was in a gracious mood. "So you go. Of course you must see your dear father."

At home, where she now went only to sleep, Marion picked up the **Daily Telegraph,** a stained and battered copy which could only have found its way there by means of Fowler. It had plainly been used to wrap a baby's disposable diaper and it was enough to make her decide to have the locks changed forthwith. Just the same, she glanced at it before going to bed, turning first to the births, marriages, and deaths, as she usually did with newspapers. Halfway down the deaths column was announced the demise of Bernice Maureen Reinhardt in the Royal Free Hospital, Hampstead. Eighty-seven years old, beloved mamma and grandmamma, greatly mourned by her devoted Morris, Emmanuel, Hephzibah, David, Lewis, and Rachel. Marion had had no idea Mrs. Reinhardt had so many descendants. She had kept them very dark. Surely one of them might have let her know, a great friend like she was left to find out from a newspaper rescued from a waste bin.

She put the paper down and went to examine the bottle of morphine sulfate. No use for Mrs. Reinhardt now. Still, the world was full of old ladies and Marion was slow to accept defeat. It was essential to find out if the morphine was tasteless or if it had the kind of taste that would blend unnoticeably with Avice's favorites: tiramisù and tarte tatin. Unlike most women, Marion only felt truly secure when alone in her own flat after dark. There was no possibility then of her doings—seldom entirely above-board—being witnessed.

She took the bottle, labeled NOT TO BE TAKEN INTERNALLY, out of the bathroom cabinet. She was rather frightened of it but she had to find out. Unscrewing the cap broke the seal and she took it off. It was probably colorless but she couldn't tell because the bottle was of brown glass and she had forgotten what it looked like. If she dipped her little finger in and just touched the tip of it on her tongue, would that be dangerous? Could she get hooked? Marion was very reluctant to try. She remembered the hallucinations that had resulted from her mother's regular dosage, troops of white-robed people trailing through the room, haggard faces looming out of mist and receding again. Or would she develop a craving for the stuff, like Fowler for drink and various narcotics?

Gingerly she placed the tip of her finger on the surface of the liquid and quickly withdrew it. A tiny globule adhered to the skin. She dotted it lightly onto her tongue. It was faintly sweetish, slightly metallic. So might a coin taste if dipped in icing sugar, thought Marion, fancifully for her. It would, she supposed, scarcely affect the flavor of a tiramisù.

She waited rather nervously for an hallucination but after an hour had passed and none came she reflected that this was far too soon to think about taking any action in this area yet. The land must be spied out, Avice's financial affairs investigated, what relatives and friends she had and, most significant of all, the situation with those two most precious of Avice's possessions, her rabbits.

There were things Ismay thought she would never do. At all costs some measure of dignity had to be maintained. Better suffer in silence, be like that girl in the play who never told her love but let concealment like a worm in the bud feed on her damask cheek. Bear the agony but never show it. That was what she thought when there was no suffering and no agony. Now she told herself, if I don't find him, if I don't speak to him and ask him, I may miss the only chance

I have of getting him back. It may be that he is only waiting for me to come to him and say I'm sorry, I should never have let Edmund come here, I should never have shared with my sister. Was she to humiliate herself like that? What would she care for humiliation if Andrew was back with her?

Try the wine bar in the evening. He sometimes went there after his day's work was done. On two evenings in succession she went down to Brief Lives and waited for him just inside a passage that led into one of the Inns of Court. It was a narrow winding passage such as might have figured in a novel of Dickens but lit at intervals by modern lamps attached to its walls. She stood between two of these lamps, away from direct light, and waited for him to come.

Apart from a man who passed her very close by and said "What're you doing later, sweetheart?" she was undisturbed. He didn't appear and she went home after two hours, disconsolate. Had he not only deserted her but all his old haunts as well? She was no longer on the edge of hysteria, her heart pounding, her mouth dry, but empty now, cold, despairing. The next night she was in the alley a little earlier. It was April but very cold and she huddled inside the sheepskin coat which had been Andrew's present at Christmas the year before.

It was just after six when he came, but not alone. He was one of a crowd of young men, all laughing and making wisecracks, who went into the bar together. She had thought that simply seeing him would cause her to cry out, even fling herself upon him, but the reality was different. She shrank against the cold brick wall of the passage. He was a very long time in there. They served food, she remembered him saying. Perhaps he had stayed to eat his dinner there. People came out of Brief Lives and fewer and fewer went in. The City died at night. The West End might throb with noisy life, be filled with loitering crowds who made fast walking impossible, but here there would soon be solitude and silence. Then, when she felt she had spent her whole life in this Dickensian passage, when she was frozen with numb hands and feet, when it was almost nine, he came out. Alone. He began to walk rapidly in the direction of Waterloo Bridge.

She followed him. The sight of him, even the back of him, had a curious effect on her. Few people were about, but it was as if there were none, that he and she were the only living creatures in the world, that he would walk and she would follow him, at this same distance apart, forever. He would never turn, she would never call out, she would never see his face again, hear his voice. They would be like that pair of lovers she remembered reading about at university—were they called Paolo and Francesca?—doomed to drift forever in the void, blown by the winds. But they had been together, eternally embraced. Ismay thought she wouldn't mind the wild winds and the darkness and loneliness if she were with Andrew, in his arms, for always.

The idea was so wonderful and so painful that, as he crossed the street into the Aldwych and she followed him, she could no longer resist and called out to him on a passionate anguished note, "Andrew!"

He either didn't hear or didn't want to, though she thought she detected a sudden stiffening of his shoulders, a momentary faltering of his step. She called again, "Andrew!"

On the pavement outside the doors to a restaurant he turned and looked at her, unsmiling. He stood staring like someone who knows immediate escape is impossible. Here, not very far from Brief Lives, the streets were no longer unfrequented. People were everywhere, waiting at traffic lights to cross the road, entering bars and spilling out of them, and two couples, hand-in-hand and arm-in-arm, passed between him and her. For a moment he was invisible and she thought, he will go, he will get away from me. . . . But when the couples had gone into the restaurant he was still there, standing with his head bent and his arms hanging relaxed, the picture of exasperated patience, as if he had given up the struggle. She approached him, no longer afraid, no longer trembling, only aware that she had caught him, she had him in her net. He stepped back under an awning, his back against a plate-glass window. She went close up to him, said on a thin high strangled voice, "What has happened to us?" And then when he didn't answer, "What have I done?"

He had such a beautiful speaking voice. After this man's voice all other men's voices were harsh or high-pitched or cockney or provincial or vulgar. He said, "It's not what you've done, Ismay. I've told you often enough, but you took no notice."

"I don't understand."

"I think you do. You brought those people into our home and though I told you repeatedly that I couldn't stand it, you absolutely refused to tell them to go."

"But my own sister . . ." she stammered, almost unable to believe what she heard.

"I don't really see that it makes a difference whether it was your sister or somebody else. That male nurse wasn't your sister. I'm afraid,

Ismay, that the plain truth is that I got tired of waiting for you to do something about it. Let's say I knew you never would. No doubt you cared for them more than for me. That's reasonable, I understand that. So I—made myself scarce."

She didn't know why the scream of horror just inside her head failed to make its way out into the shiny dark and bright of the Aldwych. It was a calm voice she spoke in. "Have you got someone else?"

It was at that moment that the girl appeared. She came out of the taxi that had stopped just behind where Ismay stood and which Andrew had been staring at while he spoke. Not perhaps as tall as she seemed to be owing to the height of her heels, she was recognizably Ismay's own type, but an exaggeration of that type, slimmer, fairer, whiter, more attenuated, her features those of an elfin creature in a fairy-tale illustration. A fur stole wrapped around her, she came up to Andrew, laid a hand on his arm, and put her face close to his.

Always able to rise to the occasion, he said, "Eva, may I introduce Ismay Sealand? Ismay, this is Eva Simber."

"Hello," said Eva Simber.

"Is she your girlfriend?" Ismay wouldn't look at her.

"I suppose that describes our relationship," said Andrew. "Yes, that's about it." The girl gave a nervous giggle. "And now, if you'll excuse us, we're about to eat."

Ismay was past dignity, past face-saving. "And that is to be it? We part like that? After two years together?"

"Better than making a scene, isn't it?"

She would have made a scene. The crowds wouldn't have mattered. The girl and what she thought would have mattered not at all. But at that moment a group of people, close together, talking at the tops of their voices, pushed their way between them, leaving Andrew and the girl on one side, Ismay on the other. When they had passed she was alone and the other two were inside the restaurant.

She stumbled away, afraid she would fall, but clinging now to an upright, a bus stop or parking notice. A woman on her own said to her, "Are you all right?"

Ismay nodded, unable to speak. She summoned up enough voice to ask a taxi driver to take her home to Clapham and, huddled on the backseat, gave way to tears and then to bitter sobbing.

· · ·

Though making it a principle not to use the key to Ismay's flat but always to ring the bell, Edmund had tried the bell push, tried it repeatedly, and on the doorstep, tried calling her on his mobile before letting himself in. He had come back for the remaining possessions Heather had left behind. She herself was spending the evening with his mother as part of their campaign to make Irene like her prospective daughter-in-law.

Always neat and methodical, Heather had left the things she wanted in three tidy stacks on the bed in her old bedroom. Edmund was packing them into the suitcase he had brought when he heard a key in the lock and Ismay come in.

He remembered how she usually danced in, threw her things down, bounced into a chair to relax. The sounds he could hear were those of a very old woman, returning home with heavy bags from a shopping trip. She didn't fall but he thought he heard her drop down onto the floor. He went quickly out of the room, calling out so that she shouldn't be frightened, "Ismay, it's me, it's Edmund."

She was prone on the floor, her face turned away from him. He knelt down beside her. "What is it?"

Instead of answering, she said in a muffled voice crying had made hoarse, "I want to die."

"Andrew? What has he said to you? Ismay, turn over, please. Look at me."

"Leave me alone. I want to die."

"You can't stay there," he said, and more firmly, the nurse taking charge, "Get up. Tell me what's happened. Come on, get up."

She did, turning to him a face that frightened him, it was so ugly with grief and pain and terror. He had never found her attractive—she was too fey, too slight and delicate, her features too childlike for his taste— but he could tell many men would. Hers was the fashion-model type, impossibly slender with thistledown hair and bush-baby eyes. All that was gone. As she staggered to her feet, fell onto the sofa, he saw that she was skeletal, her face that old woman's whose stumbling he had heard. She had become her own mother. He sat down beside her and took her in his arms.

For a few moments she let him hold her. Then she moved away, put her head in her hands, her fingertips pressed deeply into the skin. When she took them away and shook back her hair, she seemed a little restored. Without waiting to be asked again, she told him about the evening she had spent.

"He said it was my fault, Edmund. That

he'd gone, I mean. He said I preferred having you and Heather here to him. And then this girl came."

Edmund resisted the impulse to ask if she was thin and fair and wearing very high heels. Why let Ismay know her story wasn't a surprise to him?

"I don't think she knew about me. It doesn't matter anyway. She's called Eva something. I don't know. It's a name you give to lions."

"Sheba?" hazarded Edmund.

"Simba, I think. That doesn't matter either. What am I going to do? What can I do? I can't live without him."

Six months earlier, Edmund would have thought this declared intention, common to discarded lovers, an absurd exaggeration which in fact amounted to very little. But now, about to be married, he asked himself if he could live without Heather and thought that if it wouldn't be utterly impossible it would be dreadful and its extent perhaps not imaginable. The very heart of loneliness, the depths of despair.

"She came up to him," Ismay said, crying again. "She touched him. On the arm. I thought I'd die. I wish I had. Oh, I wish I had."

"You can't be alone here. Not the state you're in. I'll call Heather. We'll both stay here with you."

. . . .

Unhappy at the prospect of spending hours alone with her prospective daughter-in-law, Irene had summoned Marion to "join us for supper." She arrived early, bearing her usual gifts she had made herself, in this case chocolate fudge. Calling on Mr. Hussein an hour earlier, in the belief than an elderly Moslem gentleman would be at a loose end at six in the evening, she had found him having a patriarchal orange juice with three younger men around the ebony table. One of them let her in. He was enormous, a good foot taller than Marion, with luxuriant black hair and beard. She had never liked very tall men. They intimidated her. The other two were smaller but not much. The three of them with Mr. Hussein filled up the little room and there was nowhere for Marion to sit.

"May I introduce my sons?" Mr. Hussein indicated one after another with a wave of the hand. "Khwaja, Mir, and Zafar. This is Miss Melrose."

"Melville," said Marion, who for some reason had supposed him childless.

Accustomed to women standing about while they sat, none of the Hussein men got up to give her a seat. Marion didn't care. She eyed them and while she was wondering if one of them might be single or between marriages, their father began telling the tale of how she had given him ham for Christmas, including the detail of how he carried it to the kitchen on the end of a kebab skewer. This was the first Marion knew that in doing so she had committed a solecism. Khwaja, Mir, and Zafar all laughed uproariously and Mir (who had also shuddered) slapped Mr. Hussein on the back.

"My dad's a real comedian," he said, not looking at Marion. "He ought to be on the telly."

"I have had my offers," said Mr. Hussein mysteriously, and then to Marion, "You can see yourself out, can't you?"

She would never go there again, Marion was thinking as she sipped Irene's Bristol Cream. There was someone she wouldn't waste her morphine on. What would be the use when he was so palsy-walsy with those sons of his? Heather came down at twenty-five to eight.

"I think you've met," Irene said.

"Briefly," said Marion, and Heather said, "Hello, Marion. How are you?"

"People who make that inquiry," Irene said in a conversational tone, "don't expect a truthful answer, do they? They should, of course.

Otherwise there's no point in asking. But no, they expect to be told that you're fine even if you're at death's door."

When Heather could find nothing to say, Marion remarked that true though this was, Irene must never forget that not everyone was as clever as she was. Irene favored her with a smile and a deprecating shake of the head.

"I do actually try to answer that inquiry truthfully. I believe in speaking the truth, you see. When I'm asked how I am—and I'm usually unwell—I see no point in lying about it." To Heather she said, "I won't offer you sherry. I know you young people haven't any time for it." Ignoring Marion's affronted look at being thus excluded from youthfulness, she told an anecdote to illustrate her point. "Imagine, my sister and her husband went to a restaurant the other evening, and when they asked for sherry, the staff—not much more than teenagers actually—had never heard of it."

"Perhaps I could have a glass of wine," said Heather, having noticed an opened bottle of Sauvignon.

Her expression that of a woman who has never before been asked for drink or food by a guest, Irene said, "Oh, of course. Help yourself. You're practically one of the family now, aren't you? Well, in a way," she added.

Marion giggled, rather in the manner of the Hussein brothers. "I suppose you're a sort of common-law wife. Can you describe yourself like that if you're filling in a form?"

"There's no such thing as a common-law wife." Heather had picked up this piece of information from Andrew. "You're either a wife or you're not."

"And you're not?"

"Not until next Saturday," said Heather.

"You're getting **married?**"

"I thought Irene might have told you."

This was the first time she had called her future mother-in-law by her Christian name and the first time the marriage had been discussed, though Edmund had told his mother a week earlier. Irene looked displeased at the familiarity but realized she could hardly protest. In silence she served their first course, carrot and coriander soup. The bread was Poilâne at five pounds for half a loaf, as Irene told her guests. Heather was prevented from praising it by the ringing—or playing of a well-known phrase of Vivaldi—of a mobile. Heather fished the phone out of her bag and was about to answer it when Irene said, "Oh, really, not when we're eating, **please.**"

Thus Edmund was treated to the well-known tones of his mother saying penetratingly, "It's quite appalling the way some people can't be separated from a phone for five minutes."

"Are you all right?" he said.

Heather said to Irene and Marion, "Excuse me. I won't be long," and carried the mobile into a corner of the room. "I'm fine. What's wrong?"

He told her.

"Of course we must both stay with her."

"She won't have it," Edmund says. "She—I don't want to say it over the phone. I'm on the bus. She's got sleeping pills and she's taken one. No, it's okay, I've taken the rest away. She'll just sleep all night. I'll be home in—well, half an hour."

Irene had put their main course on the table. "I suppose that was my son?"

"He's at my sister's. He went to fetch the rest of my clothes."

"If he had to phone, why on earth couldn't he phone here on my phone?"

Tired of parrying Irene's questions, Heather said, "I don't know. He just didn't." She fell back on what she thought must be a sure-fire mollifier. "This is very good."

It was hard to tell if Irene was pleased or not. "Praise from that quarter," she said to Marion, "is praise indeed. She's a professional cook, you know. Well, in a hospital, not a restaurant."

"She'll put us all to shame, then."

Marion's remark went down badly. Irene frowned at Heather as if she had made it. They had pears in red wine. Heather ate in silence, was offered no more wine, while Irene and Marion talked about Avice Conroy and Marion's job.

"You are an amanuensis," Irene was saying when Edmund's key was heard in the lock.

He came into the room, said, "Hello, Mother," and to Heather in the sort of tone that is warmer than an endearment, "Hello." To Marion he nodded. Irene immediately asked him if he had had any dinner.

"It doesn't matter," he said.

"But of course it matters. You mustn't miss meals because of . . ." Because of what wasn't specified, but it was plain she meant this omission was Heather's fault. "I'll get you something at once. Chicken? Soup first? Or some of Marion's delicious fudge?"

"I don't want anything, thank you, Mother. If you've finished, Heather, shall we go upstairs?"

"She hasn't had coffee," said Irene. "I was going to offer her a glass of dessert wine. I know how fond of wine she is."

Heather got up, said, "Thank you for having me," like a guest at a children's party. They went upstairs. In their bedroom she sat down on the bed, her hands clutched together in her lap.

"What's the matter? You're not letting her get to you, are you?"

Heather made no answer. "Have you ever read **Tess of the d'Urbervilles**?"

"I saw the film. I'm not much of a reader. Nor are you, though. Why do you ask?"

"Oh, I don't know." She did know, he thought, but didn't want to say. "I had to read it when I was at school. Not for O levels, it was before that. I was nearly fourteen."

Puzzled, Edmund said, "Did you enjoy it?"

"When you don't read much, things you do read stick in your mind. But it doesn't matter. I'm going to bed. Are you coming?"

For the first time since he had met her he sensed in her an absence of trust. It seemed to him that perfect confidence had existed between them but did so no longer. She hadn't lied, but she had hidden the truth, and for a little while—only a very little while, he hoped, only this evening—she had separated herself from him.

Chapter Eleven

The man who had talked to her at speed dating
had so humiliated her that she considered giving the whole thing up. He was the third one
she had spoken to. He attracted her not at all,
but he was there, standing alone with a glass in
his hand, and she approached him because all
the others had paired off. Once more she introduced herself as Pam and he said his name was
Keith. The tone he used when he said it was dry
and condescending as if she hardly had a right
to ask him.

"Have you ever been to speed dating before?" It had been her opening gambit at the
two previous encounters.

He didn't reply. He looked her up and

down. "Bit over the hill for this sort of thing, aren't you? What makes someone like you want to come here?"

She felt herself blush shamefully. "I'm fifty-six. How old are you?"

"It's different for men, isn't it?" he said. "A man of fifty-six isn't old. He's in the prime of life. Whereas a woman . . ." He left the sentence unfinished, looked about him. "Time to move on to the next lucky lady," he said and walked off.

She hadn't moved on to the next lucky man but had gone home. Beatrix was sitting where she had left her, lightly and slowly wringing her hands. Pamela poured herself a triple gin with a very small amount of tonic in it. The words the man called Keith had used to her rang in her ears. It was as if an actual voice were inside her head repeating what he had said.

She would have to give up the whole business. After all, she'd been doing it for three years now, off and on, there'd been month-long gaps, but she'd always gone back to it. Yet she'd never met anyone who remotely set her pulse racing or lifted up her heart or made her say, "Oh, yes, **yes.**" There had never been anyone who seemed to think in the way she did or want to do the same things as she did or read the same books or like the same kind of music.

On the other hand, none of them had been rude to her or insulted her until now. With most of them things had never reached the point of lovemaking. Of those who had, she totted up the sorry total of four who had been impotent—two of whom said their impotence was her fault—three who had behaved while making love in such a brief rough way as to make ludicrous that decorous term, and one who had wanted to chain her to an exercise bicycle and paint her body with tomato soup.

She had often told herself what she wanted. A man of about her own age (her **advanced** age), not especially handsome but attractive to her, a good conversationalist, funny, clever, fond of the theater, someone who would take her out and spend the night with her, occasionally take her away for a weekend, be a best friend. Oh, and that phrase she was embarrassed to use even to herself: "a good lover." Was that impossible to ask? Apparently. So she might as well give up and look ahead to the barren desert of real old age.

Until she read about "romance walking" in the evening paper. You signed up for romance walking first by filling in a form on the Internet. Pamela studied it with foreboding. You were asked for your date of birth, eye color, hair color, and if not exactly your weight, whether you were slim, well-built, or overweight. Surely no one would admit, publicly, on a website, to being fat. If she were fat as against being a bit overweight she would stop now and give up the struggle as she had thought of doing so many times before.

The romance walkers met in a pub. The group Pamela was scheduled to join were to meet at the Eagle and Child in a village near Epping, accessible only by car or by taxi from Blake Hall station. Not many Central Line tube trains went to Blake Hall and she had to wait more than half an hour for one to take her there. The Eagle and Child was just about within walking distance but not really when you would be walking the romance itinerary for several hours. She had to wait again for a taxi, most being out already, taking romance walkers to the pub. She sat outside the station worrying about her sister whom she had left on her own, having watched her carefully to see she took her pill. Either Ismay or Heather would have sat with Beatrix or at least looked in on her several times but Pamela felt she couldn't ask them. Not with Heather's wedding the next day.

A thin drizzle had begun to fall. If she had any sense, Pamela thought, she would use her return ticket **now** and go back to London. But the taxi came, the driver showing no surprise at being asked to drive her to the Eagle and Child. A group of ten people, five men and five women, were inside eating sandwiches and drinking lager and Diet Coke. For a moment Pamela wondered why five of each and then realized one of the women must be the guide or organizer. The one pointedly looking at her watch before she smiled and introduced Pamela to the others.

They were all, Pamela thought, between fifty and sixty years old. All looked fit and energetic. In a kind of embarrassed panic she hoped didn't show, she thought she was by far the heaviest of the women. All were wearing jeans or fashionably cut trousers, she alone a skirt. She felt far from hungry. She felt a little sick but still she had a sandwich and drank some water.

"Time to pair you up," the organizer said. "Now, Marilyn, you've been chatting to Bill here, so I think that means you enjoy each other's company. Off you go then. Got your maps? Remember you have to be back here by four sharp."

A very thin woman and the shortest and fattest man set off rather sheepishly. Their departure left two nondescript men; a tall, thin, bent man; and an equally tall dark man with a beard. Easily the most attractive, Pamela thought. The remaining women seemed older, one completely white-haired, another heavily made up, the third with very obvious false teeth she flashed a lot. She was paired off in brisk fashion with the tall bent man and neither looked very pleased about it.

The organizer cast her eyes over the remaining six. Pamela was sure she disliked her for being a little late and not apologizing. She expected the nondescript balding man to be allotted to her and waited with a sinking heart.

"Now Pamela or Pam as I expect you prefer to be called, I've seen your eye on Ivan here, so why don't you two get together."

No doubt there had been times when Pamela had suffered worse embarrassment, but she couldn't remember any. She got to her feet, the blush burning her face.

"Got your maps? Back here by four, please."

Pamela thought, if only he would smile. Show he doesn't hate the idea of spending two hours with me. But perhaps he does, perhaps . . .

"Come on," he said, and then, "Cheer up."

He stood back to let her pass ahead of him through the doorway. The rain had stopped. Green countryside and woodland stretched before them. "I was hoping it would be you, Pam," he said as they took a footpath skirting a meadow and a hedge. "The others were such a bunch of dogs. I couldn't believe it."

In the excitement of being preferred, she forgot she didn't like men who called women dogs or being called Pam. In a moment he'd ask her to tell him about herself.

"Let me tell you about myself, Pam," he said.

They were married, quietly and quickly, Heather not daring even to glance at her sister until it was over. But Ismay remained dry-eyed, though she didn't smile much. A hire car was there to take them all to the restaurant in Marylebone High Street Irene had insisted on. Arriving, Edmund expected to find his mother there and perhaps Heather's aunt Pamela. Both were there, uneasily eyeing each other, but so were Joyce and Duncan Crosbie, Barry Fenix from next door in Chudleigh Hill, and Avice Conroy. Marion Melville would no doubt have been there too, Edmund remarked afterward to Heather, if she hadn't been looking after Avice's rabbits. He was white with anger, but there was nothing to be done but take their seats and be pleasant. Congratulations were bellowed or murmured by all the guests, who indicated the wedding presents they had brought and stacked on a separate table thoughtfully provided by the management.

Edmund didn't kiss his mother. He managed to smile at her and thank her for the bulkiest-looking present, as yet unopened, and the very ugly string of jet beads she had made for Heather. Under the table he took Heather's hand and squeezed it so tightly she gave a little whimper. He whispered, "Sorry," and she whispered back, "I love you," which made everything all right, even having this bunch at his wedding. Champagne was served. He had to admit his mother had done them proud. Joyce asked him if he and Heather were any nearer getting into their flat and he had to say, not really.

"At the rate we're going it could be late summer."

"They're very happy being with me," said Irene in her loud, commanding tones. "The rooms they have are practically an apartment in themselves. In fact, now they are married I see no reason why they shouldn't stay where they are. Give up this elusive flat. I can always let them have an extra room if they need it."

And then Heather surprised—and delighted—him. In her quiet, measured way she said, "It's kind of you, Irene, to offer us a home with you, but we'll be moving out. We're going to rent a studio flat until we get our own."

It was what he had wanted all along. "Just as soon as I can find somewhere to suit us," he said.

"When you get back from your honeymoon, is that it?" Barry Fenix, in a white Nehru jacket and rather tight trousers, uttered these words in an arch and rather lubricious way, as if there were essentially something naughty about such a vacation.

"We shan't be having a honeymoon," Edmund said. "Not yet. Not when we're not sure where we'll be living." He smiled at Heather, looking into her eyes. "As soon as we're settled we'll go somewhere wonderful. Somewhere on the other side of the world," he added as if he'd have liked to be in this paradise at present.

"India," said Barry. "That's the place. Kerala or Goa."

"The Seychelles."

"Or Tahiti."

"Patagonia is the new place," said Avice, who had never been west of Cornwall or east of Innsbruck.

"We'll see," said Edmund and, announcing that there would be no speeches, with Heather's hand covering his own, proceeded to cut the cake a waiter had carried in to strains of the Wedding March from **Lohengrin.**

Ismay, who had eaten very little, nibbled at her slice of cake. She was thinking, inevitably, of Andrew, if roles could be reversed and she Heather and Andrew Edmund. This was quite a nice restaurant. They might have had their reception (or whatever you called it) here. But realistically he would probably want somewhere like Le Gavroche. Now he would be there with Eva Simber. Tears welled up in her eyes and, excusing herself, she got up to go to the ladies'. There she was, weeping quietly into the embossed and scented tissues the restaurant provided, when Heather found her.

"Oh, Issy, what is it? No, I know. It's still Andrew, isn't it?"

"Not 'still.' It's always. It's always going to be Andrew. Imagine if you were me and it were Edmund who'd left you."

A shadow seemed to pass across Heather's face, but she said nothing and hugged Ismay. After a while they went back to the party. Everyone could see Ismay had been crying. Her eyes were red and her makeup was smeared and blotchy, causing Avice to remark to Joyce on the way home that she thought Heather's sister was supposed to be so good-looking. The people around the table pretended nothing had happened except for Irene, who asked in an old-fashioned ward-sister's kind of voice, "Is something wrong?"

No one answered. Heather turned to her and said, "Edmund and I want to thank you for doing this for us. It's been lovely. And now we'd like to open our presents."

Their taxi stuffed full of bed linen, a breakfast set, an electric mixer, an espresso coffee maker, and Irene's gift of a microwave, Heather and Edmund were driven home to Chudleigh Hill.

"We ought to have brought your mother with us," Heather said. "There's room in the taxi."

"Creep," said Edmund, kissing her.

"It's better than being enemies, isn't it?"

"Oh, much. Did you mean that about moving out?"

"Of course. We'll start looking tomorrow—if you still want to."

When they heard Irene go out, taken to the cinema and a meal by Joyce and Duncan, they came cautiously downstairs as if they were children entering a forbidden room. "Or as if we think she hasn't really gone out," said Edmund, "or got Duncan to drop her off by the back entrance."

In the hall Heather stood still and looked up at him as if she had a very daring question to ask. "Could we not go out, Ed? Could we eat something here? Would you mind?"

"I wouldn't mind a bit, but I insist on the champagne. Back upstairs then?"

"I'd like to stay here for a few minutes. Well, half an hour. As long as it takes."

Heather walked into Irene's living room and took off her coat. She kept it over her arm as if she were afraid that to drape it over a chair would leave some trace of it behind for her mother-in-law to discover.

"Here, give me that," Edmund said and took the coat out into the hall.

When he came back Heather was standing in front of the bookcase. "I can't find it," she said. "I suppose she hasn't got it."

"What are you looking for?"

"That book I told you about. **Tess of the d'Urbervilles.**"

"Why? Do you want to read it again?"

She didn't answer. "Sit down," she said. "Sit opposite me."

"I'll sit **beside** you."

"No. Sit opposite me. You see, you might

sit next to me and then move away. And that would be the worst thing in the world."

"Heather," he said, "what is this? What's going on? D'you think we could go upstairs again and have our champagne? This is our wedding day."

She nodded slowly, her lips pursed, as if she were thinking of something that must be done and done now, this evening, something she would love to put off but could no longer avoid. "This book," she said, "**Tess of the d'Urbervilles,** it's about a poor girl who's had an affair with a rich man who seduced her. Well, he raped her, really. And she falls in love with man called Angel Clare—can you imagine a man called Angel?—and they get married. And on the night after their wedding—like ours tonight—he confesses to her about some lover he's had, and she thinks it's all right for her to confess about her past to him, but it's not. He won't forgive her and he leaves her. That night."

Edmund didn't laugh, but he felt like laughing. "Darling Heather," he said, "when was this? A hundred and fifty years ago? What do people care about that sort of thing now? They're proud of it. That nurse at the hospice, what's her name, Rebecca, was going about the other day doing a sort of survey as to which of the girls had slept with the most men. Besides," he added, "we've already told each other about our lovers—and we wouldn't make a very good showing on Rebecca's list."

"That's not what I want to tell you about," Heather said, her face more serious than he had ever seen it. "You see, Angel says whatever it is she has to tell him it will be all right. It doesn't matter. But when she does tell him it matters. Do you see what I'm getting at?"

"Whatever it is," said Edmund, leaning toward her and taking her hand, "it will be all right."

"Will it? Will it?" Suddenly she jumped up, keeping hold of his hand, pulling him up with her. "It's not worth telling you. It's too stupid. Let's go out after all. Can we?"

"You can do what you like on your wedding day."

Chapter Twelve

The woman next door, whose name was Sharon, was walking around the garden with her sister, holding her arm, nodding and murmuring "Yes" and "If you say so," while Beatrix moaned that nations shall see their dead bodies three days and shall not suffer them to be put into graves. Beatrix shouted when she saw Pamela and asked her if she had eaten up the little book she had seen in the angel's hand and was it sweet in her mouth but bitter in her belly? Sharon looked very disgruntled. Pamela tried to explain that Beatrix had swallowed her pill that morning the way she had been for the past week and that this was an unexpected departure.

"I don't know about that," Sharon said. "I found her wandering in the street shouting all that rubbish about dead bodies and whatever."

Later, reaching under a chest of drawers for Ivan Roiter's card, which she had dropped on the floor, Pamela felt, glued to the underside of the bottom shelf, a series of uneven lumps. She crouched down and peered. There were ten of them and they were chewing gum, each one containing a whitish capsule. All the lumps were rock hard except one which was still spongy. There was no mystery now about the street wandering and the declaiming.

Now she would have to decide whether, without cruelty, she could ban chewing gum altogether. Wouldn't Beatrix just find some other way to avoid swallowing her capsule? She was quiet now. The spongy lump of gum must have been yesterday's, not today's, for Pamela had stood over her, watching the movement of her throat as the capsule and the water went down. But still she dared not leave her.

Would she be able to do so for long enough to go out with Ivan Roiter ever again? One day. Maybe next week when she had got Beatrix back into her ideal regimen of taking a pill every day. She looked at the card. On it, under his name, was the single word "Actuary." That meant they should have something in com-

what she was doing. Their mild brown eyes rested blankly on her when she took letters out of envelopes, glanced at invoices, examined forms. Avice, whose anthropomorphism was excessive, often remarked that if her pets could talk they would have some amazing tales to tell.

Her search yielded only one useful piece of information. After leaving no drawer unopened and no cupboard door untouched, she had found just one letter of interest. The postcard from one of the will beneficiaries and the letter from the other told her merely that the weather in the Isle of Man had been "horrendous" and the nephew's wife was expecting a baby in July. Marion was interested only in the letter from Mr. Karkashvili, Avice's solicitor. In it he accepted her invitation to lunch followed by will altering at a date in May. Nothing in the short letter mentioned the details of any new provisions Avice might be making, only that she would be doing so. Marion restored it to its envelope, idly wondering, as she often did in this situation, if paper took fingerprints.

Downstairs, the rabbits having lost interest and disappeared through their flap, Marion made herself lunch with a gin and tonic to precede it and a glass of wine as accompaniment. The result was that she fell asleep, but she was a light sleeper, as such people often are, and was roused to full wakefulness by the sound of Duncan Crosbie's car. It wouldn't have been in Marion's nature to be found reclining on a sofa, bleary-eyed, so when Avice walked in she was prancing about plumping up cushions, putting rabbit pellets and greenery into dishes, and running to refill water bowls.

"How did the wedding go?"

"Well, of course, we weren't actually at the wedding. It was a nice lunch, but it might have been just any lunch, if you know what I mean. Edmund wouldn't have any speeches. How are Figaro and Susanna?"

"Out having a lovely time in the sunshine," said Marion fondly.

While she was dozing a wonderful idea had come to her. Not only was it brilliant, but it was practical too and foolproof. She was so pleased with it that she longed to put it to Avice straightaway but she stopped herself. This must be subtly handled. She would wait for Avice to raise the subject first. Not Marion's plan, of course, that would be too much of a coincidence, but the general matter of her will, perhaps by mentioning Mr Karkashvili's projected visit.

· · ·

Getting to speak to Andrew, which had been so difficult for Ismay, Heather found easy. She left a message on his land line and, to her surprise, he called her back. But she wasn't desperate, she wasn't in love with him. He didn't use her Christian name. No one could be as icy as Andrew, his tone more distant than if he had been talking to a stranger.

"What can I do for you?"

Go back to my sister. "I wanted to tell you that—well, Issy's very unhappy. I thought that if you felt bad about her, but you felt—well, that she wouldn't have you back, if you felt awkward about it, I want you to know that she would. She loves you. She would have you back."

She had never before spoken to him at such length. A near-silence had always been observed between them and now he was silent. For so long that she thought he had replaced the receiver and was on the point of putting hers down when he said, "I can't do that. It's over."

In a small sad voice Heather said, "Are you with Eva now?"

"That's not your business, but if you mean is she with me at this moment, no. If on the other hand you mean is she my girlfriend, yes.

Absolutely. Considering you and your swain were the cause of my leaving, I think this is a piece of impertinence."

"That's not true!" Heather spoke so loudly that Edmund heard her before he came into the room. She shouted, "It had nothing to do with us and you know it!"

She put down the receiver and turned to him a flushed face. "Don't tell me not to get in a state. Don't tell me he isn't worth it."

"I wasn't going to," said Edmund, laughing. "But you could forget him and let me know what you think of the flat."

Heather took several deep breaths. After a moment she said, "It's a much classier area than we had in mind. I mean, it's practically Belgravia."

"It's Victoria, it's over a shop and it's very small."

"Five hundred pounds a month, Ed. That's quite a lot of money."

"With luck we won't be there long."

"With luck," said Heather. "You say there's a park near to it?"

"Well, it's near the park, St. James's Park, no less."

"It means we'll have to put off our honeymoon even longer."

"I know. We'll have to have our honeymoon in Victoria Station."

His mother remained very still when he told her. She looked like a character in a myth or fairy story in which people are turned to stone, petrified where they sit. Irene had been threading beads onto a string and now she sat with her needle poised between forefinger and thumb, the half-completed necklace held in the other hand an inch or two from her lap. Gradually she turned on him her Hecuba face, desolate from the loss of husband, children, and power.

He said, though she hadn't spoken, "I'm only going to live a couple of miles away."

"It isn't the distance," she said, speaking slowly and deliberately. "It's the callous indifference to my feelings. After I offered you the chance to live here for good. I suppose she put you up to it."

"On the contrary, it was originally my idea."

"At your wedding," Irene said as if he hadn't spoken, "I said to you to give up the flat, to stay here. I made you a distinct and, most people would say, very generous offer. And this is how you treat it. I'm not proud, Edmund, and I **am** forgiving. I'll go further. I'll have half this house converted into a self-contained home for you and—your wife." Her temporary surge of affection for Heather had already died. "Even though she isn't the woman I would have chosen for you, I'll do it. Whatever anyone could accuse me of, it isn't selfishness."

"No, Mother, no one's accusing you of anything. I'm to blame. I've decided to go and I'm going." Remembering that the woman his mother would have chosen for him was Marion Melville, he added, "It will be fine. You must be our first guest."

Her hands started to move as she thrust the needle through the hole in the next bead. She looked at the work, not at him. "You seem to forget that I'm not strong. You always have. I don't know how many times I've told you that it's only because I don't give in to it, I don't let it take me over, that I'm not totally incapacitated. But the fact remains that I couldn't possibly make it to Victoria. That is out of the question."

"We will come and see you here. We'll come regularly. We aren't deserting you."

Depressed, Edmund was learning that when you have been afraid of someone for years, under her thumb, and deceiving yourself that you give in to her only for a quiet life, once you begin to assert yourself it's a start, not a constant. From time to time you go right back to where you began. You get tired, you yield, and you shrink. You never really get over it, for you have been formed and molded into this shape over the long years. A few months, a single year, of showing strength and asserting himself wasn't enough to rise above the subservience of years. He would just have to keep on struggling.

Heather now said to him, "I know you don't want to talk about it, but if I can't get anywhere with Andrew, why shouldn't I try Eva herself?"

Fowler had done his best to be law abiding. He had sat on Marion's doorstep for four hours, waiting for her to come home, and had only moved into the back when a woman from farther down Lithos Road told him that if he stayed there she was calling the police. The back regions next door were neat and pretty, but these were squalid, a yard of broken concrete slabs, a garden in which weeds had grown up through the piles of builders' junk left there a dozen years earlier. Fowler, settling himself on the steps that led down to a long-disused privy, thought he had never seen such gigantic weeds, some of them surely ten feet tall and with the

leaves you see on exotic house plants, the kind
of thing you expected in a rain forest but not in
London NW6.

Marion had had her locks changed. Fowler
was genuinely upset to find his sister would go
to such lengths to keep him out. A tear or two
had trickled down his cheeks when he discovered that the key he had had cut no longer fitted. But he had waited long enough. Where
was she? Was it possible she had found a
boyfriend and wouldn't return all night? This
was a novel idea Fowler rather liked. The
boyfriend would have a home of his own, Marion might move in and his long-held dream of
living here be realized.

Meanwhile, he was very hungry. What
money he had he had spent on skunk and not
very good skunk at that. Its effects had worn off
even before he reached Lithos Road. He longed
for a drink or two or three. The sun had set
long since and it was starting to get dark. She
was his last hope. Next to a water butt in which
the larvae of mosquitoes cavorted on the
scummy surface, a short flight of steps led
down to the basement area. Fowler went down
and took stock of available means of ingress.
The back door had four panes of glass in it. It
also had bolts top and bottom. Regretfully he
turned to the only window down here, the one

in Marion's bedroom. Breaking it would let the cold in. It might be May but the nights were very chilly, not even frost free. Still, she should have thought of that before she changed the locks. Needs must when the devil drives. Fowler unwound the scarf he wore, very long and of red wool never washed in its twenty years of existence, wrapped it several times around his right hand and arm, and gave the window a hard punch. He was in Marion's bedroom, cut and scratched but not seriously, five minutes later.

The bed looked as if it hadn't been slept in for a week. Fowler couldn't have said how he could tell but he was sure of it. He went upstairs, found to his satisfaction that she had acquired a new bottle of gin, not Bombay Sapphire but nearly as good, and poured himself a liberal measure. That was better. On his last visit the fridge had been half full. This time there was nothing in it and the door was left open for it to defrost.

He addressed himself as he often did: "What are we going to do about that, Fowler?"

Some inner adviser told him to look in cupboards and sure enough there was plenty of food in cans. He made himself a supper of a tinned steak pie, which he heated in the microwave, artichoke hearts, bean sprouts, and reconstituted dried potato. It was ten o'clock. He put his dishes in the sink and went back downstairs with his third gin and there, feeling virtuous, he swept up the broken glass into a dustpan. The temperature had fallen about fifteen degrees and the room was icy. If he was going to sleep in there he had better do something about the window. He patched it with sheets of newspaper, which he secured with tape, and after watching a television program about a lot of fat people going on holiday to Miami, went to bed in Marion's clean sheets.

After the best night's sleep he had had for years—he seldom slept in so comfortable a bed—he got up at midday. It took him ages to find keys to the new lock, but he did in the end, five of them on a plastic keyholder hidden in a drawer where Marion kept her jewelry. Fowler thought it base to steal a woman's jewelry, so he left it where it was and took just one of the keys. The chances were she wouldn't remember whether there had been five or only four.

An occasionally sentimental man, he mused for a while, as he ate eggs and baked beans, on his childhood with Marion, how loving she had been, how fond of him. One particular incident came back to him when he remembered her saying to a lady their mother knew, "This is my little brother. I do love him lots." A tear fell onto the glistening surface of one of the fried eggs. In case she came back before he returned tonight he ought to leave her something to make up for breaking that window.

Fowler fished about in the ancient drawstring bag he had found on a skip a few weeks earlier, and came out with a pedometer discarded in a bin in South Molton Street and a flagon of cologne. The cologne had been used up but its container was very pretty, an ornament in itself. Marion didn't care too much for ornaments, she said they were just more things that needed dusting. Why waste this one on her? Fowler had found a bottle in the back of her bathroom cabinet with a label on it that immediately put out inviting signals. He decanted the contents into the cologne flagon, having first taken a sip. Just what no doctor would order. Now to fetch his backpack and see if he had something with which to effect a substitution.

The first time Marion stayed in her house overnight, Avice went nervously to bed, disliking the idea of someone who was almost a stranger sleeping in the next room. In all the forty years she had lived there only her friend

Deirdre, domiciled in the Isle of Man, had slept there and then not often. There must have been something unacceptable to rabbits about Deirdre, for Figaro and Susanna had stayed in the garden all the time she was there. They accepted Marion. Only too well, as she noticed next day when Marion told her they let her stroke them and fondle their long ears. Avice felt a spasm of jealousy. How could they, after all she'd done for them? But it proved Marion was a suitable person to look after them and, by extension, a suitable person to occupy that spare room. Moreover, she got up at six, opened the rabbit flap, and swept up any scattering of little black droppings that might have accumulated during the night. By the time Avice came down, Figaro and Susanna had been fed and their water bowls filled.

For the next two nights Marion went back to her own home, returning with presents, two fleecy paw-printed towels and a bag of salad leaves from the farmers' market in the Finchley Road. Rarely given to demonstrations of affection, Avice kissed her on the cheek and listened with unusual patience to Marion's tale of how her flat had been broken into and her bed slept in while she was away. Marion knew very well that Fowler was the culprit and that it was Fowler's blood all over her clean sheets. No doubt he had cut himself while breaking her window, but she wasn't going to tell Avice all that, only that a break-in had taken place. She didn't want her new employer thinking she came from a family of criminals, but she liked her to believe her rabbit carer suffered her own misfortunes.

She stayed that night and the next, angry with Fowler and not at all sure he might not be back in Lithos Road even now. In spite of having an unusually good memory, she couldn't remember if, when she changed the locks, she had been given five new keys or six. In a decimal system five seemed the more likely number, one for her to keep in her bag and four extras in the drawer. But six was half a dozen and an even number and somehow more the kind of number a locksmith would prefer. She just didn't know. Four remained in the drawer and she had one in her handbag. But had there been five in the drawer and had Fowler taken one? Or only four in the drawer all along? It was no good, she couldn't remember. She could phone the locksmith and ask, but explaining would be too embarrassing. She could have the locks changed again. But no, not **again.**

Marion couldn't get to sleep. No matter how often she wielded the dustette, the currants reappeared. If her brilliant idea worked, they needn't think she'd observe the condition. Those two would be off to a fur farm within days. And on the subject of her will, why hadn't Avice said anything about Mr. Karkashvili's visit? Perhaps she, Marion, would have to start the ball rolling.

The trouble with Avice was that she wasn't—well—communicative. She talked a lot about rabbits, the many she had kept in her long life, but very little about her past, any friends she might have had or her family. Marion had known Mrs. Pringle for only a year but by the time she left she knew all about her children and the late Mr. Pringle, all the houses she had lived in, Mr. Pringle's business dealings, the cars he had possessed, and the various holidays they had been on together. Avice had television, but she didn't watch it much. She listened to the radio and she read paperback novels, which she brought back to the house in batches of six or eight from West End bookshops. When she was reading with rabbits hopping about around her feet, she didn't like being talked to. She appeared extremely fond of silence.

Marion began to list in her mind the kind of openings Avice could make which would give the ball its initial push. Any reference to her declining health, for instance (if it was declining), to her advanced age, to wills, to intestacy, to funerals (other people's of course, not her own), to rabbits' longevity, to **Fur and Feather** magazine, to inheritance tax or to those exempt from it, and to solicitors. Marion waited. She pranced off home, scuttled back, shopped for Avice, fed the rabbits and swept up after them, sat watching them while Avice went in the tube to Hatchards to buy books and Waitrose to buy fish, and nothing was said by Avice about any of the subjects on the list. And then, one day in the middle of May, a letter came for her with an Isle of Man postmark.

Reading it, Avice broke her silence to speak on the only subject that would have loosened her tongue at that hour of the morning. "My old friend Deirdre has died. This is from her cousin. Imagine—isn't that sad?—she's left behind her lovely cat and the cousin doesn't want it. Have you ever heard anything so callous?"

The leap of something in her chest, that breathless jumping, followed by brief light-headedness, which always came to Marion at times of excitement, made her momentarily dizzy. These symptoms also raised her voice a few decibels. Squeaking a little, she said, "Couldn't you take the cat?"

"Oh, no. Good heavens, no. Poor sweet thing, but how would it react to Figaro and Susanna?"

Eat them, thought Marion. Her voice restored to normal, Marion said, "Was your friend—er, well off? I mean, was she comfortable?"

"Fairly, I suppose," said Avice with the condescension of someone who owns a street of houses in Manchester. "She had her savings. Why?"

Marion drew a deep breath. "What your friend really ought to have done," she said, "was leave some of her money to—well, to someone on condition they took care of the cat after she passed away."

Avice raised her eyebrows. She hardly seemed as gripped by the suggestion as Marion had hoped. But give her time. The idea had been planted and needed a while to germinate.

"If Deirdre had intended to do such a thing, who would this 'someone' have been? Not me. I wouldn't have been interested. And obviously not the cousin."

Bugger Deirdre, thought Marion. Let's talk about you. "No doubt there'd be difficulties, but nothing that couldn't be got over."

"This 'someone' might renege on her undertaking and turn the poor cat out or even, unthinkable as it is, have him or her put to sleep."

Marion felt herself blushing. This had been

exactly her own thought when she broached the subject. "Oh, well, it was just an idea," she said.

Still, Avice would think about it now, Marion thought. She wouldn't be able to help herself. And she'd know she must make up her mind in the next two weeks before Mr. Karkashvili came.

Ismay had almost forgotten the existence of the tape. She had ceased to care what had happened that day in August when Guy drowned. If she thought about it, it was to wonder why she had so involved herself in that whole business. It was nothing to do with her. She had been living in a dream world, a fantasy place where she imagined she could have told a man his girlfriend had killed someone. Reality was now, this cold unhappy region where she was alone, a solitary forsaken woman.

Looking along the shelf for an old Emmylou Harris tape, she found **Rainy Season Ragas** and put it in her handbag. Next time she went out she would throw it away. She would dispose of it—out of her life and out of danger of falling into the wrong hands, any hands. Most evenings now she spent upstairs with Pamela and Beatrix. Occasionally she went over to see Edmund and Heather, but, although they made her welcome, she always felt she was intruding on their private bliss and that if they could be completely honest about it—of course they couldn't—they would prefer her not to come. After all, what was she but the specter at the feast, the mourner at the wedding party?

Pamela always seemed pleased to have her company, doleful though it was. As for Beatrix, she was either glued to her radio or making her biblical comments about man-faced horses with women's hair and stings in their tails in a quiet wavering voice. Ismay sat down beside her mother and picked up the **Evening Standard** Pamela had been out to fetch. The lead story was about a man who had been attacking young girls in west London. Solely for the sake of the alliteration, it seemed, he had been given the absurd name of the West End Werewolf. So far, though an attempt had been made to strangle one of them, no girl had been seriously harmed. Ismay wasn't much interested. She turned the page, then another and another, and saw Andrew's face.

"And they had a king over them," said Beatrix gently and with a knowing smile, "which is the angel of the bottomless pit."

He was in what looked like a club and next

to him was Eva Simber. Both were smiling, but at each other, not the camera. Rather than simply happy, they looked involved with each other, as if they shared a secret no one but the two of them would ever know. Andrew held a cigarette in his left hand. The other rested against Eva's long slender neck and seemed to be caressing it. Ismay found she could read no more than the first words of the caption, "Socialite Eva Simber" . . . The print blurred and became a jumble, an obscure foreign language.

"Are you all right?" asked Pamela.

She couldn't bear the thought of discussing that picture. Pamela would be sympathetic, indignant, kind, but still she couldn't bear it. "I'm fine," she said.

Pamela began talking about the romance walking. "I've met this man. His name is Ivan Roiter and he reminds me a bit of Michael."

"Is that a good thing?" Ismay made herself recall that Michael Fenster was the man Pamela was living with, was engaged to, at the time of Guy's death. "Do you want to be reminded of him?"

Pamela flushed deeply. "I loved him, you know. Perhaps I'm only saying that Michael was my type and so is Ivan. But, there. He hasn't asked me out yet. I may never hear from him again. If he does I must admit I don't look forward to telling him about Beatrix. About me living with her, I mean." Pamela thought, but not aloud, of the two or three men who had been put off from the start by what one of them had called "your crazy sister." "I always find it hard to believe she went this way just because Guy died."

"Yes, well, I suppose she was in love with him." More than that Ismay wasn't going to explain. She didn't care. She cared about nothing but Andrew, Andrew's absence from her life and presence in Eva Simber's. She said it again: "She was in love with him," and the simple utterance of that phrase, words which inevitably carry a charge of emotion, brought the tears rushing to her eyes almost without warning, rush and spill over on a sob. She turned her face into the chair cushion and wept.

"Oh, darling," Pamela cried. "I'm so sorry, so very very sorry. Was it something I said?"

"Oh, no, oh, no. I'm always—always on the edge of tears. The least little thing. I didn't want you to see. . . . Have you looked at the paper yet?"

Pamela took it and looked at the photograph of Andrew with Eva Simber. She put her arm around Ismay and held her niece's wet face against her shoulder. "Darling, darling . . ."

Helping herself in a slow methodical way

from a box of chocolates, her ear pressed to the radio, Beatrix took absolutely no notice of her daughter's tears. As far as she was concerned, there might have been no tears, no words spoken, no pain. After a while she shut the lid of the box, pushed the radio away, and closed her eyes. The handbag slid off her lap onto the floor.

Chapter Thirteen

The previous day's **Evening Standard** had described her as a socialite. Eva knew what the word meant—she was a frequent reader of **Hello!** and **OK!** magazines—but she would have preferred to have been described simply as "lovely" or "captivating." She dropped the paper on the floor and got ready for her run.

The term "jogging" was unacceptable to Eva. It sounded like a heavy-footed animal, a hippo perhaps, or just a big person with thick ankles and a stomach. Others might jog; she ran—on light feet in Ruco Line silver sneakers and very short shorts and a T-shirt as white as snow. Eva had a number of white and pale-colored T-shirts which, instead of washing, she had dry-cleaned and which she threw away after the third wearing. Around St. James's Park she ran each morning except Thursdays. On Thursdays she went swimming in the morning and to yoga in the afternoon.

Eva had never had a job or earned anything. She had no need to. When she came home from her Swiss finishing school her father handed over to her a portfolio of reliable but fairly adventurous stock and bought her the flat, which was the ground and first floors of a house in a street that ran parallel with the Vauxhall Bridge Road. It was very kind of Daddy, of course, but a pity it was in Pimlico. The only place to live really was Mayfair or, just possibly, Notting Hill, the Kensington end and well away from the route of the Carnival.

The diaphanous scraps she wore, see-through shifts, transparent drapery with hemlines to the middle of her slender white thighs, revealed the shape of the body beneath, milk-white as a marble statue. Eva's hair was no darker than barley stems, reaching to the middle of her narrow straight back, and she was as attenuated as a twelve-year-old, with tiny breasts and a stalk for a waist. She might have been a child star playing Tinkerbell in **Peter Pan.** When she went running she braided her hair, not into two but six plaits so that afterward, when she undid them, her hair was crinkled from crown to tip like a Spanish infanta's. It framed her small flying-fox face in a pale golden mist.

Running around St. James's Park, she followed the same route each day. If she had diverged from this itinerary she would have been afraid of getting lost. Although she lived in London and considered nowhere else in the British Isles a possible place to live, she knew only Bond Street and a few streets in Knightsbridge. When she ran, a bottle of pure spring water was all she carried. She paid no attention to the trees or flowers, scarcely noticed Buckingham Palace ahead of her; and if anyone had asked her if you could see the London Eye from the bridge or if there were really pelicans, she couldn't have answered. The contents of her mind occupied her, whether she would have time for a pedicure as well as a facial later in the day, how little she could manage to eat when she had lunch with Mummy at Fortnum's, and why they wouldn't let her have True, her Labrador, with her in London.

It was nearly nine when she returned to her car, the smart Mercedes Daddy had given her for Christmas, which she had left in Birdcage Walk. A parking ticket was on the windscreen. Daddy had said he would pay her parking fines, but he had been difficult about it lately, she had so many. Still, she soon forgot it. After all, it was only a ticket. She never took parking offenses seriously unless her tire was actually clamped.

She was back in the flat, unweaving the braids, when the phone rang. Andrew, probably. She let it ring twelve times. Keeping men in suspense was her policy. Eva always answered it with her name, which she thought distinguished.

"Eva Simber."

The voice was a woman's. Strange because the only woman who rang on the land line was Mummy. "My name is Heather Litton. You won't have heard of me. You don't know me."

"No, I don't," said Eva. "Look, I've just come in from my run and I need a shower. What do you want?"

"My sister is called Ismay. Ismay Sealand. You'll have heard of **her**."

Cautious now, Eva said in a way the Swiss finishing school would have deplored, "So what?"

"You're going out with Andrew Campbell-Sedge, aren't you? No, I know you are. He was Ismay's boyfriend. They were practically engaged."

When she paused, Eva said, "So?"

"Are you in love with him?"

"Am I **what?**"

"I can't do this on the phone," said Heather Litton. "Could we meet? I'd really like to talk to you."

"Talk about what? I don't **know** you. I don't know what you want."

"I want you to give him up."

"You're mad," said Eva. "I'm going to put the phone down. Good-bye."

Not as sophisticated and detached as she liked people to think, Eva felt rather shaken. When Andrew phoned should she tell him? Should she even break her rule and phone him? Pinning her newly crinkled hair on top of her head, she stepped into the shower. She had long ago mastered the art of so twisting and contorting her body as to stand under the very hot cascade without wetting her head. You looked so ghastly in a shower cap even when there was no one to see you.

Perhaps it would be a good idea to phone Andrew and tell him or perhaps it would be better not to. Or should she tell Daddy? Daddy would tell her simply to forget it. He would treat this development the way he treated all her concerns and those of her mother and her sister. "Women's nonsense," he called them. Or "a storm in a vodka breezer," which he thought very funny. He wanted her to marry Andrew. It would be what he, in his incredibly outdated way, would call a "good match." Money should ally itself with money, in his view, and Andrew was the sort of person who would one day be on the Queen's Bench. Some other fine day, because he was made of the right material, he might become Lord Chancellor or, if this office no longer existed, Attorney General. Eva didn't care. She didn't want to marry anyone but just have a good time with a lot of men and get her picture in the papers.

She dialed one-four-seven-one, proud of herself for remembering it; she was told that she had been called at nine thirty-one that morning and was given the caller's number. She wrote it down, more to convince herself that she really was grown-up and efficient than for any use it would be. The last person she wanted to speak to was that woman.

Arranging their portable possessions in the two rooms over the shop in Rochester Row, Heather and Edmund had it all done by eight. They sat down side by side with mugs of tea on the table in front of them and Heather told him about the phone call she had made. "I'm determined to get to speak to her, Ed. I thought I could do some running myself. We really ought to take some exercise, you know, you and I. We don't have any. I thought I could run around St. James's Park. She'd just come in from her run when I phoned, so I think she goes out at seven-thirty, and where she lives it's bound to be St. James's Park."

"What are you going to say to her?"

"Don't look like that. I'm going to be nice. I thought I could find out how serious she is about Andrew and if she's not, if it's just a bit of fun, I'm going to get her to give him up."

"Why should she?"

"I don't know why, Ed, but I think I would if someone asked me the way I asked her and if I didn't love the man. Nothing would have made me give you up. Anyway, no one asked me. I wouldn't have if they had. But that's because I love you."

After Edmund had finished kissing her and whispering that they ought to go to bed **now,** she said, "I'm going to appeal to her better nature. I'm going to tell her she's very beautiful— her picture's in the **Evening Standard** and she is—I'm going to say, you could have anyone, so please give him up for my sister's sake."

"You've no guarantee he'd go back to Ismay or she'd take him back."

"She would," said Heather.

• • •

"I'm doing my run," Eva said in the indignant tone someone might use to say she had an appointment with the Queen. "I can't just stop in the middle."

"Five minutes," the woman said. "We could sit on this seat for five minutes."

"You're the one who called me!"

"That's right. You wouldn't talk on the phone so I came to find you here. Please sit down for a minute."

Eva, who was dressed in a pink satin jumpsuit, sat down reluctantly, first brushing fastidiously at the seat. This interruption of her morning workout she considered a great nuisance. The woman beside her belonged in a category she deeply disapproved of. It puzzled her that any girl in her twenties could set foot outdoors without eye makeup. And to have short fingernails that had never had the attention of a manicurist! She noticed the wedding ring on the left hand. Someone must have married her, but surely no one Eva would have looked at twice. Only the very uncharitable would have called her overweight but she'd never get into a size ten again, if she ever had. Nice hair or it would be if she had it properly cut. Having summed up Heather Litton, Eva let her eyes come to rest on the woman's knees in what were probably Gap jeans and said, "Well? What is it?"

Instead of an answer she got a question. "Did you tell Andrew about my phone call?"

"What's that to you?"

"I'd just like to know if you told him."

Eva shrugged. "No. No, I didn't. I thought it was all too stupid. I mean, asking me to give up my boyfriend just because of someone else he's got tired of. Why tell him?"

"It doesn't matter. Do you love him?"

"That's not your business."

"Okay, it's not. None of it's exactly my business. It's yours and my sister's and Andrew's. I'm interfering, I know, but I think I've got good reason." Heather was looking at her with deep earnestness and Eva recognized sincerity in her blue eyes. "But if you love him," she went on, "if you mean to stay with him and maybe marry him—well, I'd understand. I love my husband and no one could make me give him up. He's the great love of my life. But if it's just a fun thing, if you fancy him and it's sex and whatever and nothing more, couldn't you give him up and find someone else?"

"Quite a speech," said Eva.

Heather went on as if Eva hadn't spoken. "He was with my sister for two years and I think they'd have stayed together, maybe for always, if you hadn't come along. You met him at that Christmas party at his parents', didn't you?"

"What if I did?"

"I know you did. That's when he started—leaving Ismay. That was the beginning of it. It's not a very long time. You could give him up now and it wouldn't be much of a split. You've known him less than six months." Heather looked into her face and Eva was very conscious of her superiority in looks over the other woman. "I'm pleading with you, Eva. He doesn't mean all that to you, does he? He means the world to my sister. Her heart is breaking. When he went he took away everything that made life worth living for her. He'd go back to her if you weren't there."

Eva got to her feet, shaking her head vigorously. "I won't give him up. I don't **want** to." She was aware she sounded like a petulant child but she didn't care. "If he knew he'd think I was mad. No one does that sort of thing. No one gives up a man because someone she doesn't know asks her to. It's crazy."

"You could be the first."

Eva began to run. She called back over her shoulder, "Don't follow me. I don't want to see you again." Inspired to utter the worst insult she could think of, she added, "You're such a **bore.**"

If Ismay could have heard Heather's words she would have agreed with them entirely. Of course she would take Andrew back. She loved him. Nothing could change that. Eva Simber couldn't love him, not yet. She had only known him six months, if that. Ismay forgot that she had fallen in love with Andrew at first sight, the first moment she saw him across that crowded room—like in the song. As Heather had done, she found Eva's address in the phone book and looked up Sark Street, SW1, in her London atlas. Unlike Heather, she had no clear idea of what she would say to Eva Simber or even if she would go so far as to speak to her at all. Perhaps she would simply note where she lived, walk about a bit to catch a glimpse of her if she came home or went out. It was also possible, she thought miserably, that she might see Andrew. That would be terrible, but it would be glorious as well.

Once her idea had taken shape she was unable to rest until she had put it into practice.

Now her ally, Pamela was the only person she discussed this with and she advised her strongly against it. "What good will it do? You'll only make yourself more unhappy."

"I couldn't be more unhappy."

"Then better stay the way you are. If she sees you she'll despise you and if he does he'll just be exasperated. People don't like being chased. It doesn't take much for them to call it harassment."

"You know something, Pam? I don't care. I just don't care."

The next evening she had a reception she was organizing for a client. It was in Westminster and it ended at eight-thirty. The night was fine, still light at nine, and she decided to walk, to take the Horseferry Road and cross Vincent Square. The place was quiet and there was little traffic, Maunsel Street a garden of spring flowers and the grass in the square as green as a parakeet. Tears gathered behind her eyes and flowed silently down her cheeks. She had nothing to wipe them away with but the backs of her hands. I shall be "all tears," she thought, I shall turn to stone like that woman whose children all died. The woman was in classical mythology, but she couldn't remember her name or what had happened to her.

Emerging into the Vauxhall Bridge Road, tales of the West End Werewolf came into her mind. The girl he had tried to strangle had described him: young, not very tall, brown hair, clean-shaven. Thousands of men fitted that description. Anyway, he attacked at night and, though after nine, it was still light. The only people about were a couple of middle-aged Asian men, a young girl on her own walking fast, and a woman with a child in a buggy. She crossed the road and found Sark Street around the back of Pimlico tube station.

Eva's flat was the top of a narrow white-brick terraced house with steps and pillars. Lights were on in every window upstairs. Ismay marched daringly up the steps to the two bells and read Eva's name. She thought, I could ring the bell and fetch her down and talk to her. I could show her my tears. She held her forefinger, quivering with fear, an inch from the bell and then she lost her nerve and retreated down the steps. Eva wouldn't be at home, anyway. Girls like Eva never were at home in the evenings, seldom before three in the morning. The lights meant nothing.

Ismay went back to the Vauxhall Bridge Road, found a small humble café, occupied by two couples, two men, and a solitary girl like herself, and bought herself a filter coffee. She sat over her coffee for a long time while it grew dark outside. Brightly lit red double-deckers went past. A fire engine roared and howled on its way to the Embankment. She had had nothing to eat at the reception and quite a lot to drink. She bought herself a stale Danish pastry and a chocolate bar. Then she walked back to Sark Street where not a soul was about and Eva's lights were still on, unchanged from when she had last seen them.

There was no point in staying. There had never been any point in coming. Torturing herself, she imagined Andrew dancing with Eva in some dimly lit place where the music was soft. Andrew was a good dancer, especially at the tango. She walked back to Pimlico station and got into a tube to Brixton.

It was far more crowded than she had expected and she had no hope of a seat. She got out at Stockwell and found the Northern Line platform densely packed. It was a crush to get onto it at all. That always meant only one thing: that no Northern Line train had stopped here for maybe twenty minutes and meanwhile passengers had poured onto the platform from the street and, like her, from the Victoria Line. The public address system emitted its usual incomprehensible announcements, the accent Chinese, the interference with transmission an ear-splitting crackle. Whatever the voice had been saying, a train appeared, clearing perhaps a third of the people who waited. Within a minute or two a mob surged through the entrance, most of them young men, drunk and noisy. Another train came and this time she got on. She was carried on, pushed from behind and jostled on either side, shoved and pulled, buffeted to stand up against the opposite doors, clinging on for dear life on to one of the uprights.

The train started with a lurch. She reached for her handbag to adjust the strap on to her shoulder. It was gone.

Chapter Fourteen

Edmund heard Heather put the receiver down. He was in the living room of their flat, hanging the few paintings he had brought from Chudleigh Hill, polishing the glass and renewing the picture cords, and Heather was in the tiny hallway.

"I could hear you," he said when she came in. "You sounded quite friendly."

"If we are, isn't it better that way?"

Edmund turned around and looked at her. A deep red flush colored her forehead and cheeks. He had never seen her look like this before and he now realized he was witnessing some powerful emotion which somehow changed her face, but he was unable to say what that emotion might be. Fear? Shame? Pity? No, it was anger.

"What is it?"

"Nothing," she said and her voice was low-pitched and slow. "Nothing really."

"She won't give him up? No, of course not. Did you ever seriously think she would?"

"I hoped." Heather gave a cry of rage, of fury, and clenched her hands. He had never seen her lose control before and he stared. "I hoped she'd do a—well, a good action. She's not in love with him. She's more or less said." She grew calmer and took a deep breath. "You said we sounded friendly. She talks to me now like I was a friend of hers. She calls me by my name. But she won't budge. She wants to keep hold of him."

"I'm not surprised."

She turned on him and he expected something he had never had from her, shouting, reproach, anger, perhaps insults. But she put her parted lips together, touched her hot cheeks with her fingertips, and came up to him to kiss him.

"I shall try again, Ed. I can't give up."

"I can see that."

"I forgot to tell you. Issy's had her handbag stolen, her Marc Jacobs bag."

"Who's Marc Jacobs?"

"You sound like some old judge. They never know who anyone is. He's a designer. Luckily, she always carries her keys separately but the thief took everything else, her wallet with quite a lot of money in it and three credit cards, her mobile, her diary. It happened when she was getting into the tube."

"Coping with all that may at least take her mind off Andrew."

"It won't," said Heather, thinking, though fondly, that that was just like a man, a man's judgment.

Eva hadn't told Andrew and she hadn't told Daddy. When Andrew came around to take her out to dinner she had asked him if a socialite was the same thing as being in the Labour Government, and he had laughed so much that his face had turned unbecomingly red. She had shouted at him not to be so mean and beastly and his laughing some more had put an end to her speaking to him at all for the next hour. As for Daddy, he'd probably advise her to tell the police. Daddy loved the police almost as much as he loved the army and was thrilled to see so many of them carrying guns these days.

Besides, telling Andrew would require bringing her own feelings about him out into the open. Young as she was, Eva was the kind of girl who believes it is best never to show a man how you feel about him and lethal to let him believe you will hang on to him at all costs. And anyway, she wouldn't and she didn't really know how she felt about him. The truth was that if this Heather persisted she probably would give him up, simply to avoid trouble. If she persisted, and it had begun to look as if she would.

She had phoned again two days after their meeting. It was early in the morning and Eva was still in bed, it being Thursday, her day for going to the swimming pool and her yoga lesson. Heather said her name and asked if Eva had thought any more about what she had said in the park.

"No, I haven't. I **told** you. It's not your business. Anyway, he wouldn't go back to your sister."

"Is he there now?"

"He's just gone." It wasn't true. Eva knew it was weakness on her part to answer Heather Litton's questions, but Eva didn't want the woman thinking theirs wasn't a full sexual relationship. "D'you know what he told me?" She was driven to be spiteful. "He told me he doesn't know now how he let himself be seen about with your sister for so long."

"I don't believe that," Heather said.

"Believe what you like. It's true." Eva sat up in bed, wishing there were someone to bring her coffee and orange juice and half a piece of crispbread as there was at home with Mummy and Daddy. "Look, what's in this for you, for God's sake? Andrew wasn't your boyfriend."

"My sister means a lot to me. I don't like seeing her suffer."

"Well, I'm sorry if she's suffering. I didn't mean to cause her pain. I couldn't help Andrew falling in love with me."

Eva was dimly aware that she was starting to be—well—almost **on good terms** with Heather. She couldn't help it. Though not much older than she, Heather had a motherly manner, a way of talking reasonably and patiently that Eva wasn't used to in her contemporaries, still less her own mother. "She'll get over it, Heather," she said rather desperately. Using that Christian name made it worse. "People always do. She'll meet someone else."

"I used to think that but now I don't know. I don't think so."

"People always do," Eva said again. "I have to go."

"St. James's Park again?"

"No, it's not. And I don't want you following me anywhere. Is that clear, Heather? I don't want it. It's harassment."

"Okay, I'll phone you tomorrow."

Eva didn't answer that. She said good-bye and put the phone down.

Avice lifted her eyes from the paperback she was reading and told Marion Mr. Karkashvili would be coming to lunch on Thursday.

"That's an interesting name," said Marion as if she had never come across it before.

"Yes, it's Georgian, dear." Avice explained rather condescendingly that she referred to Georgia in Asia and not Georgia in the United States. "His grandfather came here from Tiflis or whatever they call it these days."

Marion waited expectantly. She had been waiting for over a week now. But Avice was still occupied with nomenclature. "If it had been me I'd have changed it to something more English. Carter, perhaps, or Carville."

"Will you go out for lunch or have it here?"

Avice hesitated for so long that Marion wondered if she meant to answer at all. Finally she said, "I don't know, dear. He'll have to come here even if we eat elsewhere. The trouble is Figaro doesn't like him."

"I hope he's never done anything unkind to him," said Marion in a suitably indignant tone. "Rabbits are like elephants. They never forget."

"He's never had the chance," said Avice in the sort of tone that implied there was no knowing what outrages her solicitor would perpetrate if left to his own devices.

"I could take Figaro into the dining room while he was here. I mean I'd have some of that cow parsley he likes all ready for him and then he'd come in very happily."

"That's an idea. But I think we best eat out."

Her tone was neutral and unenthusiastic. Marion waited and then, suddenly, she understood. Avice was thinking. Avice put the piece of red ribbon which had come off a box of chocolates between the pages to mark her place, and pondered on her suggestion. Not the one about taking Figaro out of harm's way but the other one, made after she received the news of Deirdre's death. Marion could understand her hesitation. A large sum would have to be involved and she hadn't known Marion long. But who else could she ask? And how much should the large sum be? Asking Mr. Karkashvili would be unwise, especially as he seemed to be an animal hater. Should she give Avice a prod? Not yet. If Mr. Karkashvili was coming on Thursday she must make up her mind soon.

The restaurant in Pinner village Avice suggested was Italian and called La Mandritta. It didn't seem very upmarket to Marion, who had phoned the place and made the reservation. The man who answered the phone sounded as if he wasn't used to people ringing up and booking tables. Especially for lunch, he said. "Most just come and take potluck."

Marion didn't like the sound of that, but what was it to her? She wasn't going to be eating there. She was going to be at home with those rabbits and meeting Mr. Karkashvili when he came back with Avice to redraft her will. After Avice had gone off to meet him at La Mandritta, Marion did one of her little dances. She tripped around the living room in a kind of flamenco style, wishing she had some music. Her dancing frightened the rabbits, who plunged through the flap into their hutch as soon as she waved her arms about.

The previous night she had gone off to bed despondently. It was more than a week since she had been back to Lithos Road, sticking close to Avice being the wisest thing to do. Avice had passed almost the entire evening immersed in what she called "the new Julie Myerson" while Marion watched television, necessarily turned very low so as not to disturb Avice. They had both had some hot chocolate at ten, and that was when Avice first mentioned the events scheduled for the following day.

Marion, to use her own words, perked up a bit at that. But all Avice said was that she thought she and Mr. Karkashvili would be back at the house by three at the latest and would Marion like to make tea when he came?

Half an hour later she was sitting up in bed, massaging her face with antiaging night serum, when Avice knocked at the door and came in. Marion eyed her warily. She had just come to a decision. She'd go home tomorrow and maybe not come back. Avice, who was holding the photographs of Figaro and Susanna that Marion had fetched from the pharmacy that day, asked if she might sit down.

"It's your house," Marion said not very graciously.

"Yes, but your room, dear."

"Was there something you wanted?"

"Well, yes. Oh, dear, I find this quite embarrassing. I'm so afraid you'll say no. That's why I've been putting off asking for days— well, weeks."

Marion knew now. "No need to be embarrassed with me."

"Well, you may not say that when you hear what I've got to ask."

Oh, get on with it, Marion thought. Spit it out.

"You must just say outright if you can't take

it on." A deep breath and Avice spat it out. "Do you remember when I heard about Deirdre's dying you said she ought to have left money in her will to someone who'd look after her cat?"

"Did I?" said Marion.

"Oh, yes, you certainly did, dear. Well, would you?"

Say how much, Marion prayed. How much? "Would I what, Avice?"

"Take care of Figaro and Susanna when I— when I pass on? I thought fifty thousand. Would that be enough?"

Marion would have liked twice that but dared not ask for more. The whole scheme might come to grief if she did. "I think that's very generous, Avice," she said in a humble submissive voice, and then—this took more self-discipline than Marion had ever summoned up before—"May I give you my answer in the morning?" She couldn't resist adding, "Very first thing in the morning."

Avice said in a tone anyone else would have found pathetic, "Rabbits seldom live beyond six years old, you know, and mine are nearly two now."

Tea was ready when they came back from the restaurant. Marion poured it out and handed biscuits like a servant. Mr. Karkashvili was a slender, not very tall man and, with his small pale face, resembled President Putin. He kept giving Marion the sort of looks that imply, "Go, go, leave us, get out." He never once smiled or said thank you. With great dignity, Marion passed him the last biscuit, said to Avice, "I'll be in the dining room with Figaro if you need me," scooped up the struggling rabbit and departed, leaving those two to make the arrangements that would enrich her, for at seven-thirty that morning she had said yes. "Yes, I will. Of course I will."

And enrich her soon, Marion thought, remembering the morphine.

Chapter Fifteen

It was the excitement of Mr. Karkashvili's visit, Marion said, that and eating La Mandritta's spaghetti alle vongole, which had made Avice ill. The doctor, who came quickly because he was private, disagreed. Avice, he said, madly in Marion's opinion, wasn't as young as she used to be. As if he or anyone else was. Miss Conroy had been doing too much and her heart—he only slightly varied this favored cliché of his—wasn't what it used to be. The pain Avice said she had felt predominantly on her left side, caused him alarm. He wanted her to have an ECG even though she assured him the pain was gone now.

"I can't go into a hospital," Avice said. "I

was in hospital once. I had my appendix out. The nurses were horrible, they called me by my Christian name. Besides, I have to think of Figaro and Susanna."

"I'm sure your cleaning lady will look after them," said the doctor.

Marion hadn't been so incensed for years. To be taken for the cleaner! And Avice didn't correct him. She didn't say, this is my friend or this is my personal assistant. All she did was carry on refusing to go into, or even **to,** the hospital and the doctor finally gave up attempting persuasion and told her she must rest and take things easy. Once she got over his insult, Marion was pleased with the way things were going. It would make her task with the morphine easier if Avice had suffered a prior malaise. Of course, it also meant she, Marion, was virtually a prisoner in Pinner. Someone had to give Avice what she called her "heart medicine," see she rested, and feed the rabbits, and who else but Marion?

After a week of this, Joyce and Duncan Crosbie arrived. Apparently, they and Avice had a long-standing engagement to go together to the Chelsea Flower Show. Avice had completely forgotten this date, though Marion got the blame for forgetting it from all of them.

"You could have told me she was ill," Joyce

said, going out into the kitchen where Marion was making coffee for everyone. "I'd have been straight over."

Marion said nothing. She was thinking it might be a good idea to send for Joyce as soon as Avice succumbed to the morphine, but not too soon in case she summoned help. When, after the coffee had been drunk and the biscuits eaten, Duncan said that they wouldn't go to the flower show now but stay with Avice, Marion said, "In that case I'll just nip out to see my poor old father. I haven't been near him for a week and he does so rely on my visits."

No one attempted to hinder her. She skipped down the road to the tube station, the first time she had been able to give vent to her feelings since the making of Avice's will. She ran and danced and, on the corner of the street, executed a kind of pas de deux. People stared but there weren't many of them about.

In spite of her resolve never to go near him again, she rang Mr. Hussein's doorbell. The door was answered by Khwaja, the tallest and largest of the Hussein sons, dressed this time in a very expensive-looking dark-gray silk suit. He recognized her at once and before she could speak, said with a twitching of his lips, "Ah, it's the lady who gave my dad the unclean meat."

He had a habit Marion particularly disliked, that of seeming to suppress, not altogether successfully, laughter at his own words and those of the person he was talking to. Ignoring his estimation of her while blushing at it, Marion asked, "How's your father?" feeling foolish when she did so as must anyone who utters this phrase with serious intent.

"Gone on holiday to Marrakesh with Mrs. Iqbal," said Khwaja, heaving a little with inward giggles. "I had a nice postcard of a camel."

He shut the front door before Marion was halfway down the path. She got on the bus that goes to Swiss Cottage and ran the rest of the way to Chudleigh Hill. Irene had been in the living room making a necklace of carnelian and yellow amber beads and her first words were, "Oh, dear, I do so hate having to get up when I'm in the midst of stringing beads. I always feel I can see afterward exactly where I reached. The next knot is never quite right."

One must take the rough with the smooth, Marion told herself, and if today was particularly rough, well, too bad. "Avice Conroy is very ill," she said when Irene had made it clear she didn't intend them to kiss. "Her heart has gone back on her."

"Goodness, what a ridiculous expression. Gone where, I should like to know. Is she in the hospital?"

"I've been nursing her at home," said Marion.

"Avice always was a valetudinarian." Uncertain of the meaning of this word, Marion smiled vaguely. "People like me," Irene went on, "who suffer from chronic poor health, we can't help resenting the Avices of this world. I mean, their way of inventing illness is insulting to us, don't you think? We who would give anything to enjoy good health don't have much patience with imaginary ailments."

Marion couldn't have that. Her plan depended on Avice's heart trouble being taken seriously. On the other hand, she had no wish to alienate Irene. "The doctor seemed quite concerned," she said.

"Oh, well, she pays him. What do you expect?" The string of beads complete, Irene let it fall into her lap and pressed her right hand into her lumbar region. "I think my back is worse than it's ever been. I'd get you a drink of something only I honestly don't think I could get up."

"Can I get it?"

"Oh, don't bother. Not unless you absolutely can't do without the stimulus of wine." Irene had begun accusing almost everyone she knew of alcoholism, Marion noted. "If my son and that wife of his hadn't rushed off to the other side of London at the first opportunity, I'd have someone here to see to my needs. But, no, that wasn't to madam's taste. Luckily, my friend Barry Fenix will be here in a minute."

Irene's tone had softened when she spoke of this man and she sounded rather like someone half her age talking of her lover. Deciding that staying here any longer was profitless, Marion told Irene to take care of herself—"No one else will," was Irene's reply—and left. She was looking forward to a few hours at home on her own. As she tripped down the front garden path she spotted through the privet the man next door strolling down his. Marion had caught a glimpse of him in the distance before, but they had never spoken. She was surprised to see someone so handsome, if you made allowances for age and liked mustaches.

They met on the pavement between his house and Irene's. "You must be Mr. Fenix," said Marion, holding out her hand. "Marion Melville."

It was taken in a crushing grip. "Call me Barry. You've been seeing to the old lady, have you?"

If anything could have changed Marion's rough day into a smooth one, Barry Fenix's words would have done so. The old lady! "She really needs a full-time carer, Barry. And a housekeeper." Marion cast a glance in the direction of the front door he had come out of. "Her home is very big. I suppose yours is the same sort of size."

"A wee bit bigger, I think."

"Ah, but you have a devoted wife, no doubt."

Barry looked down. "Once I did. I'm a widower," he said.

"I'm so sorry. How awful of me. The minute I open my mouth I put my foot in it."

"A dainty little foot, if I may say so," said Barry gallantly. "Well, I'd best get on and see what's to do next door."

"I'm not sure—actually, she's asleep. It might be a good idea to leave it an hour or two. I hope you don't think I'm being pushy, but I do think your house is **lovely.** And the garden is beautiful."

"Since I'm not needed next door for a bit, would you like to come in and have a look around? Have a coffee or a drink or whatever."

"I'd love to," said Marion, her quiet time at home forgotten.

Eva got another phone call from the woman with the nice hair and the short fingernails. "I can't just let this go, Eva. I want to say something quite important to you."

"I suppose you think all this is important, don't you?"

Heather didn't answer. "This is about you more than about Andrew and Ismay. You're very young and I don't think you know what Andrew's like. Not yet. I hope you never will. You see, Ismay knows him. She knows how to be with him, how to make him happy and how to—well, survive while she's with him. You don't. He could destroy you."

"You know something, Heather. Andrew's like my dad. A lot like him. And Mummy's survived with him. She's still with him after twenty-five years. I'd be the same."

"Couldn't we meet and talk face-to-face?" Heather asked her. "I don't feel I'm getting anywhere on the phone."

"We did that already. It doesn't make any difference. I'm not giving Andrew up. Why should I?"

"I've told you why you should, Eva. It's because Ismay loves him and you don't. You just like him or you're attracted to him."

"Look, Heather, if you could sort of prove to me that Andrew would go back to your sister if I split with him—well, then I might think seriously about it. But you can't. Personally, I think he'd just go off and find some other girl. Isn't that a lot more likely?"

"Can't we meet and talk this through?"

"I don't see the point."

A listener who didn't know these girls would by now have believed them friends. Both had an inkling of this, but still Eva said, "I'm going to put the phone down now, Heather," and Heather said, "Okay, but we'll talk again."

They did so two days later. Heather went to be with her mother while Pamela was out and met Ismay there. Beatrix was calm, dosed up with chlorpromazine, chewing gum and silent, apart from once or twice telling Heather she would give her the key to the bottomless pit. Making tea for her mother and coffee for her sister and herself, Ismay turned dull eyes in a blank face to Heather and said in response to her inquiry that she was all right, she was just the same, she supposed she would get through it one day at a time.

"If he came back now would you have him?"

"Oh, yes. That doesn't change."

"Even though you know—forgive me, Issy, I have to say this—even though you know he'd be unfaithful to you again. He'd take up with another Eva when he felt like it. Even though you know he's completely self-absorbed and you'll always love him more than he loves you."

"Even though," said Ismay and her face was twisted with pain. "I'm the one who kisses and he's the one who lets himself be kissed. That's the way it is."

So Heather said to Eva the next time she phoned her, "She'd take him back. She told me so. It wouldn't matter what he'd done."

Eva said hotly, "Well, he hasn't done anything so very terrible, Heather. He's only split up with his girlfriend and taken up with someone else. People do it all the time."

"Can we meet?"

"I honestly don't see what for. You haven't **proved** anything. You've just told me what you say she's said. I've thought a lot about all this. Actually, our families, I mean Andrew's and mine, they're very keen on our relationship. I mean, if it led to marriage Mummy and Daddy would be—well, actually delighted. His people would be. I'm not giving him up. I just couldn't. I mean, I wouldn't be able to say the words."

"I see."

"I may as well tell you, Heather, I don't intend to go running in St. James's Park anymore, so don't think you can find me there, will you?"

"I won't think that. Good-bye, Eva."

• • •

Walking along the King's Road made Pamela feel uncomfortable. Out of place. The expression "a duck out of water" came into her head, and when she was here she knew fully what it meant. She said so to Ivan Roiter and, when he only shrugged, explained. Everyone else was so young and they looked so free, as if they hadn't a care in the world.

"I don't suppose they have," he said. "They're all living on the benefit. And that means my taxes, your taxes."

"They can't all be, Ivan. Some of them must have jobs. Anyway, that's not really what I meant."

She was always having to explain to Ivan what she meant. It wasn't so much that he didn't understand her—who could really understand somebody else?—or that he saw nothing from her point of view, though both were true, but that most of the time they seemed to be speaking different languages. Though they both worked with money, she wasn't obsessed with it, while he appeared to see everything in terms of finance. The young people they passed in this ever-lively, ever-youthful street were free, she thought, free in spirit, not constrained by time or duty or moral pressures or convention.

She was always having to explain to Ivan, but this time she didn't explain—what would be the use?

They went into a pub. Often morose but never silent for long, Ivan soon began to speak scathingly of the cost of drinks. He had never paid so much for a pint of lager, he said, and had she any idea what he had paid for her glass of wine? Nothing makes you feel so awkward as your host complaining about the cost of the food or drink he has bestowed on you, and Pamela immediately said that she would, of course, buy their second drink.

"If we have one in this rip-off place. Anyway, I don't like a woman paying for her own drinks. Especially when it's my partner."

Pamela was startled. His partner when she had only known him a few weeks? Again the language barrier rose up. What did he mean? He had kissed her once or twice, the sort of kisses you might get from a brother. She had been to his home, a nice but hardly palatial flat just off Albert Bridge Road. She had eaten half a dozen meals with him and would eat another tonight. She had never slept with him. In asking her back there again after they had eaten, was that what he had in mind?

The pub they were in provided food, but one glance at the blackboard on which the dishes were written up in chalk told Ivan that the prices were "astronomical." "A tenner for plaice and chips!" he said. "Amazing. You couldn't make it up." Ivan often said of some quite ordinary thing that you couldn't make it up and when someone had failed to organize something or other—another ongoing contention of his—that they couldn't run a whelk stall. When Pamela said that she thought it might take a lot of skill and experience to run a whelk stall, Ivan stared at her and said quite roughly, "Oh, come on. You know what I mean."

She admitted to herself that she found him attractive to look at. Ismay often talked about people having "types" and Ivan belonged in her favored category. That is, he was tall and well-built, darkish and bearded. He had blue eyes, which she also liked, and he always smelled beautifully clean and faintly cologned. His long-fingered hands were also among his attractions. She often thought of when they had first met at the romance walking and how she had been immediately drawn to him. She kept it in mind for reassurance when he said things like "The cost of everything in here is a scandal" or "My belief is we should have some say in how the government spends our tax money. It's called hypothecation."

When she said, very gently, "I know that, Ivan. I'm an accountant," he grew huffy and told her not to pull rank.

Not staying for a second drink, they set off on one of his quests for a suitable place to eat. "Suitable" meaning cheap, Pamela reminded herself with no pleasure. After five restaurants' outside menus had been perused and their prices adversely commented on, she suggested rather diffidently that if they were going back to his flat she would cook something for them there. This put him in a better mood than she had believed possible. There was plenty of food at his place. There was nothing he liked better than some home cooking in his own home. With his own partner, he added, putting his arm around her.

He had parked his car with great difficulty on a meter in one of the squares. Pamela was always rather nervous going back to find it bcause they had once done so and found a parking ticket on the windscreen. Ivan had gone mad, swearing that he had parked the car after six-thirty when the restriction was lifted, and threatening all kinds of vengeance on the Royal Borough of Kensington and Chelsea. Although she meant to make things better, Pamela made things worse by saying to him that he ought to be glad he hadn't been clamped. He swore at her then. But this time the only adornment to the windscreen was a flyer from a fitness spa, and Ivan set off for Battersea in a jocund mood.

There must be some term in psychology for these fluctuating moods of his, Pamela thought. It wasn't manic-depression or bipolarity—she had cause to know something about madness—it wasn't extreme enough for that. She could ask Edmund but the trouble with that was that she didn't want the family thinking there was anything odd about Ivan. As he drove he talked about the mother of a Greek colleague of his who had never lived in this country but who came here solely to get a hip replacement for free on the National Health Service.

In the flat she found that his boast that there was plenty of food in the house was a wild exaggeration. Certainly there were a lot of eggs and several packs of bacon. That made her suspect that he cooked himself breakfast every morning but nothing else. She found some withered mushrooms too, some slices of white bread in waxed paper and an unopened pack of butter. The terrible need for a drink, once almost unknown, strong now when she was with Ivan, almost drove her to ask for one, but just as she was getting her nerve up he walked into the kitchen with two whiskeys on a tray.

She made them bacon and mushroom omelettes, which he pronounced wonderful. Pleased that he was pleased, Pamela neverthe- less wondered if anything made him so happy as economy, the saving of a few pounds here and a few more there. He put his arm around her and told her how well they got on together.

It was only eight o'clock, and Heather and Edmund, who were with Beatrix that evening had promised to stay till eleven. She relaxed, ex- pecting him to turn on the television to a money program, which was his favorite. He of- ten said as he did so, that they had so much in common, but tonight, without more preamble, his arm holding rather tightly on to her shoul- der, he led her into his bedroom and said, "This is what we've really come for, isn't it?"

Marion got back late, long after Joyce and Duncan had gone. She had meant to be hours earlier, but she had spent far longer with Barry Fenix than had seemed likely at first. He had given her and himself a dry martini, the first she had ever tasted. It was deliciously ice-cold and came out of a silver bottle thing he told her was a cocktail shaker. "I'm a bit of a throwback, my dear," he said. "The first half of the twenti- eth century is my spiritual home. Preferably in the Far East." He had never lived there, he went on rather sadly, what with pressures of work and a demanding career, and had visited only on a package tour to Hong Kong. Besides, his wife preferred the Isle of Wight. "The mem-sahib would never go." He winked as he said, "And she held the purse strings, you know."

Marion didn't know. She hadn't the faintest idea what he was talking about but she loved his rich, fruity voice and his old-world courtesy. It was a long time since a man had opened a door for her and stood aside to let her pass through ahead of him. Edmund had done so but without Barry Fenix's grace. He took her upstairs, showed her the five bedrooms, and took her back down again to display the spacious dining room, kitchen, and breakfast room and his "snug," a kind of study with walls lined with group photographs of men in uniform and, facing the desk, a portrait of himself wearing a lot of what she thought were called "decorations." They returned to the "lounge," where Benares brass abounded, along with carved teak furniture, embroidered Kashmiri cushions and processions of ebony elephants. It made Marion wonder why Mr. Hussein didn't have this kind of stuff.

"It's lovely," she said. "You wouldn't think your house and next door were the same sort of—well, next door to each other." She had got muddled over that sentence and she amended it as best she could. "I mean, this is so unique."

"I like to think so," said Barry Fenix, pouring her another dry martini. "It's one o'clock," he said, glancing at his watch, and poor Marion, accustomed to such treatment, thought he was going to turn her out. She was getting reluctantly to her feet when he said, "Not going, I hope. I thought we could have a spot of tiffin if you can stand an old soldier's cooking."

The word was new to her. "Is tiffin something to eat?"

"It's lunch," said Barry.

By the time she left it was nearly five and if not drunk she was, in Barry's own words, "three sheets to the wind." The trouble with him was you needed a dictionary of Asian expressions to know what he was on about. But it was the only trouble. Marion thought he was very nice, a real gentleman, the likes of which you saw few these days. She had given him her mobile number on what she thought was a clever pretext.

"I'd appreciate it so much, Barry, if you'd give me a ring if Mrs. Litton seems a bit under the weather. If you could keep a bit of an eye on her. I know it's a lot to ask."

"I'll do that small thing, my dear."

Marion danced and ran speedily all the way to Lithos Road. Anyone watching would have thought she was doing high-impact aerobics. Her home appeared untouched, just as she had left it. No signs of, or scars made by, Fowler were to be seen. He wouldn't dare break another window, not after she'd told him the cost of having the last one mended. She drank some black coffee, cleaned her teeth, and set off for Pinner.

Avice, in her dressing gown, was lying on the sofa, the rabbits dimly visible in their hutch, munching away at a pile of dandelions.

"How have you been?" Marion asked tenderly.

"Not too good. Those Crosbies wore me out. In future they'll blame me for stopping them going to the flower show, you'll see. And I've been worrying about these two"—she waved a hand in the direction of the hutch—"when something happens to me. I mean it may happen any minute."

"But I'm going to take care of them," said Marion. "You know that. It's all arranged."

"That's true. I keep forgetting. I really think I could eat some supper now."

Chapter Sixteen

Whenever possible, Edmund and Heather had lunch together in the hospice canteen. The food was the same as the patients had and cooked by Heather and Michelle. Today was curried lamb with rice and dhal or spaghetti bolognese, and Edmund chose the curry because it was his favorite. "I'd have married you for your cooking even if I hadn't been madly in love with you," he said.

"Not 'madly,' Ed. There was never anything mad about us. We've always been rational and practical."

"Speak for yourself. I saw that girl this morning. I was on top of the bus going along

Ken High Street. It was just before eight and I saw her going into Kensington Gardens."

"What girl? What are you talking about?"

"That girl you're always phoning. Eva something. Eva Simber."

"I'm not always phoning her. I've phoned her three times. I suppose she goes running there now she's given up on St. James's Park. It's miles from where she lives."

"You know what these fitness fanatics are."

Heather went to the counter, fetched herself the fruit salad and Edmund the tartufo.

"Talking of fitness fanatics, it's fat-free," she said.

"What a liar you are, Heather Litton."

"Issy's coming over this evening. Remind me to get a bottle of wine."

"I won't remind you," said Edmund. "I'll get it. I'll get two."

Tartufo was also supper dessert in Avice's house, though she, to Marion's mystification, called the meal dinner and the second course "pudding." Marion hadn't made these but bought them ready prepared in plastic cups from a supermarket fridge. Carefully, she turned them out, each into an individual glass dish, and topped them with defrosted whipped cream, first dousing the one on the left (A comes before M in the alphabet) with morphine.

"It doesn't taste very nice," Avice said, leaving more than half of it.

"You must eat." What a waste, Marion was thinking, of what was probably a very expensive medicine, not to mention the work put in by all those poor poppy farmers in Afghanistan. "You have to get your strength back. Have just one more spoonful."

Avice wouldn't. Marion still hoped, though, and after Avice had gone to bed walked around the house looking at all the bits and pieces she would help herself to between Avice's death and the arrival on the scene of the doctor, undertakers, and Joyce and Duncan Crosbie. In the Chinese slippers similar to ballet shoes she was wearing, she skipped up the stairs and down again, marking a picture here, a glass bowl and a porcelain vase there, rather in the manner of a bailiff except that she stuck on no labels.

Avice slept very soundly that night. That meant little as she was a good sleeper. On her way to the shops, Marion reflected on her choice of tartufo. She should have got something sweeter and with less strong a flavor. A pear and almond tart might be a better idea. She bought one and a piece of fish called a tilapia which she had never previously heard of.

. . .

Taking a week of the holiday due to her, Ismay stayed at home. In the past she had gone on holiday three times with Andrew, once to Venice, once to San Sebastian, and once to Barcelona. His desertion had spoiled those cities for her. She could never go to them again, perhaps not even to Italy or Spain again. She wouldn't be able to bear seeing on her own palaces and paintings, seaside and panoramas, she had seen with him. Come to that, she wouldn't be able to see places she hadn't seen with him. The idea of traveling somewhere without him made her feel ill. Imagine the long solitary nights, the sight of other couples together, of lovers walking in the warm dusk, their arms around each other. It would kill her. So she stayed at home. She was unhappy at home too but not likely to burst into tears out in the street or lie down and beat her head on the ground as she would feel like doing in some beach resort.

Rather like a medieval lady who has led a racy life and been forced to give it all up and retire to a convent, she turned her attention to good works. She committed herself to sending twenty pounds a month to the Royal National Institute for the Blind, never passed a beggar without bestowing a coin, and offered frequent service to Pamela as a Beatrix-sitter. The day after she had been to Heather and Edmund's for supper, she went around to her mother's house at six, having told Pamela to stay out till eleven if she liked, or even midnight.

It was June, a month that had started off unseasonably cold but was now warm, sunny, and windless. Ismay sat by the living room window, opposite her somnolent mother, who chewed her gum as slowly as a cow chewing the cud. She watched the people going by and the cars passing, not many people and a lot of cars, and thought how everyone but her seemed to have someone. Everyone out there who went by was with someone else. Pamela, by now, would be with her Ivan. Heather had Edmund. Ismay thought bitterly that she wouldn't be surprised if she turned up here one evening and found an elderly man sitting with Beatrix and holding her hand. The previous evening, for the first time, she had seen her sister and her sister's husband in their own home and had tried—desperately hard—to be happy for them that they were obviously so happy. All she had been was envious. No, that wasn't quite true. She loved Heather. She wanted love and peace and contentment for Heather if all those things were possible, but she wanted them for herself first.

The fairly heavy drinking she had indulged in was past. Or past unless great temptation came in her way. Edmund kept refilling her glass. He and Heather drank very little, but it seemed to her that less than an hour had passed before he was opening a second bottle. The great thing was, perhaps the sad thing, that drinking made her feel better. Not good but better. When she had had two or three glasses of wine she could think how glad she was she had never said a word to Edmund about Guy's death or tried to warn him about Heather. It almost made her smile—and at the same time threatened to bring tears to her eyes—to see how obviously Heather and Edmund wanted to touch each other, to sit squeezed close together, but resisted out of kindness to her. Not to remind her—as if she needed reminding!

No one mentioned Andrew. Neither Heather nor Edmund asked her why she hadn't gone away, what future plans she had, or if she was going to try to find a flatmate. Edmund told her they were a little nearer to acquiring their flat. The people they called Mr. and Mrs. Finchley, two links down the chain, had signed the contract on the sale of their house. Heather told her they now hoped to move in in September, but they wouldn't have a holiday because they couldn't afford it.

"Not if we're going to have a honeymoon in Japan."

"Are you?"

"Somewhere over there," said Heather vaguely.

Ismay went home in a taxi because she couldn't bear the thought of the tube full of noisy drunk people and herself on her own among them. Letting herself into her flat wasn't so bad because, in the past, Andrew had seldom been there before she came in. She poured herself another glass of wine and thought about the question Heather and Edmund hadn't asked. A new flatmate was what she needed but dared not take on. Now Heather had paid up the last of her rent she was having to bear the whole of it on her own. At least I'm not spending money on a holiday, she told herself bitterly. And it's not really worth thinking about. I'm not going to look around for someone else. Because I can't have someone else here if Andrew comes back.

He may come back. People do. They split up and then they get together again. You see it all the time. He must think of me sometimes, she thought. He must remember what he loved about me, for he did love me. God knows, he said so often enough. It couldn't all go like that, in a flash, just because he's met this Eva Simber.

The tears were running down her face now but she went on thinking of it. Gulping a bit, taking a big swig of the wine, she imagined being here alone and the place looking beautiful, newly cleaned by someone, even by her, perhaps even newly decorated. She'd be wearing one of those diaphanous skimpy dresses he loved on her or perhaps only on Eva—don't think of that—and she'd be lying on the sofa reading a book and she'd hear his key in the lock. He still had a key, he must have kept it, and he'd take her in his arms and say leaving her was the biggest mistake of his life. . . .

Somewhere in all this Ismay was also thinking that Andrew was a hard-hearted cheat, a liar and deceiver. If he came back he would be good to her, a charming lover, attentive and possessive, but after a time he would go again. Some other pretty little fair-haired waif would be waiting for him. And once more he would tell her there was no one. When he finally admitted he was leaving, it would be her fault for doing this or that to drive him away, for being selfish, for putting others before him.

She knew all this, but her enduring love for him overcame it and thrust it down deep into her mind, while she still imagined him coming in and kissing her, telling her he'd made a mistake and she was his only love.

. . .

In Ivan's kitchen Pamela was preparing their evening meal. She had brought the ingredients with her, pasta and salmon and salad and a summer pudding, still in its bowl, she had made the night before. At home she hardly ever cooked anything. She and Beatrix lived on takeaway and ready meals. She asked herself why she hadn't brought something of that sort with her, as Ivan, who had been in the other room watching television, came out into the kitchen and eyed the pretty salad with disdain.

"I don't eat green things," he said.

"I hope you eat fish."

"Provided it's fried with chips. I'm a chips with everything man."

"I've noticed," said Pamela. "I thought tonight you'd like something different. If you don't want it we could go out to eat."

"Eating out is expensive. And don't say you'll pay because you know I won't allow that." He looked at the tagliolini, the pesto, the cream, and the salmon with the expression on his face of a man considering if food items were past their sell-by date. "I've got potatoes. Can't you make some chips and fry an egg or something?"

She was already learning that crossing him

led to an outburst of bad temper. To her surprise he peeled and cut up the potatoes himself. She fried his share of the salmon, and they finally sat down, not at the table, which looked as if it was never used, but side by side on the sofa in front of the television. There was no wine. Pamela didn't mind too much because she had secretly brought a flask of vodka with her, from which she had taken surreptitious sips while cooking.

It wouldn't do, she kept telling herself. There was no point in going on with it. Well, there was a point, just one, but she shied away from facing it. In spite of those preliminary words of his last time, that it was sex they had really come there for, "that side of things," as her mother used to put it, had been surprisingly good. Or was it just that so much time had passed since the last time? Years, she thought, three or four years. Ivan, who seemed to her grossly insensitive in some areas, stingy and mean-spirited, was tender and gentle and controlled in his lovemaking. She had half expected him to boast about it afterward, that seemed in character, but he hadn't. Nor had he said, "Was that all right for you?" He knew it had been.

What did it matter if he didn't take her out for meals, if he wanted to eat chips, if he moaned a bit about taxes being spent on the unemployed? He looked so good. It was nice to lie in his arms and know he really desired her. After all, she wasn't going to marry him. She wasn't even going to be his partner, for that surely meant living under the same roof.

They went to bed. And it was just as good as the first time. It was better. He remembered that she had said she should be home soon after eleven and at ten he said he would order a cab for her. They could go to the pub at the end of his street and ask the cab to call for her there. Pamela didn't much want a drink as she had almost emptied her flask, but she agreed so as not to antagonize him. Did that mean she was afraid of Ivan? Women are afraid of men, she said to herself. Men are afraid of women's minds and tongues, and women are afraid of men's violence. It seemed to her that she had hit on a great if unhelpful truth.

They walked down the street, Ivan with his arm around her. He asked if he could see her the next day, and Pamela had to say she couldn't, not the next day. She had to stay with her sister. She couldn't ask one of her nieces again so soon.

"Why not? She's their mother, isn't she?"

"They both go out to work, Ivan. And Heather's married. They do their bit, more than their bit actually, but they can't be there every evening."

"I'd have thought you could have left your sister on her own. She's not violent, is she? She won't break the place up?"

"I do leave her alone sometimes. When I can be sure she's taken her tranquilizer. But I can't always be sure."

Out there in the street, outside the pub, he flew into a rage, shouted at her, "You put your crazy sister before your partner? Is that it? You put your selfish nieces before your partner. Can't you understand how I feel about you? Does your sister feel about you like I do? Do those selfish girls?"

He took hold of her by the shoulders but not to hurt her. He held her like that for a moment or two while she trembled. Then he said in a quite different tone, a weary tone, "Oh, what's the use? I need a drink."

She refused a glass of wine, but he became angry again, so she agreed. It made her head swim. It made her afraid to talk in case her speech came out slurred. After about ten minutes, in which Ivan talked about teenage mothers living on benefit, the taxi came. It wasn't a black cab but a minicab. Pamela wasn't happy about it as she had heard too many stories about minicab drivers stealing from their fares or even raping them. Out on the pavement Ivan kissed her passionately in front of the driver and a group of young black men, who cheered and clapped their hands. She had taken it for granted that the cab would have been paid for, but it hadn't, and when they got to Clapham the driver demanded fourteen pounds.

The first ten minutes of the BBC's early evening news was all about the United Kingdom's bid to get the Olympic Games in London in 2012. Avice was indifferent to the outcome and Marion was bored. She was disappointed but not really surprised that Avice had woken up fit and well after the tartufo dessert. After all, she had eaten a very small amount of it. Tonight was to be the night, the pear and almond tart being the poison vehicle. Not that Marion referred to it like that even to herself. The word "painkiller" appealed to her far more, though Avice hadn't had a recurrence of that ache in her chest and left arm.

A horrible story came next about a lot of dogs and horses left to starve to death in a stable. Avice was upset and wanted to turn it off—thank God no rabbits were involved, Marion thought—but it was quickly over and the following bit wasn't nearly as disquieting. Avice was one of those people who prefer animals to human beings, so the news that the man a newspaper had called the West End Werewolf had attacked another girl disturbed her less.

"I don't know why they make such a fuss," she said. "What do they mean, 'attacked'? He only puts his hands around their necks and gives them a bit of a push. Turn it off, Marion, will you? I shan't sleep tonight when I think of those poor creatures."

Oh, yes, you will, thought Marion, imagining with a shudder the feel of strange hands touching her neck. She skipped out into the kitchen. Lately she'd been remembering the ballet lessons she'd had when she was a child and Fowler not much more than a baby, and she executed a couple of pas de deux and an entrechat on her way to picking the morphine bottle out of her bag. Two slices were cut from the pie and Marion poured morphine liberally over the plate on the left (M comes after A in the alphabet). For the first course she had grilled a piece of fillet steak for Avice and a piece for herself with new potatoes and peas. It was to be a particularly nice meal. After all, it was the last Avice would ever have.

Fifty thousand pounds was a serious sum of money. It should be spent wisely. With the knowledge she had gained from her employment as an estate agent's receptionist, Marion calculated that she would get two hundred and fifty thousand for her flat or maybe even three hundred. Add another fifty thousand to that and she could buy something quite charming. Not in a basement, for instance. She pirouetted about, humming a Coldplay song, and then she carried the tray into the living room where Avice waited.

It was rather unfortunate, she thought, that the principal story line in Avice's favorite hospital sitcom happened to deal with the subject of poisoning. And, to be precise, poisoning in a cake for the sake of monetary gain on the part of a nurse. It didn't, however, put Avice off starting on her slice of pear and almond tart. Starting but not continuing.

She brought a forkful to her mouth and it seemed to Marion that her hand hovered there for far longer than usual, trembled an inch or two from her lips while she made some comment on the homicidal nurse's appearance. Marion muttered something in reply. Sighing a little, Avice opened her mouth, received the forkful of tart—and if she didn't quite spit it out, she contorted her face into an expression of nausea, pushed the plate toward Marion, and said, "Taste that!"

"Mine is all right," Marion murmured.

"I can't help that. Taste mine."

One forkful wouldn't kill her, Marion thought. A crumb or two wouldn't kill her. Cautiously, gingerly, she tasted a small fragment from Avice's plate.

"It tastes as if it has been soaked in cough mixture," said Avice.

It had. Marion went out into the kitchen, poured the dregs from the bottle into a teaspoon, and drank it. Cough linctus, no doubt about it. Someone had emptied out the morphine and substituted Benylin.

Fowler, she thought, always Fowler.

Chapter Seventeen

It was so green. Like the country but not quite like. Eva had never been in Kensington Gardens before, or if she had it was because Daddy had brought her when she was little. They had lived quite near. She tried to remember where but even the name of the street eluded her. She didn't really know London, only lived in it. You had to. It was either London or a big house in Gloucestershire. Anywhere else was unthinkable.

She had driven up to Notting Hill and left the car that had been Daddy's birthday present on a meter in somewhere called Linden Gardens. It was funny a park being called Gardens and a street too. You didn't have to put money in the meter until eight-thirty, which was just as well as she'd brought none with her. This morning she was wearing one of her white T-shirts, the one with lace around the neckline, and mid-calf-length pink pants, and she kept stealing glances at her reflection in the windows of parked cars.

The unfamiliar green space was full of trees she didn't know the names of. Mummy said she didn't know the names of anything. It was a disgrace, seeing what her schooling had cost. Some of the trees looked like Christmas trees and some had their branches sweeping the ground but their leaves were too big to be weeping willows. Eva ran along an avenue of trees, passing other joggers and race walkers, and meeting men running in pairs. These gave her admiring glances. But most people she saw were walking dogs. Eva liked dogs. She especially liked True, a Labrador named after one of John Peel's hounds, and would have had him with her but Mummy said keeping a dog in London was cruel.

It was a fine sunny day, early enough for the trees to cast elongated shadows across the sleek turf. Eva turned right and took a ride that cut through these shadows, heading for a tall tower block on the edge of the park. She passed a statue of a man on a horse and a fountain, a little house with its own garden and a fence around it, and more trees and tall bushes with flowers on them. All the other runners were left behind. At one point she had seen a great glassy lake to her left, but that was far behind her now. Almost her last words to herself before she got lost were, "I mustn't get lost." Then she was.

Eva had no idea about noting landmarks when you were out in a strange place. A strange-shaped tree, for instance, an unusual building, a glimpse of something known through the branches. If there had been such signs to look out for on her return she hadn't noticed them. She could still see the tower block, which didn't seem to fit in with the rest of the scenery, and directly ahead of her a peculiar tall kind of spire, a bit like a church but huge, with steps around it and gold all over it and statues clustered on it. She seemed to remember seeing it once before when she'd been to visit her friend in Queen's Gate years ago while they were both still at school, but she didn't know what it was and something about it, its size, its strange colors, the gilding on it, unnerved her.

Veering sharply away from it, she crossed the turf between the tallest trees she had yet encountered and at a place where four paths met at a kind of crossroads, came upon a signpost with four arms. The trouble was that she didn't know where any of the places were that the arms pointed to. Kensington Palace, for instance, the Royal Albert Hall, Exhibition Road. Knightsbridge was familiar because of Harrods and Harvey Nicks but she didn't want to go there now.

The path she took led her past a big shallow pond that looked as if it ought to have boats on it and children playing but didn't. The early sun had gone in and a wind sprung up. Now to the left of her was something that looked like a formal garden, the kind of thing friends of Daddy's had where they lived near Cheltenham. The Campbell-Sedges, of course. It was at their place that she'd met Andrew last year. Apparently, they had known each other since they were kids, but she could never remember things like that. Maybe she'd marry Andrew if he asked her. She liked the idea of a baby. Everyone knew a baby was the best accessory you could have. Look at Britney and Kate Moss. If she had a baby, newspapers might treat her more seriously. Of course she'd have a cesarean so there wouldn't be any pain.

Beyond the garden and the big house she could see a towering church spire and what might be the back of a street. She had no idea where she was or where she was heading for.

For some reason she had left her bottle of water in the car and she was growing thirsty. That reminded her of where she had parked the car and when. She never wore a watch when she was running. What time had it been when she started? Hours and hours ago—well, an hour. Traffic wardens wouldn't be about yet, not before nine surely.

The path led her through trees that formed another avenue. Ahead of her a spaniel was running, just one solitary dog in the whole park, its owner, a young black man in vest and jeans, strolling behind it. Eva could hear footsteps but they weren't his. They were behind her.

It wasn't really like being in the country anymore, for the path was neat and weed-free, and the trees more like Kew Gardens than the Cotswolds. A person could go around and around this place and never find a way out or never find the way she came in. If she didn't find the way she came in how would she ever find her car? She had forgotten the name of the street where she put it, remembered only that it was somewhere in W11.

The man and the spaniel had disappeared, though she hadn't seen them go. They must have turned off at this little path on the right. The footsteps behind her were still pattering steadily along and somehow, without looking back, she knew that whoever it was had no dog with him. Or her. Dogs made you feel safe. If she had had True with her she wouldn't be in a state now, wondering if she'd ever get out, find the car, find her car key, which she'd meant to tie to her shoelace but hadn't.

The only way the man and the spaniel could have gone was to take this little path which turned off to the right. There seemed to be no other turning. Eva didn't ask herself why she felt unsafe or why an unknown man and his dog made her feel safer, but it was so, and she had begun to dislike those footsteps behind. At the entrance to the path, where a tall bush with dark leathery leaves stood on either side like guardians of the place, she stopped and looked back. There was no one. The path she had followed, wide, sandy, straight, stretched behind her between a wall of trees.

At this point or after this time, in St. James's Park, she would have drunk half the contents of her water bottle, but she had left it in the car. Her mouth was very dry and she was aware that it was dry because of anxiety as much as thirst. Fear dried your mouth, Daddy had once told her, though she couldn't remember why. She took the path the man and the dog had taken, that they **must** have taken, unless the earth had swallowed them up. Above her, between leafy branches, ran another narrow path, a lane of sky, gray, cloudy, but lit by a pale sun.

Stopping at that junction of ride with path had put an end to her running. She would walk the rest of it, walk now until she came to a street, a pavement, gates perhaps, until she saw a bus, heard a fire engine, a car horn. All she could hear now was those footsteps. Patter-patter. Then they stopped. Whoever it was must have left the path and taken to the turf, the grass that was always out there, beyond shrubs and trees and hedges.

The path was petering out and becoming the brown dusty floor of something like a wood, a thin sparse wood, and beyond it she saw what she'd almost lost hope of seeing. Be-tween the trunks of trees, a long way behind them, a red double-decker bus passed. There must be a road. It could even be the Bayswater Road. She remembered the name now and would have run toward it, but she could see that ahead of her was no way out of the park. She would have to return to that hated path and walk on to where she thought the gate must be. Still keeping her eyes on the spot where the bus had been, she took a step back-ward, then another. A second bus passed, going the other way. As she peered, trying to locate the gate, she heard the faintest sound, a whisper or rustle behind her, and slowly turning her head, felt a cold finger touch her neck.

Eva screamed. She felt her legs buckle and sink as the finger became a hand, became two hard strong hands, and closed together, digit tips meeting.

A traffic warden found her car at eight forty-one. Spotting it, doing the paperwork, and summoning the clampers would add another one to his tally and enable him to reach his target. As he filled in the forms and began attaching them to windscreen and driver's door, he felt, as well as satisfaction, relief that the driver hadn't come back to abuse him, assault him, or spit in his face.

Chapter Eighteen

"That poor girl," said Edmund, handing Heather the **Evening Standard.**

"I've seen it," Heather said. "I wonder if Ismay knows. She never reads a paper these days. Eva really was lovely, but not like a woman. Like a child of twelve."

"Andrew Campbell-Sedge fancies twelve-year-olds. Haven't you noticed?"

She could live for ten years, thought Marion. At least ten. There had been a man of a 109 having a birthday party on breakfast television that morning. Was she going to stay with Avice in spite of this setback? Perhaps for a while. She remembered the will. That still stood and would endure. But she wouldn't allow herself to be a slave, tied to the place. It was time for her poor old father to have a serious illness which required her frequent presence. She was thinking along these lines, wondering whether to give him cancer or coronary heart disease, when her mobile rang. The sound it made was the first few bars of "The Entry of the Queen of Sheba," and Avice asked her rather crossly if she'd left the wireless on.

Her caller was Barry Fenix. "Do you remember me?"

"Of course I do, Barry. Once seen, never forgotten is what I always say. How are you?"

"Fighting fit as ever. I was just wondering if you'd pop over and have a look at the old lady. I saw her in the garden this morning and I thought she was looking a bit frail."

"I could do," said Marion. "Just let me consult the diary." "The" diary sounded so much more official and important than "my." She did a little dance on the spot, the cough linctus temporarily forgotten, before picking up the phone again. "Say five o'clock this afternoon?"

"You couldn't manage anything before that?"

Not if she was wise. Not if she gave an hour to Irene, then went in next door at drinks time. If she hung about a bit, dinner was likely to be suggested. . . ."Five it must be, I'm afraid, Barry. I've a very full day."

It might, in any case, be wise to turn her attention back to Irene, never mind the insults. They were incidental to the job. Avice, after all, could change her will at any time. Will changing was almost an **occupation** with her. Irene disliked her daughter-in-law, was sure to fall out with her son. Marion told Avice that the call on her mobile was from a paramedic who had found her poor old father unconscious on the floor. She must go to him at once and couldn't say when she'd be back.

The tube journey from Pinner to Finchley Road was a long one and Marion never cared for the enforced sedentary position it demanded but she had bought the **Evening Standard** to help her pass the time. There she saw that a man was helping the police in their enquiries into the murder of a blond girl called Eva Simber. The West End Werewolf, possibly.

In the big Sainsbury's around the corner from Lithos Road she bought herself a packet of hair dye in a shade called Poinsettia and a pair of rubber gloves. Barry had remarked on her hair and its lovely natural shade. Last time the tinting and cutting had been done by Kevin at Have a Nice Hair Day, but she was far too short of funds to go in for that again. While she

waited for the evil-smelling pink paste to take
effect, her mind dwelled once again on Fowler
and the cough linctus and the awful waste of all
that morphine going down his throat. That label she'd put on the bottle would have had little effect on someone whose specialty was using
substances most people wouldn't dream of taking internally.

Marion put on a very tight green top, a
boho chic skirt, and the slippers that looked
like ballet shoes. It was youthful attire which
suited her girlish figure. No coat would be
needed this fine afternoon. Of course she
would be a little late, it was always best with
men, and she decided to walk, or rather to skip,
all the way to Chudleigh Hill through the
pretty backstreets, all their trees in full leaf and
some with reddening berries. Marion had never
been interviewed for a newspaper or magazine,
but if she had she would have said when asked
what her secret was, "I'm an optimist, you see.
I always look on the bright side." She imagined
how lovely her hair must look, ruby red and
gleaming in the sunshine. Anyone else would
have brooded on that morphine business, but
she wasn't one for rancor. You had to move on.
You had to think of yourself, a useful maxim.

"I've a confession to make," Barry said

when he answered the door to her. "There's nothing wrong with the old lady. I made it up."

"Mr. Fenix!"

"Barry," said Barry. "I wanted to see you again and I didn't feel quite up to saying that on the blower."

"Well, I don't know what to say. You are **awful.** I think I'll just pop next door all the same. Just for half an hour."

"Not a minute more, mind."

Nothing like this had happened to Marion for years. She wanted to dance and sing and shout, but she had to walk decorously up to Irene's front door, ring the bell, and put on a concerned face. Irene was in a fairly good mood. The Crosbies had asked her to go with them to Crete for a fortnight in September.

"Well, 'asked' isn't the word. Begged me is really what it was. I said I'd think about it. I don't really know if my back would stand it." Irene opened her workbox and took out a half-finished string of blue beads. What does she do with all that rubbish, Marion asked herself. "I've been suffering from a lot of flatulence lately. That wouldn't be very convenient in a hotel, would it?"

"Any sign of Edmund moving into his new flat yet?" asked Marion, stirring it.

"You don't suppose they ever tell me anything, do you?"

Three quarters of an hour later she was back
ringing Barry's doorbell. She rightly thought
that what he liked her for was her vivacity and
this evening she felt more vivacious than she
had for weeks. She smiled, she laughed at his
jokes, she admired all his possessions. Gin and
tonic helped. He said his favorite type of
woman was "your natural redhead." She was a
little vixen and he was ready to bet she had a
hot temper. At seven he suggested he take her
out to dinner in Hampstead. It was a good dinner and neither tartufo nor pear and almond
tart was on the menu.

He drove her home to Lithos Road. Marion
was praying all the way that Fowler wouldn't be
there, sitting on the doorstep waiting for her,
and her prayer was answered. Barry kissed her
wetly before opening the door for her to get out
of the car. She hadn't liked it but, waving gaily
to him, reminded herself that there was no gain
without pain.

Ismay found out from Pamela.

"It's just been on the news that they're questioning another man in the Eva Simber murder," she said.

Ismay held herself very still. It felt as if the color had gone from her face. "Who did you say?"

"You know, Eva Simber, the girl who was murdered in Kensington Gardens—oh, it must be at least a week by now. Don't you ever see a newspaper, Issy? Don't you watch television?"

"Not much if I can help it. You say Eva Simber was killed last week?"

"That's right. You didn't know her, did you? The name sounds familiar."

"I met her once," said Ismay distantly.

She got herself something to eat, found a half-full bottle of wine in the fridge, and went to sit with her mother. The shock of hearing of the death of an enemy can be as great as when the victim is your friend.

Beatrix said dreamily, "The earth shall be filled with the glory of God as the waters cover the sea."

"The waters **are** the sea, Mum."

Ismay wondered why she bothered, for Beatrix took no notice but, removing a lump of chewing gum from her mouth and squeezing it in her fingertips like plasticine, abandoned hymns for the Book of Revelation. "Blood came out of the winepress," she remarked in quite a cheerful tone, "even unto the horse bridles, by the space of a thousand and six hundred furlongs."

Eva Simber was dead. Ismay repeated these words over to herself. She later felt it was to her credit that instead of rejoicing, she thought, how terrible, how awful. A woman walking her dog had found the body. The paper said police had DNA from Eva's fingernails where she had scratched her attacker, but it would take some time to try to match it with any possible suspects. A second man was helping with inquiries. There was no mention of Andrew.

The police must also have been questioning him, Ismay thought. They'd be bound to talk to the boyfriend, and Andrew had been Eva's boyfriend. There was no good deceiving herself over that.

She picked up the phone and dialed Heather's mobile. She and Edmund were in a wine bar on their way home from work. "Did you know?"

"Of course we knew, Issy. I knew you wouldn't—well, not at first. You never read the papers or see the news."

"Why didn't you tell me?"

"I didn't want to upset you."

"**Upset** me?"

Heather said nothing.

"Why did you think you'd upset me? Didn't you think I'd be glad? Oh, I know I'm awful. I'm terrible being glad someone's dead. But didn't you know I'd be glad? Now she's gone Andrew will come back to me."

"I doubt it," said Edmund after she had rung off.

They finished their drinks and went out. Under a shady overhanging tree Heather lifted up her face and smiled at him. He felt overwhelmed with love for her, a feeling so strong that it made him breathless. She came into his arms with a sigh of pleasure and he kissed her as passionately as if they were in their own home, away from all eyes. "I love you so much."

"Not more than I love you," said Heather.

The street in Battersea where Ivan lived was some way from Kensington Gardens, but still Pamela felt nervous walking to his house from a distant bus stop. Women are always on edge after the murder of a woman in the city where they live, even if it didn't take place on the doorstep.

Ivan had suggested the last time they met that she hire a permanent live-in carer for her sister so they "could get a real relationship go-ing." She had asked him what he meant and he said, "Well, move in together."

"I'm not ready for that yet, Ivan."

"Why aren't you?" he said. "At our age we can't afford to hang about. We know how we feel about each other."

Did they? Did **she?** "I couldn't leave Beatrix with a carer. For one thing, I couldn't afford it."

"Wouldn't those selfish nieces of yours help with that? I'd be prepared to help."

She was amazed. After the business with the minicab and his unwillingness to eat out, she had put him down as cheap. His cheapness had been the main thing she saw as a stumbling block to a permanent relationship. Yet here he was offering to pay toward the care of her sister.

"It's good of you to think of it." As she said it she seemed to see Beatrix's poor blank face, the pale eyes that recognized no one for more than a few minutes at a time, and to hear that voice uttering the ancient pronouncements of a fanatic. "It's very good of you," she said, and then, weakly, "I'll think about it."

She had thought about it. She had thought of little else. He must love her if he, a man care-ful with money, could make an offer like that. Why did it matter so much to her that while he'd take her to pubs, he was so reluctant to go to any restaurant superior to a workman's café? For years she had eaten every meal at home with Beatrix. Restaurants were hardly essential in her life. It was true that his constant harping on what he called "gravy train passengers," those whose sole income was derived from state-funded benefits, grated on her. But it was a small matter to set against his attractions, his fondness and need for her, and his recent generous offer. Why then was she going to say no?

"I want to go on seeing you, Ivan," she said when she was inside his flat and, to her surprise, he had produced a bottle of wine and a packet of crisps that looked as if it had been around for a long while. "It's just that I think it's early days to move in together. Organizing something satisfactory for my sister would take time. It might not even be possible."

He raised his glass, said, "Cheers," then, "You know, I'm not altogether sure I believe in this sister of yours. I wonder if you haven't invented her."

"Oh, Ivan, why would I?"

"How about to create a distance between us? To make it impossible for us to be really close?"

"Of course I haven't invented her."

"I'm not convinced. I think I'll come and see her. See if she really exists. I could take you home tonight, couldn't I? As a matter of fact, I **ought** to take you home. It's a bit remiss of me not to."

She had resolved not to bring the food this evening. It was a habit she shouldn't get into. He surprised her again by producing two fillet steaks, frozen peas and carrots, and two panna cottas from a supermarket.

"Not fish and chips, then?" She smiled as she said it but he didn't return her smile.

The idea of his taking her home was very unwelcome. Meeting Beatrix didn't matter. She would stare at him or not stare at him, closing her eyes. But Ismay would be there. Pamela had never before shied away from introducing any friend to her nieces, but now the fear of what he might say to Ismay, what effect his manner and way of speaking might have on Ismay, made her wince. Heather would be even worse. She was less tolerant. When she realized she expected those close to her to **tolerate** Ivan, Pamela felt very miserable.

She cooked the food and they ate it. Ivan talked about his job and the various disagreements, not to say vendettas, he had with colleagues. People were envious of him and therefore had it in for him. Pamela had always believed that when a man claims to have many enemies the fault must to some extent lie with him, but she couldn't let herself adhere to that when it was Ivan. If she was going to think like that she might as well go home now and never come back.

They went to bed. Eating supper, going to bed, had become routine. She thought it very early in their relationship to get into a routine, but she could tell he was a man who liked an orderly life, geared to the clock, and she couldn't really fault that. The pleasures of love-making were overshadowed for her by the knowledge that he was coming home with her, that Ismay would meet him, and she shouldn't be thinking like this.

It didn't happen. He broke with his timetable and fell asleep. She got up, wrote him a note that said, **I'll phone. See you soon. Love, Pam,** and went out into the street to begin the frightening walk to the bus stop. A few people about would have made it less sinister than this emptiness. There were always cars. At night, she thought, it was easy to have the illusion that the cars, the streams of them, were driverless automatons, moving of their own volition. One single person appearing ahead of her, walking toward her, or behind and following her, would be the terrifying thing, just one. This wasn't the West End, of course, it was too far south, but now she remembered that one of the Werewolf's victims had been walking on Wimbledon Common when she had felt his hands on her throat.

Surely Ivan shouldn't have condemned her to this? She remembered that it was she who had left him. He had been asleep. He hadn't sent her out into the night alone. And hadn't she spent the whole evening hoping he wouldn't come with her?

The bus came and she got on to it.

More prudently than her aunt, Ismay hailed a taxi the short distance to home. It was twenty past eleven. She was wondering if Andrew still lived in Fulham or if he had moved in with Eva Simber. Suppose she were to phone him on his old number? Or on his mobile? She could phone like an old friend, just say she was sorry about Eva. No, she couldn't. Her voice wasn't capable of that.

For the first time for a long while she went to bed without having a preliminary drink. She slept more soundly than she had for weeks.

Chapter Nineteen

It occurred to Edmund that the police might come to see his wife. After all, even though she wasn't a friend of Eva Simber's, she had set out to meet and talk to her in St. James's Park, and had made at least three phone calls to her. A woman phoning another woman asking her to give up her boyfriend for the sake of her sister was hardly a normal way of making contact with someone. He said so to Heather.

"Do you think so?" Heather said.

"They may want to ask you if Eva ever mentioned to you a man who'd threatened her or stalked her. Something like that. They'll ask everyone who knew her that sort of thing."

"I didn't really know her."

"I'm just warning you, darling, so you won't be alarmed if the police come."

"I don't think I'm the alarmed sort," said Heather.

Ismay phoned later in the day to ask Heather if she thought Andrew should somehow be told she was waiting for him, had never given up on him.

"No, I don't. That would do more harm than good. You'll just have to be patient."

"So you do think he'll come back to me?"

"Just be patient, Issy. Wait for him to come back or not come back. You haven't much choice, have you?"

The police never came.

Working the area of the West End he called his "manor," Fowler left Oxford Street behind him—useless for really good stuff—and made his way down South Molton Street. He was having a bad morning and suspected that the bins had been recently emptied by Westminster City Council. It was the wrong time of day for them but that meant little. They could have changed their time or taken on temporary staff ignorant of the rules. He crossed Bond Street and Regent Street, and made a foray into Soho, far from his usual haunts. A bin in Old Compton Street, surrounded by a detritus of chicken bones and call girl cards, yielded a broken flowerpot and a cigarette packet labeled SMOKING KILLS and containing eight dog ends.

Fowler trailed southward. Months, even years, had passed since he had investigated the bins of Leicester Square, but there was a chance one of those binge drinkers who infested the place by night might have left behind a half-empty lager can or even dregs in a wine bottle. Glad that he had made it last, he had a little morphine left in the cologne bottle and, on the steps of St. Martin in the Fields, he sat down and sipped it. Not for the first time he wondered why Marion had kept morphine sulfate. Not for his use, certainly. She might be a secret addict. If that were so, there would be more in the flat, concealed in hiding places he knew nothing of.

It wasn't long before the visions started. Troops of white-robed pilgrims walking along the kind of paved streets Fowler's imagination placed in Babylon or Nineveh, headed for a vast stone palace from some obscure period of prehistory. Skull-faced figures sat about on broken rocks and read from parchment scrolls. He was unaware of falling asleep but very aware of a foot prodding his ribs and moving him on. Only half awake, he muttered to himself,

"Buck up, Fowler, wakey-wakey," drifted up St. Martin's Lane, wove across the street between cars with unsympathetic drivers, was nearly run over in Little Newport Street, where Marion had once told him their grandfather had been born, and finally came to rest, leaning against the wall of one of the great cinemas of Leicester Square.

His hallucinations had subsided into a vague grayish fog, populated by moving shapes, so that London looked as it must have done in the days of pea-soupers. It was inadequate to obscure the waste bin that stood two yards from him, a bin full almost to overflowing. Fowler was usually methodical about his emptying procedure, but this time he picked out object after object, plastic and paper, bottle and packet, much of it coated in grease or tomato ketchup, and strewed them across the pavement. Halfway down was an unexpected find, a large stone-colored handbag. Fowler pulled it out and wiped off its thick dappled surface traces of what seemed an effusion from the leather itself but which smelled like salad cream. He allowed himself briefly to hope that whoever had discarded it had forgotten to empty it of cash, cards, and saleable items, but he was a realist and he quickly undid the zip.

A label inside said MARC JACOBS. Maybe that was the owner who had thrown it away. No cash, no credit cards, not much at all. The fog was beginning to clear. Fowler sat down on the pavement with his feet in the street and examined the bag's contents. A woman passerby stopped beside him and began lecturing him on dropping litter.

"All of us are standing in the gutter," Fowler remarked to her, "but some of us are looking at the stars."

Although Ismay knew Eva Simber was dead, it took her a while to absorb it into her mind as a fact. It was a long time since she had read a newspaper, but now she read two every day, a morning paper and an evening, not so much to discover the latest police moves as to see yet another photograph of Eva. It was as if these pictures and the sensational captions underneath them made her death real. This was the work surely of one of those strange half-crazy men whose description and faces seldom appeared in the newspapers until they came up for trial, itinerant men who had no occupation, no permanent relationships, were probably illiterate, had been in and out of prison. The West End

Werewolf who had put his hands around women's throats and run off laughing had now killed.

Of course she thought of Andrew. How was he? What did he feel? Nothing much, she hoped. Conventional feelings of pity only, pity and a certain amount of horror, but no grief. Later she began asking herself what he would do now. She meant, will he come back to me, but it was a while longer before she let herself answer with a strong affirmative.

Gradually, she began to hope he would return. If only for her shoulder to cry on. She told herself she was a fool to believe simultaneously that he would care very little about Eva's dying and that his grief would be such as to need comfort. Both could hardly be true. Very soon she found herself back in the situation she had been in when he left her, believing it was Andrew every time the phone rang. She had a new mobile number now, replacing that of the one which had been stolen. Suppose he was trying to call her on her mobile and couldn't get through. Suppose he was trying to text her. He might be trying now, at this moment.

The temptation was to drop everything else and concentrate on her new relationship.

Plainly, Barry was falling in love with her and his love must be encouraged in subtle ways. It wasn't in Marion's nature to confess, even to herself in the long watches of the night, that she might be a less than attractive woman, that she was aging, that the prospects of romantic happiness for her were receding daily. In her own expressed estimation she was exceptionally good-looking, clever, hardworking, accomplished at everything she turned her hand to, and possessed of a charming personality. Sometimes, complacently, she told herself she suffered from high self-esteem. Still, she recognized that a prize like Barry Fenix had to be worked for, studied for. Irene Litton might hardly seem to be in the running, but that was a shallow person's assessment. Years older than herself, fat—well, fattish—ridiculous with her beads and her imaginary illnesses, she was nevertheless well-off, the owner of a fine house and **on the spot.**

But she mustn't neglect her other commitments. In spite of having been let down (as Marion saw it) over that business with the morphine that never was, she was still in Avice's employment. More to the point, she was still in Avice's will. Unlikely as it now was that Avice would die of poisoning, die she would. Eventually. She was eighty-four. Marion would go

back to Pinner that night, make sloppy over-
tures to those rabbits, make Avice's supper and
do her shopping tomorrow. Then there was
Fowler. Unusually for her, she had let him in
when he rang her front-door bell. She needed
someone to talk to, boast to, really. She might
even let him stay the night.

Where anyone else would have remarked to
her brother "I've got a boyfriend" or, even,
cryptically, "I'm seeing someone," Marion said
to Fowler, "I'm thinking of getting engaged." In
a way, it was true. She was thinking of it all
the time.

"It's not the thing to say congratulations to
the lady," said Fowler. "You have to wish her
well." He came over and kissed her, a wet,
bristly kiss that was just tolerable. The smell of
him, compounded of sweat, cannabis, and
cheeseburger, was not. "I haven't done that
since we were children. I often kissed you then.
I expect you've forgotten."

"You were more fragrant then."

Fowler ignored this. "When is the happy
day?"

Marion saw that she had gone too far. "I
didn't say I was engaged. I said I'm thinking of
it. He is considerably older than I am. Inciden-
tally, he's an expert on Oriental matters."

"Has he got any money?"

"Lots and lots," said Marion, "and a very nice big house in Hampstead. Well, West Hampstead."

"Pity. Still, beggars can't be choosers."

"Speak for yourself. And talking of beggars, how dare you break in here and steal my morphine?"

"It was the bottle. It looked like cough mixture and that reminded me I'd got some cough linctus out of a bin and then—well, the rest is history."

They argued for a while, not acrimoniously. Fowler put an end to it by asking for a drink. Anything alcoholic. He wasn't fussy. If he wanted a drink he'd have to have a shower first, Marion said. She'd wait here till he had cleaned himself up and then she'd give him a small whisky but not the single malt she had appropriated from Avice's stock. He could stay the night if he liked. Just one night, mind.

She heard the shower running and top-volume sounds from her CD and disc player he'd taken into the bathroom with him. She tapped on the door to tell him the neighbors would complain. He came out wearing her bathrobe. "What'll you do with this flat when you're married to your old bloke?"

"He's not old. He's sixty-two." Keep it for a bolt-hole, she didn't say aloud, while she was waiting for the divorce (and the alimony) to be settled. In case he turns out to be a pervert or snores or something.

"I could take care of it for you." Clean, sweet-smelling Fowler gave her one of his winning little-boy looks.

Marion held out her hand. "I'll have my player, thanks very much. I hope you haven't let steam get in it."

"If you have a baby, could I borrow it? Just for the morning?"

Marion screamed.

She would have preferred to tell him somewhere other than on his home ground. A restaurant or even a pub would have been better. When she had suggested it, he had said he supposed this was because it was such a long way to come. He'd come to her, only her crazy sister would be there and he had a feeling she didn't want them to meet.

Pamela hadn't liked hearing Beatrix called crazy, though she was. She hadn't pursued the subject either. What was the point? What was the point in trying to reconcile the things he said with her own standards? She wouldn't need to, for this was the last meeting they would have. It was September now and she'd been seeing him since the beginning of July. But enough was enough. She had tried to make it work but had failed. Maybe he had tried too—in his way. She would tell him at once, not put it off. His lovemaking she'd miss, though not his going to sleep afterward and his leaving her to get to the bus stop in the dark and being rude about her family. And a host of other things.

Since she had come to this decision she had worked out carefully what she would say to him. She had done her best to imagine his replies. He would argue, of course. He'd probably accuse her of ingratitude. And he'd constantly say he didn't understand. What had he done? What had he omitted to do? He'd probably ask if there was someone else. People did ask that in this sort of situation. But ultimately he would have to accept. Pamela just hoped the ultimate, the inevitable, wouldn't be too far off. You can always just leave, she told herself. All you have to do is say good-bye and go.

It was ever the way. Things never work out how you've planned them. People are different in reality from the way you've seen them while making scenarios in your mind. For one thing, they're less consistent. They surprise you all the time. He had laid the table, made a salad, ordered Indian takeaway, opened a bottle of red wine. "You see, I'm learning," he said.

She nodded, took the glass of wine he gave her. How much easier it would be to sit down at the table with him, make conversation, listen to yet another story about some family he'd heard of, living on the benefit and buying a car and going on holiday to Lanzarote. She nearly yielded to temptation. She drank some wine, set the glass down, said, "It isn't working, is it, Ivan?"

He was putting dressing he'd evidently made himself on the salad and he didn't look up to answer her. "What isn't working?"

"Us," she said. "Our relationship. It doesn't work, it won't. We're too different. We've nothing in common. We don't see things in the same way. Is there any point in going on with it?"

He sat down opposite her. "Of course we've things in common. We both work with figures, don't we? We're the same sort of age. I don't know what you mean, 'We don't see things in the same way.' I'm a man and you're a woman. We're bound to be different. The bed part's all right, isn't it? I don't notice you complaining about that."

"I'm not complaining, Ivan. I'm not complaining about anything. I'm simply telling you I don't think this thing, relationship, affair, whatever it is, will ever work for us. Don't you feel that yourself?"

"I'll tell you what I feel," he said. "I feel you're doing this for a bit of excitement. Liven things up. It's too dull for you. It's too static. Sitting down at a table with me, eating, having a drink, having a conversation, all that's too boring for you. Time we had a row, that's what you're thinking, aren't you? Or d'you want the bedroom first and the food later, is that it?" He was standing over her now. "You can have it, only why go to the bedroom? What's wrong with the sofa? What's wrong with the floor?"

He was a big man. She felt she'd never fully realized that before. A big man with big hands and strong muscles. He took hold of her by the shoulders and pulled her to her feet. His face was close to hers now, their bodies pressed together. He made an iron hoop of his arms, locking his hands behind her back and tightening them. She struggled and he dug his fingers into her flesh.

"Ivan, let me go," she said. "You haven't understood me. I shouldn't have expected you to understand."

"I understand all right."

He picked her up. She might have been a child, he lifted her so easily. Only a monster would have flung a child down as hard as he flung her. She banged her head on the sofa arm and bounced up and down, the springs jangling. On the third coming down he grabbed her shoulders and pressed her into the cushions. She knew then. She knew what he meant to do. Lying on her, smothering her with his beard and his hot breath, he tugged at her underclothes, tearing silk and when he met resistance, pinned her down with his left hand, groped with his right.

"No, Ivan." It came out as a strangled groan. "No, Ivan, don't. Stop, please, stop."

"Please don't stop," he shouted at her. "I won't, I won't, don't you worry."

So this is what rape is, she thought. I will give in now. I will relax and let him go on so that he doesn't injure me. I won't struggle. Afterward he'll say I agreed, but it doesn't matter. How can sex you want be so different from sex you don't want, yet with the same person? It hurts a bit but not much. It's not that it hurts but that it's such a violation. As if one were a house, used to being cherished and cared for, made as beautiful as can be, and then a burglar breaks in and plunders, destroys everything and shits on the carpet. A hysterical laugh bubbled from her mouth. She couldn't stop and it maddened him. The things that happened maybe would never have happened if she hadn't laughed.

He tugged out of her and, pulling himself to his feet, struck her hard across the mouth. "Shut up, shut up. Stop that laughing. I'll stop you if I have to kill you."

He dragged her out of the room, across the hall floor to the front door. Her hurt head hurt more as it thudded against the floorboards. He's going to put me out of that door and let me go, she thought. Her jaw throbbed where he had hit her. I wonder if I can open my mouth, if I can speak. My bag is inside there, I've no money to get home with. A sudden shaft of pain stopped thought and made her whimper. He had to let her go to open the door. She got to her knees, then, holding her face, tried to stand but fell. He pulled her upright, pushed her out of the door. She swayed but kept on her feet until his hand, pushed hard into the small of her back, knocked her over to stumble and fall. It would have been better to have stayed like that, on all fours, and crawling weakly across the floor. But she struggled to get to her feet, to cling to the banister rail and scramble down the stairs. She felt his foot in the small of her back and she screamed. The scream was loud but not loud enough to fetch someone from the floor below. Pamela teetered on the edge of the staircase, lost her balance, and fell.

She failed to grab the rail in time and she fell down, down, down the dark well, bouncing on the treads, plunging to the bottom.

It happened very fast. The awful helplessness she felt, her inability to hang on to carpet or banister, was driven away by the pain, the stab of pain renewed on every tread of the stairs. Not an ache but a fiery burning that made her scream aloud when she hit the hall floor, her leg twisted and caught under her.

The Indian takeaway man ringing the doorbell brought a new pain, the shrillness assaulting her ears, but it galvanized her into desperate sound and she shouted to him, "Help me, help me. Call an ambulance. Please help me."

Upstairs Ivan went into his flat and closed the door.

Chapter Twenty

The contents of that bag, and perhaps the bag itself, would make a nice engagement present for Marion. As soon as she was out of sight, passing through the ticket barrier at Finchley Road tube station, he had nipped back into the flat and taken the bag out of his backpack. There wasn't much in it. Once he had made sure of no money or means of getting money and no mobile to sell, he had rather lost interest. That was before he knew of Marion's matrimonial plans. Until he had taken that shower he hadn't really known that she possessed a tape and CD player. This chap of hers liked Eastern stuff so he might appreciate the tape of Indian music called **Rainy Season Ragas,** which had been inside the inner pocket of the bag, along with the quite expensive-looking ballpoint pen and the stick of concealer, whatever that might be. Neither he nor she would have any use for the photograph of a dark man hugging a fair-haired girl, and this he had thrown away.

Fowler wrapped his gifts in a picture of tigers in a rain forest, which was a page of the **Sunday Times** magazine, wrote **With love from Fowler** on the back of a heating engineer's calling card, and helped himself generously to the single malt Marion hadn't seen fit to give him. Settling down with his drink, he flicked through his sister's address book. What a lot of wealthy friends she had! A Mr. Hussein in Perrin's Grove, Hampstead; a Mrs. Litton in Chudleigh Hill a mile or two south of that; a Mr. and Mrs. Crosbie in Ealing. Surely there must be something there for him.

"I haven't told the police," Pamela said. "I told the ambulance people I fell downstairs. They brought me here and I told everyone I'd been in a friend's flat and I missed my footing at the top of the stairs. I think they wanted to know where the friend was in all this, but I just didn't say any more."

"But why?" Ismay looked at her in bewilderment. "You've got a broken jaw, a compound fracture of your left leg, and three broken ribs, and you won't say he did it? He ought to go to prison. I don't understand you."

"I don't suppose you do. He raped me, too. I didn't tell you that. How could I tell them? A woman of my age meets a man through a crazy thing called romance walking. She can't wait to get into bed with him and then she's got the face to say he's raped her. You think I could go into court and say all that? I could be cross-examined and asked about my sex life?"

"When you put it like that, yes—well, I do sort of see. But I can't bear to think of him getting away with it."

With difficulty, Pamela turned away her face. It was still swollen and purplish-blue with bruising. "How's Bea? How are you managing without me?"

Ismay shook her head. "All right, change the subject. Heather said she's told you we're fine. After all, I do live in the house. Sharon next door's been coming in while I'm at work. Heather and Ed take it in turns to stay overnight. And now they've said they'll give up that flat of theirs—they've only taken it for two months—and move in with Mum. I think that's marvelous of them. And you mustn't worry about anything."

The orthopedic ward was full. On one side of Pamela was a very old woman who had had a hip replacement and on the other someone nearer her own age who was the victim of a hit-and-run driver. The television was on all day.

"I don't want to watch it, but there's nothing else to do. Isn't it odd the way when someone gets murdered like that girl Eva Something it's all over the TV for days and in all the papers with a photo of the victim every day, and then it suddenly stops? If they don't find someone for it, it sort of fades away and you never hear any more. Then, one day years later, someone refers to it as an unsolved crime."

"I thought they'd arrested that man they call the West End Werewolf," said Ismay.

"They let him go. He wasn't the right one. I mean, he wasn't the Werewolf and he wasn't the killer either. Just ask me. I see every news and every police program. This is my supper coming. No, don't go. I shan't eat much. It's just as awful as they say. Have you noticed in those hospital sitcoms on telly you never actually see any of the patients eating?"

A tray was set down in front of Pamela on a folding table. On it was a small salad of bruised avocado, withered lettuce, and a piece of raw carrot with a small round pie and boiled potatoes to follow. Pamela asked Ismay to pour her some water from the jug and pass the glass.

"When Edmund came in he told me he'd been afraid the police might want to talk to Heather because apparently she knew this Eva. You know how they want to talk to the victim's friends. Not that Heather was a friend, but she did know her."

"Heather knew Eva Simber? I don't believe it."

"That's what he said." Pamela hesitated. "I suppose you know—I'm sorry, Issy, but I'm sure you do know—Eva was seeing Andrew? I didn't know, but he was on telly."

"Andrew was on television?" Saying the name brought the blood to her face.

"Only for a minute or two. He was with her parents, appealing for the person who killed her to come forward."

"I didn't know." All Ismay could think of was, if she had been murdered would he have gone on the television to appeal to her killer?

"Edmund didn't say it had anything to do with that, but I'm sure it must have," Pamela said. "I mean, Andrew having been your boyfriend. I wondered if she'd—well, told Eva about you and how Andrew had treated you. It's a possibility, isn't it?"

Ismay sat very still. She had been looking at Pamela, but now she turned her eyes away and down into her lap. "What, asked her to give him up, d'you mean?"

"I don't know, Issy. It did cross my mind. It would sort of be like Heather."

Ismay had been going to resume her urging of Pamela to go to the police and tell them what Ivan had done, but now she had lost heart. She kissed Pamela and told her she would come again in a day or two.

"Maybe I shouldn't have told you," Pamela said. "I could be wrong, anyway. I do wonder sometimes if you know how much Heather cares for you."

It hadn't escaped Marion's notice that whereas, once upon a time, fifty or so years ago, tradition had it that if you slept with a man he wouldn't want to marry you, the reverse was now true: He wouldn't marry you **unless** you'd slept with him. Barry Fenix, however, was getting on a bit. Marion didn't know how much he was getting on. In telling Fowler he was sixty-two she had merely uttered the first likely number that came into her head. He might be older, though hardly younger.

Did that mean he clung to the prejudice

and bigotry of half a century ago or had he moved with the times? She would have to find out first. Perhaps she could steer the conversation around to modern morals. The trouble with that was that there never was much conversation, only Barry talking about India and she saying how wonderful he was and what a lot he knew.

Marion's sexual experience was very limited. Over the decades there had been two affairs, entered into more for status and kudos than love, and neither had lasted more than a few months. The lovers said she was frigid, and though she hotly denied the charge, attributing the coldness of her response to their clumsiness and lack of attraction, privately she told herself it was true and she was glad of it. A lot of trouble was saved. It was a dirty, untidy business at best. As far as she was concerned, sex was to be used for manipulation and possibly blackmail, though it would hardly come to that with Barry. If she did sleep with him, would he know she wasn't a virgin? Would he expect her to be? Would he care? Again, that depended on what he thought of contemporary morals.

She was going out with him again that evening. She kept a tally and this was the seventh time, which possibly meant something. First to call in at Avice's and explain why she had scarcely been near Pinner for the past week. Sitting in the tube train, she thought about the ultimate reason she must give for failing to turn up six days ago. Her poor old father had passed on. But this was so rash and final. If she told Avice that, she would have nothing left to supply her with an excuse for future absences. Surely she must save up Dad's death for when Barry's engagement ring was on her finger or even when her wedding had been fixed.

She found Avice, with Figaro at her feet, sitting in front of the coffee table on which lay a fresh batch of paperback novels. She looked cross. Marion reminded herself that Avice was a frequent will changer and the arrangement she had come to with Mr. Karkashvili might be altered at any time. Also, she needed the miserable wage Avice paid her.

"I'm so sorry, Avice," she said. "My poor dad's gone into a coma. I've been sitting at his bedside hoping against hope he'd come to and recognize me. I've been holding his hand. It's seventy-two hours since I've had my clothes off."

"Well, of course I'm sorry about your father," Avice said, stroking Figaro's head, "but there is such a thing as a telephone."

"They don't allow mobiles in the ward where he is. Now I'm here, let me see what I can do. If you'll just jot down a few things I'll run up to the shops, shall I?"

In the pet shop in Pinner Village she bought a packet of rabbit treats. Gifts for her pets were a surer way to Avice's heart than giving her chocolates. She changed the peat which covered the concrete flooring in the hutch bedding and made Avice's lunch. She would return tomorrow, she said, but now she must go back to her comatose father.

On superficial examination, Fowler appeared not to have been back to Lithos Road, though Marion was sure he once again had a key to the flat. She had been too preoccupied to ask him. Besides, he would have denied having it or else asked her in that lugubrious way of his if she'd prefer him to break in. She couldn't afford getting someone in to mend more broken windows. But the big dread of her life remained: Suppose she brought Barry back here and they found Fowler in the flat. However besotted with her Barry might be, she was sure he'd retreat at the sight and smell of her brother.

He liked to watch for her from his window and see her hopping and skipping (his words) down Chudleigh Hill. Marion always did it as fast as she could and popped in through Barry's side gate in the hopes Irene wouldn't see her. Of course, once she had Barry's ring on her finger,

Irene could see her all the time, the oftener the better, but spotting her now might lead to attempts to put a spoke in her wheel.

Barry was cooking for her at home that evening. She sat on the sofa beside him, her shoes off, her feet tucked under her and her head on his shoulder while he played strange music he told her was made by sitars, tablas, and tambouras.

"It's what they play in India, little one," he whispered into her crimson hair. "Didn't know that, did you?"

"I'm very ignorant, Barry," she said humbly, "but I'm learning. You're such a good teacher."

The curry was particularly spicy and Marion made the mistake of helping herself to lime pickle. Even a tiny spot of that on her tongue burnt like fire. It was the hottest thing she had ever tasted. She choked and cursed under her breath and had to be plied with iced water, tears streaming down her face. But she hardly need have worried. Barry loved ministering to her, dried her tears, said she was a poor little kitten, and gave her a kiss on her forehead.

After dinner there was more tabla music and cuddles on the sofa. Barry told her how he had seen the Indian rope trick done by a man in Brick Lane while he was pursuing his inquiries there (whatever that meant) and Marion told him about her friend Mr. Hussein who came from Ladakh and his son Zafar who had, she said, been madly in love with her. "And did you reciprocate?" Barry asked this in quite a different tone from his usual facetious banter.

"Pardon?" said Marion.

"Did you respond to his—er, ardor?"

"Oh, no, Barry. Of course not! What an idea! I've never been like that, never."

"Not that sort of girl, eh? That's what I like to hear."

The altar before bed then, thought Marion, relieved. As she had half believed, he was living in the middle of the previous century. Perhaps even before Indian independence came about, some time, she vaguely believed, in the nineteen forties. She must remember to ask him for the precise date. He'd like that.

He drove her home, attempting quite a passionate kiss before she got out of the car. But Marion, remembering her icy chastity, pushed him gently away and flitted up the path to her front door, waving as she went.

Ismay came away from the hospital angry with Heather, determined to go straight to Victoria and have it out with her, but Pamela's final words came back to her. "I do wonder sometimes if you know how much Heather cares for you." Of course she knew. Hadn't Heather killed Guy to save her? Heather would do anything for her. The question seemed to come out of the air and present itself to her: Is it possible she has done something else for you, something enormous and terrible? Is it possible she has killed Eva?

Ismay was on a bus going to Victoria. She was upstairs in the front seat. The question was such a shock that although the bus was coming up to where she wanted to get off, she sat quite still without moving and let it rumble past the stop. Could this be what she had feared for twelve years? That Heather, who had done it once, would do it again? The situation wasn't quite a parallel with the drowning of Guy but was close enough. Eva hadn't set out to injure her, but without Eva, Andrew wouldn't have left her. Removing Eva wasn't a guarantee that Andrew would return to her but it was the only step anyone could take to make it a possibility.

I can't have it out with her now, thought Ismay as she got off the bus. I can't mention it to her. Is it possible she could have done it? Would she have known Eva went running in Kensington Gardens? Come to that, how well had she known Eva? So much of this was new that Ismay felt her head reeling. That girl with her skimpy transparent clothes, her socialite's lifestyle, her country family—much of this had appeared in the newspapers—and her lack of a job or an aim in life, was so nearly the antithesis of Heather that it was hard to believe they could even have spoken to each other. Ismay no longer felt the resentment she had in the hospital over what had seemed like interference on Heather's part. It no longer angered her to think of Heather asking this girl to send Andrew back to her. It hadn't worked anyway, had it?

But she wouldn't go to Heather and Edmund. She needed time alone to review what she had discovered. If she had discovered anything. Sleep was very slow in coming that night. She lay in the dark and, because that was hopeless, put the light on again. Her grief over the loss of Andrew—like a bereavement it had been and still was—had almost emptied her mind of all other concerns. Her long-held worry over Heather and what Heather had done (or possibly not done) had been pushed out of the way. If her mind was a cupboard, Heather and Guy had gone to the back of the top shelf, hidden and almost out of reach. Now the things Pamela had said had brought it to the front, into the light of day, and with the sight of it came a cold, sick feeling of dread. It was terrible enough knowing that Heather, as a child, had killed a man. Ismay understood now that there had been some element of fantasy in her fears that she might kill again. It had been a possibility but a remote one. There was nothing remote about Pamela's reasoning and what she had inferred from it.

I will listen to the tape again, she thought. I will listen carefully to what I recorded for Edmund but which I never gave him. Could I give it to Heather now? Could I do what I should have done years ago? Could I sit down with her and be gentle with her and **ask** her? "Did you drown Guy for me and did you kill Eva Simber to send Andrew back to me?"

She got up and began to look for the tape. At one point she had put it in a plant pot but she remembered taking it out again. Where had she put it? She looked in all the obvious places—what **were** the obvious places? Were there any?—and ended by ransacking the flat, turning out cupboards and emptying drawers, all of it in vain.

Just before morning, when the dawn was coming and gray light filled the room, she dreamed of climbing the stairs, a much steeper and longer staircase than in reality, up and up to where Heather, in her wet dress, stood at the top. But the farther she climbed the more the stairs lengthened ahead of her, and though she stretched out her arms, Heather turned away and retreated, disappeared, leaving pools and trails of water behind her.

Chapter Twenty-one

A little early in getting to Chudleigh Hill—she had been rabbit-minding while Avice went to a matinée of **The Woman in Black** with Joyce and Duncan—Marion was about to slip into Barry's house by way of the side gate when Irene came out of her front door with a pair of pruning shears in her hand. "You must be getting absent-minded, my dear," she said in rather a cheerful tone for her. "This is where I live."

"Goodness, I'll forget my own name next," said Marion with great presence of mind. She didn't like pruning shears. Fowler had nearly chopped off one of her fingers with a pair just like Irene's when she was ten. She still had the scar. Fowler had intended no harm. She wasn't so sure about Irene. "I can't stop long, I'll just pop in and out."

Bristol Cream sherry was produced, the pruning shears were laid down on the table, and Irene was off on a long diatribe about her next-door neighbor. He was sulking, she said. Just because she had made it plain she wasn't interested in "anything like that." It was very silly of him to hide himself away just because romance was out of the question. Why couldn't men realize they weren't all God's gift to women? Even worse was Edmund's behavior. To be fair, it wasn't his fault but that wife of his who had undue influence over him.

"They've given up their flat and moved in with her mother in Clapham. She's mad, you know. The mother, I mean. Mrs. Rolland, she's called. I suppose Edmund's wife thought she'd get free attention from him, though what he can do I don't know. It's not as if he were a doctor or even a psychiatrist."

"Mad?" said Marion. "My goodness."

"There's a sister living downstairs. Esme or something. Her boyfriend walked out on her and she's having a nervous breakdown. That means nothing these days. She's probably mad too. These things are hereditary, you know."

Marion made her escape after about ten

minutes. Irene came out with her, remembered after they had said good-bye that she needed to dead-head the dahlias and had left the pruning shears inside. While she was gone Marion rushed into Barry's garden and had just got inside the side gate when she heard Irene returning and the snip-snip of her decapitations.

"How's my kitten?" asked Barry above the soft keening of a raga. Marion thought he looked very strange in an embroidered silk coat over his flannels, a kind of turban on his head with a feather and a jewel on it. She lifted up her face for a dutiful kiss. "I'm in my best bib and tucker for your birthday, my dear." He was the only one who had remembered it. "I hope you don't think it too much like fancy dress."

"Not on you, Barry. You look gorgeous."

"The old lady caught you, I see."

Marion had heard or read somewhere that men like women who are kind and generous toward other women. "Poor thing. She's so lonely. I had to go in for five minutes."

"Ten," said possessive Barry. "I was counting. Would you like your birthday present now or in the restaurant? I've fixed it up that they're bringing your cake after the main course and one of the waiter-wallahs is going to sing 'Happy Birthday to You.' So shall we save the present till then?"

"Anything you say," said Marion, hooking her little hand over his arm and pretending to be enraptured by the music. It was always an Asian restaurant, but she was getting used to it.

"I don't suppose you're going to tell old Barry which birthday it is?"

"Oh, just somewhere between thirty and death," said Marion with a giggle.

Pamela was sitting in a wheelchair and she wasn't alone. A man was with her, someone Ismay thought she vaguely recognized, associating him with Guy, though she couldn't place him. Pamela held out her hand and Ismay bent down and kissed her.

"Do you remember Michael, Issy?"

Then she did, of course. This was the man who had been engaged to Pamela at the time Beatrix married Guy. This was the man who had left her a week before they were due to be married. "How are you?" she said.

"You were a little girl when I last saw you."

"I was fifteen."

He was looking at Pamela as if he had fallen in love with her all over again. He took her hand, kissed her in a tender way, and left, promising to come back the next day. Ismay said good-bye and looked inquiringly at Pamela.

"I know what you're thinking. He apologized for all that."

"Bit late in the day, wasn't it?"

Pamela went on as if she hadn't spoken, "He said it was partly due to Guy's dying like that. He said he felt he couldn't be connected to our family when he'd actually hoped something like that would happen."

"What on earth do you mean?"

"He said that when Guy had that virus and just seemed to get worse and worse he hoped he—well, he wouldn't get better."

"You mean, he'd die?"

Pamela winced. "You're not usually so blunt, Issy. But yes, he hoped he'd die and then Michael would get his job. And then Guy did die. Maybe he killed himself. Michael felt so much guilt about that he thought it would be best if he just—disappeared. After all, he was offered Guy's job but didn't take it."

"I don't think he ought to feel guilt about anyone but you," said Ismay, who thought the story sounded like an excuse and not a very clever one. "How did he know you were here?"

"He ran into Heather at the hospice. His mother's in there. She's dying."

"He must spend all his time hospital visiting," said Ismay drily, and then, on an impulse,

"When he was with you did he have a key to our house? I mean, did he have access to a key?"

"Why on earth do you want to know?"

"Take it that I just do. Did he?"

"I suppose he did," said Pamela.

Michael had hated Guy, had wanted his job. He had broken off with Pamela over the guilt he felt for wishing Guy dead. Or because he had killed Guy? Ismay asked herself that question as she went home in a taxi. It was far more likely that he had felt guilt because he had killed Guy than over some tenuous neurotic fear of being associated with the family of a man he had wanted dead. He had a key or access to Pamela's key, which amounted to the same thing. Could she, after all this time, find out where Michael had been on the afternoon Guy died? Could she now take the enormous and frightening step of asking Heather if Michael had come into the house that afternoon? Or even if he could have come into the house without her knowing?

It was a long time since she had thought about Guy's death. Her loss of Andrew had driven most of that away. It had returned to her mind because today was the anniversary. Thirteen years ago to the day it had happened and always on the day the memories were stronger. If she didn't dream about it she had a waking dream in which once again she saw Heather on the stairs in her wet dress and heard her say, "You'd better come."

Did her thinking of it now mean she was beginning to get over Andrew? Hardly, for with that thought and its many possible repercussions, he came back into her consciousness so that she was asking herself, what does it matter now? What can it matter after so long who killed Guy, if anyone did? All I want is Andrew. I don't want answers. I want him. I can wait. If someone said to me that he would come back in five years, in ten, I would be happy. I would wait, I would be patient. I shall never get over him. But if I knew that one day I would see him again, he would love me again, I would be dizzy with happiness. Sometimes I feel I would die of it.

For all that, when she was back in the flat, had put her head around their door and said hello to Edmund and Heather, she began once more hunting for the tape. She looked in all the places she had looked in before, and then it occurred to her it might be in her clothes cupboard, in the pocket of a coat or jacket. It wasn't. She never carried anything in her pockets but in her handbag.

Perhaps that was where it was, in one of her handbags. Ismay had a lot. She took them out of the cupboard and laid them on the bed, opening each one and removing the contents. This yielded a lot of receipts and credit card chits from various shops, which she prudently tore into pieces; several dozen tissues; and a miscellaneous assortment of paper clips, coins of tiny denominations, ballpoint pens, a floppy disc, and a notepad; but no tape. Of course not—she remembered now. The tape had been in the bag that was stolen.

She felt a little mild relief. It wasn't falling into the hands of anyone she knew. Any thief finding it would have thrown it away as he had thrown away all the other things in the bag except the money, no doubt, and the credit cards.

Her mind returned to Andrew. She sat down and closed her eyes. I didn't like him smoking, she thought. I had asked him to give it up. Oh, God, now I'd let him smoke all day and all night if he'd come back to me. I love my sister, but I'd turn my back on her for him. I'd never see Heather and Edmund again if it would mean having Andrew back. I'd give everything to have him back. . . .

· · ·

Barry had a great many tapes of this Indian music of his and not many CDs. Must be his age, thought Marion, pretending to scrutinize his music library after they had come back from the Maharanee. It was a wonder really he hadn't got it all on LPs, he was so old-fashioned. Her present from Barry she had been given in the restaurant. Not a sari, which she had feared, but a beautiful Indian dress, apricot-colored, embroidered with crystals and sequins. "I want to see you in it," he said.

She gave a little girlish shriek but ran away into his bedroom, rather regretting she couldn't give him his reward now. But it wouldn't do. It would put the kibosh (a favorite Barry word) on all her well-laid plans. The dress was very small but not too small for her. Thank God she was wearing her beige patent shoes with the heels like needles.

He actually gasped when she appeared. "Well, you are a beauty," he said. "That must be saved for a very special occasion and I think I know what that occasion will be."

So did Marion and she went home feeling more elated than she had for a long time. Before driving off, Barry took advantage of his position as dispenser of largesse and organizer of birthday parties by kissing her more ardently that usual, his tongue lightly brushing her teeth. She'd give him something next time and make him some halva. Or wasn't that Indian?

Barry wasn't the only one who had remembered her birthday after all. Fowler had been back again and left her a present. She unwrapped it. Quite a nice handbag, surely not one of his bin finds. Marion examined it carefully. Of course it wasn't new, that was too much to expect. There was a scratch on one side near the bottom and the strap was a bit scuffed. But still it was good leather and a lovely color. She opened it and saw the Marc Jacobs label inside. Although the bag remained unchanged, in her eyes it was immediately enhanced and increased in value by this label. Nothing inside it, or was there? She rummaged around and brought out a tape.

Rainy Season Ragas. Just the thing to take over to Barry when she'd made the halva.

Chapter Twenty-two

The West End Werewolf had been arrested. There was no murder charge, but as is the way in these cases, everyone knew because the newspapers knew that as soon as enough evidence had been amassed, he would be charged with causing Eva Simber's death as well as numerous assaults on young women in the western suburbs. His name was Kevin Dominic Preston from Hounslow. He was twenty-one, an unemployed painter and decorator.

Watching television, Ismay saw him brought to court in a police van, mobbed and threatened as he was hustled into the building with a coat over his head. A woman in the crowd threw something in his direction and a policeman caught her by the arms. Ismay turned it off. She wondered if Andrew had watched it. If he had loved Eva he would have wanted her killer caught. Perhaps he was very unhappy. She understood something. You want your lover to be unhappy if he is unhappy over you, not over someone else. The death of your rival should cause him to rejoice, not grieve, even though this makes him into a monster.

The first time Irene saw her sneak through the side entrance into Barry's back garden she thought Marion had gone to the wrong house. The second time she saw her, on this occasion going boldly up to his front door and calling something through the letter box, she had a panic attack. Her heart raced, she moaned and choked, laughed and then wept.

She phoned Edmund, but by the time he arrived it was over and she was lying prostrate, unable to speak above a whisper.

"Has something happened, Mother? Have you had a shock?"

She wasn't going to tell him. "I'm **subject** to panic attacks. You ought to know that after all this time."

"Can I make you a hot drink? Get you something to eat?"

"If that's the best you can offer. I realize it's not as if you were a doctor."

Edmund went back to Clapham and Beatrix but to Heather as well and she made everything all right. "Sometimes I think if we could choose our mothers I'd rather have yours than mine."

Heather laughed. "Mine's never been so calm and—well, happy, since you've been looking after her. And she never sticks her pill on her chewing gum anymore."

"She never gets the chance," said Edmund.

In Chudleigh Hill Irene made her weekly evening call to her sister. "Do you happen to know if Marion Melville still looks after those animals for Avice?"

"Oh, my dear, she works for her. She gets a wage."

"Works?" Irene was in her Lady Bracknell role increasingly these days. "In what capacity?"

"I don't know. Cleans out the rabbits. Does a bit of shopping. Makes her appointments for her, such as they are. She **sleeps** there. Or she does sometimes. Not so much since her father's been so ill."

"Could you let me have Avice's phone number? I used to have it, but it seems to have been mislaid." She spoke in a slightly menacing tone as if the mislaying had been done by some servant and retribution would quickly follow. "I've got a pencil. I'll hold on."

As she usually did these days while on the phone, Irene positioned herself in the drawing-room bay window, the better to see comings and goings next door.

Joyce came back with the number. "Here it is. Now, how are you? I'm told that the proper answer to that these days is 'good.' All the young say it."

"I'm not at all good, Joyce. I've just had a panic attack and I've a severe pain in my chest. I think it may be pericarditis."

"Oh, dear. If you're meaning to phone Avice now, the chances are Marion will answer."

"No, she won't," said Irene. "I've just seen her going into next door."

Marion was on her way to see Barry but hadn't brought the tape or the halva. She had assembled the ingredients for the halva—honey, sesame seeds, nuts and saffron—and then discovered from a footnote in the cookery book that it was a Turkish sweetmeat. As for the tape, she thought she ought to have a look at it before giving it to Barry. She had taken it out of its Perspex case and examined it. Wasn't it rather peculiar to have a plain black tape cassette in a case with a picture of a man in a turban sailing on a blue lake? Maybe it wasn't **Rainy Season Ragas** after all. Typical of Fowler! She had no time to test it now, what with all this running between Pinner and West Hampstead.

No time either to plan surreptitious ways of getting into Barry's house. She would have to trust to luck, and luck was against her. Irene was stationed in her bay window, talking on the phone. When she saw Marion she waved and smiled. It was the kind of smile you gave, Marion thought, when you wanted to reassure people but actually intended betrayal. Perhaps Irene had been bad-mouthing her to Barry.

If she had, there was no sign of it in his behavior. She was in his arms almost before he had closed the front door and, nestling close to him, she murmured to herself, "Ask me then. Go on. Ask me. Propose."

Avice was sitting on a footstool, grooming Figaro with a comb and a rubber brush with spikes on its back that looked a bit like a sea urchin. The rabbit sat completely still, showing neither pleasure nor distaste, and reacted not at all when Avice had to get up to answer the phone.

"You **are** a stranger," she said.

"Is Marion Melville there, Avice?" Irene knew very well she wasn't.

"She's a friend of yours, of course. I'd forgotten. Would you like me to give you her mobile phone number? These things are a mystery to me, but I understand with one of them you can run someone to earth **anywhere.**"

Inspired, Irene said, "Where does she say she is, Avice?"

"That's a strange tone to use. As a matter of fact, she's visiting her father. He's ill in hospital."

"He's dead," said Irene.

"That must have been very sudden."

"He's been dead for twenty years."

"I see." Avice said an abrupt good-bye and absent-mindedly returned to her grooming. It was Susanna's turn. Unable to concentrate, she pulled out a tuft of fur on the teeth of the comb and Susanna fled through the rabbit flap. After she had apologized profusely to the absent animal, Avice found a pencil and wrote on the phone pad: **Speak to Mr. Karkashvili tomorrow.**

. . .

Pamela was going into rehab, where she would have daily physiotherapy. After a fortnight, if she improved the way they expected, she could come home. The rehab center was in Berkshire and it was proposed that Pamela should be taken there in an ambulance, but Michael Fenster insisted on driving her.

"We can stay on for another couple of weeks," Edmund said.

"But you've got possession of your flat." Ismay tried to keep dismay out of her tone.

"Not till next Monday," said Heather. "We can move all our stuff in. We can still be here and be with Mum."

Ismay argued. "But I can easily manage. Now Ed's got Mum taking her pills regularly she'll be in the habit of it. She'll be fine. I can come home at lunchtime. It'll only be for a short time."

"Issy, we'll stay. We'll stay as long as it takes. Now tell all about Michael. Has he come back to her? Will he move in here with her? He used to be quite fond of Mum—only she was different then."

Ismay thought of how different she was and of what had made her change. If Edmund left them alone, could she ask Heather **now?** Take her chance and say to Heather, "You were alone here that afternoon, you were in your bedroom, that room that's Pamela's now. Did anyone come into the house? Did Michael come? Or was no one here but you all the time?" Edmund wouldn't go. He and Heather were about to sit down and eat their supper. She could say to Heather, "Come downstairs later, will you? There's something I want to ask you." Edmund would come too. It was impossible.

It's always been impossible, she thought. I've had twelve years to do it in, thirteen years now, and I haven't done it. I'm never going to know because the fact is I haven't the nerve to ask her. I never have had. I never shall have.

"I'd better go if I want to see Pam before eight."

"Tell her Ed and I will be in to see her tomorrow," said Heather.

She poured herself a glass of wine and started the tape. Whatever she had expected, it wasn't a human female voice. The woman's first words meant nothing to her. "My stepfather was called Guy Rolland. He was thirty-three when he married my mother and she was thirty-eight." Marion stopped the tape. This wasn't what Barry had told her was a traditional Hindu musical form. She felt a sharp pang of disappointment. Romantic Indian songs were just what she needed to bring Barry to the point.

Afterward she didn't know why she hadn't abandoned it. Barry was coming to dinner ("To see my kitten's little nest"), but there were still two hours to go before his arrival, time to get back into her tracksuit and run down to HMV and pick up a CD. They were bound to have Indian music and she could buy it on her Visa card. It was the idea of getting out of that dress and back into it later that stopped her. Full of anti-Fowler rage, she pressed the "tape on" button. The voice said, "My father and Heather's had been dead for three years." Heather. Marion's attention was caught by the name. She stopped the tape and rewound it. She knew a Heather. Just one woman called that and she was sure she'd never met another.

She played the tape again, heard "Heather," was given no clue as to the identity of the speaker; but then came a name that was very familiar to her. "Edmund, I have to tell you this, and this seemed to me the best way to do it." Marion felt a dizzying adrenaline rush. She took a mouthful of her Sauvignon and listened to the rest of it.

Barry arrived a little early, admired her in the dress, and gave her one of his sloppy kisses. Marion thought he seemed taken aback by the modesty of the flat, but perhaps that was all to the good. He would be even more keen to rescue her from it. She had turned down her bed in an inviting way and sprayed the covers and curtains with room fragrance, but it wasn't exactly an invitation. She knew by this time it was marriage or nothing.

The lamb vindaloo was a great success and Barry seemed to believe that the chutney was her own make and not Waitrose's. But Marion couldn't concentrate the way she usually did when she was with Barry. The tape got in the way. Phrases and expressions she had heard kept repeating themselves. This Guy character dying in the bath, Heather in a wet dress, water splashes on her shoes, the woman called Beatrix—their mother?—going off her rocker, the other girl, the sister, not wanting to leave Heather alone in case she did it again. But who was the sister? Marion thought she'd listen to the tape again after Barry had gone and see if there was any clue on it as to where this sister lived and what her name was. Maybe it was enough just to find out if Heather had a sister. But, yes, of course she did. Marion remembered now. It was all coming back to her. Heather had mentioned a sister. Irene had mentioned her at that dinner when Heather had had to ask for a glass of wine and again when she had said the sister was having a nervous breakdown.

"What's wrong, kitten?" said Barry. "You're very quiet. Come and give old Barry a cuddle."

So Marion sat on the sofa beside him, put her head on his shoulder, and curled up her legs so that he could rest a hand on her thigh. She had tried to lay her head in his lap but he reacted uneasily and she shifted to a more decorous position. After he had said he loved her and had never known anyone like her, she began to be confident that the proposal was imminent, but nothing came and at eleven, rather the worse for drink, he used her phone to order a taxi to take him home.

"I may be retired," he said obscurely, "but still it wouldn't do for someone like me to be over the limit."

Marion managed quite a passionate goodnight kiss and waved as the taxi moved off. At least Fowler hadn't turned up. She began to wash the dishes. Marion would no more have gone to bed leaving dirty crockery and cutlery about than she would have let Barry know details of Fowler's lifestyle. Washing up wasn't a particularly onerous task. It allowed her to dance about, picking up plates, balancing glasses and stacking cups and, later, stretching upward to put things on high shelves. The by-now cold remains of the curry she put away into the fridge and saved the cold rice too. It would be tomorrow's dinner. Now Avice had given her the push and taken her out of her will, Marion was starting to feel the pinch. Another couple of weeks and she'd have to become a "job seeker," living on whatever the Department of Work and Pensions would allot her.

I wonder if I could sell the dress, she thought. She played the tape once more before going to bed.

Ismay got out of the tube at Clapham South and began the walk home. She thought about the women of her own age who lived in Hammersmith and Acton and Shepherd's Bush and who, since Preston's arrest, had felt safer now he was locked up. Even here was west enough to be risky. While he was free she had been conscious all the time of the need to be streetwise, to keep to well-lighted places, preferably frequented places, never to take short cuts along alleys or narrow dark lanes.

Their street was never thronged with people, only packed with cars, cars lining pavement edges on both sides. Someone (a man) had once told Ismay that if what he called "one of those lowlifes" approached her she should jump on the hood of a car and scream. She didn't think she could jump onto a car, and even if she tried such a safety measure she was sure her pursuer would be better at making the leap. But things really were safer now that Preston was under lock and key. She came to the house with the pineapples on the gateposts and climbed the steps under the glass canopy to the front door.

As soon as she let herself in she smelled it, something she hadn't smelled in there for months. Cigarette smoke. No one who smoked came here—except one person. Her heart seemed to swim up inside her rib cage and knock against the bones. Because her mouth had dried, the little cry she gave was halfway to a gasp. Her hand shook as she unlocked her own front door.

Andrew was sitting on the sofa, smoking a cigarette and reading the **Evening Standard.**

Chapter Twenty-three

"I would have come back before but it seemed—well—unfeeling, with Eva dead in that terrible way. I waited a decent interval." He held her in his arms. From the moment she came home and found him there he had held her. Eva was nothing, Eva was dead. "It was those two being here that made me leave in the first place," he said. "I couldn't stand sharing our home with them." That old excuse again, but all she heard was "**our** home." He thought of it as **his** home as well as hers. "They're not likely to turn up, are they?"

"No, Andrew," she said. "They won't turn up."

They won't turn up because they're upstairs.

Don't think of that. She wanted no alloy to her happiness that night. Don't think of them, she told herself. Don't think how they offered to stay on, maybe for weeks. And I was grateful, I was **pleased.** He pulled her down on the sofa and began to kiss her with little soft kisses, whispering how much he loved her, how he had always loved her, and she thought of nothing much anymore (except how happy she was) until it was deep night, the mad after-midnight hours and he was fast asleep in her bed.

She got up and did something she couldn't remember ever doing before in the nighttime. She made herself tea. Then, for the first time, she saw and smelled the flowers he must have brought with him. Without eyes or sense of smell for anything but him, she had failed to see the chrysanthemums, big, luscious, expensive ones—like everything he indulged in— stuck in an inch of water in the kitchen sink. She fetched a vase, put them into it because, though she hated them and they reminded her at once of Guy, Andrew had given them to her. Carrying the vase into the living room, she sat down on the very spot where he had sat earlier that evening when she had found him there. I think too much, she whispered to herself. It would be better for me if I didn't think, if I could just enjoy, live and be happy. But it's beyond my control. Never mind Heather and Edmund upstairs. They're not in **here.** They're not living with me, it's not the same as it used to be. Andrew may never find out or by the time he does they'll be gone. Is he going to move in with me here? I don't know. I only know he said "our home." It's mad to worry about something when you don't really know what you're worrying about.

What I've got to worry about is something real, something that's happened. Andrew's come back to me because Eva's dead. Because someone—Preston, I thought—killed Eva. But Heather knew Eva, she'd talked to her on the phone and maybe met her too. Heather killed Guy to save me and now she's killed Eva to save me in another way. To bring Andrew back to me. Was it possible?

Of course it was. It was exactly what she had feared, only she had thought that when murder was committed again it would be to protect Edmund or even their children. She hadn't considered herself once more as the beneficiary of an act of Heather's, but so it was. And it had worked. It had brought him back to her. Killing Guy had saved her from his attentions, and killing Eva had brought Andrew back and made her happy. She asked herself, what shall I do?

After a while, the smell of the chrysanthemums, bitter and medicinal, drove her back into the bedroom and there she gazed down on his sleeping face. It was dark still but enough light from street lamps came through the curtains for her to see him. She thought of a story she had once read of the girl called Psyche holding up a lamp to look down at her lover Eros while he slept. A drop of hot oil fell on him and he leapt up and ran away from her forever.

"I think I'll move in here," he said next morning.

"Oh, Andrew, please do."

They were having breakfast. "I told Seb I very likely would in a week or two. Give him a chance to find someone else to share with him."

"Suppose I'd said no." She smiled to make it seem a joke.

He took another piece of toast. "There wasn't much chance of that."

No, there had never been any chance of that. She felt cold, though it wasn't cold. Wasn't that what she wanted, that he should take her entirely for granted? That he should rely on her always being there, his lover, his home, the place he could always come back to? Why not? Why not? I said I'd wait forever, she thought, and now he's come back and the waiting's over. I should be as happy as the day is long. I **am** happy.

"Where are those two now? Still with his mother?"

If it had been anyone but Andrew she would have thought him obsessed with Heather and Edmund. "They've got a flat," she said. It was true in substance if not in intent. She changed the subject swiftly. "Something I've just thought of. I had my handbag stolen but I'd kept my keys in my pocket. If they'd gone I'd have had to change the locks and then you wouldn't have been able to get in."

"Are you glad the keys weren't in your bag, my darling?"

"You know I am, you know it."

Upstairs Edmund was giving Beatrix her capsule embedded in a Black Magic strawberry cream chocolate, her favorite. When she had chewed it up and swallowed it he let her have a stick of chewing gum. She switched her radio on too low for anyone except herself to hear and squashed her right ear against it. Heather was at the front window, looking down on the steps, the bushy front garden, the pineapples on the gateposts, and the roadway.

"Andrew has just gone out of the gate and down the street," she said.

"What?"

"I told you he'd turn up."

"I didn't believe you. D'you think he's come back for good?"

"Depends what you mean by 'for good.' Until another little blond fairy turns up."

"I hope we don't have to meet him," said Edmund. "What time are you on today?"

"Not till one. I'll stay here with Mum."

Ismay came upstairs after he had left. Heather put her arms around her and held her close. "I know," she said. "I've seen him."

She couldn't stop herself. "Has he seen you?"

Heather released her. "Not so far as I know. I saw him from the front window about half an hour ago."

Although Beatrix, as usual, had taken no notice of her arrival, Ismay went up to her and kissed her cheek. "I stood upon the sand of the sea," said Beatrix, "and saw a beast rise up out of the sea, having seven heads and ten horns and upon his horns ten crowns and upon his heads the name of blasphemy."

"I suppose he doesn't like it that we're up here," said Heather.

In a low voice as if Andrew could hear Ismay said, "He doesn't know."

"Would you like some coffee?"

"No, thanks."

"What did you mean by 'he doesn't know'?"

"Just that."

"No, you didn't." Ismay couldn't recall her sister ever before speaking to her in that cold, resolute tone. "You meant you don't want him to know. You want us to hide ourselves, pretend we're not here and Mum's alone. Because if he thinks we're living here he won't want to come here. That's it, isn't it?"

"Please don't be cross, Het."

"I'm not cross, though I may be in a minute. Andrew will just have to put up with us. We won't pretend. I know I can speak for Ed. We're not going or pretending we've gone. We're not sneaking in after dark. It's only for a fortnight anyway. You'll have to see him at his place."

"He's coming to live with me."

"When? Now?"

"In a couple of weeks. When Seb Miller's found someone to share the flat."

Heather lifted her shoulders in a little light shrug. Turning her eyes away from her, Ismay thought, I must be mad, I'm feeling a bitch because **I ought to be grateful to her.** She's given Andrew back to me and here I am asking her and her husband to disappear. "Forget what I said, Het."

"Of course." But Heather spoke in the same

cold tone. "I'll try. Ed says we ought to forgive, but forgetting takes longer, maybe a lifetime." She smiled but it was a rueful smile. "Changing the subject, do you know a woman called Marion Melville?"

"I don't think so."

"She's a friend of my mother-in-law. She phoned and said she wanted to get in touch with you. Ed took the call and gave her your address. Was that okay?"

"I suppose so."

"Do you know what she wants?"

"Does she work for a charity? Once I gave a donation to a children's charity and ever since all the other children's charities have been appealing to me."

"Then you're used to saying no," said Heather.

"Where did you get it?"

"In a bin in Soho," said Fowler.

Marion wrinkled up her nose. "You are so disgusting." For once she hadn't waited for him to turn up but had sought him out, finally running him to earth in Conduit Street outside the Kenzo shop. Now they were sitting on the bronze seat at the bottom of Bond Street, Fowler between the statues of Churchill and

Roosevelt, and Marion on Churchill's knee, sharing a packet of salt and vinegar crisps. Fowler had bought them with half his morning's takings.

"Has your old chap come up to scratch yet?"

"Has **what?** "

"It's what they used to say in olden times when a girl wanted to get a guy to propose. Has he?"

"It's not your business," said Marion. "I've lost my job, but I've got my eye on another one."

"You won't need another one if you marry the old boy. You'll have to seize time by the forelock. Did you come all the way down here just to find out where I found those Indian songs?"

"Don't flatter yourself. I'm on my way to Clapham. I've got friends there."

Marion trotted off without saying goodbye. The street named by Edmund Litton was a turning off Clapham Common Road and great walker though she was, she decided she couldn't get from Bond Street to Clapham on foot. It would have to be the Northern Line tube. On the way she would think the whole thing through and make up her mind what to say when she rang the doorbell and Heather's sister answered.

She had chosen a Saturday because the sister wouldn't be at work. Edmund had told her that. He had also asked her in that abrupt, not to say rude, way of his what she wanted. Marion had answered, "Oh, this and that," in an airy tone. She walked through St. James's Park to Westminster. By then her feet were hurting. The pointed shoes with kitten heels weren't ideal footwear for a trek on hard pavements. She didn't want to arrive limping, but there was no help for it. She couldn't afford a taxi—they were even more expensive on a Saturday—still less a pair of flat shoes, even supposing she could bear to put her dainty feet into such things. At last Embankment station was reached and she could sit down in the train to ease her feet. She got out at the wrong Clapham station and after another quarter of a mile she was in a discount store buying a pair of blue flip-flops. She could just about afford that and the relief was overwhelming.

She saw the house and guessed it was the right one before she read the number. Edmund had mentioned the pineapples on the gateposts. Steps ran up to the porch and the front door under a funny glass arrangement, creeper climbed over the brickwork, and the bells told her there were two flats. Before passing between the gateposts, she studied the house, noting the stained glass in the heavy black-painted front door, the open window on the upper floor, the newspaper still trapped in the letter box, and the untended front garden. That newspaper was suddenly withdrawn; the door opened and a tall, dark-haired young man came out, slamming the door behind him and running down the steps. Of Marion, standing beside one of the gateposts, he took no notice. She stayed where she was until he was out of sight, climbed the steps, and rang the bell under the card which said "Ismay Sealand."

The woman on the doorstep Ismay had never seen before. She was a little thin woman of forty-something with stick-like legs and bony feet thrust into blue flip-flops. The flip-flops, which would have been passable with a sundress, looked very strange with a check tweed skirt and a red sweater that matched her curly crimson hair. Ismay said, "Hello."

"Hello. I'm Marion."

"Oh, yes. My sister said you'd phoned."

"Can I come in?"

It was said aggressively, rather as if people one didn't know had a right to come into one's house anytime they liked. Ismay, who had been feeling the purest intense happiness, a happiness all the greater because Andrew had gone out, leaving her to savor her joy and bliss in his absence and in the knowledge he would return, thought, what would he do? He's much better at these things than I am. She knew what he would say and she said it, but politely, "I'd like to know what this is about."

"You are Ismay Sealand?"

"Yes, of course. Sorry. Didn't I say?"

"No, you didn't. Can I come in, then?"

Ismay stepped back and closed the door after her. "Are you collecting for something?"

"You could put it like that." The tone wasn't aggressive this time but strangely menacing. "D'you live on your own?"

Ismay knew she ought not to have answered that. She ought to have asked the woman what she wanted, but she was so happy that Andrew was back and with her, that he would return soon and be with her all day and night and every day and night, she was so proud of him, that she said, "No, with my boyfriend. I expect you saw him go out just now."

"Maybe." Marion sat down. She had begun to feel aggrieved. There was something wrong with the way things were ordered that this girl had a man like the one she'd seen coming out of the gate and she was stuck with old Barry. Still, old Barry had the money and by the look of the place there wasn't much to spare around here. "I'll come to the point," she said. "Have you lost a handbag?"

"I had a handbag stolen," said Ismay. "Why, have you found it? Have you got it?"

"I've got what was in it."

Just six words but as they were spoken, as Ismay realized what they implied, all her happiness vanished. It was as if the sun had been shining, warm and bright, but a cloud had come and covered it and the world was plunged in darkness. "I don't understand," she said, though she did.

She might have been less distraught if she had known how uneasy her visitor was feeling, how doubtful of how to proceed. There was something innocent and gentle about Ismay, something sweet and trusting, which Marion had seldom encountered. She was undeterred, but she was a little daunted. However, she went on, accompanying her words with a defiant stare, "You know what I've got so I don't need to spell it out. You never gave it to Edmund, did you? I wonder why not. I could play it to him. I could take it to the police. Or what about the boyfriend? What does he do?"

"What do you mean?"

"Do for a living. Not a policeman, is he?"

"He's a lawyer."

"I could play it to him. Ah, you don't like that, do you? I can see it in your face."

"What do you want?" Ismay's voice had grown higher-pitched and more childlike.

"A hundred pounds now and a hundred next week and then we'll see."

It didn't occur to Ismay not to meet this demand. Only the victims of blackmailers who are strong-willed and experienced in dealing with those on the criminal fringe resist them and go straight to the police. With most people, going to the police comes later, as a last resort. The possibility of telling someone else and asking for advice did flash across her mind—flashed and vanished. Telling Andrew, to whom she should naturally go for support, was out of the question. You don't tell the object of the blackmailer's threat that you are being blackmailed. Edmund or Heather or both of them would have to be told about the tape—unthinkable. Pamela? The only possibility—but Pamela was incapacitated and far away. . . .

Marion had understood her silence and waited with apparent patience. In fact, she felt more than usually jumpy, half expecting someone else to come into the room. Hadn't Irene said those sisters' mad mother lived here? What she most feared was that Edmund would arrive and be unpleasant, even throw her out. The boyfriend coming back would, on the other hand, have its advantages. She had sat down opposite this silent girl—how old was she? She looked about sixteen—for much longer than she usually remained still. Unable to put up with it any longer, she jumped to her feet and began walking up and down. Upstairs someone was moving about. She could hear footfalls overhead.

Suddenly the silence was broken and Ismay said, "I haven't got a hundred pounds in the house."

It was victory. Marion's troubles were over. "We'll go out and find a cash machine."

"All right."

She was afraid the boyfriend might come back. Marion could tell that Ismay wanted to get out of here as fast as possible before he returned. He hasn't gone far then, Marion thought. Maybe to fetch a newspaper or milk or something. Now she too wanted to leave before he came back. It wasn't beyond possibility that if this silly girl's self-control snapped she might blurt everything out to him; then Marion's plan would come to nothing.

"Let's go, then."

Ismay's cotton trousers and T-shirt weren't warm enough for an autumn day, so she put a cardigan around her shoulders. As they went out into the street, Marion almost laughed out loud when she saw Ismay looking to the right and then to the left to make sure the boyfriend wasn't coming.

"What's his name?"

Ismay didn't have to ask who she meant. "Andrew Campbell-Sedge."

"Posh," said Marion.

The bank with a cash dispenser outside was about a hundred yards along the main road. Marion noticed that Ismay's hands were shaking as she brought a credit card out of her wallet. She was so nervous that she took no precautions to hide the four digits she keyed in. Marion had excellent sight and a good memory for numbers, and repeated this one to herself over and over along with what she had read on the card over Ismay's shoulder. Some idea that secrecy might be a good idea impelled her to lead Ismay into a phone box where she shut the door on the two of them and held out her hand. Ismay said nothing but counted out five twenty-pound notes and held them out to her.

"All I want now is your phone number."

"What for?"

"Like I said, you haven't heard the last of me."

This number she also committed to memory, but as soon as Ismay had gone she wrote it down along with the pin number and the card's start and expiry dates. Getting home took a long while, but once she was there she rooted through the stack of mail-order catalogs that had come through her letter box in the past week.

Half an hour later she had spent two thousand pounds on a bathroom cabinet in a flat-pack, a lifetime's supply of pastel-blue bed linen and towels, six cashmere sweaters, four pairs of trousers, two suede jackets, and, for Barry, a framed picture of a sultan in turban, surcoat, and scimitar, gazing into the eyes of a maiden in a sari. On second thought, she also ordered him a silk dressing gown printed with Indian dancers.

Chapter Twenty-four

That pure perfect happiness was gone. It had lasted no more than a few hours. Trying to look at the situation dispassionately, Ismay knew this was Andrew's fault, not hers. Nor had it anything to do with Edmund and Heather. They had done nothing but selflessly stay in the upstairs flat to look after Beatrix when they would have greatly preferred to move into their own new home. Andrew had made her afraid of him. Without overtly threatening her, he had made it plain that Edmund and Heather were so obnoxious to him that he wouldn't remain under the same roof with them. While still believing they were living in Crouch End, a great distance from Clapham, he spoke of them often, referring to Edmund as "that male nurse" and to Heather as "your little gorgon of a sister." Ismay protested but not very strongly.

Though he was there almost every night, he still hadn't moved in, but she was afraid all the time that he would find out that Heather and Edmund were living upstairs. Having tried unsuccessfully, she was now deeply ashamed of having made her sister think that she would like them to be gone. She remembered painfully Heather's hurt reaction, her suppressed indignation. Never again would she hint at what she wished for, yet she increasingly wanted it so powerfully that she felt her desire must show itself without words. She dreamed of Andrew's finding out and created for herself fantasies of his anger and the accusations he would make of deceit, lying, and prevarication.

Then there was the Marion Melville threat. She had heard no more, but the first week wasn't yet over. Every time the phone rang she thought that was who it was. If Andrew found out the nature of the threat, that a tape was in existence in which Ismay had spoken of her sister's causing the death of their stepfather, he might not be surprised—he hated Heather enough to believe it without difficulty—but he would cut himself off from the Sealand family. He might not go to the police, though it was likely he would, but he would never see Ismay again. She knew that as forcefully as, **more** forcefully than, she knew of the rage he would feel and show if he discovered the presence in the house of Heather and Edmund.

Yet he had been seductively sweet to her since he came back—not that she needed seducing. Every day red roses arrived, one on the first day, two on the second and so on. The chrysanthemums had soon died. His lovemaking was better than it had ever been, as if there had been no Eva, and he gave the impression of being, and always having been, entirely monogamous. He took her out to dinner to places she would have thought far beyond his means. He laughed at her protests.

"Nothing is too good for you, my darling," he said, and then, quoting something and in a mock dramatic tone, "'All that I have is thine.'"

When they were about to go out, while she waited for him, she stationed herself in the hall, listening for movement from upstairs, hoping with all her strength that one of them wouldn't appear down the stairs or enter by the front door, but not knowing what she would do if they did. She pictured herself falling on her knees to Edmund, begging him to hide himself, and his acquiescent if contemptuous shrug. As for Marion—suppose he answered the phone and she lightly hinted at her purpose in calling. A light hint which, to others might pass over their heads, would immediately be seized upon by Andrew, dissected, and give rise to inquiries she felt it would kill her to answer.

Marion would phone. Somehow she knew it. Added to her anxiety was the beginning of money worries. She didn't earn enough to stand that sort of strain on her resources. Yet the thought of saying no to Marion, of telling her, as the melodramatic phrase has it, to do her worst, was unthinkable. If I lose him again it will kill me. I shall die.

The next day, again a Saturday, when Andrew was back in Fulham, packing his things for the move, though she told herself she wouldn't seek Edmund out, she stayed where she could hear his tread on the stairs and when she did came out into the hall.

"So you and Andrew are together again," he said but smiling, looking pleased for her.

"Yes." Impossible after that opening to say what she had meant to. But she stumbled on awkwardly, "I've got a week's holiday owing to me. I could take it from Monday week if you like and then you and Heather . . ."

"Heather told me how you felt," he said.

You tell each other everything, she thought. Without effort, without fear. How lucky you are. She said nothing but, turning away her eyes, feared she might start to cry.

He put his arms around her and hugged her tightly. "We're going on Thursday. Heather's found a carer till Pam comes back."

The doorbell rang. It was the delivery man bringing Andrew's eight red roses. She held them to her face, their velvety coldness, their scent as of fresh wet leaves. A thorn scratched her cheek. As she went back into the flat the phone was ringing. She knew it was Marion before she picked up the receiver.

"Is he there? I wouldn't want to be the cause of making you any sort of . . ." This was one of those sentences Marion couldn't cope with and she began again. "I wouldn't want to embarrass you. I can call back."

"He isn't here," Ismay said.

"Right, then, there's another hundred owing." As if she were a legitimate debt collector, Ismay thought. "I could come over or we could meet."

I don't want her in my home again. She contaminates it. Anyway, Andrew may come. I don't know long he'll be fetching his stuff. Seb's got a car. Seb may drive him and it won't take long. A bold idea came to her. "Why don't I come to you?"

Of course she wouldn't want that. "I'll meet

you in the middle of Hungerford Bridge at eleven."

Ismay had read enough thrillers and seen enough TV dramas to know that, to safeguard themselves, blackmailers should take precautions against their victims bringing the police with them to venues. It would be wiser, for instance, for her and Marion never to meet again, but for the money to be placed by her where Marion could collect it. She should have been asked for the notes to be in three (or even four) different denominations and taken from separate cash dispensers. This carelessness or ignorance on Marion's part told her that her blackmailer was naïve or inexperienced at this kind of work or both, but she had to face the fact that it made no difference. She would no more have brought the police into this than she would Andrew.

Luckily (and strangely, since he paid for all their entertainment and extravagances), while she and Andrew had been apart she had spent less money than when he was with her. Perhaps it was because he wasn't there to admire her hair or any new clothes she might have bought. The result was that for a time she could meet Marion's demands. But not for long, not for months. . . . She shuddered at the thought. Yet she must. Andrew must never in any circumstances hear that tape. Marion, she acknowledged, had picked her victim wisely, more astutely than she knew.

"I haven't got any money," said Marion. "It's no use asking me. There isn't any gin either. I'll be frank with you, Fowler. At present I've got a hundred pounds a week to live on and that's all. I've got the council tax to pay and the water charge, whatever they call it. You wouldn't know about these things."

"When we were little you gave me all your pocket money one week because I wanted a Bounty Bar. You lent me one pound sixty-five to buy Ma a birthday present."

"Yes, and I'm still waiting to have it back."

"Where's the hundred quid coming from? Your old chap?"

"Ask me no questions and I'll tell you no lies," said Marion. "You can stay here tonight if you want, but there's no drink in the place and nothing to eat but baked beans."

On her way to Embankment tube station, she rather regretted the impulse that had resulted in her offer. What if Barry brought her home? She would worry about that later. In the hall at the top of the escalator she watched her ticket vanish into the machine and wished it had been a return. Could she walk back? It was a very long way.

Lying in her path, ignored by everyone else, was the orange-colored plastic case of the Freedom Pass. Marion picked it up and walked purposefully to the ticket window as if about to hand it in. This of course she had no intention of doing but, sure she was the cynosure of no eyes, veered around toward the exit. Inside the case was the pass, the "oyster" card itself, and the identity card, issued to those over sixty and ensuring them free travel on tube trains, buses, and suburban line trains in the capital.

Luckily for her, this one was for a woman, a dark-haired woman looking years younger than her age. Must have been taken when she was about thirty, thought Marion. Loath as she was to add nearly twenty years to her age, she recognized that needs must when the devil drives. Besides, no one looked at your picture when you used the pass, she had noticed that, and noticed too that getting on buses, people didn't need to do more than wave it at the driver.

Ismay was already waiting in the middle of the bridge. It was, as usual, crowded with people. She didn't speak, so Marion didn't. She handed over an envelope. It might be a bit risky to count it with all these people about, but Marion just took a peep inside to check it was all there.

"It'll have to go up next time," she said. "I said we shall have to see and I've—well, I've seen. A hundred's not enough. I can't live on it."

"How much?" Ismay asked meekly.

"I'll phone you when I've decided."

Ismay turned her back and walked across to the South Bank. Feeling good, Marion contemplated the river in the morning sunshine, the London Eye, the Palace of Westminster, and the Royal Festival Hall. It was a fine day, as days often are in the middle of October. If she had been acquainted with Wordsworth she might have said that earth hath not anything to show more fair. The sentiment was there.

She had a free trip back to Finchley Road. All her mail-order goodies had arrived while she was out. Fowler had taken them in and left them stacked on the kitchen counter. For half an hour she amused herself putting away the linens, changing the sheets on her bed for new pale-blue ones, and trying on the cashmere sweaters. Finally she selected the lilac one to wear for her date with Barry that evening.

Chapter Twenty-five

There was a chance Andrew would never discover the presence of Heather and Edmund upstairs. Not much of a chance, Ismay acknowledged, unless she could bring herself to persuade them to watch for his comings and goings and conceal themselves when he was likely to leave or arrive. Some vestige of pride or good sense still remaining with her, balked at this. She could—just—have tried it with Heather but not with Edmund. She was sure he would refuse her. Apart from that, she would have to face making the request and meeting his eyes. He was kind, he was one of the kindest people she knew, but she remembered the look he gave her when the eight roses had come and she had received them so rapturously, not a contemptuous look but one full of pity and regret.

Four days to go before they left. Andrew was out of the flat all day, and when he came home in the evening neither Heather nor Edmund had yet come home. Andrew hadn't asked her who was looking after her mother. It never occurred to him to think about things like that, caring for the sick, preparing meals, shopping and cleaning. They were done and someone must have done them, but for him they always had been. They happened, just as water came out of taps when you turned them on and illumination from lightbulbs when you pressed a switch. She had told him where Pamela was, who this new man of hers was and when she would be returning, but he had shown minimal interest. He hadn't yet met her mother.

Her days with him had been a kind of honeymoon. Or, rather, to create a honeymoon atmosphere was obviously his intention. She felt mean and base when she responded with less than her old delight—she feared she gave the impression of loving him less—because her worries oppressed her. She might be in his arms, she might be making love, when the thought would come to her in spite of herself that she was being blackmailed, followed closely by the everlasting anxiety of her doubts about Heather. The substance of her stress she might hide from Andrew, but she couldn't pretend the stress wasn't there, only tell herself that once Heather and Edmund were gone, things would be a little easier. Meanwhile she prepared herself for another phone call and for parting with twice what she had paid to Marion Melville last time.

Michael Fenster had been due to bring Pamela home on Thursday lunchtime. Ismay and Andrew would both be at work. Because he worked shifts, Edmund would be at home to receive them. Things happened differently, though not at first disastrously. Michael arrived on Wednesday evening, letting himself into the house with Pamela's key. It was just after seven and Ismay and Andrew were going out, first to dinner and then to a club where they were meeting Seb Miller and his girlfriend. For Ismay it wasn't a particularly happy arrangement. True, she would be with Andrew, this new adoring devoted Andrew, but she couldn't forget how she had humiliated herself to Seb, phoning him and begging him to tell her where his flatmate could be found. Still, once she had faced him, things would be easier next time.

Hearing someone come into the hall, she

thought at first it was Edmund, though she had believed him home already. She prepared herself to detain Andrew until he had gone upstairs, but then she heard Pamela's voice and she went out to her. Andrew followed. Pamela looked pale and thin, but she could walk, though with a slight limp.

"We're a day early, Issy. I should have let you know, but I couldn't wait to get home."

Ismay kissed her, introduced her and Michael Fenster to Andrew. Smiling, looking a little shy, Michael shook hands and said, "Pleased to meet you." Ismay saw what no one but she would notice, the faint curl of Andrew's upper lip, his invariable reaction to a solecism.

Then Pamela asked the question, the question Ismay hadn't allowed for in all her anxious predictions and fraught fantasies. "Are Edmund and Heather in, Issy?"

She felt a deep thick flush burn her face. Beside her, Andrew's intake of breath was almost silent. "I don't know," she said.

"Well, you're obviously going out so we won't keep you," Michael said. "I'll fetch Pam's case in a tick," and, in a way which would once have won Ismay's admiration, he lifted Pamela in his arms and carried her up the flight of stairs. She heard Heather's voice as he reached the top.

Andrew opened the front door. Their taxi had drawn up outside behind Michael's car. Andrew went outside, told the driver he wouldn't be needed, came back, ushered Ismay into the flat, and shut the door behind them. She thought, I won't say I can explain. I won't. I will not sink to that. He won't leave me for this. She said nothing.

"Sit down."

She thought he would ask her what she had to say for herself. He didn't. "What is it with you, Ismay? Are you really so committed to those two, so **in love** with that pair, that you lie to me, deceive me, go to all sorts of lengths to keep from me the truth that they have been living upstairs all the time I've been here? Why? What is it about this dull, plebeian, lower-middle-class couple, these **chavs,** that has so enslaved you?"

"I'm sorry," she said.

"You're sorry. Those words should carry with them an implicit promise of amendment, but in your case they don't. You've done it before. No doubt you think you can do it again."

"It will never happen again, Andrew. They're going tomorrow. They take over their new flat tomorrow."

The phone rang. The voice of Marion Melville said, "Hello?" This is the ultimate, my

Apocalypse, my hell, thought Ismay. This is where I lie down and scream. Of course she didn't. "I can't talk now. Can you call back?" She put the phone down.

"Was that your sister?"

"No."

"I find it hard to believe anything you say. Let me just say to you, I'm going out now. Alone. I don't know when I'll be back if ever. I can't live under the same roof with those people."

Last time he had gone she had cried. She had wept uncontrollably, sobbed through the night, lain on the floor crying bitterly. For some reason it was different now. She said aloud to the empty room, I can't bear it, and then she began to bear it, dry-eyed, still, staring at his roses, the fresh, the dead, and the dying, all in one vase, kept like that because she couldn't bring herself to throw away those that had faded.

For the first time for years, Beatrix showed a flicker of emotion when her sister came into the room. She held out her hand to Pamela, who, uncertain whether to take it in a handshake or clutch it, lifted it instead to her lips. Beatrix looked at her hand, frowning, and touched the spot where Pamela's lips had rested. Then she offered her a chocolate.

"Well, I've never known you do that before," Pamela said.

Beatrix nodded to Michael in a moderately friendly fashion.

"This must be your doing, Edmund," Pamela said. "I hope you're not thinking of going."

"Tomorrow," said Edmund. "We must. We've waited to get into our flat for nearly nine months."

Heather brought them a bottle of champagne and four glasses. "To celebrate your homecoming." She glanced at Pamela in a meaningful way, said, "Perhaps something . . . ?"

"Not exactly," Pamela said. "Michael has asked me to marry him. He says he'll live here with me and Beatrix or we can live in his house and bring Beatrix, but I won't do that."

"She says she won't put that burden on me. It wouldn't be a burden. I've always been fond of Bea."

"I hope he'll stay with me. I hope he'll be my—I won't say boyfriend—my lover. And forever or whatever we mean by that."

Edmund raised his glass. "To you. I was going to recommend marriage. I like it. But I know when I'm beaten."

· · ·

The mail-order dressing gown and the picture of the sultan with his bride were received by Barry with a gratitude that exceeded Marion's expectations. He insisted on putting on the dressing gown over his shirt and trousers and only removed it to change before they went out. Marion had a good look around the living room while he was upstairs. The books, which she had never examined before, were mostly histories of India and biographies of British and Indian luminaries. But there were also a number of works on forensics, a couple of accounts of pathologists' investigations, and quite a lot of true crime, especially wife murder. Having a suspicious mind and, in common with her brother Fowler, unsuppressed criminal tendencies, she wondered for the first time how Mrs. Fenix had met her death. It might be prudent to ask. Come to that, what had Barry done before he retired? She fancied Irene had told her he had been a civil servant.

Barry came out and drove her to St. John's Wood to the new Indian restaurant called Pushkar. He wore a white jacket over his pin-striped trousers and a white cap, which Marion could have accepted without embarrassment but for the presence of so many authentic Indian diners. It seemed to her that two or three of them exchanged amused smiles. He was rather taken aback when she asked him about his wife's death, said, "Heart," and reverted to the subject of the mail-order dressing gown. She thought he ought to take his hat off while they ate but relaxed a little when she saw that no one else had done so.

In spite of its auspicious beginning, it wasn't turning out one of their more successful evenings. Barry had only once called her kitten, and he was strangely silent and seemed nervous. As they ate beef madras and sag gosht she racked her brains for something to say, asked him how he liked the lilac cashmere sweater, got a smile and the response "Smashing," and once more had to cope with the unusual silence.

"There's something I want to ask you, Barry," she said.

The look he gave her was preoccupied.

"It's—well, what sort of work did you used to do when you . . ." She had got muddled and tried again. "I mean, what was your . . . ?"

Barry cut her short. "There's something I want to ask **you,**" he said and his voice was low and serious.

He must have somehow found out about her demands for money from Ismay Sealand or even her attempts with the morphine. If he had it was all up with her. She said nothing. She just looked at him with the winsome timid eyes of the small animal with whom he identified her.

He swallowed and his face reddened. He picked up a fork from the table and set it down again. "Marion," he said and paused, looking away.

"Yes?" She knew what it meant to feel her heart was in her mouth.

It was coming now. She waited, breathless. "I love you," he said. "Will you marry me?"

She was forty-four and it was her first proposal. She had been working toward this end but had no idea what to do now she had got there. Her instinct was to scream with joy, but she managed to restrain herself. Slowly, trembling, she nodded her head. She nodded in a quite uncharacteristic way, almost shyly, as if she were awestruck. What might have happened next she later speculated, but before Barry could speak or act, an Indian man had come up to their table and was addressing her. It was Mr. Hussein.

"Good evening, Miss Melville."

Collecting herself, Marion was pretty sure he hadn't come up to them with simply greeting her in view. Until now he had generally been rude to her. He had been about to reprove

Barry for some incorrectness of dress but seeing her there had deterred him.

"Won't you introduce me to your friend?"

"Not a friend, sir," said Barry. "No longer that. Her future husband. Miss Melville has just done me the honor of accepting my hand in marriage."

In the manner of his son, Mr. Hussein looked as if he was suppressing an almost uncontrollable mirth. Marion didn't know why. She thought Barry's little speech quite moving. He and Mr. Hussein chatted for a few moments about the name of the restaurant, which appeared to be a place in India. Barry had of course never been to Pushkar but he knew quite a lot about it.

"Beautiful lake," he said, "and the Snake Mountain."

Mr. Hussein's lips twitched. "Not forgetting the internationally renowned Camel Fair."

"Miss Melville and I may go there for our honeymoon."

"Ideal," said Mr. Hussein with a broad smile. "Of course you're aware that, as it is a holy place to the Hindus, alcohol, meat, and even eggs are banned there. Unlike," he added before strolling back to Mrs. Iqbal, "this restaurant."

• • •

Knowing it was an imprudent thing to do, a mad thing to do, Ismay had walked about on Clapham Common half the night. Nothing happened. The people she encountered took no notice of her. One of them was Fowler Melville, in unfamiliar waters, but he didn't know her and she didn't know him and they walked in opposite directions to each other like a white-sailed frigatoon and a dirty British coaster passing in the night.

She went to work in the morning, more dead than alive, afraid to phone Andrew on his mobile, even more afraid to phone Seb Miller in Fulham and ask him yet again where Andrew was. When she got home a message awaited her. It must be from Andrew, it had to be— please, God. It was from Marion Melville, a jauntier than usual, confident voice.

"Okay, two hundred this week, please. I can't wait until Saturday, so let's meet tomorrow, same time, same place. Mind you call me to confirm."

Suppose Andrew had been there and had taken the call or listened to the message. But even if he had been there and taken it, that would be better than his not being there at all. Anything would be better than being without him. Late in the evening she remembered that this was the day Heather and Edmund were moving out. They would be in their own home now. With their two keys each, their new things, and their new phone. She had written down the number and she ought to phone them. For a long time she sat by the phone, doing nothing. Pam must be upstairs, but she didn't phone her either. At nine she walked down the road to take two hundred pounds out of the cash machine. A foolish act after dark, but she no longer cared about things like that.

In bed but unlikely to sleep, she began wondering if he had another girl somewhere, a girl kept in reserve for times like this. Someone he could phone, after weeks of absence, and say, "Hi, it's me. Can I come over?" Since he had come back things were different from what they had been before he went away. He had been sweeter to her and yet more autocratic, while she had been less able to stand up for herself. She was more in love with him than ever. She finally slept, only to dream he was back, that he had come into the room to tell her Heather was dead.

She took the tube to Waterloo and walked on to Hungerford Bridge from the South Bank. Marion also took the tube, but for her it was a free ride as she used the Freedom Pass she had picked up at Embankment station. Having employed the "oyster" card to get through the barrier at Finchley Road, she began to worry once she was in the train that inspectors might get on. Then it would be all up with her, as she plainly wasn't Hilary Cutts, aged sixty-three. Of course, inspectors seldom did get on; she could remember it happening only once. What bothered her more than this precise anxiety was that she was worrying at all. She never worried. Perhaps it was because she had read in Fowler's **Big Issue** that all oyster card details were now kept in a database. Well, getting out at Baker Street where she had to change lines would be the solution. That and not getting into the Bakerloo Line train.

It came in and she got into it. No inspectors did but she jumped out at Charing Cross just the same to be on the safe side. Remember the data base. She skipped along the Strand and dropped the Freedom Pass into a waste bin. A pity, but using it was too risky. What a funny thing it would be if Fowler found it. He'd be bound to bring it to her. He always did, like a cat bringing home a mouse to its owner. She was still laughing to herself when she met Ismay on the bridge.

The girl looked like a famine victim or a camp survivor, pale, wan, her eyes dark-ringed.

Marion said a sprightly "Good morning" and put out her hand for the money, her left hand so that Ismay could see the ring on the third finger, a beautiful ruby ring Barry said came from Delhi. An envelope was put into it in silence. "As you can see, I got engaged since I last saw you. I shall soon be Mrs. Barry Fenix. I'm telling you so as you know who it is when I'm giving you a ring."

Whatever reaction Marion hoped to provoke in her victim, it wasn't to make her break into a flood of tears and run away across the bridge. Marion shrugged, smiling, catching the eye of several passersby to show them how mature, sensible, and restrained she was.

Ismay got a bus home. She had been back no more than ten minutes when Andrew walked in. She gave a little involuntary cry. She allowed him to hold her in his arms and kiss her, but that was all she did, resting her head limply against his shoulder, trembling from so many tears. When she finally lifted her head she made herself say, and the effort was enormous, "Andrew, we have to talk."

"Oh, darling," he said, "not that awful cliché, please. I can't bear it. Come on, do something about your poor face. I'm taking you out to lunch at the Fat Duck."

Chapter Twenty-six

"We've had an invitation to Marion Melville's engagement party," Heather said to her husband. He was putting up bookshelves in their new living room. "The man she's marrying lives next door to your mother. Did you know about it?"

"I know my mother hoped he was marrying **her.**"

"You don't want to go, do you?"

"Wild horses might drag me. Especially if you were riding them. When I've finished here we've got to talk about our honeymoon."

He didn't finish there because a phone call from his mother, gasping that she was having a panic attack, fetched him to Chudleigh Hill, and in fact the shelves were destined never to be completed nor to contain a single book. Irene was lying on the floor with, beside her, the party invitation that had either fallen or been placed there. Edmund felt her pulse, listened to her heart, and said there was nothing wrong with her. He helped her to her feet while she muttered to him that he wasn't a doctor.

"It's breach of promise," she said when she was seated in an armchair. "I shall definitely go. To this travesty of an engagement party, I mean. I shall tell everyone how he—well, he . . ."

"Trifled with your affections," Edmund said. "No you won't. Because if you continue to make these threats I shall tell Barry he'd be wise to cancel the party or postpone it and not invite you next time. And I'll tell him why. Is that clear?"

She looked up at him, perplexed, and he knew that at last he had won. He threw the invitation into the waste bin. "Heather and I," he said, "would like it very much if you'd come to tea tomorrow. I know you'll remember it's Heather's home and you're the guest. See you about four."

She said, "That will be nice, dear."

Leaving her, he thought a little kindness was called for before they parted or perhaps he was simply reverting to his old cowardice. "It's a secret where we're going for our honeymoon, but I can tell you. In the strictest confidence. No one else knows, least of all Heather."

It was pathetic, her very obvious joy. "I won't tell her."

"It's a place called Kanda. In Sumatra. Beaches and sunshine and beautiful green forest. Quite exotic for two people who have never been east of Greece."

The invitation to Mr. Hussein and Mrs. Iqbal was accepted, Mr. Hussein remarking to her that it would be "good for a laugh." His sons were not invited. Marion had admitted to Barry that she had a brother but said he was a recluse, almost a hermit. He wouldn't come if asked. She invited Avice Conroy, reasoning that there was nothing damaging Avice could say about her except that she had invented a sick father and no one said that sort of thing at parties. Avice sent an abusive letter declining and telling Marion she had changed her will.

Marion made her by now regular phone call to Ismay. It was answered by a man she guessed to be the boyfriend she had seen on her visit to Clapham. She put the phone down without speaking and before trying again considered what the consequences might be if the boyfriend, who sounded a masterful man, were to squeeze the truth out of Ismay and **take steps.** He might. He was a lawyer, she had said. And Ismay was a poor little thing with no spirit. Take no risks, Marion, but keep trying till you get her. She realized she was addressing herself by name the way Fowler had once told her was his habit. Her evening attempt was answered by Ismay and, mindful of the additional expenses she must incur as a bride, she again asked for two hundred pounds.

The "talk" with Andrew had never happened. Ismay thought of all the psychotherapists and counselors and agony aunts she had heard of who advised their clients to "talk it through," never apparently understanding that there are some people, many people, who refuse to do this, who simply dismiss the suggestion with a "there's nothing to talk about" and clam up or walk away. Andrew was one of them. More than anything she would have liked to sit down with him and tell him frankly how she felt, how terribly his departures made her suffer, and receive from him some explanation, some reason for his using her the way he did. I must be a masochist, she thought, and knew he would tell her she was. Would he admit he could be sadistic? She should also, she confessed to herself, sit down with Heather and finally, after all these years, get the truth from her about Guy's death. And Eva's death. This was beginning to seem more of a possibility than talking to Andrew.

If Marion Melville continued with her demands for money—and there seemed no reason why she shouldn't—the time would come when she would have to talk to Heather. Somehow she knew her sister wouldn't lie to her. If she asked her directly Heather would tell her the truth. And then what to do with the truth when she had heard it? Go to the police? Her thoughts went back to those late summer days when Guy was newly dead and the police had questioned her mother, Heather, and herself. They had been gentle with her and Heather, asking nothing about their relations with their stepfather but concentrating on their whereabouts that afternoon. Two police officers, detective constables, and their superior had briefly appeared to speak to her mother. She couldn't remember their names except that the inspector's had been a bird's. Sparrow or Swift or Parrot. No, none of those. The policemen had believed them when they said they had all been out together, shopping for school uniforms. Beatrix, cleverly, had said Heather had been with them but hadn't actually gone into the shop but waited outside.

They would probably be retired by now, those policemen. Why was she thinking of them now when she hadn't for years? Because, if the tape found its way into their hands, she would have to meet them again or their successors. It hardly bore thinking of, yet it was almost preferable to the tape being handed to Andrew. When he had heard it he would leave and this time he wouldn't come back. But the police would come once he had spoken to them.

Her savings were almost used up. One more envelope containing two hundred pounds to Marion Melville and that would be the end. The end of all our lives, mine and Heather's and Edmund's, her mother's and Pam's and maybe even Michael's. Not Andrew's, though. Andrew would leave and find himself a new little blonde. Achieving all this was in Marion's power. Nothing could stop her. Paying out thousands of pounds would keep her silent while it continued—but it couldn't continue. The money wasn't there.

"You don't want him to meet me, do you?" said Fowler. "It's not very kind, not when I've brought you a whole box of floppy discs."

He had found them in a bin outside the Dorchester, rainbow-colored ones, apparently unused.

"They're no use to me," Marion said. "I haven't got a computer."

"If I can find one I'll give it to you for a wedding present."

"No one throws away computers in waste bins. And, no, I don't want him to meet you. I may be engaged but that's not marriage, is it? Engagements can be broken and you're enough to put any man off."

Fowler helped himself to the last of the gin from Marion's fridge and the last inch of tonic in the bottle. "Have you told him about me? Does he even know I exist?"

"If you must know, I've told him you're a recluse."

"Chance'd be a fine thing," said Fowler, lighting a cigarette. "Do you know what a remittance man is?"

"No, I don't."

"It's someone like me. A wastrel, a ne'er-do-well, a loafer, a layabout, a freeloader, a black sheep, a sluggard, a hobo, a bum, a tramp, a—"

"Oh, give over, do."

"In a minute. A remittance man is all those. His relatives pay him to stay away. Right?"

"If you reckon on me paying you to stay away from Barry, you've got another think coming."

"I'm not asking for money," said Fowler. "Well, I am but no more than usual." Dirty, unkempt, and unshaven as he was, he looked at her with the limpid eyes of innocence. So had he eyed her when he was six years old and in pursuit of a tranche of her pocket money. "What I want is this flat."

Andrew had hired a car and they were going away to a country house hotel for the weekend. From the brochure it looked a glamorous place, a converted stately home, once a refuge for Charles I, later its owner host to George III. It was surrounded by twenty acres of parkland, it had a spa, a gym, and a pool. Before they could leave, Ismay had to pay her weekly hush money to Marion Melville. Two hundred pounds was almost all she had left in her account until her salary was paid into it in a week's time. Leaving Andrew in bed, she walked down to the cash dispenser, feeling that this was the last week of her life. Marion would ask for more next time and she couldn't pay it. Andrew would receive the tape in the post or, more likely, taking no risks, Marion would deliver it to him herself by hand. Ismay imagined the consequences. First of all there would be the kind of inquest he was so good at, the demoralizing kind he had instituted over her concealment of Edmund's and Heather's presence in the house, but far, far worse. She knew him so well. She envisaged his astonishment, half feigned, his lawyer-like interrogation of her, his threat that of course she understood he couldn't "just let this go," then his slow considered decision to go to the police and finally his farewell. Good-bye, this was the end, it couldn't be helped, but she must understand that in the circumstances, in his position, he could hardly be associated with someone whose sister. . . .

She had arranged with Marion for the meeting to take place earlier than usual. And at Clapham Common tube station, not Hungerford Bridge. She couldn't be away too long. Andrew would be suspicious as it was, wanting to know where she had been and what she had been doing. If she had been shopping, what on earth had she bought, knowing they'd be away for the weekend?

She withdrew the money. That made six hundred pounds this woman had extracted from her. It was rare for her to go to Clapham

Common station, Clapham South being much nearer her own home, but she had lived here all her life so there was nothing to surprise her. Only perhaps something which had temporarily slipped from her memory. Phoenix Road. She passed the end of it and the pub on the corner called the Phoenix, noted the name, and wondered why it suddenly seemed to her so important, so relevant to her life as it now was, so **vital.** Something in the picture on the pub sign? She didn't think so. It was just a bird looking rather like a pheasant rising out of a fire with red and yellow flames. Nothing there . . .

Of course. It came to her suddenly. Phoenix was the name of the detective inspector who had come to the house just once to talk to her and her mother and Heather. Not Parrot or Swift or Swan but Phoenix, the bird that is reborn from the flames that have incinerated it. Hope sprang, like the fiery bird, and made her breathless as if she had run instead of walked the distance.

Marion was there before her, in ra-ra skirt, tight sweater, and kitten heels. She looked pleased with herself.

"How's Barry?" Ismay said.

"Goodness, what a memory you've got! He's fine, thanks."

"Here's the money." Ismay passed her the envelope. "So you'll be living next door to my sister's mother-in-law."

"It looks like it. I'll phone you about next week's installment."

Marion went to get a train home. Watching her pass through the barrier, Ismay marveled at herself. All this was very unlike her. This was the kind of thing people like Marion did, not people like her, but if she didn't go ahead with it she wouldn't enjoy her weekend. Even being alone with Andrew in that lovely place would mean nothing if this wasn't resolved, or set up to be resolved. She took her mobile out of her bag and asked Directory Inquiries for the number of Phoenix, initial B, at 56 Chudleigh Hill, West Hampstead, NW6.

"How do you spell that?"

"P-H-O-E-N-I-X."

"There's no one of that name."

She had never seen it written down. Perhaps there were other ways of spelling it. "Try beginning with an F. F, double E, N-I-X or maybe F-E-N-I-X."

One of those must have been right. The recorded voice came on. "The number requested is . . ." and four digits followed the 7624 area code. Ismay dialed it.

A rather deep voice said, "Hello?"

"Is that Detective Inspector Barry Fenix?"

"It's ex–Detective Inspector now, my dear. What can I do for you?"

She cut the connection.

Chapter Twenty-seven

The remittance man was sitting on her doorstep when Marion reached home. She had not
changed the locks again, so there was no reason
for him to be there except, as she put it to
herself, out of malice. If he did it often enough
the time would come when she had Barry with
her. Beautifully dressed Barry in his immacu-
late car, helping her out, escorting her to her
door, to find this piece of human refuse litter-
ing the step. And Fowler was looking particularly awful, his face and hands black with
dirt. It was months since his hair had been cut
and it hung in straggly rats' tails to his shoulders. Now the weather was growing cold, he
had resurrected the red wool scarf and wound it

around his neck over the collar of a thickly grunge-encrusted black plastic jacket with a broken zip. He had surrounded his seat on the step with a detritus of food packaging, a plastic sandwich case, an empty quarter bottle of gin, several apple cores, and the remains of a meat pie on a polystyrene plate.

"I was just saying to myself," he said, "Fowler, I was saying, what's she up to, out all this time? Been to see lover-boy?"

"No, I haven't, and it's no business of yours."

"I've always understood that one's family was one's business, even in these degenerative days. If I clear up this mess, will you cut my hair?"

She was looking for ways to get out of the trap he was setting for her. If she were to clean him up and somehow keep him clean, maybe pay him a little, would he withdraw his threat? Once she was married to Barry it wouldn't much matter what Fowler did. Of course, marriage wasn't what it had been in their parents' day, the permanency, the tie that binds, but it still carried a fair amount of security. . . . She sent Fowler off to shower and wash his hair. A man wouldn't leave his wife because she turned out to have a brother who was a dosser, but a fiancé might leave his fiancée. Fowler really wasn't bad-looking when he was cleaned up. If his hair was no longer golden and curly it was quite a pleasant straw color. She sat him down in a chair, spread towels on the floor, and began cutting.

"Are you going out with him this evening?"

"What's that to you?"

"You know what, Marion. I won't be here, anyway. I've got an engagement with a skip in Highbury, but I could come back on, say, Wednesday."

Filthy again by then, she thought. "I could give you a bit," she said. "I mean, say, twenty pounds a week."

"I remember," said Fowler, reminiscing, "our dad telling me that when he was young twenty quid a week was a fortune. The height of a girl's ambition was a handsome husband and a thousand a year. Can't imagine, can you? It's nothing now, couple of drinks and a packet of cigarettes."

"I'd throw in a new pair of jeans and one of those army greatcoats."

"I don't want a greatcoat," said Fowler. "I want this flat."

"I expect you'd like a big white wedding," said Barry. "No reason why not. I can afford it."

"No, darling, I don't think so. It'd take so long to organize. Actually, I just want to be your wife as soon as possible."

"Do you, kitten? Camden Register Office, then, and we'll be off to India. How about three weeks' time? I reckon it has to be three weeks."

He returned to his perusal of **The World Scanner's Guide to the Asian Subcontinent.**

"Will you fix up the wedding, then?"

"Of course I will, kitten. I'll pop over there this afternoon."

"And it'll be just us?"

"We'll have to have witnesses. How about that brother of yours? And maybe an old colleague of mine."

"From the Civil Service?"

"That's right," said Barry, his mouth twitching rather in the manner of Mr. Hussein and his sons. What was so funny about the things she said she couldn't imagine.

Mr. Hussein came to the engagement party and brought one of his sons with him, Khwaja, the tallest and best-looking one, accompanied by a glamorous wife in gold lamé shalwar-kameez. Marion, in her Indian gown, felt quite equal to her. She had hoped for the chance to crow over Irene Litton, but Irene stayed away, though Edmund and Heather were there. Barry appeared to have no relatives or none whom he wanted to invite, but by far the majority of guests were former colleagues of his in the Civil Service, all now retired. Marion thought them the dullest bunch of men she had ever come across. She smiled and simpered when Barry introduced her as his "lovely bride-to-be" but soon skipped away with the excuse that she had to "see to the refreshments."

These were in the hands of caterers, all Pakistanis, and the food was splendid Mogul delicacies, Barry's favorite, covering two long buffet tables. She picked up a plate of samosas and handed them to Heather and Edmund.

"When's the wedding, Marion?" said Edmund.

"In two weeks' time. We're going to India on our honeymoon the next day. That's the best part of a wedding, don't you think? You didn't have a honeymoon, did you?"

"We're starting ours a month after you," said Heather.

"Are you going abroad?"

"I don't know. Ed is planning a secret destination."

Marion smiled tightly. If everyone was going to look at her like that, with suppressed amusement, she'd be seriously angry. And this woman had no business to look at anyone like anything, not after what she'd done. Drowned someone! Well, Edmund would know, the whole world would know, once that sister-in-law of his had run out of cash. Marion trotted off to greet Joyce and Duncan Crosbie. Every time the doorbell rang she feared it might be Fowler. She hadn't invited him, of course she hadn't, but somehow he had found out about the party and though he said he had a date with a couple of men he called job seekers in a pub in Harlesden, she couldn't rely on his not turning up here. Maybe she'd take some of this food home for him. There was so much of it, leftovers were bound to be abundant. A bottle of wine too wouldn't be missed. She realized, uneasily, what lengths she was going to to keep him sweet.

Another glance in Heather Litton's direction reminded her of the tape. Since she began her extortionate demands she had carried it with her everywhere she went. It wasn't safe to leave it in the flat with Fowler about. It was in the pretty little jeweled handbag that was yet another gift of Barry's and she had left it lying on a chair, on an arm of which one of the dull colleagues was sitting. With a sweet smile, Marion retrieved the bag and, imagining her feelings if someone had robbed her of the tape, quickly checked. No one had. She hooked the bag strap over her shoulder to be on the safe side and advanced in a hostessy way on Edmund and Heather once more. They were talking to Joyce and Duncan Crosbie. Marion took Edmund's arm and smiled up into his face.

"You and I were very close once, weren't we, Edmund? You used to walk me home from your mother's. She—and not only she—had high hopes we might have a future together. But it was not to be and here we are with completely different people. No doubt it's all for the best."

Joyce flicked her eyes up and down Marion's Indian dress. "How's your father these days, Marion?"

Marion made her escape with the excuse that guests' glasses needed refilling.

Heather and Edmund left the party early to call next door on his mother. Irene was entirely dressed in black, hung with handmade strings of jet and onyx.

"The noise from next door has been fearful. I had always supposed that if one's house was detached, one could hear nothing from the next house, but I find I was mistaken. Surely it isn't necessary to have the windows open at the end of October. Was **she** there?"

"If you mean Marion, Mother, since it was her engagement party, inevitably she was."

"You know, I consider your going to it, not to mention my own sister and her husband, a betrayal of me personally."

"That's a pity," said Edmund, "but nothing can be done about it now."

Heather had said nothing, believing that any comments on the party and the party guests would be unwelcome. At last she asked Irene how she was and felt the choice of inquiry had been tactful as her mother-in-law launched into a litany of ailments: backache, exhaustion, pins and needles in the legs, numbness on waking (if indeed she had slept), persistent cough, and general malaise.

"I find it much easier to be tough with her now." Edmund put his arm around Heather as they walked down the street. "And the result is I feel guilty. I'm so sorry for her, but I daren't show it. She spends hours at that window, watching the comings and goings next door and fermenting hatreds. If Barry Fenix had to get married, why couldn't he marry her instead of Marion? They're both obnoxious, but my ma is marginally less awful."

"I don't understand why anyone marries anyone except you," said Heather. "You weren't really close to her, were you?"

"What do you think?"

"Ed, what are we going to do about Issy? She's never been over to see us in our flat. We haven't been asked to Clapham. I've phoned her, but she's only once phoned me and that was from work."

"Andrew," said Edmund as they went into the station at Finchley Road and Frognal.

"Yes, of course Andrew. She doesn't say, but I know that's why. He'll divide me from her. That's what he wants."

"Is it making you unhappy?"

"Well, put it like this. You make me so happy, much happier than I've ever been in all my life. So that's all right. This thing with Issy, that's a kind of secondary unhappiness. It's always there and I'd like it to stop, but I reason that although she's crazy about him now, she'll have to get over it. He can't last. He's so awful and she's bound to see that sooner or later. One day she'll sort of—I don't know . . ."

"The scales will fall from her eyes, as your mum might say."

"That's right. And she'll give him the boot and we'll be like we were before."

• • •

"Darling, I hope I'm not unreasonable but I can't say I find your aunt's boyfriend entirely congenial. At least he's not living upstairs, though I suppose that will be the next step."

"I don't think so." Ismay wanted to sound warm and accommodating, but she found it impossible. Her voice was low and despondent. "Pamela lives with my mother and she doesn't like the idea of anyone else being there." She made a renewed effort to be strong. "You haven't met my mother yet."

"No, I haven't, have I?" Andrew lit a cigarette. The smoke caught at Ismay's throat, but she knew that if she allowed herself to cough he would accuse her of putting it on. "Do I have to?" He said it in the tone of a man willing to do anything to please, but she knew what the result would be if she said, "Yes, you do." Things would be said that were so hurtful that she couldn't contemplate them at this stage of her life, this crux.

Marion Melville had phoned ten minutes before he came in and asked for four hundred pounds. "Only two more weeks," she had said brightly, "and then you can have a break. I'll be away on my honeymoon. Clapham Common station on Saturday morning?"

"No, I don't think so," Ismay said. "I'll come up to you this time. There's a café in West End Lane called Ayesha's. Do you know it?"

"It's at the bottom of Barry's street," said Marion.

"Possibly. I'll see you there at eleven."

How it could it be, she thought as she put the phone down, that she could be so positive, so strong and in control, with other people, yet so feeble with Andrew? She was like two different people, two souls in one body. He would take her away from Pamela now as he had separated her from Heather. The time would come, and it wasn't far off, when he would ask her not to go upstairs and see her mother. And she would comply. Because she couldn't lose him.

The four hundred pounds would be for Marion's wedding dress. Barry had offered to pay, but her pride wouldn't allow that. He'd be paying for everything **after** they were married, she told him. Something dignified, she had in mind, but suited to her type. Not white but possibly pale pink, one of those ankle-length skirts that were all over frills and lace and bows.

When Barry drove her home after the party, Fowler was nowhere to be seen, but on the kitchen counter she found a note with "I want the flat" on it in large print. She tore it up and went to bed.

She and Barry were spending most of every day together now. He wanted it and not letting him out of her sight except at night made her feel safer, for as the wedding approached she found herself acutely aware of how unlikely it was that someone like her should marry someone like Barry. Barry who was rich and had a house as big as Mrs. Pringle's and a Mercedes-Benz, and she who lived by her wits. It wasn't like Marion to be nervous and even less like her to be afflicted with low self-esteem, but on the previous evening he had told her his wife (to herself Marion referred to her as his first wife) had had a lot of family money, all of which she had left to him. And this man was marrying **her.** Nothing could go wrong now, could it?

Fowler professed to be hurt that she hadn't asked him to the party and now didn't want him at her wedding. "You've got to admit I clean up all right," he said, though he was dirty again by this time and had put gel he had found in a bin on his nice clean hair. "When we were little you promised we'd live together when we were grown up. That was when you had that Wendy house in the garden and you used to ask me to tea. Well, Penguin bars and Lemsip. I sometimes think it was drinking all that Lemsip that started me on those substances."

"I haven't got a Wendy house now."

"No, you've got a flat," said Fowler.

She had to make an excuse to Barry for not coming around to his place on Saturday till midday. She told him she had a fitting for her wedding dress. Men didn't know about these things. He wouldn't be able to tell the difference between a skirt from Dorothy Perkins and one from Chloé. Still, it might even be Chloé when she'd got that four hundred pounds.

Extremely devious herself, she wondered what was prompting Ismay to come all the way up here for their meeting. Clapham was about as far again in the opposite direction from central London as West End Lane. Could it be a trap? But of what sort? It was possible—remotely possible—that Ismay could have told the police and one of them would be with her, in plain clothes of course, sitting at a nearby table. But if she had done that she would have to be prepared for certain dire consequences. If they failed for some reason to listen to the tape, no one could prevent her coming out with what was on it. And she would, right there in public in Ayesha's. Even then nothing could be done to her. She'd take the greatest care to check the place over before she entered into any transaction. In fact, this time she might suggest she and Ismay take a walk to some open space, even Hampstead Heath, before the money was handed over. If only all this weren't happening quite so near to Barry's house. . . .

While to walk through the streets between the Finchley Road and West End Green and then take Chudleigh Hill was by far the quickest way to get there, Marion dared not pass number fifty-six. If Barry saw her he would want to come with her. Instead, she took Acol Road and ran up West End Lane. She was early. Ayesha's was a very small café with bead curtains over the doorways and statuettes of many-armed goddesses on the counter, run by a very large and handsome Indian woman in a mauve sari. Not one of the four tables was taken. Marion sat at the one nearest the window where she could keep an eye on the street. Though it was possible Ismay might have taken a bus, the tube was more likely and she would be expected to appear from the direction of West Hampstead station. Within two minutes she did.

Her appearance was less haggard and strained than on previous occasions. Resigned herself to fate, Marion thought rather dramati-

cally. For the first time at any of their encounters she greeted Marion with a "hi." Both of
them had realized that they could hardly meet
in a café without buying at least a cup of coffee.

"What would you like?" Ismay asked.

"Me? Oh, nothing. You have something."

Ismay came to join her at the table, carrying a cappuccino. She sat down, said, "Once,
quite a long time ago, I met your future husband. That was when he was Detective Inspector Fenix. You didn't tell me he'd been a
policeman."

Marion stared. She said nothing. Ismay
took a sip of her coffee. "You didn't know, did
you? No, I thought not. All right. I don't like
doing this. It's blackmail and I think it comes
more naturally to you than to me. It disgusts
me, frankly, but I must do it. I'm not giving
you any more money and if you say to me that
you'll carry out your threat, I shall tell Mr.
Fenix what you've been doing. He might think
a bit differently about you then, don't you
think?"

"You can't do that," said Marion.

"Well, I can and I will if I have to. We could
go around there now if you like. Number fifty-
six Chudleigh Hill, isn't it? He's an honorable
man and I don't think he'd listen to the tape,

but he wouldn't marry you either. By the way, can I have the tape, please?"

Marion took it out of her handbag and handed it over. The shock of what Ismay had said, the revelation about Barry and then the threat, had been so great that she doubted if she could stand up. She felt as she imagined a very old woman who has had some sort of seizure must feel, broken, weak, dazed, and disorientated. Ismay put the tape into the bag she still carried on her shoulder and drained her coffee.

"I'm sorry I can't save that poor man from marrying you," she said as she left. "He's a good chap and he deserves better."

It was a full ten minutes before Marion felt able to get up. She might not have done so even then if four people hadn't come into Ayesha's and Ayesha herself begun hovering. Once out in the street, away from the joss stick scents of patchouli and cardamom, strength began to return. She hadn't got her four hundred pounds, but that was not the worst of it. She was the blackmailer blackmailed and it wasn't over yet, what with her other blackmailer set on getting her flat. But she was still engaged to Barry, she was still getting married on Thursday week.

He was delighted to see her half an hour

earlier than the promised time. "I thought we might try Afghan today for our lunch. And then I'll drive us to Hampton Court."

"Lovely, darling," said Marion. "Why didn't you tell me you'd been a policeman?"

He laughed. "How did you know?"

"A little bird told me. Why didn't you say?"

"I did try, kitten. I kept dropping hints. I was going to tell you that time we met Tariq and then at the party I did say I wanted you to meet Superintendent Bailey and ex–Chief Inspector Ambury only, honestly, sweetheart, you didn't seem interested."

Ismay had been brave and strong. She had stood up to Marion Melville and said things and made threats of which she would hardly have believed herself capable. Now reaction had set in and careless what any passerby thought of her, she sat down on a wall and began to cry.

A very pretty young woman crying in the street soon attracts attention, mostly from hopeful men. Two of them asked her what was wrong and one offered to buy her a drink. Realizing that she must pull herself together, she got up, rubbed at her eyes with the one tissue she had, and began thinking what excuse to make to Andrew for her absence. One great worry at least was over. She had no doubt Marion had passed out of her life forever. She had handled that. Could she handle those two other great quandaries? One of them she could and must. The time had come to confront Heather and, after thirteen years, ask her for the truth. That which had for so long seemed impossible, insurmountable, she began to see as necessary and essential. Now there was no possibility of anyone else asking her, she must do it.

As for Andrew, if she wasn't to be ruined and ultimately destroyed, she must refuse to let him divide her from Heather and Pamela, whatever the cost might be. She was in the tube by this time. She leaned her head back against the seat and closed her eyes when she thought of what that cost was.

Chapter Twenty-eight

The fact that Marion had found out for herself what his occupation had been convinced Barry she was fascinated by his reminiscences, and reminisce he did. India might be his first love, but he ate in Indian restaurants every day, dressed up in Indian clothes whenever he felt like it, and was going to India in a week's time. Ever since his wife's death there had been no one to talk to about the old days in the Force unless a former colleague came around for a drink, but now there was Marion, avid and all ears to hear about his cases, his adventures, and his triumphs.

She understood this and though she was bored stiff, saw it as a good thing in these last crucial days before she became Mrs. Fenix, and it was, so to speak, too late to do anything about it. She listened, smiling and admiring, to the case of the Wandsworth Widow, who had done away with three husbands and would have seen off a fourth but for Barrry's intervention, and the mystery (until Barry solved it) of Bernard the Balham Burglar, who broke into flats and cut off locks of hair from the heads of sleeping women. Daily she expected to hear of the Clapham man found drowned in the bath, but he never spoke of that.

Her own past history troubled her sometimes. What would Barry say if he knew of the frozen grouse and partridges, the pots of caviar, and the Stilton cheese she had appropriated from Mrs. Pringle? Or the silver, glass, and jewelry brought home from Avice Conroy's? Then there was the morphine. Avice hadn't died—Marion would have worried less about the ornaments if she had—but she had intended her death and that was attempted murder. Not to be forgotten, though she tried, were all those things that were not against the law but of which she knew Barry would deeply disapprove: the lies about her father, her efforts to fix Avice's will, her keeping the morphine instead of handing it in. For a whole week she had kept and used on trains and buses someone else's

Freedom Pass. It wasn't that her conscience bothered her, she had once told Fowler that she didn't know what he meant by the term, but rather that if Barry found out about even one of those things the wedding would be off.

Marion had much the same attitude to her coming nuptials as upper-class Victorian brides-to-be had to theirs. Or so authors tell us. Only let her once be married and then all those offenses against the law and morality might come out. In the case of the Victorians, it was usually debts to be settled because once married, the husband would be liable for his wife's, but there was little else he could do short of leaving her. Barry could leave her of course, Marion thought, but she'd still get half the value of his house and no doubt maintenance. Only let her be married.

During these last days she barely had enough to live on. That four hundred pounds would have made all the difference. It was hardly a question any longer of buying a wedding dress. She scarcely had enough to eat. She told herself she'd starve to death but for dinner out somewhere with Barry most evenings. When they got to whichever Asian restaurant he had picked this time, she had to restrain herself from falling on the food and stuffing it into her mouth with her fingers. The debts for Barry to settle in the sweet by-and-by would be her council tax and the electricity, gas, and water bills, none of which she had paid and which were perilously overdue.

The rich never think of these things. It seemed not to occur to Barry that when she lost her job she would also lose her income. He never asked, he never mentioned the subject. Perhaps he thought she had savings or had gone on the benefit and she rather wished she had. It was too late for that now. Of course, she had thought herself assured of an income from Ismay. One evening when she was at 56 Chudleigh Hill and Barry was cooking dinner for her—the scent of meat and spices coming from the kitchen made her feel faint with hunger—he asked her what she was going to do about her flat.

"It won't be any use to you, kitten, after Thursday. You could let it. You'd better allow me have a look at the tenancy agreement if you do. Or sell, of course."

"I don't know, darling. I'm not very good at business matters. You can be sure I'll consult you before I do anything."

"That's my kitten."

After they had eaten dhansaak, dahin, rice, and poppadoms (Barry critically, Marion voraciously), they spent the rest of the evening perusing the travel agent's brochures on Kerala. Pushkar had been given up on grounds of its vegetarianism and a preponderance of camels.

"The Land of Green Magic," said Barry. "I can't tell you how I'm looking forward to showing you India, kitten."

She knew better than to point out that he could hardly do so since this would be his first visit. Just before ten he said he would drive her home. Although she liked the lift, her terror of finding Fowler on the doorstep outweighed the pleasure. As always lately, she said she could walk or take the tube, and as always, he said he wouldn't dream of it.

"You never know what scum is hanging about out there after dark," said Barry, the ex-policeman.

It was true. She didn't. As they went out to get into the car and Barry was saying that Wednesday was the last time they would have to do this, a man of indeterminate age and appalling filth, unshaven, with straggly hair and a grunge-encrusted plastic jacket over ragged jeans, a dirty red scarf wound around his neck, emerged out of the dark between the street lamps. It was Fowler. Marion clutched Barry by the arm, afraid that this time she might really faint.

Fowler looked her in the eye. He held out

his hand and addressed Barry. "Got the change for a cup of tea, guv?"

She knew then. This was a threat, not the end of the world, not the collapse of her hopes. Her brother was better at blackmail than she was. But she was just as good an actor. She had her bag open. "Oh, the poor man," she said to Barry. "I must give him something."

"I wouldn't," said Barry.

She had little enough. She handed him one of her three last pound coins.

"Thank you, madam," said Fowler. "You're a lady." And, giving Barry a nasty look over his shoulder, he went on his way up the hill to West End Green.

"I hope I'm not unreasonable, darling. Of course I'm not trying to stop you seeing your sister. She **is** your sister, though I'm naïve enough to marvel at the disparate types found in one family. I simply don't want to have to go near her or that closet queer she married. If they come here, perhaps you'll let me know in advance so that I can make sure I'm out."

Ismay lifted her eyes to meet his. "Does the same go for Pam and Michael?"

"Come on, Issy. You know I'm not unreasonable. I don't care for him. I'm not mad about her, come to that. But of course I wouldn't dream of stopping you going up there to see your mother. You must know family is highly important to me. And you can have them all down here if you like." He smiled at her, took her hand. "Once a year," he said. "Anyway, we're not going to live here forever, are we? What do you think of the idea of moving out and buying a flat? This place isn't ideal and it's a long way out."

She had lived here all her life, but she would move if he wanted to. "If it's what you want. It would be a big step for me."

"Mary Queen of Scots is supposed to have said to Bothwell that she'd follow him to the ends of the earth in her shift. I'm only asking you to go to Chelsea."

He had booked them into a suite at the Savoy for Tuesday night. It was her birthday, which was perhaps a good enough reason, though he had never done anything like that before. Dress up, he had said. It's important. That day, first thing in the morning and before he was up, she took the tape out of the bag she had been carrying it in ever since Saturday and tugged it out of the spool inside the cassette. It was very cold outside. She put on her winter coat, took one of the ashtrays he used and a box of matches, and went out into the back garden, down to the end, and there under the trees she put the shiny brown length of tape onto the ashtray and set light to it. This was the only way she could think of which would utterly destroy it. The tape smoldered, then flamed, half-melted, and turned black. She dropped the remains into the dustbin by the back door and went into the house.

At six that evening she got out of the tube at Charing Cross and bought an evening paper. Immediately she wished she had stuck to that old rule she had made never to look at newspapers. That had been after that photograph of Andrew with Eva was in the **Evening Standard.** Eva was in this one too, a big picture on the front page, and the headline beside it was MAN IN COURT ON EVA DEATH CHARGE. Ismay stood still up against a shop window, reading the story under it. Not Kevin Preston, not the West End Werewolf, but a completely different man, someone called Kieron Thorpe, aged nineteen, from Harrow. She thought, Heather killed Eva. It's Heather who should have been in that court, not this nineteen-year-old, this boy. She would have to do something now. She couldn't let Kieron Thorpe go to prison for fifteen years when he'd done nothing.

But she put the paper into a waste bin. Andrew mustn't see that face, Eva's face, on this special day. If only she could push away the story and the name as easily from her mind. She walked along the Strand to the Savoy, thinking about it, trying not to but still thinking about it. About a boy of nineteen going to prison for something he didn't do. What must Heather feel? What must Heather ever feel? She found she didn't know. She hadn't the faintest idea of what her sister's thoughts might be. Except on one subject. She knew Heather loved Edmund, but it seemed to Ismay that she knew nothing else about her.

She was shown up to the suite. Andrew was already there and the room was full of red roses. He put his arms around her and kissed her as if he had fallen in love with her anew, or as if it were three years earlier, when they had first met.

"Would you like to go down for dinner or have it up here?"

"What would you like?"

"No. This is your evening and your night. You say."

She would have liked to dress up and go down for the sake of showing Andrew off as hers, but she sensed he would prefer being up here, so she said, "Here. This room is so lovely. And the view."

"Good. I'm glad. There's something I want

to say to you and I'd rather we were alone to say it."

A hint of alarm, like a cool breath on her skin, touched her. Something about the photograph in the paper? Something worse?

When Fowler turned up, letting himself in with his key, not even bothering to ring the bell, Marion was delving through her wardrobe for what to wear the day after next. It was no longer even a question of a visit to Dorothy Perkins, not even an excursion to Asda. She was too skint for either and it had to be something she already possessed but preferably an outfit Barry hadn't seen before.

"Something old, something new, something borrowed, something blue," said Fowler, plucking a battered artificial rose from the pile on the floor.

"There's no problem finding something old," said Marion tartly.

"I've brought you something new. At any rate, it was new when they threw it away. It came out of a bin in Conduit Street and that's a classy area." He pulled out of his backpack a flounced pink skirt with frilly hem which he had wrapped up in the **Evening Standard.** "Look, it's still got the price tag on it. Folks are amazing what they throw away. You even get a free paper with it. You can read all about the Kensington Gardens murder."

"I'm getting married the day after tomorrow, remember," said Marion. "I'm too busy for reading." She held up the skirt against herself. "Actually, it's just what I had in mind."

"Can you spare the change for a cup of tea, guv?"

"Oh, shut up. I'll never forgive you for that."

She found something blue, a length of ribbon. Maybe she could tie it around her leg like a garter. What could she borrow?

"Shall I come along and give you away?" asked Fowler.

"You don't need anyone to give you away in a civil ceremony."

"I'll be a witness then."

"We've got our witnesses."

"I'll be there. You can count on me. Waiting on the steps to throw confetti."

"You can have the bloody flat," Marion screamed.

She had a bath and put on a diaphanous white slip of a dress. He liked her best in black or white. What was he going to say to her? The idea came into her head that it was something about Eva. That he was still mourning Eva, she had been so sweet and good—something like that. But he had never yet shown signs of mourning her. It could be something different. He had said it was her special day. She did her face, combed her newly washed hair, and went back into the bedroom.

"You are so beautiful," Andrew said. "Who would look at another woman if you were there?"

You did, she thought, but she didn't say it. Not on this special day. It was seven and their dinner was due in half an hour. While Andrew opened the champagne she thought about Eva and the boy they were saying had probably killed her—a paranoid schizophrenic, a madman, a poor deluded creature?—and then she thought how Pam had once said you could never trust a man who opened champagne without spilling a drop. Andrew withdrew the cork with practiced dexterity, a foamless maneuver. But she already knew she couldn't trust him, didn't she? He handed her one of the tall flutes.

"To you," he said. "To us." And then, taking her left hand, "Will you marry me, Ismay? Will you be my wife?"

· · ·

"Do you remember," Heather said, "the day we were married, I said something to you about Tess of the d'Urbervilles and her marrying a man called Angel and them confessing to each other? And you said no one does that anymore. You meant about sexual things. Maybe they don't, but I didn't mean that. I meant something else, but I couldn't tell you. I lost my nerve."

Edmund said, "There's no need to tell me anything."

"There is. I'm going to tell you now. I must."

Chapter Twenty-nine

It should have driven everything else out of her mind and for a while it did. Her ring was so beautiful, the solitaire diamond so big that for a moment or two she doubted if it could be real.

"Of course it's real," he said, laughing. As if any serious person, anyone who was anyone, would give a girl anything but the most precious of stones!

She was dizzy with happiness, thoughts of Eva gone, the nineteen-year-old Kieron Thorpe gone, or apparently gone. Even then, though, she knew they hovered under the threshold of her conscious mind. Did there always have to be a worm in the bud?

Andrew put the announcement of their engagement in the **Daily Telegraph.** She read it
over and over, it was so wonderful to see their
names coupled together: Andrew Jefferson, son
of Mr. and Mrs. Campbell-Sedge, and Ismay
Lydia, elder daughter of Mrs. and the late Mr.
James Sealand. But in opening the newspaper
to find the engagements page, she saw another
photograph of Eva beside the proceedings in
the magistrates' court where Kieron Thorpe
had been committed for trial.

A feeling came to her that this exciting
time, this glorious time of being congratulated
and fêted and loved, must be limited, would
fade soon and gradually depart. And then she
must confront Heather. At last, after all this
time, she must know and act. Would that be
the end of her engagement, the end of everything joyous and good and life-enhancing?

Something blue was her shoes, something old
the skirt, and something new the tights she
bought in Church Street market for fifty pence.
A string of pearls she had pinched from Avice
she told herself she intended to give back so that
it would do for something borrowed. Brides
should turn up a little late for their weddings so
as to seem shyly reluctant, but Marion's nerves

saw to it that she was on time, even a little early. Barry's sister and the policeman called Ambury were the witnesses. The wedding passed uneventfully. Her sensations were those not uncommon to brides who are desperate to be married—that is to have the ceremony performed and the union made legal—more than to be loved and desired, a feeling of unreality, of a dream too good to be true, of faintness. Coming down the steps from the registrar's office she had to cling to Barry's arm and even so almost tripped on the hem of the frilly pink skirt. She saw the world, streets, buildings, people, faces, a dog, trees, cars, and buses through a pale golden haze, not entirely the consequence of the sun shining through November mist. She had done it. She had married this wealthy man with his Mercedes and his two-million-pound house, and she would never again be in want. Cheating and petty thievery could be put behind her. Lying and prevarication too. The time had come when she could afford to be good and she would be, a shining example of goodness, especially to people like Irene Litton and that sister of hers. They would admire her. She would be called a lovely woman. That Mrs. Fenix, she's a lovely woman.

In the taxi she snuggled up to Barry and said, "Can I tell you something, darling?"

"What's this then, a confession?"

God knew what he thought was coming. "I don't know what you'll think," she said, prolonging his suspense.

"You'd better try me, kitten." He sounded quite anxious. Maybe he thought she was a bigamist or having a lesbian affair.

"Well, sweetness, I've given the flat to my brother Fowler. He's got nowhere and nothing and you and I—well, we've got so much."

His arm already around her waist, Barry gave it a squeeze, the fact that she had promised to consult him forgotten. "You're an angel, do you know that? The most generous woman I know."

He and she and Alan Ambury and Barry's sister Noreen had "tiffin" at a Sri Lankan restaurant with a wedding cake and flowers everywhere. Having done the gracious hostess bit for ten minutes, Marion escaped to the ladies'. Fowler had moved into the flat the moment she left it. She phoned him on her mobile.

"I've done it. I'm Mrs. Fenix," she said.

"Congratulations. I never thought you would. Not when it came to the crunch."

"Nor did I," said Marion.

· · ·

Admiring Ismay's ring, Heather said she was happy for her. She knew how much she loved Andrew. They had been together for a long time and must know each other really well. Ismay noticed that "for her" and that her sister failed to say that Andrew was nice or someone she'd like for a brother-in-law, and she didn't blame her for that. Heather never lied. Or, rather, Heather had never lied since she went along with their mother's lying and said a downright no to Detective Inspector Fenix's question as to whether she'd been at home that afternoon. Since then she had always told the truth—so she would tell it now.

"I saw the announcement in the paper. Marilyn at work showed it to me. She said you must be very grand and I said, no, you weren't but Andrew was."

"Quite right."

Ismay was suddenly overwhelmed with love for her sister. What did it matter what she had done thirteen years earlier? She had been a child, hardly into her teens. No, it didn't matter much, but it mattered what she had done last summer. What she did for me, she thought, for me. And it worked, what she did. It brought Andrew back and now I'm engaged to him and I'll be his wife, and when we've been married for half a century I'll look back and remember my sister gave me this. No, I won't. I'll remember Kieron Thorpe who served fifteen years in prison for what she did for me.

"I brought a bottle of wine. Shall we have some?"

As Ismay opened it and filled two glasses she thought how much she needed it to help her through what she was about to do. For now she knew she must do it and today, tonight, before Heather and Edmund went away.

"Does Andrew know you've come here?"

"Of course he does, Heather. He's not set against you like that. He'll come around." To her truthful sister she had told a lie and another to Andrew. He didn't know where she was. He thought she was at a friend's office-leaving party. I need this wine. I shouldn't live like this, but I do and when I'm married to Andrew I always shall. To brace myself for the lies I shall have to tell him. To fortify myself against the lies he will tell me. For his infidelities and for my daily stress. It's that or Saint-John's-wort or Prozac—or worse. "Heather," she said, "can we talk? I have to ask you something."

"All right. What is it? If it's about Andrew, yes, I'll come to your wedding. I'll even be a bridesmaid—a matron-of-honor, they call them when the bridesmaid's married—and I'll be as nice as I can to Andrew, but, you know, Issy, I can't answer for Ed."

"It's not about Andrew. It's about Eva Simber."

Heather raised her clear and calm blue eyes to Ismay's, innocent, childlike eyes. "Oh, yes, poor Eva. I see they've got someone for killing her. He's only nineteen." She paused, then said, "I met her, you know."

"You asked her to give Andrew up."

Heather looked surprised that she knew. "Yes, I did. That was the point of talking to her. She wasn't my sort of person and I certainly wasn't hers."

Ismay was breathless now. Hyperventilating was what they called it and now she knew what it meant. It affected her voice, which came out at the first attempt in a whisper. She tried again. She was staring at Heather and she took a deep breath, unclenched her hands, and spread them flat on her knees. She tried to speak evenly. The words she used, just the words themselves, shocked her. "Did you kill her, Heather? Did you?"

In Heather's incredulous stare she had her answer, but she persisted. "Did you?"

"Did I kill Eva?" Heather spoke roughly. "Are you mad?"

"Don't be angry."

"Of course I'm angry when you ask me something like that. What sort of a question is that? Of course I didn't kill her," Heather said. She seldom got cross, but when she did Ismay was afraid of her anger. "Why do you ask a thing like that? I can't believe it. You think I'd go into a park and strangle someone? You think I'd plan something like that? Do something like that? I wouldn't be surprised if Mum had asked me that but not you."

Ismay said in a small, almost humble, voice, "You never tell lies, do you?"

"I suppose I do sometimes, little ones, like saying I can't go out somewhere when I can, that sort of thing, but no, I try not to."

"You know why I thought you'd killed Eva?"

"For the reason I'd talked to her, I suppose. To make her give Andrew up."

"That, yes. I thought you'd killed her for me."

"Well, thank you very much. I'm not a psychopath. Just for your information, Issy, I think she was on the point of giving him up the last time I talked to her. Next time she'd have agreed, I'm pretty sure she would have, only there wasn't a next time because Kieron Thorpe killed her."

"I'm sorry," said Ismay.

"You didn't suspect any of your friends of killing her, did you? You didn't think Pam might have. You suspected me. You thought it was me because of Guy."

It was what she had waited for these past thirteen years. The truth would come now, she knew it. It should be happening at home in the house Andrew was going to take her away from, not here in this new, pretty, newly furnished flat. Truth can be told everywhere, she said to herself, it has no home, and she wondered if she had made that up or was quoting from something she had read.

"You did kill Guy, didn't you? You did drown him? I haven't been wrong all these years? It wasn't Michael, was it? Michael wasn't in the house that afternoon?"

Heather looked steadily at her. Her face was no longer indignant or incredulous but sad, as if she had carried a great sorrow for years and perhaps she had. "No, you haven't been wrong," she said. "Michael—God, no." A silence fell. They sat there like two people who have just met and can't speak the other's language. Then Heather said, "I think you've just been wrong about why."

"You did it for me. Because you thought I needed protecting from Guy. You thought I didn't like the way he came on to me. But I did. I encouraged him. I was fifteen—what did I know? Then he got ill. He was very ill, you know, he had a terribly high fever. Mum thought he was going to die. I must have been very selfish. I just saw it as keeping him from me. I used to hope he'd come to my room at night and get into bed with me and his illness—well, it postponed that. You haven't got much patience when you're a teenager."

"I know that," said Heather. "I mean I know all that, what you're saying."

She had gone very white. Heather was normally very healthy-looking with tanned skin and pink cheeks, but now all that color seemed to have drained away. Lines appeared between her eyebrows and above her cheekbones. She aged ten years. Ismay watched her hands curl into fists and clench hard. "I know how you felt about Guy," she said, "and how he felt about you."

"You can't have. You were thirteen."

"I know because he told me. I don't know how to put this, Issy, but he wasn't—well, a good person. People used to say someone like him was wicked, but 'wicked' means something else now. It means nice or extraordinary. Guy wasn't either of those things. He was a pedophile."

Ismay didn't know why she was appointing herself his defender. She felt Heather was being unjust. "You can't call a man a pedophile because he fancies a fifteen-year-old who sets out to attract him. I really did do that. I sort of lay in wait for him. If he came on to me, I came on to him."

She hesitated, realizing suddenly that she was doing it, she was talking about it to Heather. The impossible was happening, the something she had known she would never do. Here she was, doing that impossible and Heather was answering, white-faced, stricken Heather with her clenched hands and eyes that stared. "I suppose I was in love with him," she said. "He was a sort of forerunner of Andrew. Andrew looks a bit like him, don't you think?"

"More than a bit," said Heather. She let herself slump forward, dropping her shoulders in a conscious effort to relax. Her voice was steadier. "That was why I found it so hard to talk much to him. I found it hard to be ordinarily nice to him and of course he noticed. But sometimes I'd find him sitting in the flat and I'd fancy for a moment it was Guy sitting there." She looked suddenly cold but didn't quite shiver. "I really hated Guy," she said.

"Would you tell me what happened that day?"

"The day I drowned him?" It was horrible to hear her say it so openly in that stark, cold voice. "Can I have some more wine, please? I said that to my mother-in-law once and she said she'd never known a guest in her house ask for anything before. Sorry, I'm stalling."

"But you did drown him?"

"Oh, yes. Of course I did. I'll tell you. I'll tell you now and I won't put it off any longer." Heather took a long, slow draft of her wine and shivered a little. Then she began. "You remember I was going to go out that afternoon. I was going to play table tennis at my friend Greta's. Guy was in bed. I suppose he was asleep. I don't know. I never went into that room when he was in it. Greta phoned and said not to come because she had to go with her mother to see her gran in hospital. I went out into the garden. Do you remember that swing seat we had? I sat on that with a book I was reading. It was **Tess of the d'Urbervilles** and I thought it was the most boring book I'd ever read. But I did finish it—oh, yes, I finished it. Somehow I can't leave a book I've started unfinished.

"The French windows to the balcony were open and just before four I saw Guy come out onto the balcony in his dressing gown. He saw me and he called out, 'Hi, Heather. Lovely day, isn't it?' It was, but I didn't answer. I didn't look up. A bit after that I heard the water running. I'll always hear that sound, Issy, the running of water, the flowing of water. It's not that I don't like water, the sea, swimming and all that, but it seems to have an importance in my life sort of out of proportion. Anyway, I sat there, trying to read that sad, miserable book, and soon I heard the running water stop and I knew Guy must be in the bath.

"The day before when Guy was downstairs I'd been in their room to borrow a comb because I couldn't find mine. While I was there I must have taken my cardigan off and left it on a chair. It was a warm day but starting to cool down and I needed my cardigan. Nothing would have made me go into that room when I knew Guy was there, but he wasn't. He was in the bath.

"I went upstairs and into their bedroom. I couldn't see my cardigan. Mum had put it in my bedroom, but I didn't know that then. The door to the bathroom was wide open. He must have heard me, though I was careful not to make a noise. He called out, 'Heather, would you bring the shampoo in here, please?' I didn't want to. I didn't believe he'd wash his hair in the bath. But I did take it in. I don't know why."

"He was in the bath and he called you in? A girl of thirteen? Heather, is that true?"

"Oh, yes, it's true. This is all true. You know I won't lie. I went in and he was in the bath and the bath was full of foam. You know how it is with a foam bath. You can't see the person's body. I remember I was thankful for that. You could later—when the foam went. I put the shampoo on the shelf thing by the taps, not looking at him, and then he said something to me. Something awful or I thought it was at the time. It **was** when you think how old I was. I mean, how **young.** I thought, I'll stop this now, now before it's too late, and I picked up his feet and lifted them up high and his head went under—and you know the rest."

Chapter Thirty

It was very silent in there, high up above London. From the window in daylight you could see tall landmarks, the dome of Saint Paul's, the Post Office Tower, and in the distance on a fine clear day the silver-gray shine of the river with an unidentifiable bridge over it. Tonight, in the winter dark, it was just a spread of lights, some still, some winking in varied colors, one which flashed brightly every few seconds. Ismay walked away from the window and sat down again.

Heather said, "What are you going to do?"

"I don't know. You said I know the rest. I don't really. What did you think **you** were going to do?"

"After I'd drowned him? He fought and struggled but he was weak, Issy. Under the water he was so white, sort of parchment color. I could see him very clearly because all the foam had gone. Funny thing, wasn't it? All the foam had gone. My dress was wet and my legs were wet. I dried them on a towel but not my shoes. I didn't think of my shoes. You asked me what I thought I was going to do. I thought I'd run away. It was the only thing I could do, though I didn't know where I'd go or anything.

"That's why I came downstairs. I hadn't heard you and Mum come in. I hadn't any money or any clothes with me, but I came down because I thought I'd go out of the front door and run away. You were there, looking up at me, and I couldn't speak. Mum spoke to me. She said, 'Why are you so wet, Heather? Where have you been?' and then I spoke. I said, 'In the bathroom. You'd better come.' "

"And we did and found Guy drowned. Someone must have phoned the police, but I don't remember who. Not me."

"It was Pam. Mum phoned Pam. She came straight over. The police came later. And a doctor, though anyone could have seen he was dead. All the time I was thinking I couldn't run away now. We didn't talk to each other at all, you and I and Mum. Mum wasn't in the sort of state I'd have expected. She was calm. I was terribly frightened, Issy. When the police came, the inspector and the other one, I thought they'd take me away, and then Mum told them we'd all been out together, buying school uniform, but I hadn't gone into the shop, I'd waited outside. I suppose even then I knew she'd said that so that if they questioned the shop man he'd say I didn't try on any clothes. And I said that was right. And you said the same." She paused. "You say I don't tell lies—well, I did then, about as big a lie as anyone could."

"The inspector is the man Marion Melville married."

"Really? I suppose we lived in his jurisdiction or whatever you call it. I wonder if he remembers. After he'd gone and the other one had, I expected you and Mum to ask me what really happened and I couldn't understand why you didn't. I thought Pam might, but she had other things on her mind. That was when Michael left her. Why didn't you ask?"

"I don't know. I suppose if we didn't ask we could go on accepting Guy had done it himself. That it was an accident, I mean. One thing we did do. We tried it out to see if you could have done it. Mum got into the bath and I lifted her feet up and her head went under and she couldn't have pulled herself up till I let go. So we knew you could have done it."

"If it wasn't all so ghastly," said Heather, "I could laugh. At the idea of you and Mum doing that, you know. Was it knowing all that which drove Mum crazy?"

"I don't know. No one knows. It was easier for me. After all, presumably she'd loved Guy. She had that loss to bear. And she couldn't have known why you'd done it. I did."

Heather looked at her curiously. "Why did I do it, Issy?"

"For me," Ismay said. "To save me from Guy. Even if I didn't want to be saved, you thought I ought to be, didn't you? Nothing had happened, though I'd wished it would. I knew you'd done it for me and I think that's the reason I never told anyone."

"I didn't do it for you, Issy. I did it for me."

It was as if she were trying to speak a language in which she'd only had a few lessons, a strange tongue whose grammar she hadn't even begun to master. "What do you mean? I don't understand what you mean."

Heather nodded. "That night we stayed at Pam's—do you remember that?—and we both came downstairs because there was a wasp in our room. Do you remember?"

"Of course I do. That was when Guy first saw me."

"He saw two girls, Issy, not one. He saw me as well. I think we both attracted him, but you—you have to forgive me for this—showed pretty plainly what you felt. And you were older. That was part of the trouble. Did you never wonder why you got all that kissing and fondling but nothing more? Why he never did what you wanted and came to your bedroom?"

"I suppose I thought there wasn't the opportunity. Or maybe he was scared of going that far."

"He wasn't scared," Heather said. "He came to mine."

This time Ismay was silent, looking down at the empty wineglass in her hands, not daring to meet her sister's eyes. Outside, halfway up in the sky, that single light flashed on and off, on and off. She was as Heather had been when she had come down those stairs, speechless.

Heather went on, "I don't want to hurt you, but since I'm telling you all of it, I have to tell you this. Guy wanted you at first, but he stopped wanting you because you so plainly wanted him. Does that make sense? I said he was a pedophile. He kissed you and had you sitting on his knee to distract attention from me. But I was the one he wanted because I didn't want him. That's the kind of man he was. He told me so. He said, I need a girl who looks like a woman but who's innocent like you are. You don't want it now, he said, but I'll make you like it. You'll see. That was when he came to my room and—well, did it to me. There was only the once. He got ill after that. What could I do? I couldn't tell Mum. It's the old story. That's how men like Guy operate. She won't tell and if she does they won't believe her."

It was surely the longest speech Heather had ever made.

"He actually had sex with you? He raped you?"

"Yes, you could call it that. I didn't struggle, though. I was afraid he'd hurt me. Well, hurt me more."

Ismay put her head in her hands. Just for a moment. "What did he say to you when he was in the bath and you went into the bathroom?" she asked. "You said he said something awful to you."

"Yes. Maybe if he hadn't said it I'd never have drowned him. He said, 'How about coming into the bath with me, Heather? The water's lovely.' "

"Oh, God, Het. He deserved what he got."

"I don't know how many times I've heard those words. 'The water's lovely.' Every time I've been to the seaside. It always makes me wince."

"Let's finish the wine. Do you know, I can tell you now, I was so worried about it all when you met Ed that I thought I'd have to tell him, sort of not let him marry you without knowing this thing about you." She poured the last of the wine into their glasses. "I never did tell him, of course."

"Oh, Ed knows," said Heather. "I told him."

"You **told** him?"

"I had to. A few days ago, actually. I told him everything."

"What did he say?"

"He said he loved me and we'd never talk about it again. He didn't exactly say I was justified, but that's what he meant. And we have talked about it again. He does love me and things are just the same—I think—but still . . . he never used to be sad, Issy, but he's sad now."

Was Heather justified? Ismay didn't know. If she had fought off his advances and killed him in self-defense, well, yes. But in cold blood? A calculated move because he had disgusted her? "Do you think you were justified?"

"No," said Heather. "Not really. Do you?"

"I can't say. I don't seem to know anything anymore."

"What are you going to do? If you're going to do anything, would you let us have our honeymoon first? For Ed's sake?"

They heard his key in the lock. He came in, kissed Heather, kissed Ismay, and began talking about his mother. Ismay thought his eyes were unhappy, in a steady, accepting, resigned sort of way.

In the days that followed, Ismay spent as much time as she could with Heather, not as difficult as it might have been, for Andrew was occupied in house-hunting. And it was "house," not "flat." His father had promised him the deposit on a mortgage if he would consent to buy a mews house. Douglas Campbell-Sedge was prejudiced against flats. His children lived in stylish houses in fashionable places. Ismay went with Heather to buy clothes to wear in a hot sunny climate at Christmastime, sundresses and swimming costumes. She told Andrew she had been looking at furniture and carpets for the new house.

Edmund and Heather left for their honeymoon in the middle of December. On the same day Andrew took Ismay to look at a little house

he had found in a pretty mews in Chelsea, cobbled and with antique lampposts and troughs
for flowers, looking, he said, as mewses should.
She liked it, he told the estate agent they would
have it, and that evening he got in touch with
his solicitor. Ismay didn't know he had a solicitor, but, on reflection, she saw that of course he
would have one, inevitably.

Marion and Barry came back from India.
He had been disappointed in the subcontinent.
There was a great deal more dirt than he had
expected, and the widespread poverty got him
down. There were too many people about who
reminded him of that poor wretch who had
asked for change outside his house the evening
before they were married. The food, too, failed
to come up to expectations, the meat and fish
being tasteless and tough compared with what
he got at the Maharanee and the Pushkar. He
wasn't, however, disappointed in his wife, who
was sweetness itself, something which went a
long way to consoling him for the gas, electricity, and water bills that Fowler had forwarded
and were waiting for him on his return. Although they were careful not to drink the water, they both came back with what Barry called
"tummy bugs."

Christmas chez Litton was a livelier affair
than it had been the year before. Joyce and

Duncan Crosbie came, and brought Avice Conroy with them. Her new Croatian au pair was rabbit-minding. The unexpected guests were Marion and Barry Fenix and their friend ex-Superintendent Alan Ambury, who had promised to come in "just for drinks" the day before. Marion had made her peace with Irene, humbling herself and apologizing profusely— she had done much the same with Avice—for, as she put it, she could afford to do so now. Much to her relief, Barry's impressions of the subcontinent had put him off Indian dress and he came in a new charcoal worsted suit. Marion was in Alexander McQueen with Prada shoes. There was a lot of kissing and expressions of re-gret that Edmund and Heather weren't there.

"They've gone to a place called Kanda in Sumatra," Irene told everyone. "No one else knows, but Edmund naturally confided in me."

Barry and his wife went home for Christ-mas dinner—curried turkey, for Barry's disap-pointment in India didn't extend to his own cooking—and they took ex-Superintendent Ambury with them, but not before he had asked for Irene's phone number and given her his.

Andrew met Ismay's mother at last. He seemed embarrassed by the experience, a condi-tion Ismay had never seen him suffering before.

He managed to be polite to Pamela and Michael but was visibly relieved to make his escape and take Ismay out to lunch at San Lorenzo. She thought about Heather and Heather's confession more than she liked. Every day she thought about it and about Edmund knowing and what she should do. If anything. Kieron Thorpe had been committed for trial to a higher court. Andrew said it would be months, maybe even a year, before the trial took place. At least Heather had had nothing to do with that.

She faced Andrew across the table and ate the delicious food and drank champagne. He had given her a gold bracelet for Christmas. She was wearing it. She thought, I must decide about Heather. Perhaps I have decided—to do nothing. In a minute Andrew would wonder why she was so quiet, he would ask her why. She looked up and saw that he had turned his head. His eyes were fixed on a girl who sat waiting, alone, at a table nearby, a fair-haired, pretty, waif-like girl in a translucent white dress. It's nothing, she said to herself, it means nothing. He turned back to her and smiled.

The earthquake and hurricane and floods in Indonesia and Sri Lanka dominated news broadcasts from the day after Boxing Day onward. "Tsunami" was a new word to most viewers, but it was soon on everyone's lips. Southern India, the Thai coastline, the islands that Irene still called the East Indies, though she wasn't quite sure what the term comprised. She talked about it on the phone with her new friend Alan Ambury.

"Sumatra," he said. "The Nicobar Islands, the Andamans."

"Sumatra?"

"Places one has never heard of, like Banda Aceh."

"My son is in Sumatra."

"It's a vast area, Irene. I shouldn't worry."

"You don't want to worry about that," Andrew said to Ismay, signing the contract for the purchase of their house in Chelsea. "I remember when some mate of my mama's was in a hurricane in Guatemala or she thought she was. Of course I got on to my pal in the Foreign Office, but it was all a storm in a teacup if you'll forgive the pun."

Ismay said, "But the worst-hit place is Kanda in Aceh, and Ed's mother called to tell me that that's where they went."

Andrew's casting up of eyes showed plainly what he thought of any family connections of Edmund Litton's.

· · ·

She watched television, one news after another. The water wasn't lovely. One huge wave and then another and another, the engulfing of land, the destruction and sweeping away of fragile structures. Four British citizens staying in a beach hotel in Kanda . . .

"Their names cannot be released until next-of-kin have been informed."

Next-of-kin would be Heather's mother and Edmund's mother. Ismay lived, moved, wandered in a daze. She was afraid to show much to Andrew, but at last she couldn't help herself and she threw herself into his arms, begging him to find out, to tell her the worst, anything to end this. He didn't fail her.

"You're wonderful," she said. "What would I do without you?"

"You don't have to do without me," he said.

He gave her a drink and went into the bedroom to phone the pal in the Foreign Office in private. When he came back, after a long time, enmity forgotten, quarrels past, his face told her. He held her close, telling her she had no need of anyone else. Hadn't he said he would love her forever?

About the Author

Since her first novel, **From Doon with Death,** published in 1964, Ruth Rendell has won many awards, including the Crime Writers' Association Gold Dagger for 1976's best crime novel for **A Demon in My View,** and the Arts Council National Book Award, genre fiction, for **The Lake of Darkness** in 1980.

In 1985, Ruth Rendell received the Silver Dagger for **The Tree of Hands,** and in 1987, writing as Barbara Vine, won her third Edgar from the Mystery Writers of America for **A Dark-Adapted Eye.**

She won the Gold Dagger for **Live Flesh** in 1986 and, as Barbara Vine, for **A Fatal Inversion** in 1987 and for **King Solomon's Carpet** in 1991.

Ruth Rendell won the **Sunday Times** Literary Award in 1990, and in 1991 she was awarded the Crime Writers' Assocation Cartier Diamond Dagger for outstanding contribution to the genre. In 1996 she was awarded the CBE, and in 1997 was made a Life Peer.

Her books have been translated into twenty-five languages.

Ruth Rendell has a son and two grandsons, and lives in London.

LP
M
REND

Rendell, Ruth

The water's lovely